The Art School Murders

A novel

Robert Dodds

Also by Robert Dodds:

For adults:
RATTLESNAKE AND OTHER TALES (Polygon)
SITTING DUCK
THE GARDEN OF EARTHLY DELIGHTS
SECRET SHARERS
PARADISE POR FAVOR

For children 8 – 13:
THE MIDNIGHT CLOWNS (Andersen Press)
NIGHTLAND (Andersen Press)
THE SECRET OF IGUANDO (Andersen Press)
THE MURRIAN (Andersen Press)

For teenage reluctant readers:
THE HAUNTED MOBILE (A&C Black/Bloomsbury)
PITCH DARK (A&C Black/Bloomsbury)

About the author:

Robert Dodds grew up in Yorkshire and Kent. He went to Oxford University to study English, and then became a teacher and lecturer. After several years working in England, Mexico, and the USA, he settled in Scotland, where he worked for twenty-three years at Edinburgh College of Art.

No murders were committed at the college during this time.

Visit robertdodds.com to read more of his writing

For Theo, Coralie and Aila

Copyright © 2021 Robert Dodds

The right of Robert Dodds to be identified as the author of this work has been asserted by him in accordance with the Copyright, Designs and Patents Act, 1988.

All rights reserved.

ISBN-13: 979-8732524178

Cover image by Laura Dodds

AUTHOR'S DISCLAIMER
This is a work of fiction. The characters bear no deliberate resemblance to any real person living or dead.

CHAPTER 1

**The city of Forthburgh, in Scotland.
September 1989**

The woman's voice ran in a continuous, breathless stream.

"Oh... hello? Is that the police? I can hardly think straight... I'm ringing to report an awful thing... it was my Trudi that found it... in the woods... she wouldn't come back when I called, so of course I had to go scrambling after her up into the trees. I got all muddy. Bark, bark, bark! She just wouldn't come back. And I'm not surprised given what..."

"Could you give me your name, please?"

"Oh... of course... I'm Eleanor Brown. Mrs Eleanor Brown. Trudi's a basset ... they have the most remarkable sense of smell..."

"And your address and phone number please?"

"Oh... it's 44, Inverbeith Terrace... such a terrible..."

"In Forthburgh?"

"Yes."

"And what is your phone number?"

"It's 556133"

"And you're saying your dog found something, Mrs Brown?"

"Yes. Oh... such an awful..."

"What did your dog find?"

"Well, it almost looked like a giant hedgehog at first. Spiny things sticking out all over it! But then I saw the face. Oh... God help me, I'll never forget that face! And of course Trudi had to go licking it all over. I had to pull her off."

"What was it, Mrs Brown?"

"A body, of course! The body of a man. Naked, with these... these kind of thin sticks all sticking out of him. They looked like paint brushes, you know? Artists' paint brushes. Bristling like a hedgehog he was..."

"Where was this?"

"In the woods. Deil's Glen."

"Right. If we send officers out to your house now, can you take them to the location?"

"Oh... I don't want to see that again! I'll have nightmares as it is."

"You won't have to approach close enough to see. Just to point it out to the officers."

"Oh, all right. I see it's starting to rain. Have I time for a cup of tea? I'm all shivery."

"The officers will be there very soon. How long ago did you find the body?"

"Oh... I came straight back to the house, as fast as I could walk."

"Approximately at what time?"

"Let's see... it's ten to nine now. It must have been about eight thirty."

"Did you see anyone else nearby, or on your way back?"

"No. It was looking like rain. Sometimes there's other people walking their dogs, but it was looking like rain. And now it's started. It's coming on heavy now. Oh dear... that poor man's face!"

Inspector Coupar Cruickshank, thirty four years old, lean and boyish-looking, clicked the 'off' button on the cassette tape recorder and settled back in his chair. Both emitted a small groan.

The uniformed officers first attending the scene had done an indifferent job. Six out of ten, at best. Of course, the heavy rain hadn't helped. All sorts of possible evidence might have been washed away. No footprints or fingerprints to be found. Only one useful thing had survived the deluge. He had it on his desk in front of him now, dried out. A small piece of paper, rectangular, about three inches by two. It had been curled up into a tight tube, like a cigarette, and stuck into the dead man's nostril. The ink – red ink – had run in the rain, but some of the block capital letters were still just legible; unfortunately not all of them. He had puzzled over it for half an hour. It looked like two separate words, one beginning with an 'A' and the other, possibly, with an 'I'.

Unless the dead man had stuck it up his own nose, this was likely to be some sort of message from the murderer, and as such a very useful clue. But the rain had buggered it up.

"The rain's buggered it all up!" was precisely what Detective Superintendent Dennis "The Menace" Scott had remarked to him in the woods at Deil's Glen, fingering the bristling grey brush that he accommodated on his upper lip.

Dennis Scott had been called out at once and was the Senior Investigating Officer. Since he was already up to his oxters in another murder case - a strangled disc jockey - he was displeased at being summoned out into the rain at half past nine in the morning to contemplate an additional body. He eyed his deputy doubtfully. Coupar Cruickshank was new to his team, and just now looked like a boy scout who has lost his compass.

"You can get started without me, Coupar. You've done murders before, haven't you? Before you were transferred to Forthburgh?"

"Two."

"Solved?"

"No."

"What, neither of them?"

"I was only the deputy. Like now. The files have been passed on to a new D.S.I.O."

"Chance to improve your score then, Coupar. One out of three wouldn't be bad. Get cracking and report back to me this afternoon."

Then Senior Investigating Officer "The Menace" gave a final tug to his scrubbing brush moustache and lumbered heavily away under his stripy golf umbrella, probably to have his second breakfast, Coupar thought.

Coupar trudged back up to the single track road that was the nearest vehicular access to the crime scene. The rain, and the coming and going of police vehicles had now obliterated any useful tyre tracks that might have been left there.

This was not going to be easy.

Back at the station, where an incident room was being noisily set up next door to his own office by Detective Constables Price and Waterhouse, consequently displacing the station's much loved ping-pong table, Coupar listened to the tape of Eleanor Brown again, and then jotted down his first thoughts:

Unknown male victim, appears to be in his mid or late thirties.

Bizarre state of the body suggests pre-meditation by the killer.

Some kind of nutcase by the looks of it.

Murdered elsewhere and then brought to the wood?

But no vehicle access close by so would have to be carried.

Someone strong therefore? Or more than one killer?

More likely murdered on the spot?

Most likely murdered by a man? Or two men? Or a woman? The murderer a powerful woman? Or women?

So, unknown man murdered by unknown nutcase or nutcases.

Coupar Cruickshank ran his eye over these notes and sighed. The first task was to identify the body, and the other avenue to explore was the most salient evidence: the sharpened artists' paint brushes that had been thrust into the victim's flesh. Seventy five of them. At the scene he had thought they looked new. There were no paint marks on the wood or the bristles. Forensics hadn't finished with them yet, but he would be prepared to bet there'd be no fingerprints. He went out of his office and stuck his head through the doorway of the incident room.

"Waterhouse - check art shops to see if anyone's been buying paint brushes in unusual bulk."

Waterhouse, himself unusually bulky, looked at him with his blank walrus face.

"Art shops?"

"Yes. There must be art shops I suppose in Forthburgh."

Waterhouse shrugged.

"Use the telephone directory. Yellow Pages."

"Yes sir."

"And after that, if you don't turn anything up, take yourself off to Deil's Glen and spend a couple of hours talking to joggers and dog walkers or the like. See if anyone's seen anything odd lately."

"Yes sir."

"And Price, take the polaroid of the dead man's face to the art school and see if anyone there knows who he is."

Price scratched his right ear and then his left ear.

"What polaroid?"

"Go and find what's-his-name… the photographer."

"Larry?"

"If that's his name. He took plenty of photos. Get one of the face."

"Yes sir. Shall we stop setting up the room then, sir, to do this?"

There was always something about the way Price said "sir" that suggested insubordination. If Waterhouse was a walrus, Price was a weasel. Wiry and sly looking.

"Of course. The room can wait."

"We'd better take the table tennis bats and the ping-pong balls away – can they go in your office, sir?"

"Yes, yes. Give them to me."

Price and Waterhouse went off. He heard Price make some remark and then a low chortling sound from Waterhouse.

By the time Coupar was eating his lunchtime sandwich, Price had phoned him from the art school. It hadn't taken long, with the aid of the polaroid, to find someone who could identify the victim. The dead man was Steven Sidling, Head of the Department of Sculpture, recently re-named 'The Department of Ambient Interventions'.

That evening he went over to Lisa's flat. She opened the door to his ring, and pecked his cheek perfunctorily, like a hen without much appetite. She wasn't capable of looking unattractive, with her slim figure, luxuriant blonde hair, large eyes and regular features. However, she had done what she could by wearing shapeless tracksuit trousers and a baggy non-matching top, and refraining from hair-brushing or make-up. Following her into the living room he found the sofa strewn with laundry and an ironing board set up in the middle of the floor. She returned to it and took up the iron.

"Weren't you expecting me?" he queried.

She raised a quizzical eyebrow.

"You always come on a Thursday night."

"I just thought – you know… with the ironing…"

"I thought you could pop out and get fish and chips? Or there's a frozen lasagne in the freezer. I've not had chance to do the ironing all week."

"Okay. Fish and chips. That's fine."

"You have a good day at work?"

"Depends how you look at it. They found a body this morning. A murder. The Menace has put me in the driving seat."

Lisa's lustreless mood was transformed. Her eyes shone. She put down the iron.

"A murder! That's your first one!"

"There's murders every week or two."

"Yes, but *you* don't get them, do you? Why have you got this one?"

Coupar shrugged.

"The D.I.s who usually do murders must be busy already. The Menace came straight to me."

"It'll be a chance to impress him then, eh?"

"Possibly. There's not a lot to go on yet, though."

"Early days, if the body only turned up this morning! Come on, I'll get us a glass of red and you can fill me in."

She switched off the iron at the plug.

"You know…" he started to warn her.

She bobbed her head up and down, a hen reinvigorated.

"I know! I know! You're not supposed to *tell* me anything. But you can trust me, Coopsie! I won't breathe a word to anyone! Move the laundry and make a space on the sofa and I'll get us that red wine!"

CHAPTER 2

August 1988- December 1988

ABOUT A YEAR EARLIER....

Steven Sidling gave himself a metaphorical pat on the back. This cushy number – *Head of Sculpture* at Forthburgh School of Art - was now his for life – or for as much of his future life as he chose to spend in Scotland. Outside the three eleven week terms of the academic year he would in any case be free to pursue his own ends, wherever the fancy took him. But Forthburgh was where he wanted to be for now, anyway. The dust needed to settle in London before he showed his face down there again. London might be a big city, but, like most of its denizens, he only frequented a limited range of locales, and he had started to feel that his regular habits made him unsafe. The situation there was untenable, for now.

It had all started with an exhibition. Limited edition photographic prints of some of his *ambient interventions* had been on show at an up-and-coming gallery in Wapping. At least, the owner, Tiny Prodger, had described it as up-and-coming. However, the prints had been on the walls there for a couple of weeks with no sales. Then a buyer – a city slicker looking to diversify his investments and simultaneously tart up his penthouse apartment – had approached Steve privately. He wanted all the prints. Sixteen of them. Steve curtailed the arrangement with Tiny Prodger's gallery and then sold them privately to the slicker, avoiding the gallery commission. All would have ended well but for his own loud mouth. He'd boasted of his shrewd move to a blabbermouth, and word had got back to Tiny.

Tiny, six foot four and ugly as a manatee, was not your average art gallery owner. In his earlier days he had been a professional boxing trainer. He still kept his hand in at a boxing club he owned near the gallery. In a phone call to Steve he had let it be known that he had friends at the club with some rather disagreeable tendencies. One or two of them were inclined to play fast and loose with the law. One or two of them were bare knuckle fighters. These friends were unfortunately homophobic, and, if given to understand that Steve was a poofter as well as a cheat, would enjoy nothing better than to rearrange his facial features to their own preferences. Steve tried to persuade Tiny that the buyer had only appeared on the scene after the end of his show in the gallery. Tiny said he didn't buy that story about the buyer, and put the phone down with a final imprecation. Nothing had come of it, but still it preyed on Steve's mind as he walked along a quiet street in Fulham, or emerged from a club late at night in Kensington. Tiny might have thought putting the frighteners on him was a sufficient revenge – or he might just be biding his time.

He was under no illusions about why he had been offered the job here at Forthburgh School of Art. The Principal, a popinjay clad in primary colours named Edgar Peabody, who was chair of the interview panel, had clearly made up his mind before he even entered the room. He flattered himself that Peabody must have seen him as a catch, with his international reputation. Besides, from what he had seen of the other candidates, he didn't have strong competition. They had been left in a room together while waiting to be called in to the panel. There was a morose bearded fellow, the insider candidate who had been in the institution for years and quite possibly regarded himself as a shoo-in now that the incumbent had retired. He had barely spoken. Then there was a woman with purple dyed hair, an air of intense inner pain and an almost impenetrable accent. These attributes would surely count against her, in spite of her status as Hungary's premier exponent of post-communist works in rusted iron recovered from abandoned military hardware. His third rival for the post, a rotund fellow defiantly dressed in grubby jeans and a t-shirt, was plausible in conversation, but the glance at his portfolio that he had vouchsafed revealed his achievements to consist only of some gigantic wooden polo mints in a Derbyshire field and what looked like a malevolent concrete jelly baby glowering across a Midlands railway station concourse.

After the interview's positive conclusion, he went straight to a grimy phone box located just outside the art school and rang Derek. Derek McCafferty was the prime reason for applying for this particular job.
"So, did you get it?"
"Yep. I'm coming to live with you in Forthburgh!"
"Fantastic! Champagne tonight!"
"Mmm – sounds good! Well, you're stuck with me now!"
"That's what I wanted."
"That's what I wanted too. I'm over the moon."
"See you later darling!"
"See you later, gorgeous!"

A few weeks later, in early September, Sidling made his way to his future place of work so see how the land lay. Between the imposing columns and looming pediment of the main entrance, a wide man in a dark jacket was smoking. He observed Sidling's approach without expression. There was something toad-like about his general appearance; a giant smoking toad.
Sidling smiled politely and attempted to skirt around him.

"The buildings are closed. Vacation," the toad said, making a barrier with his arm.

"Ah. I'm Steven Sidling, the new Head of Sculpture. I was told that staff could access the school outside term time."

The large man took a drag from his cigarette and blew it not so very far from Sidling's face.

"Got any ID?" he grunted.

Luckily Sidling's driving licence was in his wallet. The man looked at it suspiciously and handed it back.

"Are you…," Sidling hesitated. What might this surly brute's position be?

"… are you a janitor?"

"I'm the head janitor."

"Ah, good."

It was not good, but Sidling was determined to make the best of it. He held out a hand.

"Pleased to meet you."

The man looked at his hand as if it might be carrying some unknown virus. Then he shook it as briefly as he could.

"And your name is…?" Sidling suggested.

"Miggs."

"Good. Pleased to meet you Mr Miggs."

"It's just 'Miggs'".

"Okay. Pleased to meet you, Miggs. I wonder if you could tell me where my office is located?"

Miggs sighed, as if imparting this kind of information was outside his remit.

"Go into the entrance hall and turn left. Ground floor. You'll see signs to Sculpture. In the first studio there's a wooden staircase going up. It's at the top of that."

"Excellent, thank you!"

Half way along the broad corridor leading from the entrance hall, something occurred to Sidling. He retraced his steps. Miggs was just re-entering the building, exhaling his final lungful of smoke.

"Er… is the office kept locked?"

"Aye."

"Could I have the key then, please."

Miggs passed wordlessly behind a counter and entered a room on the other side, visible through a glass partition commanding a view of the entrance hall. Sidling observed him opening a narrow cabinet and running his hand along a row of keys suspended from hooks. He returned with one, which he gave to Sidling with an air of reluctance.

"You keep this one. We've only one spare, so don't lose it. Change of lock due to lost key is charged to whoever lost the key."

"Thank you," Sidling replied, forcing a smile with difficulty, and set off once more along the corridor.

On arrival, he surveyed his new office with dissatisfaction. He had already discovered, on the occasion of his job interview, that Forthburgh Art School's 'old' building, outwardly a gracious and imposing edifice in the Beaux Arts style of the nineteenth century, was inwardly a guddle of half-arsed adaptations to its modern usage. This particular office seemed to have been jammed as an afterthought into what was intended as an internal roof space. The exterior window vanished into the floor as if it had slipped down at some point in the past and never recovered itself. Presumably it was only the upper portion of a much larger window. The top of his share of the window was approximately on a level with his stomach, so only when seated could he see through it to the vista of spires and steep-pitched roofs that surrounded the art school like the set of a gothic horror film.

This unsatisfactory office would have to be dealt with, in due course.

He re-locked the door and descended the rickety staircase that connected this eyrie to the rest of the sculpture department and embarked on an exploratory stroll around his new domain, which he'd only briefly taken in when he attended his job interview. He found a linked series of airy high-ceilinged studios, some cleared out after the departure of the graduating students, others filled with the untidy detritus of the second and third year students who would be returning at the end of September. Apparently, a Scottish art degree required four years of study. First year students attended a general course in a different building with different staff, and would not be his concern. He noted a number of half-finished works that the general public would have no difficulty in identifying as 'sculpture'. That would all have to change.

A sound of hammering started up somewhere. That was odd. In all the vacation-becalmed studios and corridors he hadn't seen a soul. He followed the sound to its source, a small studio with a north-facing window looking towards the soaring bulk of the city's castle. The door was wide open, and he went to the threshold and peered in. Because he was wearing soft-soled moccasins, his approach was a silent one.

It was the big bearded fellow who had been the internal candidate for the job. His name came back to him… Duncan McBane. He had his back to the door, and he was driving a metal wedge into a great lump of stone with a sledge hammer. How the heck had that stone been manoeuvred into this space? As Sidling stood there, the man delivered a final mighty blow and the stone split in two. The two halves – each the size of a refrigerator – peeled away from each other and the metal wedge clattered onto the wooden floor. McBane stepped back quickly to save his toes from being crushed, set down the sledgehammer, and wiped his brow with the back of a hairy arm. Sidling cleared his throat to announce his presence, and McBane swivelled around swiftly and eyeballed his new boss.

"Hi there!" Sidling said, raising a friendly hand in the air.

McBane's features maintained their granite impassiveness, but his lips, almost invisible beneath their hirsute curtaining, twitched a little.

"Ah… Mr Sidling."

"*Steve* please! We're in an art school, let's have no formality! I see you're at work on something, Duncan?"

McBane's eyes drifted to the two substantial pieces of stone at his feet.

"Aye."

"Something for yourself? Or a commission?"

"It's to be for Shobbs."

Did McBane have a cold?

"Shops?"

"Shobbs Prison."

"Oh?" Sidling said encouragingly, and waited for more.

But nothing more came. Sidling realised he was dealing with that breed of Scot who allowed only the minimum amount of personal information to escape into the world at large. He girded his loins, mentally.

"How interesting. What will it be?"

Now McBane couldn't escape that question. Not unless he was prepared to be outright rude. Sidling observed the man's dark eyebrows lowering a little, like furry animals trapped in a corner, crouching.

"I'm doing two heads."

"Heads? What sort of heads?"

"A prisoner and a warder."

"Where is it… are they… to go?"

"One on either side of the new entrance gates. On top of pillars."

"How will people know which is the prisoner and which is the warder?"

McBane shot him a look of disdain.

"The warder will have a cap on his head."

"Ah."

He waited a little, to see if McBane would come up with a conversational topic of his own. A deep silence pervaded the art school around them. Outside, a church bell began to toll.

"Well, I'll let you get on," Sidling said at last, admitting defeat.

McBane nodded.

"See you later!" Sidling added, with a pleasant smile. Let this hairy brute see what good manners were!

There was no reply, only another small twitch under the beard. It might have been a smile, or it might have been a grimace of pain. Sidling turned and walked away down the corridor. Clearly McBane had attended the same charm school as Miggs. Pray God all his future colleagues were not cast in the same mould as these two! Behind him, he heard a grunt, and a grating sound made, he assumed, by a very large piece of stone being dragged over wooden floorboards.

A few weeks later, entering the staff canteen and surveying the faces that were becoming familiar, Sidling was just beginning to feel at home at Forthburgh Art School. After queuing for his coffee and Kit-Kat he made for the corner table where Arabella Wood from the Fashion Department was just about to sit down on her own. She didn't get on with her boss, Leonora Hunt, the Head of Fashion, and so she and Leonora always took their coffee breaks at different times. He had made her acquaintance during the first week of term when he had ventured a compliment on one of her outfits – and they had hit it off immediately. Today, her slender figure was clothed in a mini-dress with alternating bands of gold and black material. Her earrings sported antennae that poked upwards and forwards through her long curly dark hair. As he joined her, it occurred to Sidling that this waspish appearance accorded well with her sting-in-the-tail sense of humour. He was not averse to sitting with the other sculpture staff, or going into the student canteen with some of his students – after all, he had new loyalties to work on in both camps. But his preference was for half an hour of scurrilous gossip and badinage with Arabella, who was a woman after his own heart. Like him, she had bold, revolutionary ideas for her department. But unlike him, she didn't have the power to implement them. She looked up with a grin as he sat down opposite her.

"Hi Steve!"

"You're looking pleased with yourself."

"Am I?"

"Like the Cheshire Cat," he suggested.

"Oh dear, is it so obvious?"

"Good night in the sack, was it?"

"No. David's in Bristol for a conference."

"A *dentists'* conference?"

"Apparently they have them."

"Well - one can amuse oneself, Arabella."

"Well, amusing oneself might count as a good night in the sack for you, but I prefer company."

Sidling chortled.

"Well, there's something making you look cheerful, admit it."

Arabella smirked.

"Oh, it's nothing. I just got one over on Leonora, that's all."

"How?"

"Long story, but in a nutshell, she'd got one of our best final year students all geared up to create a Forties style collection for her degree show. Leonora can't get enough Forties revivalism. But I had a long chat with Gwendolyn this morning and she's going to change tack. We talked about a collection of outfits for the robots manning a spaceship in the thirtieth century."

"Quite a shift."

"Gwendolyn is malleable. The Forties thing was only because she couldn't come up with a good idea of her own and had fallen prey to Leonora. It was an idea off the top of my head. I told her not to mention it to

Leonora until she'd done some preliminary sketches and so on. I don't want her being talked out of it."

"You're a devious type."

Arabella shrieked with delight. Out of the corner of his eye, Sidling caught one or two heads turning. But Arabella's noisy outbursts were part of the fabric of life in the staff canteen, and the heads quickly returned to their previous business.

"You're not so *undevious* yourself," she replied, reducing the decibels somewhat.

"There's no such word."

"You know what I mean. How are the *Ambient Interventions* going?"

"It's early days. I've started sowing the seeds among the students."

"Not the only seeds you've been sowing?"

Sidling adopted a blank look.

"I don't know what you mean, Arabella."

"Nothing, nothing. I just wondered about that hunky, dark-haired boy from... where is it? Latvia?"

"Artjoms?"

"Is that his name? I like it. Artjoms. Good name for an artist."

"He's Estonian. What about him?"

"Don't try to look so innocent. I've seen you chatting him up around the place!"

"I'm not chatting him up. Or only about ambient interventions."

"So far."

Sidling was unable to supress a grin.

"So far," he agreed.

"You'd better be careful. Staff/student relationships... murky waters."

"It's an art school for God's sake. Aren't we expected to be lechers and deviants?"

"You're mixing it up with being an artist. An art lecturer ...."

"Lecherer?"

"Pay attention! An art *lecturer* has to be a pillar of respectability and a model citizen. Like me."

Their eyes met and then they both burst out into their characteristic noises of hilarity: Arabella a seagull who has just found an abandoned chip wrapper and Sidling a raccoon calling for a mate.

Heads turned again, among them that of Duncan McBane, seated at the far end of the canteen with his usual coffee mate Angus Campbell from the Painting and Fine Art Department. Angus had just returned to work after a heavy cold, and so was not familiar with the newcomer. He turned his circular-framed spectacles on Duncan.

"Who in Christ's name is that?" he enquired, his ruddy, whisky-veined nose wrinkling in disgust.

"Fucking Sidling," Duncan replied.

"Oh, aye – your new boss, eh?"

"Unfortunately."

"From down south, isn't he?"

"Aye."

Angus ran his fingers through his lush ginger beard, a sure sign that some notion was struggling towards the light in his brain.

"He'll be back off to London within a year or two, will he no?" he suggested after a few seconds.

"I wouldn't be so sure. I think he's got personal reasons for being here."

"Oh aye? Scottish wife?"

"He's not married. But I've heard him talk about his *partner*, and I happened to see him last week prancing down the Regal Mile with a fellow in a pink Pringle jumper."

"A poof, then?"

"I'd say it's more or less certain."

"So he's probably not trying to get into that Fashion lassie's knickers."

"No way."

"She's no bad looking, that Arabella – in spite of her weird outfits."

"Aye, she's a bonnie lass," McBane concurred. "A bit noisy though."

Angus Campbell leered like a satyr.

"You'd know about it when she cums, eh?"

McBane snorted.

"Aye! And so would the neighbours!"

They sipped their coffees, mulling over that.

"Have you no had a beer with him yet then, or anything?" Angus said after a few moments.

"Who? Sidling?"

"Aye. A bit of personal chat, eh?"

McBane shook his head and shrugged.

"I wouldn't want to."

"Have you never heard the expression 'know your enemy?'"

"He's not my enemy."

Angus Campbell nodded seriously for a moment or two, running his fingers through his ginger beard. Duncan waited patiently for his friend's train of thought to arrive at the station. Finally, Angus winked.

"But you hate his guts anyway, eh?"

Mc Bane leaned back in mock horror, and then they both laughed. Low secretive chuckles. From the other end of the canteen, another bout of shrieking hilarity reached their ears.

Angus looked at his friend for his cue, and they mouthed the words together.

"Fucking Sidling!"

They chuckled again.

As Sidling's first term as Head of Sculpture progressed, he found himself drawn more and more to the student Arabella had teased him about. Artjoms Ubags. The Estonian was a fine physical specimen, around six feet tall and muscular without being overly bulky. He had jet black hair worn quite long, with an unruly lock that flopped forward regularly over one of his eyes. Sidling was charmed by the casual sweep of the hand with which Artjoms cleared this obstruction from his vision every few minutes. He observed that he seemed quite influential among his peers, in spite of being somewhat aloof and enigmatic. Leafing curiously through his file, Sidling saw that he was twenty five years old, a little older than most of the other students in his year group, and that he had worked as a lumberjack in his native country after finishing secondary school. Hence the fine musculature, perhaps.

Artjoms reacted very positively to Sidling's ideas of taking sculpture out of the studio, the gallery and the usual kinds of public space into less obvious environments, where it could surprise and disrupt. Ambient interventions, in a word... or two words. 'The Department of Ambient Interventions.' That would be something! Sidling was itching to make his mark on this stuffy old institution, and getting rid of the boringly obvious 'Department of Sculpture' label would be a fine symbolic stroke. Maybe it could be achieved in time for the next academic year, if he could only gain sufficient traction. Artjoms – talented, influential, and delightfully handsome - was a good place to start.

The trouble was, that after some long talks in the studio, and an evening drinking bout that somehow ended up in Artjoms's flat with one empty bottle of Scotch and two full condoms, it was becoming apparent that Artjoms was a very complicated young man indeed and was developing an excessive interest in Sidling himself. On two murky evenings in late November, walking home from the art school to the Victorian suburb where Derek had his flat, Sidling had experienced a prickling sensation at the back of his neck, and turned around to look behind him. Both times, a shadowy figure that might or might not have been Artjoms was a hundred yards or so away, stopped dead in its tracks like a statue. Was he following him home, to find out where he lived? Did he already know? Did he also know about his partner, Derek? Could he be jealous? This was all worrying.

In the light – or dark – of these troubling episodes, Sidling decided that the drunken sexual encounter with Artjoms would most definitely have to be a one-off. Admittedly, he wasn't averse to one-night stands when Derek was away on business, but the one-night rule was a rigid one, in every respect. After all, wasn't it primarily to be with Derek that he'd applied speculatively for the job at the art school? Their relationship, which had started with occasional meetings when Derek was visiting London for work reasons, had evolved into the most stable partnership he'd ever experienced. He'd never shared a home with anyone until now. The free-wheeling life of an internationally acclaimed artist (the phrase was not uncommon in gallery catalogues and press reviews, and it always gave him a smug little thrill) had previously suited him well. He was *un citoyen du monde*. He'd long since lost count of the men he'd shagged in various corners of the globe, although some encounters – like that with the Vatican priest in a discreet corner of Saint Peter's, or the vertiginous rogering by a Polish crane operator – were particularly fond memories. While habitually sceptical about the concept of 'being in love', he recognised that his feelings for Derek were different from those he'd felt for any previous lover. There was an innate gentleness about Derek that contrasted with the rougher sexual partners that had always previously appealed to Sidling. But he had succeeded in developing in Derek a taste for the kind of role-play that he himself found stimulating. What was completely new though was the calm and satisfying domesticity of his new life with Derek in Forthburgh. Perhaps, at thirty five years old, he was 'settling down'?

Anyway, this was one apple cart that he didn't want to upset. Derek didn't know about his one night stands, and he certainly didn't want him to know about Artjoms. Artjoms had now to be kept at arm's length emotionally and physically, but cultivated and influenced nonetheless as a useful ally in his quietly germinating plan to supplant 'Sculpture' with 'Ambient Interventions'.

"You know, Steve..." Artjoms addressed him one day when they were alone in the studio where Artjoms was nominally based, "... you know, I think I have new inspiration to share with you! I think I see connect between your ideas of sculpture as intervention, and folklore of Estonia and other Baltic countries."

"Oh?" Steve replied.

"Yes. For example your hedgehog building that you once made. The building you cover with spines – or *spikes* you would say?"

"The German town hall project?"

"Yes. The hedgehog is in some Baltic folklore a symbol. Is symbol of... what do you say... regeranation?"

"Regeneration?"

"Yes, 'regeneration' and fertility. Just like you are regeranating... sorry... regenerating... in this art school the idea of sculpture. You are fertilising it with seed of new thoughts, new ideas."

"Ah, yes," Steve replied.

"So, yes. The hedgehog..." Artjoms continued, warming to his theme, "... so in Latvia, for instance, in wedding songs, they might call the bride the *she-hedgehog*, and they might call the married women there *the mothers of hedgehogs*."

Artjoms was to be cultivated and humoured, but sometimes he went off on some baffling tangent. Where was he headed now?

"Really? I had no idea," Sidling said. It sounded downright perverse to him. What bride would enjoy being compared with a hedgehog?

22

"So – my idea is to make marriage this concept of the she-hedgehog with other folklore idea from my own country Estonia, Steve. This is the idea that we can go to a crossroads at midnight and call up the Devil."

Artjoms looked expectantly at Sidling as if he might burst into applause at this brilliant juxtaposition. Sidling considered his response carefully.

"Interesting…" he said, as a holding position.

"Yes. It is interesting. So… probably you hear of our Estonian folklore idea of *kratts*?"

"Er… no, I don't think so Artjoms. Have you mentioned them before to me?"

"I don't know if I mention it, but is a very well-known thing in Estonia. The *kratt* we can say is kind of supernatural servant. We can get one by going to the crossroads at midnight to call up the Devil. Then with only three drops of our blood we can get the kratt."

"That's a very reasonable price."

Artjoms didn't spot the humour.

"Yes, it is good price. But on other hand the Devil… well, he gets to keep your soul when you die. And this is my idea: that I make some kratts and put them at the different crossroads in places in Forthburgh. What do you think? Is a good idea, no?"

"Interesting… er, what will these kratts look like? Hedgehogs?"

"No, no. That is just where idea comes from to me. This is beauty of idea: each kratt will have different features, but they will all have common features also. The kratts will be inspire by different people who have sold their souls."

"Politicians, for example?"

"Yes, I think politicians very suitable. Perhaps Margaret Thatcher will be one. She has sold her soul for this poll tax, no? The tax that everyone here in Scotland is protest about?"

"So your work will be quite political?"

"Not only. Some will be more positive things. I will make one special for you, Steve, even though you haven't sold your soul. In fact, you are a man with great soul."

Artjoms fixed his deep brown eyes on Sidling's, and a tentative smile illuminated his handsome, habitually serious features. Sidling repressed a strong impulse to take him in his arms, here in this deserted studio. That would be a very bad idea.

Back in his cramped and unsatisfactory office, Sidling was still dwelling on the agreeable Artjoms. What if he had given in to temptation and invited him up here to this private place, and locked the door? He was just starting to experience a stirring sensation in his trousers when his telephone rang.

"Yes?"

"Steve?"

"Yes, who's that?"

"You don't recognize your old pal's voice?"

A nasty feeling like a heavy stone falling into the pit of his stomach made Sidling shudder.

"Is that Tiny?"

"Well done mate! Indeed it is me! Tiny Prodger. Art dealer and boxing gym owner. How are you doing there? Scotland suiting you is it?"

Sidling didn't reply. He felt his tongue cleaving to the roof of his mouth, which had suddenly gone dry. His hitherto tumescent cock was shrinking like a snail pulling in its horns.

"Nothing to say? I'm sorry, mate. We used to have lovely chats, didn't we – you and me – when we was in business together. Anyway, I just wanted you to know that I've kept tabs on you. Just in case you thought you'd been forgotten. Do the words 'twenty per cent' mean anything to you?"

"Listen, Tiny…"

"No. *You* listen! Twenty per cent was what you owed me when you sold them photos. But you know how it is. Inflation and all that. Now that twenty per cent seems to have turned into fifty per cent. I'm guessing you got about ten grand for them. So the two grand you could have given me then has turned into five now. That's capitalism, that is. Wonderful thing, in its way."

Sidling found his voice.

"I told you, Tiny. I sold those prints well after our arrangement came to an end."

"Well, we don't quite see eye to eye then. Pity. Anyway, thought I'd just let you know that I know where you are. Might pop up to Forthburgh one of these days. Beautiful city I believe. Never been there. You know how to get in touch, Steve. A cheque for five grand, that'll sort all this out. Cheerio now!"

The phone went dead. Sidling stared at the fanciful gothic spires and turrets outside his window, receding down the slope towards the Brassmarket. A "beautiful city..." There would be nothing beautiful about it with Tiny Prodger prowling its streets.

He'd been a fool to let this thing stay unresolved! And now the bill for his folly had escalated. Perhaps he could borrow five thousand off Derek? If he could spin a story to Derek that didn't reveal his own embarrassing duplicity in the affair, then perhaps the best thing would be to finish this business once and for all. Could he come up with a convincing story? Should he come clean, and risk diminishing himself in Derek's eyes? Perhaps if he could raise the original two thousand that would be enough to keep Tiny away. He had to do something! He had felt safe until now here in Forthburgh, but he couldn't go on living with this sword of Damocles suspended over his head.

CHAPTER 3

September 1989

Coupar made a quick assessment of the man entering the interview room at the police station, the first interviewee on his list. The man who shared the victim's address.

Mid-forties, but pulling out all the stops in an attempt to hide it. The hair was recently cut and styled, its rich coppery tint forming an incongruous topping to the lined skin of neck and face. A bulging belly was held unwillingly in custody by the waistband of designer jeans. Dark bluish shadows under the man's bloodshot eyes suggested sleeplessness. Perhaps he'd been crying.

The bulky figure of Constable Waterhouse waddled into the room behind the man, shut the door, and eased down onto a chair beside it. He glowered suspiciously at his charge, like a bull walrus guarding his harem.

"Mr McCafferty?" Coupar verified.

"Yes."

"I'm Inspector Coupar Cruickshank. I'm the deputy chief investigating officer in the matter of the murder of Steven Sidling."

"I see."

"Please sit down."

Surprisingly, the tight jeans permitted this manoeuvre.

"I'll be tape-recording this interview, Mr McCafferty. I take it you have no objection?"

"No... no, of course not."

Coupar pressed the record button on the cassette player on his desk, and adjusted the position of the little microphone so that it pointed squarely between them to pick up both voices. He spoke slowly.

"Investigation into the death of Steven Sidling. Interview One. Interviewee Derek McCafferty. Twenty first of September Nineteen Eighty Nine. Interview conducted by Detective Inspector Coupar Cruickshank, in the presence of Detective Constable Neville Waterhouse."

He sat back slightly, and went on in a more conversational tone of voice.

"Mr McCafferty, could you confirm for me if Steven Sidling was a paying tenant at your address, or if he was a friend?"

"A... friend, yes. We shared the household bills. There was no tenancy."

"Can you tell me about what you were doing two days ago, on the day he was killed?"

"I was at work as usual all day."

"And in the evening?"

"I was at home."

"Were you expecting him to be with you?"

"Absolutely. I was surprised when he wasn't at home after I returned from work. But I was seriously worried when he still hadn't appeared by bedtime."

"That was unusual?"

"He would normally phone if he was going to be late."

"Did you do anything to find him, when he hadn't come home later?"

"There was nothing I could do. I thought of ringing one or two mutual friends, but I didn't want to start a panic. Or set stupid rumours flying. It wasn't... well... it was unusual, but not entirely unknown..."

"What? That he would stay elsewhere overnight?"

Derek McCafferty ran a hand down the side of his head, as if wiping something away.

"It happened one or two times."

"Mr McCafferty, it will assist me greatly if you can be frank in this matter. Were you and Steven Sidling in a relationship?"

"Yes. I'm sorry. Somehow I thought you'd know that, or assume that."

"We try not to make assumptions, Mr McCafferty. Facts are what we're after, in a situation like this. Hard facts. So, you were alone all that evening?"

"Yes."

"And you came straight home from work?"

"Yes."

"What time did you leave work?"

"About six thirty."

"What is your place of work?"

"I'm with Granville and Barker."

"Investment management?"

"Yes. On Drumscleuch Terrace."

"Were there others there at six thirty, when you left?"

"I left at the same time as one of the other fund managers. We walked along the street a little way before parting."

"And after that time, did you see anyone else?"

"No… well… I did go out at about nine o'clock. To get fish and chips. Steve had said he was cooking supper, so I'd waited and by then I was starving."

"You must have been a little angry?"

"More worried than angry."

"Do they know you at the fish and chip place?"

"No. I hardly ever go there."

"Did you speak to the staff? Anything that they might remember?"

"It was a big woman who served me. A big woman with black hair. I had the exact change and she said that was helpful."

"And the rest of the night you were at home, on your own?"

"Yes."

"Did you sleep well?"

"Not really. I was worried. I heard a downpour of rain."

"But you stayed in?"

"Of course I did. I looked out of the window at some point, and it was sheeting down."

"Otherwise you might have gone somewhere to look for Steve?"

"No. I wouldn't have any idea where to look."

"But you looked out of the window to check the weather?"

"It was just because the rain was coming down so hard. I wanted to see. I think I fell asleep more soundly after that, at least for a spell."

"What do you know about how Steven's body was found?"

"What I read in the papers. It was horrible."

"We were too slow to stop some of the details getting out. It isn't helpful for us."

Without warning, Derek McCafferty's face crumpled up. He groped in a pocket for a handkerchief, and sobbed into it. It sounded like a gasping for air, interspersed with desolate whimpering. Coupar exchanged a look with Waterhouse, who gave a slight nod. Coupar interpreted that as confirming his own thought: this was not a piece of play-acting.

On the other hand, you might murder someone and still be racked with grief.

After a long minute, the sobs subsided. Derek McCafferty wiped his face with the handkerchief. His eyes were redder than ever.

"I'm sorry, Inspector. Please go on."

"Do you have any thoughts on who might have wanted to kill Steven, Mr McCafferty?"

McCafferty shook his head.

"That's what I've been dwelling on. Who could do a thing like this? And the only thing I can think of is that he was frightened of someone in London."

"Who?"

"He didn't give me a name. It was something he didn't want to talk about."

"Why was he frightened?"

"I can only guess. I think he'd done something he was a bit ashamed of, and he didn't want me to know about it."

"But what sort of thing?"

"I think it must have been to do with money. He once said that he'd done nothing illegal, but that from a certain point of view he'd not acted as he should have done."

"But you think he'd made an enemy of someone?"

"Definitely. He made a bit of a joke of it once or twice. Called the person *my London enemy*. I tried once to get the whole story, but like I said, I think he was embarrassed about what he'd done."

Coupar jotted down *London enemy?* on his notepad.

"Have you any other information you think might help us, Mr McCafferty?"

"He was a great guy…"

Derek McCafferty's face began to crumple again.

"… a great guy. So full of life… I can't believe he's gone…"

Coupar flicked off the cassette player.

"We'll probably have to interview you again, Mr McCafferty. Obviously you'll want to help us find out who did this?"

"Of course. Of course. What kind of maniac…?"

His voice faltered, and a tear appeared at the corner of an eye. He pulled out the handkerchief once more.

"Would you have any objection to me coming over to your flat and taking a look at Steven's personal possessions? No uniformed officers will come. Quite informal – I'm not applying for a search warrant."

Derek McCafferty dabbed at his eyes.

"You can do that, of course. Anything that will help."

"And… just one more little thing before you go. Would you mind writing something down for me on this sheet of paper? Just a couple of words, in block capitals?"

"What do you want me to write?"

"Just write *amplify independence.*"

"What?"

"*Amplify independence.*"

"In block capitals?"

"Yes, please. It will be helpful."

Coupar spent that night at Lisa's. He was surprised when she phoned and invited him around. It wasn't one of their regular nights. They had been in a relationship for over a year now, but there had been no talk of shared accommodation. They had a well-trodden routine for togetherness. He spent two nights a week at her place, and on one other night they'd go out together to the cinema or to a restaurant. On those nights they'd kiss goodnight at a bus stop. It kept the relationship 'fresh', as Lisa said. Coupar wasn't so sure. He never felt entirely certain about Lisa's commitment. She was nearly ten years younger than him, and very attractive. Working as a receptionist at the sports centre, she would be in daily contact with all kinds of athletic young men who might try to chat her up. And the demands of his job sometimes meant that the thrice weekly routine was diminished. Sometimes he only saw her once a week.

There was no mistaking her pleasure in seeing him this evening though. She opened the door with a glass of wine in hand and a big smile on her face. She was wearing the low-cut spangly top that was generally a reliable clue that seduction was on her agenda.

"Hi Coopsie!" she said, planting a wine-flavoured kiss on his lips. "Come in and tell me how it's going!"

"How what's going?" he said, following her into the living room. The main light was off, and only a couple of lamps illuminated the space.

"Don't be silly," she giggled, pouring him a glass of wine. "The case, of course! I've been reading about it again in today's paper. They've called it *The Hedgehog Murder!*"

"I know they've called it that. It's a real nuisance."

"What is?"

"Details like that getting out. At least they don't know about the note."

Lisa sat down next to him on the sofa, and snuggled up close.

"Note? What note?"

Coupar cursed inwardly. He'd forgotten that he hadn't mentioned the note to Lisa.

"I shouldn't say."

She pulled away slightly.

"You don't trust me?"

"Of course I do. But I really shouldn't..."

"What did the note say? Where was it?"

"It was..."

He hesitated. Lisa rested a hand on his thigh.

"Go on!"

"...it was in the victim's nostril."

Lisa's eyes widened.

"God! That's creepy! And what did it say?"

"It was wet, with the rain. There were two words, in capitals. But I couldn't make them out."

"Not at all?"

"No. Impossible to read."

He was fairly sure that one word began with 'A' and the other with either 'I' or 'L'. But he'd blabbed enough already.

She nodded. The hand on his thigh gave a little squeeze.

"Do you mind if I tell Dan?"

Coupar looked at her, surprised.

"Dan?"

"At the sports centre. He's one of the tennis coaches. He's writing a crime novel. He loves details like that."

"Of course you can't tell him!"

She looked a little pouty.

"I told you, it's important to keep some details from the public," he explained. "There's always a chance that the killer will reveal himself by mentioning something that isn't widely known."

"Or *her*self?" Lisa suggested.

"In theory. But I think we're dealing with a man."

"Or a transsexual?"

Sometimes, Coupar thought, Lisa's thought processes were just baffling. She looked at him expectantly. No, she definitely wasn't making a joke. He sighed.

"Yes, in theory, we could be looking for a murderous transsexual."

CHAPTER 4

October 1988 – February 1989

Duncan McBane was in the little room designated as 'the Sculpture library'. It was more often used as an informal coffee and farting station by the department's technical assistant, Rory Coggs, a rosy, rotund young man with curly hair who looked like a cherub who had fluttered out of a Raphael painting. But it did contain an untidily stacked bookcase, as well as a low table, and three wonky plastic chairs, on one of which Duncan perched as he thumbed through the library's latest addition – a book about Steven Sidling written by some pretentious London dickhead, and donated to the library – with a flamboyant signature on the title page – by Steve Sidling himself.

Duncan would not have liked anyone to see him showing an interest in this book. He was disgusted that someone like Steve Sidling would have a book dedicated to him at all. But he was looking at the photographs it contained of Sidling's work on a *know your enemy* basis. It was his pal Angus Campbell who had put that idea into his head. If he was to orchestrate resistance to the kinds of change that Sidling had started to talk about, then Angus said it was necessary to know what he was up against. Occasionally even slow-witted Angus could come up with a good idea.

The first few illustrations – poor quality black and white photographs - revealed that Sidling's earliest works were graffiti perpetrated during his sixth form schoolboy years in Sheffield. One of these featured on the cover of a Sunday Times magazine in 1972, having been 'discovered' by an influential art critic and gallery owner who was prospecting for talent 'up north'. The graffiti was on the side of a large brick building, and featured a gigantic cartoonish hedgehog with a speech bubble saying 'fuck off!' Sidling's meteoric rise to art world success proceeded apace through his art college years, when he developed his 'ambient interventions'. As far as Duncan could make out from the photographs, these always consisted of inserting something ugly and incongruous into an otherwise inoffensive setting. For his degree show he dressed down a bunch of out of work actors and created a 'homeless village' of cardboard boxes photographed at dawn in front of Buckingham Palace. The press loved it.

For the next thirteen years he was a darling of the art world as he travelled Europe and America 'intervening'. He was lavished with Arts Council and private funding. The book concluded with a double page spread of his biggest project, executed a year or so ago, in which the town hall of some unfortunate German city had been wrapped in brown sacking and furnished with hundreds of protruding spikes. It was a return to the hedgehog of early days, as noted by the London dickhead in the caption beneath the picture.

Duncan closed the book with an irritated snap and threw it back on the table where it had been artlessly left on display, no doubt by the arch interventionist himself. He fell into a dark reverie. This Sidling had floated effortlessly into prominence like a puffed up balloon, in galling contrast with his own more modest artistic success, chipped splinter by splinter out of the hard unyielding stone of his medium. It was relentless dedication to his craft that had pulled him free of the violence and self-loathing of his early years; a long, hard road to travel. Like Bunyan's pilgrim he had escaped from a Slough of Despond. Now he felt as if his feet were sinking once more in that swampy ground. Why on earth had Principal Peabody and the rest of the interview panel delivered Forthburgh School of Art's Sculpture Department into the hands of such an iconoclast? Were they mad? Did his own proud roll call of eminent Scottish figures standing in monumental splendour in town squares and parks throughout the land count for nothing? They had received a slap in the face, these eminent Scots, just like him. They had all been spurned in favour of an upstart southern meddler whose misguided travesties didn't warrant the label of 'art', let alone the even higher distinction of 'sculpture'!

Such were the brooding thoughts that Duncan shared with his pal Angus Campbell in the pub that evening. They were in the Tap of Poverty, the nearest drinking hole to the art school, and consequently a frequent haunt of staff and students alike, despite its charmless décor and bar staff. On Fridays he and Angus would generally down a few bevvies there after work, neither having a home to go to, to speak of, or a woman to go home to either.

"Well, we've got a prick in charge of Fine Art as well..." Angus remarked, wiping the foam from his third pint of heavy from the ginger shrubbery around his mouth ..."Peabody's filling the place with his own kind."

Duncan snorted.

"It's always the pricks that get the plum jobs," he replied.

Angus nodded. His fingers went foraging in his beard. Presumably his beery thoughts were off on a new track.

"Speaking of pricks, are you absolutely sure that Steven Sidling of yours isn't banging that Arabella Wood?" he said at length.

Duncan shook his head.

"He's definitely not shagging any woman."

"I know you think he's a poof, but..."

"He's definitely a poof."

"… but I've observed them, you know? They seem pretty close, him and her – and the noise they make!"

"Just pals, that's all, I guarantee it."

Angus gave him a wink.

"Bet *you* wouldn't mind giving her one!"

Duncan took a sip of his beer.

"Eh?" Angus prompted slyly, his eyes narrowing behind his round spectacle lenses. "You've told me before that you quite fancied her!"

"Maybe a little. But it's never going to happen."

He took a longer draught of his beer. Angus ran his fingers through his beard again.

"She's a big pal as well of that Hermione Cutter."

"What?"

"Pals. Her and Hermione Cutter."

"Who?"

"Arabella Wood."

"No, numpty! I mean who's Hermione Cutter?"

"Hermione Cutter? Ach… you'll know her face. She comes in three days a week, I think it is. Takes drawing classes."

"Oh aye. I think I've spoken to her once or twice. Tall, thin woman, greyish blonde hair, a bit nervy looking?"

"That's the one. Her and Arabella are like that."

He wrapped his two forefingers together as a demonstration of their closeness.

"You're not saying…?" Duncan looked at him, surprised.

"Ach no, Hermione's married. And I don't think Arabella Wood is that way inclined either."

"How do you know all this about who's friends with who?"

Angus tapped the side of his nose.

"I just keep my eyes open, Duncan. Besides, I get on all right with Hermione. She's a pharmacist, apparently."

"A pharmacist?"

"Aye – or used to be before she took up painting. Unusual, eh?"

"I suppose so... but then you used to be a rent boy before you started painting."

Angus roared, and slapped his hand on the table.

"Fuck off, McBane!" he said amiably.

When they'd finished their fourth pints, Angus made his way off to continue the evening at his local, which was on the other side of town from Duncan's abode. Duncan decided to call in at The Bull's Tail on his way home. This was a bit of a posh pub, and he didn't take to the clientele, nor they to him. But it was on his walking route, and they had a fine collection of single malts. A nice single malt was what he fancied before he took himself on to his own local for the rest of the evening. An evening that would most likely end with a craving for a carry-out curry, to be consumed in the squalor of his flat, like most Friday nights.

As he sat nursing his Talisker and mulling over the general unfairness of the universe, he was startled by a familiar noise nearby, as if a seagull had got trapped in the pub and was screeching for the exit. It was the subject of his recent conversation, Arabella Wood. She must have already been sitting in the adjacent booth when he came in. He hadn't seen her, and the pub's music and chatter had until now masked her voice. But now that distinctive voice was rising to a pitch of indignation.

"You're selfish! That's all! And you don't give a damn about my feelings!"

A low murmuring male voice could be heard in reply. Not a voice that Duncan recognised. Arabella's tirade continued.

"If you'd said that right at the start, it would have been different. But you let me just go on in the dark, didn't you!"

The male voice rose a little in volume in protest, but the words were still indistinguishable.

"Well that's it, then! Just go! Just go!" Arabella shrieked.

Duncan heard a muttered male voice saying "Fuck!" and then a well-dressed man with thick black hair made his way swiftly across his range of vision, moving away from the booth and out of the door of the pub. Not anyone he'd ever seen before. After a pause he thought he heard sobbing. Yes, it was Arabella sobbing.

He swirled his whisky around in the glass and took a thoughtful sip. Should he do anything? It would be very awkward if she chanced to see him sitting here, within earshot of that dust-up.

He slid silently and unobserved out of his own seat. He felt sorry for her. Perhaps it was the drink talking, but he felt he could comfort her. And, in spite of her unfortunate voice, and her ill-judged friendship with Steven Sidling, he did fancy her! Indecisively at first, but then making up his mind, he traced a circuitous route around the far side of the bar and then approached Arabella's booth from a new direction, as if he had just come from buying his drink and spotted her there.

"Arabella!" he said, expressing surprise and pleasure. Then, as if noticing her distress for the first time, he added a note of concern. "Are you okay?"

She dabbed at her eyes with the tissue already in her hand and mustered a faint smile.

"Oh... hello Duncan! I'm sorry... just had an upsetting moment."

"Would you rather be on your own?"

She continued dabbing for a moment, and then shook her head.

"No, no. Have a seat Duncan. It'll do me good."

He observed that her wine glass was empty.

"Can I get you a drink?"

"Oh... yes, thanks. A sauvignon blanc please. The New Zealand one."

Duncan went to the bar and bought a large glass of the wine and another single malt for himself. When he returned, Arabella had clearly made an effort to pull herself together. The slight smears of running mascara had been wiped away, and fresh lipstick applied. She received her drink with a smile, and immediately took a big gulp from it.

"I've just broken up with my boyfriend," she said.

Duncan arranged his features into a look of sympathetic interest. His eyes flickered to the plunging neckline of her red blouse, and back up to her face. Circumstances might be propitious, he thought, depending on her mood and alcohol intake. It wasn't as if they needed to get to know each other. That spadework was already done, although they hadn't ever gone beyond superficial conversations.

"Do you want to tell me about it Arabella?" he said, assuming the most sympathetic tone available to him. It sounded more or less okay to his ears.

Arabella shook her head slightly.

"I don't want to bore you."

Duncan thought he detected an interrogatory glance at him.

"You won't," he assured her.

"Well, I'll keep it short. His name was... well it doesn't matter. He's a dentist."

"Is that how you met?"

She snorted and smiled at him. Duncan felt this was already going well.

"No. He's not my dentist. We met at a party in the Georgian Quarter."

"How long ago?"

"Only three months ago. And it's all been a lot of fun, until I got wind of something a couple of days ago. Someone mentioned that he'd bought a house in Bristol."

"Bristol?"

"Yes. So I tackled him about it tonight. Turns out he's moving to a dental practice down there. It's been lined up for nearly a year. Someone retiring. And he never said a dicky bird to me about it. He was just going to slope off without a care in the world. I was just a fling, right from the start, and I didn't get it. I thought we were building something together."

"A house somewhere?"

Arabella snorted again and then laughed.

"No, you idiot! Not a house. A relationship. A long term one."

Duncan nodded. She'd called him an idiot in an affectionate way. That was extremely positive, wasn't it?

"I suppose I was half prepared for tonight," she went on. "Knowing about the house in Bristol. That was the worst moment, when I first heard of that. I came here more or less expecting we'd break up. The bastard never even tried to suggest I should go to Bristol with him!"

She put on a face of brisk cheerfulness and took another glug of her wine.

"I think I'm ready to move on already!"

Duncan glanced again at her neckline. If she needed help moving on immediately, he was her man. He smiled at her, and they clinked glasses and drained the contents.

"Another one?" he said.

The next morning, prodding her gently awake and putting a mug of tea down next to her on the bedside table, Duncan observed a look of bewilderment on Arabella's face as she raised her head slightly. Her eyes roamed, unfocussed, across the peeling ceiling of his bedroom and she emitted a long, low groan before she spoke.

"Where am I?" she said, in a voice about an octave lower than her normal pitch.

"My place," he confirmed quietly, taking a sip of his own tea. She winced and shut her eyes again, laying her head back on the pillow as if it were an eggshell that she might shatter. Duncan stretched out again on the bed beside her. He had a banging hangover himself.

"Oh, God!" he thought he heard her mutter under her breath. He hoped she was referring to her hangover rather than the locale or the company.

"Good night, last night, eh?" he said. From his point of view it had been a very good night indeed. He'd been celibate for about two years; wasting time making sporadic attempts to get his wife back, until a year or so ago. But last night proved he hadn't forgotten how to do it.

"What, breaking up with my boyfriend?" she croaked, and reached over to get hold of the mug of tea.

"No. I'm sorry about that," he lied. "I mean later on. I'm glad we got together. I've always liked you."

Leaning on her elbow, she looked at him now for the first time. It was a hard look to read, at least for him. Her eyes took a journey down his torso. He was in good shape, he knew, in spite of his intake of beer and whisky. That was mostly only at weekends. He worked out at the gym, from time to time, and hewing stone kept the muscles in trim. To his surprise, and relief, she put down the cup of tea and turned over onto her side to nestle against him with her head on his shoulder.

"You're nice," she said.

About a minute later she was asleep again, snoring deeply.

The next two weeks were a blur of lust, as Duncan made up for his long drought and Arabella expunged the dentist from her memories. They slept together every night, either at his flat or hers. At the art school, she continued to associate noisily with the odious Sidling, but Duncan let it ride. He didn't want to bring up a bone of contention. He just made sure that his true feelings about his Head of Department never came out into the open when he was with Arabella.

To his own surprise, over the following weeks Duncan found his feelings for this intoxicating woman growing beyond his control, like ivy climbing up a sturdy oak tree and smothering it. He suspected that, like ivy, Arabella was really using him as a convenient prop, to give her exposure to the sunlight. She liked having his arm to the round of exhibition openings, fashion shows and parties that made up her world, and demonstrating to any dentist or other previously unsatisfactory partner (Duncan identified two without difficulty by observation of body language, and suspected many others) that she had 'moved on' and was perfectly contented with her lot. He had a foreboding that it would be wise to cut off this clinging addition to his life at the root, but he was powerless to do so. Swept along in the updraft of an alien social whirlwind, and helpless prey to surges of jealousy, affection, obsession and lust, Duncan found that he was falling in love. And yet he couldn't help observing that Arabella was flighty, flirting with any presentable man who came her way.

He didn't shine very brightly himself at these social gatherings that came thick and fast, and she was increasingly inclined to tick him off for what she described as his 'gloomy Scottish outlook on life'. He objected that this was racist stereotyping. She retorted that she was Scottish herself, and therefore licensed to make observations about her fellow countrymen. The great saving grace of their relationship was the sex, which was inventive and enthusiastic, as Arabella introduced him to a number of hitherto unexplored practices. He'd never read the *Kama Sutra* – he'd only heard of it – but he imagined Arabella would be able to write a chapter or two of her own.

As well as bringing his sex life up to speed, she also took him in hand sartorially. Dissatisfied with the drab corduroys and faded fleeces that were his habitual garb, she led him, sheepish and only half-willing, into expensive shops whose existence he had never previously noticed on Regency Street. There, in a matter of hours, he parted with more money than he had spent on clothes in the previous two decades in order to fit the bill as Arabella's man-about-town.

All this was destined only to last for less than four months.

In February, they attended a private view of work by Hermione Cutter, the pharmacist-turned-painter who worked part-time at the art school and was an old friend of Arabella's. When Arabella wasn't with Duncan, she was frequently spending time with Hermione. Hermione was only a few years older than her – in her late forties – and they shared a lot of common ground. Apparently, they met up at least once a week at Arabella's flat over a bottle of wine. Although Hermione was married, her husband was often away on business, and their only child, Roland, was away at university. So she was always up for an evening of booze, gossip, and art talk. At the art school, once or twice, Duncan fell in with Arabella and Hermione briefly, but he never conversed with Hermione on his own.

Hermione was primarily a portrait artist, turning out ugly misshapen images reminiscent of the twisted angst of certain works by Francis Bacon. Her wealthier sitters sometimes purchased their likenesses, but they were more often snapped up by collectors who saw her unusual style as an investment opportunity, especially as her output was sparse. The private view encompassed around thirty works that had taken her five years to produce.

The show was hosted by a private gallery in the Georgian Quarter called The Blinking Eye, and all the staff of the art school had received an invitation as a matter of course. Arabella had pointed out to Duncan that there would be free prosecco, and suggested they might go on for dinner afterwards at the excellent Thai restaurant around the corner. She would meet him at the gallery, as she was going to go early to help Hermione 'relax' before the event. Duncan took this to mean drink before the event.

When Duncan entered the gallery it was already ringing with the chatter and laughter of a crowd well lubricated by free alcohol, few of whom were paying any attention to the paintings on the wall. He peered into the first room, looking for Arabella. Edgar Peabody, clad in sky blue jacket and tartan trousers, was holding forth in there to a cluster of bored looking individuals. He also observed Arabella's head of department, Leonora Hunt, who was languidly posing amidst another grouping in her forties garb looking, or trying to look, like Lauren Bacall waiting for her camera call.

He advanced to the next room, where he was accosted by Hermione Cutter herself, who, he quickly realised, was indeed half-cut.

"Duncan!" she exclaimed, in a tone of enthusiasm that he had never before called forth from her. In fact, he was slightly surprised that she knew his name. Perhaps Arabella mentioned him frequently. Quite tall already, she was wobbling now on high heels that brought her face to face with him. Her rather thin lips were fleshed out with abundant rouge, and her hair had been modelled into a flawless dyed blond curtain that rested triumphantly on her bare shoulders. "How lovely that you could come! You don't have a drink!"

She turned and waved a peremptory hand at a young person nearby with a tray of glasses.

"Here, Ariadne! A glass of wine for our eminent sculptor Mr McBane!"

Duncan received his glass and raised it to his hostess.

"Congratulations, Hermione! Quite a show!"

He hadn't so much as glanced at a painting yet, but there was no need to admit to that.

She fixed him with a grateful smile. Not only her lips, but her eyes too had been artificially enlarged by abundant make-up.

"Do you think so?"

He was going to have to offer more, he realised. These glasses of prosecco came at a price.

"Yes. Eh... I like the boldness of form and colour you use..."

He could see one of the portraits over her shoulder. It looked like a lump of uncooked meat balancing precariously on top of a man's jacket. He also spotted Arabella now, just to the right of the painting, nodding enthusiastically to some remark by her companion, a handsome man in a suit and tie, probably in his late forties. He felt a qualm of unease.

Hermione was looking at him out of her mask of mascara and rouge, waiting for more.

"I particularly like that one," he said, indicating with a nod the picture behind her. She half turned.

"The one beside Arabella and my husband?"

So that was who it was! Duncan experienced a sense of relief. He might reasonably expect that Arabella wouldn't be trying to get off with Hermione's husband right under her very nose.

"Yes..." Hermione went on. "That's the most recent picture here – I only finished it a week ago. I feel it may be the start of a new phase in my work. I'm freeing myself from the figurative, looking for a more... a more brutal... that might be the word... a more *brutal* style of portraying the human essence."

CHAPTER 5

September 1989

Arabella Wood knocked on the door of the little office in the art school that had now been allocated to the police. It was five in the afternoon. She would go straight home after this. It had been preying on her mind all day, this interview.

A voice called her in, and she opened the door.

"Arabella Wood? I'm Inspector Coupar Cruickshank. Please come in and sit down."

Arabella was a little surprised by how young the detective looked. Only in his early to mid thirties, she thought. He was putting a cassette into a cassette-recorder. There was an ashtray on the desk, so Arabella assumed that it was okay to smoke, and she fumbled a cigarette out of the carton in her handbag and lit it.

"Are you ready?" he asked, as she exhaled the first calming stream of smoke into the air above her. She was back up to twenty... well, twenty five... a day since poor Steve had been murdered. She felt on edge all the time, these days.

"Yes."

He pressed the record button.

"Investigation into the death of Steven Sidling. Interview Twelve. Interviewee Arabella Wood. Twenty sixth of September, Nineteen Eighty Nine. Interview conducted by Detective Inspector Coupar Cruickshank, in the presence of Detective Constable Neville Waterhouse."

Arabella glanced over Cruickshank's shoulder to where Waterhouse was sitting on a plastic chair beside the door. He was a burly figure with a big nose, and he was staring at her in an unnerving way. She suddenly had a trapped feeling. This office was very small, and stuffy with the exhalations of previous smokers. She took another long drag at her cigarette.

"So, Miss Wood... how long have you worked at Forthburgh School of Art?"

"Three years. Since Autumn, Nineteen Eighty Six."

"In the Fashion Department."

"Yes."

"So you must know most of the staff of the art school?"

"More or less. A lot of them just to nod to or say hello to, though."

"But Sidling... Steven Sidling... he was a better friend of yours than most, I gather from some other staff that I've interviewed."

"We generally had coffee together in the mornings."

"Just the two of you?"

"Usually."

"Why was that?"

"Why did we have coffee together?"

"No, why just the two of you?"

"We were just friends. We had a laugh together."

"But I gather most of the staff tend to sit in groups. The tables in the canteen are round, with eight or nine seats."

"There are smaller tables too. And sometimes we sat with other people."

"Sidling with the other sculpture lecturers and you with the fashion staff?"

Arabella uttered a short dry laugh.

"No."

"Why was that?"

"Neither of us was universally popular in our own department."

"But Sidling was the head of his department. Surely he had to get on with his staff?"

"We were both interested in changes to the way things were done. Steve had only been in the art school for a year, but he was stirring things up considerably in Sculpture."

"In what way?"

"He wanted to get away from the whole traditional aspect of sculpture. His own work was quite different. He liked the temporary and provisional: exciting bold interventions in unexpected places. He found most public art boring and uninspiring."

"And this wasn't popular?"

"At first it wasn't. But he won people around gradually – even the most doubtful ones in the end. The department and the art school's academic council agreed to a change of name, from 'Sculpture' to 'Ambient Interventions'. It was going to go ahead this academic year. It was his baby. He was excited. Now I don't know what will happen."

Coupar opened a little notebook. He put a finger on a page covered in scrawled handwriting.

"There are six lecturers in the Sculpture department, three of them part-time, and a technician."

He glanced up.

"If you say so," she replied. "I don't really mix with them, but I think I would know all their faces."

The detective nodded.

"I've spoken to all of them now. I believe there is *one* of them you know quite well?"

Arabella took another puff from her cigarette. She could guess what was coming up. It didn't have anything to do with this murder. It was her private life. She felt resentment about to break through.

"Duncan McBane," Coupar Cruickshank added.

"Did you get that from him?"

"No. One of the others mentioned that you and he had… well, had had a relationship."

"It ended last February. We had a *relationship*, as you call it, for barely four months. Does that have anything to do with anything?"

"I need to build up a picture of everything surrounding the victim – his friendships, relationships, and so on. Anything might be relevant. Would you call Duncan McBane, or any of the staff in the Sculpture department, an enemy of their head of department?"

"In what sense? Ready to kill him?"

The detective's eyes widened fractionally.

"You're jumping the gun there, Arabella... Miss Wood. No... I just mean, would you say any of them nursed a particular antipathy towards him? A really strong dislike?"

"A number of them, I daresay, at first. But, as I said before, he was winning them around. In fact I'd say he'd won them around already. Including Duncan McBane."

The detective nodded.

"Okay. What about you and Sidling? Steve Sidling?"

"What about us?"

"Were you in a relationship?"

Arabella stared at him.

"Are you serious?"

"Yes."

"Well, if you've done your homework, you'll already know that Steve was gay. Haven't you spoken with his partner Derek, the man he lives... lived... with?"

"Derek McCafferty? Yes, I've spoken with him."

"Well then..."

"But there are people who swing both ways, so to speak."

"Steve wasn't one of them. He only liked men."

"Men? Plural? Did he have other relationships?"

"What did Derek say?"

"I'm asking *you*. Perhaps you were more likely to know than Derek, as a close friend of Steven."

Arabella thought back over the sleazier secrets they had shared. She felt reluctant to betray the confidences of a dead man. But the detective was staring at her expectantly.

"He... he used to frequent certain places. Bars and clubs."

"With Derek?"

"More without Derek."

"Gay venues? Places where he might pick up a man?"

"I believe so."

"And he told you about these... adventures?"

"Sometimes, a little."

"Did he mention names?"

"Not really. They tend to stick to Christian names, apparently."

"Who does?"

"Men who like casual sex."

"Did he mention any Christian names then?"

"Not especially."

"None at all?"

"No, not that I can remember."

"What about the venues – the bars and clubs. Was there anywhere he used to go in particular?"

"There was a place... somewhere he'd only gone to maybe a couple of times. When Derek was out of town. He found it a bit frightening though."

"Where was that?"

"*The Devil's Dungeon* it was called."

"I've never heard of it. Where is that?"

"Somewhere off Drumpelier Park. A basement place. Apparently it doesn't have a sign up outside. It's a kind of private club. You needed a card to get in."

"Why was it frightening?"

"The men who went there... they were into rough stuff. S and M."

"Sado-masochism?"

"Yes. He only discovered it a couple of months or so ago."

"In the summer?"

"Yes."

"You still met up with him during the summer? Outside term time?"

"Once in a while. There's always stuff do be done, even when the students are away."

"Would you arrange to come in on the same days?"

"We'd be in touch, yes."

"How many times did you see him over the summer break?"

"I don't' know. Maybe four times, maybe five. He was away a lot. Spain on an art project. Majorca with Derek. London... although..."

"Although what?"

"There was something about London. I can't remember... he only mentioned it once. There was someone there he was afraid of, but I don't know why."

"Derek McCafferty mentioned that too. Don't you know any more?"

"No. He didn't want to go into details."

"Nothing at all?"

"No, sorry."

"Okay. So, going back to The Devil's Dungeon... was Steve into *rough stuff*?"

"I think he was experimenting."

"On the sadism or the masochism?"

"He liked to be tied up for sex. He told me that Derek sometimes did that. But it was an extra kick to be tied up by a stranger."

"You were very frank in your conversations."

"Yes. But you mustn't think... you mustn't think Steve was some sort of... I don't know... some sort of raving pervert. He was a witty, super-intelligent, creative man..."

Now she felt tears welling up. Her best friend at the art school! Gone. Murdered. Horribly murdered in some deliberate, calculating way. The newspapers' details of how he was found haunted her imagination. She took out a handkerchief and dabbed at her eyes.

"Take a moment, Arabella. I'm sorry you've lost your friend, but we have to gather as much information as we can about Steve's private life if we're to find who did this. Are you okay now?"

She nodded. That fat silent policeman by the door was staring at her like she was a hamburger he'd like to eat. She suddenly felt desperate to get out of there. She needed a quiet place in which to have a good cry.

"Are we nearly done?" she said.

"Nearly, Miss Wood. So, it's fair to say that you knew things about Steve Sidling that his partner Derek didn't know. Did you ever feel guilty? Knowing about Steve's relations with other men?"

"It was a little uncomfortable, at times. But I didn't know Derek well. I only met him for the first time this summer."

"Through Steve?"

"No, through my boyfriend.... partner."

"Who is that?"

"I don't see..."

"Miss Wood, please... anything could be relevant."

"His name is Ted."

"Ted...?"

"Ted Cutter."

"Someone who came along after Duncan McBane?"

"Yes, obviously. I don't keep several men on the go at the same time."

She scowled a little, although inwardly acknowledging that this was not entirely true. She was sometimes guilty of rather impulsive liaisons. The fat guy by the door was hanging on every word.

The Inspector uttered a dry, mirthless laugh. He scribbled something down in his notebook.

"Just clarifying the connections, Miss Wood. Just clarifying. So this Ted Cutter knew Derek McCafferty?"

"They were at university together."

"But he's not gay?"

"Of course he's not gay. Why would he be my boyfriend if he was gay?"

The detective looked thoughtful for a moment, and then took out a printed sheet from a folder and scanned it.

"There's a Hermione *Cutter* on the part-time staff list here. Any connection?"

Arabella stubbed out her cigarette.

"He's her husband."

Thank goodness she didn't have to go back into the teaching studios after this interview, with her mind in an irritated turmoil. She felt as if it had been an investigation into *her*, not into Steven's murder. Why had she been made to reveal details of her own private life to that annoying and persistent detective and the fat goggle-eyed pig at the door? It was a violation! When she got home, she made herself a good stiff gin and tonic. Ted came in a few minutes later, and she made one for him too.

"Your son left a phone message," she informed him.

"What did he say?"

"Just to give him a call."

"Okay."

She didn't like finding Roland's voice on the answer machine. It was *her* answer machine, in *her* flat. But Ted's son never acknowledged that. He only left messages that began 'Hi Dad!' His voice, a little high-pitched for a man, reminded her invariably of his mother. It was bad enough that she had to see Hermione Cutter looking daggers at her at random moments whenever they encountered each other at the art school. The frequent phone incursions of Hermione Cutter's son into her cosy Scotsbridge flat were almost as bad. The only time she had met Roland, who was now away in England at university, he had behaved with a frosty politeness that conveyed his disapproval as clearly as if he had said *I wish you were dead*.

Ted had moved in with her in June, leaving Hermione in possession of the family house in Martinside. He claimed to enjoy the Bohemian disorder and compact dimensions of her flat. But she couldn't see that lasting. He was used to living in style, and she'd seen him looking at the property pages of The Scotsman. Whether he was looking for a bachelor pad or a new home for the two of them she didn't know, and it was too soon to ask.

"I'll call Roland later," Ted said, subsiding into the sofa next to her. His neat grey suit looked incongruous against the magenta throw with its beaded fringes. She was still in her hippy revivalist phase of home décor. She couldn't afford to change her furnishings as often as her wardrobe. Friends jokingly accused her of changing her man as often as she changed her appearance. Well, Ted was one man she intended to hang on to, if she could. The equivalent of a timeless little black dress or a pair of classic blue jeans. A standby for the future. The richest man she'd ever got hold of. Rich *and* nice.

Arabella snuggled up to him, inhaling that faint aroma of musk, patchouli and sandalwood that accompanied him wherever he went. An aroma that spoke to her of masculine potency and money spent on expensive *eau de parfum*.

"What have you been up to today?" he said, taking a gulp of his gin and tonic. He was a handsome man, but he had a prominent Adam's apple that ran up and then down his neck like a mouse as he swallowed. It was only a small defect, like one of the tiny deliberate flaws that Islamic artists inserted into their works, to demonstrate that only God was perfect.

"I had my police interview after work," she replied.

"Oh... about Steve?"

"Yes."

"How was that?"

"Unpleasant. A policeman nosing into your private life. Two policemen in fact, although one of them only listened."

Ted looked slightly alarmed.

"What did they want to know about your private life?"

"Don't worry, they didn't want to know about you. Have you committed a crime?"

Ted pulled a face.

"Not recently. Go on..."

"Well, it cropped up that you were a friend of Derek's."

"Cropped up? How?"

"I'm afraid I let it slip, Ted. It doesn't matter, does it?"

"I suppose not. Although it might mean I get dragged in for an interview I suppose. Most murders are committed by the victim's partner I believe. So they may want to dig into what I know about Derek."

"I'm sorry, Ted. I shouldn't have mentioned the connection."

He patted her knee.

"Don't worry, gorgeous. I've nothing to hide. It's just a slight nuisance, if the police do follow up."

"I didn't like the detective. Cruickshank, he's called. He weaselled stuff about Steven's private life out of me. Although I suppose if it helps to catch the bastard who did it..."

"The sort of things you've told me? His clubbing?"

"That sort of thing."

"Do you think it was one of his weirdo sex contacts that... you know..."

Arabella looked down at her drink, watching the bubbles of tonic winking at the surface of the liquid. It occurred to her that Steve's life had been a bit like that – a rising bubble of effervescence and liveliness, suddenly and brutally popped.

"I really don't know. I suppose that's the most likely thing. Although there was one of his students who Steve thought had a bit of a fixation on him. A

Latvian... no, Estonian. He thought he might have followed him home once."

"Did you tell the police about him?"

"No. Maybe I should have done. But I felt it would be unfair."

"On the student?"

"Yes."

"Did he have the look of a murderer?"

"I don't know. Do murderers have a special look?"

Ted shrugged.

"I suppose not. And what about Derek McCafferty? Did you say much about him?"

"Not really. The detective asked me about him, but I didn't have much to say. Apart from that time we went to the restaurant with Steve and Derek, I don't know him."

"Derek was on the phone to me yesterday."

"Oh? Why?"

The mouse in Ted's throat carried another gulp of gin and tonic down to its destination.

"He'd had a long interview the day before with that same policeman – Cruickshank – that's his name isn't it? He was a little upset. I think he just wanted to talk things through. He's always used me as a bit of a listening post. At university I was the first person he told he was gay."

"Such a coincidence, Steve Sidling getting together with an old friend of yours."

"Life is a long series of coincidences, don't you think?"

"I suppose so. You can only see them after the event, but I suppose that's true."

CHAPTER 6

February – May 1989

As the interminable Scottish winter reluctantly dragged its feet into what was whimsically called 'Spring', Duncan felt that the Sculpture students were one by one slipping away beyond his sphere of influence. The stone carving workshops were empty. His slide presentations on the 'old masters' of sculpture were thinly attended. Steve Sidling's school of thought was beginning to prevail. Led by his preaching, and the urgings of his almost fanatical disciple Artjoms Ubags, many of the students were abandoning all efforts at acquiring the skills he had himself mastered after years of learning and practice, and were heading out into the world at large to 'intervene'. On one occasion he'd had to go and disengage a second year student from police custody after he'd climbed onto a railway line dressed as the Pope. Had Sidling directly incited this act of madness? The student, sheepish in his cardboard mitre, denied it. But Duncan had no doubt that the inspiration for such tomfoolery emanated from the new cock of the walk, the odious Sidling.

Worse – even worse than losing his grip on the students – Duncan sensed his grip on Arabella's affections weakening in the aftermath of that occasion at The Blinking Eye Gallery. Unfortunately his own feelings had crossed the Rubicon, and now there was no rowing back. In spite of Arabella's flightiness, he sought her company, and her bed, whenever he could. He thought about her all the time. His desperation began to show. He carried a small passport photo of her in his wallet, which she had given him in the early days, and he looked at it over and over again, as if possessing it were also to possess Arabella herself – a kind of voodoo doll or a talisman against losing her. When she was otherwise engaged – which was with increasing frequency – he spent his own evening brooding over what she might or might not be doing. He was in the grip of an obsession, however much he wished he wasn't. He could see the end of the road ahead, and it looked very much like a cliff edge that he would drive over with his foot still on the accelerator.

Finally, after a week without sex, and then another entire week of lame excuses for not even having a drink together, he pinned Arabella down to a rendezvous after work. She proposed meeting in The Bull's Tail. He turned over its associations in his mind as he made his way there. It had been the scene of their first get-together, and he had a fondness for it as such. On the other hand, it had been the venue for her break-up with the dentist, his predecessor. Perhaps it was a habitual location for Arabella's brush-offs. He entered the pub with a sense of apprehension.

"Hello Duncan," Arabella said, as he arrived at the booth she was already occupying. It was exactly the one from which the dentist had been dispatched. She had nearly emptied a wine glass already, he noticed. She was the fastest female drinker he'd ever known – which was hardly a cause for complaint, as it was that very trait that had caused her to fall into his arms in the first place.

"Hi Arabella," he said, and leaned in for a kiss. She gave him a cheek rather than her lips and his sense of dread deepened.

"I'll go and get a drink," he proposed. "Another glass of sauvignon for you?"

"Yes please."

He selected a Macallan for himself, poured a little water into it, and returned to his lover. If that's what she was, a fortnight after they had last been in bed together.

"So, how's it going?" he said, forcing a light and cheerful note.

"Not bad. I've prised most of this year's final year students out of the nineteen forties."

"So Leonora must love you more than ever."

"She's spitting mad inside. But she maintains a front of politeness."

Arabella took a sip of her wine. Duncan suddenly felt completely unable to make small talk.

"Arabella... I feel as if you're drifting away from me," he blurted out.

She put down her glass and examined her fingernails.

"I was going to talk to you, Duncan. Things have been moving fast this last week or two."

"What things?" he said, hot jealousy stirring like a scaly dragon in his guts.

"There's someone else I've been seeing."

Now a black tide of despair came welling up inside him, dousing the dragon's fire in a surge of bitterness.

"Oh..." he said, and couldn't go on. The black wet tide had reached his eyes. He was going to cry. Right here in this bloody pub, in front of Arabella, he was going to break into sobs!

"I'm sorry, Duncan. I wasn't certain at first. I promise I didn't sleep with him as long as... as long as you and I were doing that. I don't like overlaps."

"Overlaps..." he echoed, attempting a tone of sarcasm. But the word blended into a gulp of air, and then he *was* crying, as he knew he would. He put his arms on the table and buried his head in them, trying to hide.

He felt a hand on his heaving shoulders.

"Duncan – I *am* sorry. I could see you were getting... well... too attached to me."

The hand was withdrawn, and his tears flowed for a minute or more. He wasn't certain if she was still there. Perhaps she had fled after delivering her apology. Perhaps the other drinkers in The Bull's Tail were gathering in a bewildered knot around him, wondering what to do, embarrassed. He groped blindly in a pocket for a handkerchief, lifted his head and dabbed at his eyes. A watery image of Arabella was still there across the table, dissolving.

"But I love you!" he ejaculated.

The fragmented watery Arabella image shook its head ruefully.

"I didn't want that. We had some fun, that was all. Now I've met someone else…"

"For more fun?" he said bitterly. The tears were drying up at last.

"No. No, this is more serious. This… well… this is the kind of relationship I've been needing for a long time, I think. I'm sorry Duncan, but it could never have been like this with you. I've moved on, and you'll have to do the same."

She took another gulp from her wine glass, polishing off most of the contents, and then put it down unfinished.

"I don't think we've got any more to say at the moment," she went on. "I hope we can still be friends."

And with that she leaned forward, gave him a little squeeze on the shoulder, and stood up to leave.

"Can't we…" Duncan protested. *Can't we what?* he thought.

"There's no point."

"Who is he? At least tell me that!"

Arabella looked at him. She appeared undecided.

Suddenly it was important to Duncan to know this.

"Just tell me, and then go."

She nodded.

"Okay. He's called Ted. Ted Cutter. He's the husband of Hermione Cutter."

And with that she turned on her heel and left.

Duncan departed an hour and three whiskies later, and plodded with slumped shoulders through the rainy streets towards his flat. He splashed through puddles, beyond caring. Half way along the deserted Dolry Road, a young man emerged suddenly from a doorway without looking, putting up an umbrella that struck Duncan on the side of the head.

"What the fuck!" Duncan said, swiping the umbrella away from him.

"Oh, sorry pal!"

That apology might have been enough, if it had been uttered without an edge of amusement, and not followed by a chuckle.

Duncan swung a haymaker fist into the young man's cheek, sending a pair of spectacles flying into the roadway. The man sank to his knees with a cry. The black circle of the umbrella, released, rolled away on a gust of wind. Duncan took aim, and imparted a vicious kick at the man's ribs.

"Shit! Stop man! I'm sorry!" the young man shouted as he keeled over onto his side, flapping his hands in a feeble attempt to defend himself.

When he was down, Duncan contemplated him for a moment. His father had always imparted a final kick, if it was him or his mother that he'd brought down onto the kitchen floor. The memory of his father lent an extra impetus to Duncan's valedictory brutal punt into his victim's spine. He left him lying on the pavement groaning, and resumed his route, quickening his pace. The guy might go back indoors and call the police. The sooner he got off the street and into his own flat, the better.

The only attention Duncan received from Arabella from this time forward, when they happened to encounter each other around the art school, was confined to a nod and a forced smile. For his own part, he couldn't muster either the nod or the smile.

It was in the staff canteen that her presence was most upsetting, because there he could hear her as well as see her. He avoided it for a few days, but Angus ticked him off, and he missed it, so he resumed his usual habits. The morning coffee break was sacred to the lecturers; a ritual which extended sometimes to an hour or more, when they could all relax, chew over the issues of the day, the latest television series, or the local gossip, wallowing in the knowledge that they were being paid for their time. On most of the occasions when he went in, Arabella and Steve Sidling were ensconced in their usual corner. He tried to sit with his back to them when he could, but then he could still hear fragments of their conversation, as could the whole canteen. The jealousy that gnawed at his innards found a more ready focus there than in the almost ethereal Ted Cutter, her new paramour. Cutter was a man he had only met once - barely met at all. They had done no more than be introduced and shake hands at Hermione Cutter's private view. Instead, stoked by his dislike of all that he stood for, and all that he was trying to change in the Sculpture Department, Duncan's hatred centred itself on Sidling. Why was Sidling on such intimate terms with Arabella? Why did they greet each other like long lost friends on a daily basis in the canteen? What did Steve Sidling have that he, Duncan, lacked, that he should be the Head of Sculpture and the intimate friend and confidant of Arabella Wood?

It made him feel sick. A nasty, physical sensation, although emanating from an emotional cause.

"You look sick," Angus said, breaking into a chocolate bar. "You all right, Duncan?"

Duncan tried to rouse himself from his gloom.

"Aye, I'm fine."

"Still the Arabella thing?" Angus suggested, guiding the chocolate bar through the tangles of his ginger beard.

"Aye, I suppose so."

"She's not worth the angst, laddie! You're well out of it."

Duncan nodded.

"Do you want to hear a joke?" Angus suggested.

He didn't want to hear a joke, but this was clearly Angus's only resource for cheering him up. He nodded again.

"So... this horse goes into a pub. He goes and stands at the bar for a while, and the barman notices him and comes over and says *why the long face?*"

Angus leaned back with a grin and stared expectantly through his round spectacles at him.

Duncan gazed at Angus blankly. Was that it?

"You get it, man? *Long* face!"

It dawned on Duncan that this was the sort of thing a barman might say to a silent gloomy customer. He mustered an imitation smile.

"Very good, Angus, very good!"

"Christ! If Tommy Cooper had had you in the audience he'd have given up."

"I'll be better company in a wee while."

"Let's all hope so. It's like having coffee with an undertaker these days."

At that moment a fragment of Arabella's conversation flew into Duncan's ear like a shard of breaking glass.

"Fishface!"

It was uttered in a tone of delighted scandal, and followed by a peal of appreciative shrill hilarity, mingled with the only slightly lower-pitched tones of Steve Sidling cackling.

Duncan felt his heart turning to stone, as if a Gorgon had caught him in her gaze.

Fishface was the nickname he'd painfully and unwillingly carried through his years at secondary school. Some twelve year old wit had discerned in his rather weak jaw and wide-lipped mouth a resemblance to the goldfish that swam in a tank in the school's entrance hall. Once pointed out, the idea caught the popular imagination, and he was stuck with it until he left school. From the age of nineteen onwards he had cultivated a beard to disguise this deficiency in the chin department. The nickname had been lost in the mists of time. He had once confided in his wife, who had shrugged it off with the remark that she thought he was perfectly handsome with his beard, and she had no wish to see him without one.

This must be some coincidence. There was no way that Arabella and Sidling could have stumbled across this old cross that he had had to bear. They must be talking about something else entirely, surely?

While nodding with apparent attention to Angus's sporadic remarks, Duncan strained to catch more fragments of Arabella and Sidling's conversation. They seemed to be talking about Glasgow. Seemingly Sidling had been spending a day there over the weekend. He caught the names of a gallery and Byres Road. The next phrase that he picked up made it clear, all too horribly clear, where the reference to Fishface had come from.

Crumpets with poached eggs was the phrase, and like the final piece in a jigsaw puzzle it clicked into place in Duncan's mind, and confirmed his worst suspicions.

His ex-wife, Mary, now shacked up with a lanky journalist in Glasgow, ran a café on Byres Road. Crumpets with poached eggs were one of her signature offerings. Obviously Sidling had been a customer, they had got chatting, and the connection had been established. Then Mary – he could picture her malicious little grin – had vouchsafed the hideous epithet from his past. Fishface had risen from the grave of his tormented childhood to haunt him once more.

It was bad enough knowing that Sidling and Arabella were now familiar with this old soubriquet. But worse was to come. A week later, as he was approaching the open door of one of the sculpture studios, he could hear that a lively conversation was in full flow within, interspersed with bouts of hilarity. He could distinguish one or two of the students' voices, notably that of Artjoms, whose accented English and forceful timbre stood out from the others. Then again it came to his ears, that insidious slithering word, ending in a serpentine hiss. *Fishface!* It was Artjoms who had uttered it.

He didn't even pause outside the door, much less enter as he had intended. He passed onwards in a turmoil of impotent fury. So Sidling had revealed this old nickname even to the sculpture students! He was known widely now, as in his schooldays, as Fishface! They might not shout it out at him, but they would use it behind his back. It was too much to bear, and he vowed not to bear it. Somehow, some time, he would exact his revenge!

From this period onwards, he thought he could detect a secret smirk on the face of everyone in the Sculpture department. From Sidling to Artjoms, to the second, third, and fourth year students, the postgraduates, to even the cherubic rosy-cheeked face of Rory Coggs, the technician. The smirk was in their heads rather than on their lips. But he could imagine the little voice inside them that was chanting out at him, as if across a frosty winter school playground: *Fishface! Fishface! Duncan is a Fishface!* He began to drink more heavily, and at his local, The Pig with Wings, in Dolry Road, he fell as a consequence more often into the company of another habitual heavy drinker there, Lemmy Stoter.

Lemmy Stoter was a man of around seventy, small and wrinkled well beyond his years, who looked as if he'd spent his life trying to batter down walls with his nose. He'd served twenty years in Shobbs for the murder of a man who had run off with his wife. He wasn't shy about it. In fact he was a bit of a celebrity in the Pig with

Wings, and didn't need much encouragement to talk about his time in prison and the people he had met there. Also, after a bevvy or two, he wasn't shy about the murder itself, and his habitual conclusion never varied.

"Aye, he was a wee bastard and it was worth twenty years o' ma life to twist the knife in his guts and see him aff the scene."

Lemmy was enchanted by the fact that Duncan had made stone heads for the gates of Shobbs Prison, which he tended to refer to as if it was his own place, like a wealthier man might have a 'place in the country'. He brought up the heads every time they were drinking together.

"They heids, y'ken Duncan...they heids... are you sure you didnae have me in mind for the prisoner wan?"

Duncan smiled indulgently into his pint of heavy. This was Lemmy's usual opening gambit.

"I told you, Lemmy, they're more kind of abstract, you know?"

"Abstract? You mean they havnae got eyes and ears and that?"

"They've got them, but they're not like real ones. They're... well, monumental."

"Big, ye mean?"

"Big, aye, and also kind of... well, not detailed. Have you seen the Easter Island statues?"

"They on Easter Road?"

"No, no. In the south seas. The south Pacific."

"D'ye think I've been surfin' aboot in the south Pacific? For Christ's sake, man!"

"No. I mean have you seen photographs? They're these famous heads."

"On an island?"

"Aye."

"I havnae."

"Well. That's the kind of thing about my heads at Shobbs. They're like those."

"That's all fucking clear then. What about the wan of the warder?"

"The same. They're both like that. They're not based on a particular person."

Lemmy drained his pint, satisfied for now. He'd bring the subject up again the next time they met. His conversation was like the Circle Line in London, stopping regularly time and again at the same stations.

At this point a man entered the bar who Lemmy and Duncan didn't like. A wobbling, smirking, annoying man with opinions about everything. They shared a glance with each other.

"If I wis your age, I'd pick a fight with that lardarse!" Lemmy breathed.

"I can't get into fights in pubs, Lemmy. I've got a respectable job to keep. Besides, they'd ban me here, and this is my local."

Lemmy winked.

"Aye! But you'd *like* to give him a smack, eh?"

Duncan grinned. It was true. And maybe one day, if he could get away with it, maybe he'd do just that.

After one of these drinking sessions with Lemmy Stoter, a man who advocated violence as the universal solution to life's problems, Duncan would stumble back to his depressing, messy flat and entertain dark schemes for murdering Steve Sidling. It was only the thought of twenty years in prison that spoiled these fantasies. By the sounds of it, he didn't want to meet the kind of people with whom Lemmy Stoter had spent twenty years in Shobbs.

CHAPTER 7

September 1989

It was darned bad luck, Ricky Love remarked to his wife Boony, as he ran a rueful hand through his thick brown hair, that only two weeks into his year as an exchange lecturer at Forthburgh Art School such a grisly event should have occurred.

"So it was the body we heard about on the News was it, the one they found in those woods?" she said, dabbing at Marcus's face with a damp flannel. Marcus was encrusted with those parts of his supper that had failed to hit their mark. Being only two years old, he was unlikely to be upset by the grim topic of their conversation. He squirmed away from the flannel.

"Yes. Deil's Glen – that's 'Devil's Glen' in Scottish apparently. So today they identified who it was. A guy called Sidling. Head of Sculpture."

"Jesus! That makes a nice start to your year in the art school!"

Ricky nodded. Boony was wearing that slightly glum look that had settled on her features in the airport departure lounge in Seattle, and intensified during their first fortnight in Forthburgh, like the grey layer of cloud that seemed permanently settled over the city itself. He had a suspicion that the prompt demise of one of his fellow lecturers was being added to some list in her mind; black marks against their new home.

There was also a sombre mood in the art school, overshadowing his attempts to fit in. He felt that, because of the unfortunate timing of his arrival on the scene as a new face, he had in some indefinable way become associated with the atrocity in the minds of his new colleagues. He couldn't shake off a feeling that when they met him they were sizing him up, gauging his capacity for weird acts of violence.

Rumours about the victim were in hushed circulation. As a newcomer he wasn't directly privy to very much information, but his technical assistant, Hartley Coddler, had vouchsafed the view that Steve Sidling was a woofter who mixed in dodgy circles, and the death had probably been the result of some depraved sex game gone horribly wrong.

Coddler's generally inert pale face, like a crumpled paper bag with knitted grey wool eyebrows, was oddly animated as he gave this opinion, and Ricky had the feeling that Sidling's death was a matter for little regret in that quarter.

"Did you know him well? The Sidling guy?"

"Never spoke to him. He only came a year ago. But you got his drift. He was full of himself. No one liked him, *that* I knew."

Coddler shot him a look from under the knitted eyebrows, that seemed to say *and we're not going to like you much either!*

Ricky was suddenly reminded of that strange British movie, *The Wicker Man*. Maybe the entire art school was in on the crime, a whole secretive and sinister community collaborating to wipe out unwanted incomers? This Hartley Coddler had the look of a murderer about him. Then there was that lurking guy at the front door - Miggs, he was called - the head janitor: *he* looked like a psycho. And the Principal, Edgar Peabody, fluttering about the premises, clothed in primary colours like an escaped parrot - another weirdo.

Dismissing these thoughts, Ricky left Coddler to the video game he was playing on the Apple Mackintosh computer in the audio-visual studio. Students had not yet registered for the new academic year, so Coddler made no pretence of doing anything useful. Ricky made his way to the canteen. This was where the various cliques of the art school gathered around their circular tables. There was the mostly male muster of the painters, predominantly bearded and in their fifties or sixties. There was the conclave of the architects, some of whom wore ties and actually looked like they were here to work. There was the assembly of technical staff clad in their stained white coats as if freshly come from unpleasant experiments with rats. There were other congregations he couldn't yet identify, and then, over there, the circle he was trying to break into himself, the staff of the graphic design and commercial art department. From all of these groupings, exhalations of cigarette smoke rose and gathered at the ceiling in drifting clouds of fog.

There was none of the jokey banter going on that he'd overheard in the few days he'd been in the art school before the murder. It was a distinctively Scottish type of banter which was incomprehensible to his ears and might have been mistaken for insults and disputation if the occasional peal of gruff laughter hadn't belied it. Today, faces were long and chatter was subdued. He guessed that the murder had thrown everyone out of kilter.

He purchased his mug of coffee from the motherly lady who presided at the counter, and made his way towards the solid wall of bodies around the graphic design table, trying to think of some pleasantry that he could employ to bring in an extra chair and breach the circle. But on his way over there he caught the eye of a woman sitting on her own at a smaller table. She had long curly hair, and was wearing a black body-hugging dress that spread outwards at ankle level, reminiscent of Cruela de Vil or Morticia Addams. She had a cigarette holder poised in the air, and gave him a smile as he came near, and so he returned it, and, on impulse, changed course. She seemed more approachable than the ring of barely familiar colleagues.

"May I join you?"

"Of course!"

He sat down and offered his hand.

"I'm Ricky Love."

"Love?"

"Yes: as in affection."

He was used to offering this clarification.

"Or *desire?*"

"Yes ma'am."

"Pleased to meet you!"

As they shook hands, her eyebrows seemed to imply a question, so he added "I'm the exchange partner for Ernest Buckley in Graphic Design. He's gone for this academic year to the Woodlands Institute for Art and Design in Oregon where I work."

"Oregon! I travelled through Oregon after I left art college! I had an American boyfriend for a little while. Lovely state!"

"It is," he agreed.

"Trees and mountains… lakes… fabulous.! I'm Arabella Wood. Fashion Department."

Ricky smiled and glanced at her dress.

"I would have guessed! Nice outfit!"

"Thank you. A bit theatrical maybe. But I like to try new looks."

"Fashion… you're part of the Arts and Crafts group of subjects, aren't you?"

"Yes, worse luck. Square peg in a round hole."

"I don't think I've met any of your colleagues yet."

"They're not very sociable."

"So do you usually take your coffee alone?"

"It looks like I will do from now on."

Ricky looked at her quizzically. She took a deep drag on her cigarette holder, and expelled the smoke upwards to augment the general pall of fog above. Then she leaned forward slightly, holding his gaze and speaking in a low voice.

"I usually drank my coffee with Steve."

"Steve...?"

"Steve Sidling, who was just found murdered."

She sat back and looked away. She looked, in fact, as if she might cry.

Ricky felt ill equipped for this turn in the conversation. One minute it was getting-to-know you chit-chat, and then suddenly this.

"Oh... I'm sorry..." he muttered, and stirred his coffee for a while. "I... I didn't..."

What on earth could he say? Arabella's watery eyes turned back to contemplate him.

"I didn't know him," he went on lamely after a few moments. "I've only been in the art school a few times."

"No, of course. You're so new here. Perhaps you saw him around? Or in here, in the canteen?"

"Yes, people have described him and I think I saw him once. And heard him. He had quite a loud voice, didn't he?"

"He wasn't shy. He let his opinions be known."

"He had very blond hair, didn't he?"

"Peroxide. I told him it was a bit *passé*, but it was part of what he was."

"So... forgive me – you feel as if you've lost a good friend I guess."

Arabella nodded.

"My best friend, within these walls. We were on a wavelength."

She was definitely on the verge of tears, Ricky thought. Just his luck to put his feet right into the swamp. He sought desperately for a change of topic that wouldn't seem like a heartless evasion. Luckily Arabella provided one herself. With a straightening of her back and a smile straight out of amateur dramatics, she shook off the gloom like an invisible cloak.

"So, Ricky, have you come here with family or on your own?"

"With family. My wife Boony and our two year old, Marcus."

"And Ernest Buckley's gone to Oregon?"

"Yes, with his wife. He'll be settling into my job now."

"Have you *met* Ernest Buckley?"

"Not in person, no, but I've spoken to him on the phone - and we've exchanged houses so I've seen photos. In fact, there are a lot of photos of him and his wife around the house. Looks like they were very keen on fishing."

Arabella let out a peal of laughter.

"I can just imagine!" she gasped.

Ricky wasn't certain why this information had aroused such hilarity. It seemed out of proportion to the topic. The Buckleys looked ridiculous enough, certainly, in their tweedy clothes by riverbanks, displaying salmon they'd caught. But there was nothing inherently funny about fishing, was there? He had liked to fish sometimes himself, until he'd read about fish suffering pain on the hook. If there was one thing that could get him riled up, it was any kind of cruelty to animals.

He glanced at Arabella, who was now dabbing at her eyes with a tissue. He was beginning to suspect, in fact, that there was a good reason why Arabella Wood was drinking her coffee alone. She seemed to be teetering on an emotional tightrope.

"I'm sorry," she said, recovering herself. "I'm on edge since... you know, Steve... and I overreact to things. I cry or laugh immoderately. Let me explain about Ernest Buckley. He's an old oddball. Sartorially and temperamentally. Always wears a bow tie. Not that I have a problem with bow ties especially. It's just that... well, I hope your students in Oregon are ready for something a bit out of whack with the modern world!"

"I hope Ernest can adjust to our way of doing things there. It all seems kind of unstructured here."

"Oh, yes. It's pretty free-range."

"You don't seem to have modules…"

"You'll get the hang of it, Ricky. We give the students a lot of leeway in what they do. Student-centred, I suppose you'd call it."

Ricky nodded. He hoped it would gradually start to make sense. At present he was all at sea.

A few days later, Ricky entered the little office in the bowels of the art school that had been allocated to the detective investigating the murder case. The man who rose solemnly from the desk to lean across and shake his hand perfunctorily looked about his own age. He'd expected someone older, somehow.

"I'm Inspector Coupar Cruickshank, deputy chief investigating officer," he said in a weary way that suggested he wished he wasn't.

He glanced down at a piece of paper on his desk.

"You're Ricky Love?" he said.

"Yes,"

"Please sit down Mr Love."

Ricky sat, and Coupar Cruickshank gestured to a weasel-like man who had remained seated in the corner of the room.

"This is Detective Constable Price."

"Howdy!" Ricky said. The weasel fellow made no response, but scratched one ear, and then the other. Neither of these men wore a police uniform, but Price looked very dapper, whereas his superior looked a bit shabby, in a well-worn jacket with plenty of creases in it.

"We'll be taping this interview, Mr Love. Normal procedure."

"Sure, I understand."

Coupar Cruickshank inserted a cassette into the recorder and pressed 'record'.

"Tape Forty One. Eleven am, September the thirtieth, nineteen eighty nine. Steven Sidling investigation. Interview with Ricky Love, member of staff at

Forthburgh School of Art. Interview conducted by Detective Inspector Cruickshank. Also present, Detective Constable Price."

Having got this off his chest, he looked at Ricky in a manner that suggested a deep conviction that the murderer was in front of him. At least, that was how Ricky felt.

"How long have you known Steven Sidling?" he began.

"I didn't know him at all. I'm new here this term."

"Ah… so, what is your position here?"

"I'm on a one year exchange. A guy called Ernest Buckley is taking my job in the US, and I'm teaching motion graphics here."

"Motion graphics?"

"TV idents, commercials, animated sequences for films and so on."

"When did you arrive in Scotland?"

"The fifth of September."

"Do you have evidence of that, if asked for?"

"Sure. The art school here reimbursed me for the plane tickets. They must have some paperwork. Maybe the tickets themselves. I gave them to them."

"When did Mr Buckley leave?"

"The day before that. We've exchanged houses."

"Where are you from, in the US?"

"Just outside Portland, in Oregon."

"Can you give me the address?"

Ricky felt his face flushing a little. The name of his road was pretty well known in Portland.

"We lived at 2416 Pine Loop."

"2416 Pine Loop?"

"Yes."

The policeman hadn't reacted to the information. It had no bearing on anything here, but it would have been annoying if it had prompted a whole slew of questions.

"So, you never spoke to Steven Sidling?"

"No."

"Did you know who he was?"

"Not before he... he was killed. But afterwards I recognized him from how people described him."

"And how was that? How did people describe him?"

"Loud. Opinionated. Gay."

"Did you form the opinion that he was popular or unpopular?"

"Both. I got the impression that he polarized opinion among the staff. But I gather he was popular with his students."

"Who were your informants?"

"It was mostly just stray remarks, from various staff members. I spoke with a Fashion Department lecturer who was a friend of his."

"Arabella Wood?"

"Yes."

"Do you have any ideas of your own, Mr Love, about who might have murdered Steven Sidling?"

"No, absolutely none."

The detective sighed and clicked off the cassette recorder.

"Thank you Mr Love, you can go. Please get in touch if you hear or see anything you think is relevant to the case."

"I will."

"Oh... and... would you mind just writing down your name on this sheet of paper for me. In block capitals, if you don't mind."

Ricky did as he was asked, slightly puzzled.

The detective took the sheet of paper without looking at it, and held out a card in return, which Ricky took and glanced at. It contained the detective's name and phone number.

"Have they interviewed you too now?" Arabella asked him the next day in the canteen. They had joined the queue at the same time, and so it had seemed natural to sit together at the same table as previously.

"Yes. I couldn't offer much information about... much about it."

He felt reluctant even to mention the guy's name in front of Arabella, in case it provoked a flood of tears.

She shook her head.

"No, of course, you didn't know him."

She glanced around her, and then leaned forward confidentially and spoke in lowered tones.

"Listen though. I've got a theory. Don't repeat this because I might have got it all wrong."

"I'm not sure I want to hear..."

"No, listen. Please. I can talk to you, Ricky, because you're new here and you aren't going to spread stuff around. And you're not the police either. I just want someone to listen to my idea."

"Okay," Ricky said reluctantly. He didn't want to be Arabella's special confidant. She seemed slightly unhinged to him. Or maybe it was just Britishness.

"There's a student in Sculpture... *Ambient Interventions* I suppose we're still supposed to call it now, although God knows if that name change will survive Steve's death. Anyway, there's a final year student whose name is Artjoms, and he had a bit of thing about Steve."

"A thing?"

"You know... a *thing*. He was a little obsessed. Steve told me he followed him home once, and I started to keep an eye open and a couple of times I saw this Artjoms staring at Steve when he wasn't looking. It was creepy."

"Shouldn't you mention this to the police?"

"I don't know. I might be doing the young guy a bad turn. It might have been nothing more than a sort of crush."

"But... well, it's up to you, of course. I guess the Cruickshank guy is going to interview all Steve's students anyway."

"He's probably done it already."

Ricky thought about it a bit longer.

"I think you should tell the cops. You never know. It might lead to something."

Arabella stirred her coffee thoughtfully.

"Maybe. I'm in two minds. I'll think about it."

On his way home, Ricky was stopped in the entrance hall by the bulky lurking Miggs guy, the head janitor, who put up a flat hand like a policeman stopping someone from jaywalking.

"Yes?" Ricky said.

"You haven't got your ID card yet."

Was this a question? An accusation? An offer? There was nothing in the man's tone or facial expression to give a clue.

"No," Ricky agreed, and waited.

"We'll need a photo. Follow me."

Miggs lumbered into the little glass-windowed office behind the reception desk. Ricky followed as instructed.

"Stand there."

Ricky stood where a pudgy finger indicated, in front of a cork noticeboard festooned with scraps of paper.

Miggs opened an ancient cupboard and took out a polaroid camera. He sidled into position a few feet from Ricky. At that moment someone pinged a bell on the reception desk. It made Ricky jump, and he looked to see the source of the sound. There was a click from the camera.

The polaroid image whirred out into the world. Miggs waved it in the air for a few moments, and then put it down on the surface of the desk while he stowed the camera away. Ricky watched as the picture slowly appeared on the little glossy rectangle. It gradually revealed a startled individual with staring eyes wildly swivelled to one side. A lunatic, one might have said.

"Er... could we do another one?" Ricky suggested.

Miggs threw a glance at the photo.

"That one's fine," he said. "You'll get the ID card in the internal mail. Always have it with you."

Then Miggs plodded to the reception desk to deal with the bell pinger. Ricky took another reluctant glance at the photo. No, it just wouldn't do. He tore it into four parts and dropped it in a bin.

Miggs returned and looked on the desk for the polaroid.

"I binned that one," Ricky said, determined to hold his own. "It wasn't good enough."

Miggs looked at Ricky as if at a skunk that has made an unwelcome smell in a confined space.

"They come out of the janitorial budget, those polaroids," he announced.

Ricky chose not to answer.

"You're in the Design Department," Miggs went on. "I'll charge the extra photo to your head of department."

He took another polaroid. Ricky didn't stay to see the result. It couldn't be any worse than the first one.

Miggs scowled at the image emerging on the piece of expensive photographic paper. He took a deep breath. In due course he would find an opportunity to take down this arrogant Yank.

CHAPTER 8

October 1989

"There's nothing illegal going on here, officer."

"I'm not interested in what goes on here. This is a murder investigation. Please let me in."

The heavily tattooed man opened the door wider, and Coupar entered. Detective Constable Waterhouse came in behind him. Coupar somehow hadn't felt entirely safe coming down to these sinister basement premises on his own, and the presence of the blubbery bulk of Waterhouse gave him some sense of security. It was four in the afternoon on a dull October day, and the club wouldn't open for several hours yet. The man in black leather trousers and jerkin who had admitted them admitted also to being the proprietor. Once inside the door, Coupar put it to him that the more co-operative he was, the less unwelcome attention his club was likely to receive.

"Follow me, then," the man said, and moved on ahead like a skinny black spider along a broad passage lit by red bulbs and decorated with manacles and whips on the walls. He stopped at a doorway marked 'private' on the lintel.

"My office," the man said, and stood aside to let them enter a claustrophobic little cell with no windows. Coupar had a flash of nightmarish fear that he would be left locked in there with Waterhouse until Waterhouse was forced to eat him to stay alive.

But the man followed them in, his leather trousers creaking as he sat down behind an untidy desk, and indicated a plastic bucket chair to Coupar.

"Do you mind if Constable Waterhouse has a look around the premises while we talk?" Coupar said.

"No, no," the leather man said hesitantly. "But please – I'd appreciate it if you don't touch anything."

"Off you go, Waterhouse."

Waterhouse nodded and shambled off.

Coupar took out a little notebook and pen from his jacket pocket.

"Now, your name is…?"

"Dick. We only use Christian names here."

"Well, Dick, in a murder investigation we like to use surnames as well."

"Oh… all right. Richard Scragg."

"Thank you. Well, first things first. Do you know this man?"

Coupar displayed a passport photo of Steve Sidling that he'd got from Derek McCafferty.

Scragg examined it.

"Yes, he joined earlier this year. Is he… I mean… is he dead?"

"Do you read the papers, Mr Scragg?"

"Not much."

"Yes, he's dead. Murdered. Do you know his name?"

"He called himself Steve. I don't know if that's his real name."

"It is his real name. Steve *Sidling*. Do you keep a list of all your members, Mr Scragg?"

"Of course. But it's Christian names only – or names they've invented, we don't ask."

"Addresses or phone numbers?"

Scragg laughed uneasily, revealing little sharp teeth.

"Our members wouldn't want to share that information too widely. They generally get an introduction through an existing member, I meet them, and then if I'm satisfied that they're right for the club, they get a card with an ID number and their Christian name. That's it. I don't know any more."

"But you must talk to them after that? You must get to know something about them."

"It's not a club for polite conversation, officer. When men come in here, they leave their upper world identity at the door. This is an underworld."

"How are things paid for? You have a liquor licence, do you?"

"Yes."

"And a membership fee, I expect."

"It's a cash economy, officer. Strictly cash only."

"And you go to the bank every morning with the night's takings?"

"We don't open every night. It's Thursday, Friday and Saturday."

Coupar nodded.

"I expect you account for everything to the tax man, don't you Mr Scragg?"

Scragg shifted creakily a little in his chair.

"Of course."

"How many members do you have?"

"Around a hundred."

"And did Steve have any particular friends?"

"I don't have time to see everything that's going on. I'm busy at the bar."

"This is important, Mr Scragg."

"He only came twice, I think. He wasn't one of our regulars. As far as I know, he didn't form any particular friendships down here."

"So, what was he doing?"

Scragg smiled.

"Do you know what a 'top' and a 'bottom' are, officer?"

"No."

"Steve was what we call a 'bottom' or a 'sub'. He would make himself available to a 'dom' when he came in here. That means he would go into one of our private rooms, or 'cells', to be used."

"Used?"

"In a sexual way, officer. Perhaps tied up or in chains."

"And he *liked* that?".

"He wouldn't have come here otherwise."

"Do you have a record of who was here on the nights that Steve came?"

Scragg shook his head.

"We don't keep track of our members like that."

"And there are around a hundred of them, you say?"

Scragg nodded.

"How long ago was he here?"

"It would have been several weeks ago. Only twice, as I said."

"Okay – can you write something down on this piece of paper please?"

Coupar tore a page from his spiral-bound notebook and pushed it towards Scragg.

Scragg looked at him warily.

"What do you want me to write?"

"Just write *amplify independence* for me. In block capitals."

Scragg rummaged about for a pen amidst the chaos on his desk.

"*Amplify independence* did you say?"

"Yes"

"Why?"

"It will be helpful."

Scragg raised his eyes to the ceiling, and then wrote the words. He handed the piece of paper back to Coupar.

"I see you use a red pen for writing with, Mr Scragg."

"Yes. I got into the habit at school. The masters had to correct my work in blue ink."

"You were a bit of a rebel?"

Scragg shrugged.

"Maybe. A little."

"You've misspelled *independence*," Coupar remarked, folding the paper and putting it into his pocket.

"I don't care. Are we done now?"

"Yes. Thank you for your co-operation Mr Scragg."

At the door of the office, Coupar called out for Waterhouse, who appeared stooping and wide-eyed from a low doorway nearby.

Back on the street outside, Coupar addressed his assistant.

"Did you see anything worth telling me about in there?"

"Jeez, I've never seen anything like it. All whips and chains and... stuff. I couldn't work out what some of it was. Gave me the creeps."

"There's a hundred or so of these weirdos in Forthburgh, Waterhouse. I think we're going to have to interview them all, somehow. I might have to send you in here, undercover."

Waterhouse looked aghast. Coupar smiled inwardly. He had plenty of disrespect from Price and Waterhouse to avenge himself on.

Lisa listened spellbound that evening as they relaxed with a bottle of wine.

"A dungeon!"

"That's what they call it."

"I'd never have thought a place like Forthburgh... you know... it seems more like something from a film. New York or somewhere."

"There's weirdos everywhere. You can't tell."

"No. That's the frightening thing. They must look like normal men, you know, going around? Shop keepers. Bank clerks..."

"Tennis coaches..."

Lisa stared at him.

"Why do you say *tennis coaches*?"

"I don't know – just a joke. You're always on at me to have coaching from your mate Dan."

"He's a good coach. Everyone says so at the sports centre."

"Maybe I will."

Lisa mulled it over for a few seconds.

"Dan isn't the type to visit a dungeon."

"You never know. Even murderers look like normal people."

Coupar visited the Devil's Dungeon the next Thursday night, expecting it to be open. But the door was padlocked, and a note was pinned to it which read *DD Closed. Members who have joined in the last three months can contact Dick by phone for full refund of joining fee.*

A Forthburgh phone number followed. Coupar went straight to a nearby phone box and called it.

"Yes?"

"Is that Richard Scragg?"

"Yes."

"It's me, Inspector Cruickshank."

"Oh. Hello Inspector."

"What's going on?"

"What do you mean?"

"The club closing."

There was a pause. It sounded as if someone else was in the room with Scragg, saying something inaudible.

"It wasn't an easy decision. But you see, word got out somehow that the police had visited the club. A bloody nuisance. I never said anything, but someone must have seen you and the other guy coming in and thought you looked like policemen. You do look like policemen. Anyway, a rumour then gets going that the police are interested in who the members are, and... well, as you might imagine, that was the kiss of death. Our members value their privacy above all else, Inspector."

"How did this rumour start?"

"Hard to be sure. As I say, I think someone must have seen you going in or coming out."

Coupar breathed hard.

"I might remind you, Mr Scragg, that obstruction of the police in their duties is a crime."

"Obstruction?"

"It appears to me that you have closed the club in order to protect your members, among whom might well be the murderer or murderers of Steven Sidling."

"Far from it, Inspector. I did everything I could to persuade those members who came in to talk to me that the whole thing would blow over, and we should continue as normal. Do you think I wanted to lose my livelihood?"

Again, Coupar caught a murmuring voice behind Scragg.

"Who is with you there, Mr Scragg?"

"Only a business associate. We were having a discussion about how to start again. A clean break. In another city. Glasgow, perhaps. Or maybe Newcastle."

"Does this business associate know any of the members?"

"No, not at all Inspector. He's only on the financial side. A family man."

"Some of your members are probably family men."

"They may be, Inspector. But we don't know their private lives."

"Public lives, more like. Their private lives are what they get up to in your dungeon."

"Not any more."

Coupar sighed. They were going around in circles here.

"Mr Scragg. I want you to come into the station tomorrow at 11am."

"What station?"

"Oatmarket Police Station."

"I've got a dental appointment."

"Change it. When you come in, I want you to bring everything you have about your membership."

"It would only be their Christian names – or made up names – and their membership numbers. And the dates that they joined."

"And I'll want you to describe each of those individuals to one of my officers in as much detail as you can."

"Describe them?"

"Their physical appearance. Their voices, mannerisms, anything at all. If you've got a hundred members, you'd better leave most of the day clear."

"I don't know if…"

"And, just a reminder Mr Scragg. Obstruction – in any form – of our investigation will be a very serious matter for you. We're dealing with murder here, Mr Scragg, and you yourself are not yet eliminated from our potential list of suspects. We'll see you tomorrow."

The funeral service for Steven Sidling was held that Saturday at the Muttonhall Crematorium on the leafy fringes of Forthburgh. Coupar attended in as discreet a manner as could be managed, arriving at the last moment in his own unmarked and unremarkable car, speaking to no-one and standing at the back, so that he could survey all of the mourners. Looking at the backs of the people ranged in the rows in front of him, he tried to identify as many as he could, and observe their demeanour. Most appeared stoical, but he observed the heaving shoulders and deployment of handkerchiefs that betokened tears in five individuals. Two were elderly ladies in the front row. Perhaps one of them was Sidling's mother. Another sobber was Sidling's partner Derek, who was also in the front row. Another, further back, was Sidling's close friend and fellow lecturer at the art school, Arabella Wood. The last one was right in front of him in the back row, one of the Sculpture students, tall and male. Coupar had interviewed them all of course, and he recalled that this one was from Latvia or Poland or some such, and possessed a curious name, which he couldn't call to mind just now. Perhaps public displays of emotion were more common in his country.

There were at least a hundred and fifty people present, including several individuals whose backs he could not identify. When the service had finished, he moved quietly among those who milled about outside. With a few murmured words, he pressed his calling card into the hands of those who were strangers to him. You never knew who might come forward with some crucial bit of information. His presence was naturally noticed by many of the individuals he had interviewed in the weeks succeeding the murder. A few exchanged a glance or a terse smile with him. Perhaps some of them thought privately that his attendance was a tactless intrusion. Certainly he intercepted a look from Arabella Wood that bordered on hostile.

When the crowd had dispersed, he went back into the lobby of the crematorium, and made a note of the names he didn't recognize that were left in the book of remembrance. He wondered if the murderer had been amongst those present, and whether he had even already exchanged words with them, either here or in the interview room previously.

If they had been here, at the crematorium, would that suggest that they were now racked with remorse, or that they had come to gloat over this communal coda to their secret bloody project?

CHAPTER 9

May 1989

May came in, and Forthburgh was finally putting on its brighter garb. In Princess Gardens the tulips were standing to attention in serried ranks under the stern military gaze of the castle above. Every day at nine in the morning a cannon was discharged from the battlements with a resounding bang, sending a puff of smoke into the spring sky like a smoker's exhalation. Duncan, taking a roundabout route to the art school to enjoy the morning air and clear his head from the previous night's excesses, felt an unfamiliar surge of optimism as the cannon went off. It was as if a starting gun had signalled a change of mood. He was thinking about a new public sculptural commission that had just come his way, and later in the week, on his 'research day' (dedicated in recent weeks to lounging morosely at home), he would start work on it. It was to be a kind of totem pole, to be placed at the entrance to the woods of Deil's Glen. He would carve it from oak, a material that he had occasionally worked with before; more tractable than stone and inviting a more subtle, much more sinuous style of carving. He had considerable freedom of subject matter, beyond the stipulations that it should be approximately twelve feet tall and feature some references to the wildlife of the glen – birds, deer, foxes and suchlike. Perhaps on his research day he would take a stroll around the woods of Deil's Glen to imbibe some of its atmosphere, and then settle down on a bench somewhere and make some rough sketches. He envisaged twisting branches and leafy surfaces on the totem pole, amongst which his animal carvings would be set.

His new optimistic mood lasted about ten minutes, until the moment that he arrived in his little office in the art school and found a piece of A4 paper on his desk. Printed on it in bold type were the words *Meeting of Sculpture Department today at one pm in the lecture theatre*. Below, in smaller type, were the words *Purpose of meeting: a consultation with staff and students on a change of name for the department, to commence next academic year.*

Duncan sat down heavily, all thoughts of his totem pole banished. A change of name? What the hell was Steve Sidling up to now? Were they to be the Sidling Sculpture Department, or the Department of Sidlingism? Whatever was afoot, he had already decided on his position. He would be implacably opposed to anything Steve Sidling put forward.

The lecture theatre was surprisingly full. Not only were all the sculpture staff and most of the students there, but Duncan was surprised to see Principal Peabody perched on the front row, the only man in the room wearing a suit, albeit a suit of post-box red material. The Vice-Principal was at his side, also more formally dressed than most denizens of the art school, sporting a mustard yellow bow tie and a corduroy jacket. He felt a pang of anxiety. If the big beasts of the institution had been called forth, then this change of name business might already have secured their approval. He took a seat on the back row, away from his teaching colleagues who were near the front.

He was one of the last to arrive. He had just sat down when the lecture theatre door behind him was closed with a bang, and the buzz of chatter died down as Steve Sidling descended the steps to the raised platform at the front of the room. Already Duncan was disgusted. This entrance was obviously stage-managed, like the arrival of the star at a pop concert. As Sidling reached the dais, the lights dimmed and an image appeared on the back projection screen. At first sight it was an enormous hedgehog, but then Duncan recognized it as the German town hall he had seen in the book, wrapped up in fabric and sporting hundreds of spikes. Was Sidling here to boast about his own work? That would not surprise him greatly.

"Ladies and gentlemen," Sidling began in his shrill, self-satisfied voice, "Scholars and Sculptors, Students and Staff..."

He paused with a smirk, to allow them time to appreciate his alliteration.

"What is *Sculpture*?" he said, and allowed another pregnant pause to develop. In his head, Duncan answered *it's what Michelangelo did, and Donatello, and Bernini, Rodin and Moore and Hepworth. That's what it is, you prat!*

"Is it not something redolent of the past?" Sidling went on. "Is it not something we admire... wonder at sometimes, indeed... looking at Michelangelo's 'David' for example... but yet consigned in the main to the dusty corners of museums, or plonked unimaginatively in our public squares and gardens, perched on plinths? Is it an art form we associate with the fast-moving world of the now, here today and gone tomorrow? Evanescent, challenging, vital?"

Here he paused again and shook his head sadly, as if commiserating with mourners at a funeral.

"I have to suggest to you that it is not. I have to suggest to you that the heyday of the statue of the famous politician, the commemorative stone plaque, the carved totem pole..." (here Duncan almost spluttered aloud. Had the bastard got wind of his own recent commission?)... "the days of outworn conventional work are over. Do we here at Forthburgh Art School want to be identified with the dinosaurs, lumbering into the twilight of eventual extinction with our outmoded practices? Do we wish to be seen by the public and the art world as a fusty, dusty haunt of has-beens and dodos? Or…" here he turned briefly and gestured towards the slide of the hedgehog. "… do we want to be identified with the avant-garde of contemporary practice? Is Forthburgh School of Art a repository of the old, or a battle cry for the new?"

He paused again, and looked around interrogatively at his audience. Duncan was seething with contempt for these facile remarks (what exactly were the outmoded practices of which dinosaurs were guilty?) and hatred for the pompous self-satisfied man who was uttering them. But for the moment he contained his fury. He felt like a pressure cooker about to burst, but this was not a moment to make his stand. He was not going to stand up and declare for *a repository of the old!* Let Sidling have more rope for now with which to be hung!

"Scholars and *Sculptors*, Students and Staff…" (was that a sneer on his face as he pronounced 'sculptors'?) "… I suggest to you that our place in the world is changing. We are engaging with what is out there. We are provocateurs. We are boldly altering the shape of our environments. We are seizing opportunities and bending conventions. We are interventionists! I suggest that it is time to draw the world's attention to this fact. I propose that from Autumn term of this year, the Autumn of nineteen eighty nine, this department should be renamed *The Department of Ambient Interventions*!"

He clicked a switch attached to a cable lying on the desk in front of him and the slide behind him changed. An untidy heap of cardboard boxes filled the screen, with an unkempt bearded man huddled inside one of them smoking a cigarette. Buckingham Palace loomed in the background. He clicked again, and a tree festooned with dangling milk cartons appeared. A lugubrious cow stood beneath the branches, looking at the camera. Sidling fixed his audience with a fanatical stare.

"These are the directions of the future, colleagues and students. This is the brave new world which has formed my own artistic practice, and it is a brave new world I want to lead you into. I commend to you this symbolic step: out with the old and in with the new! Out with *Sculpture* and in with *Ambient Interventions!*"

He paused expectantly. It looked like a cue, and sure enough Artjoms burst upwards from his seat like a firework with a volley of clapping, which was taken up, to a greater or lesser degree, among the students. Duncan observed with disgust that some of his colleagues were joining in quietly. It was too much to bear. He stood up and shouted above the noise of the applause.

"Stop!"

Afterwards, he couldn't quite recall what he'd said. He wasn't a naturally eloquent person, nor was he generally comfortable with public speaking. But he had felt in the grip of some supernatural possession. The spirits of the past were gathered about him, pouring the words into his brain. A few phrases remained in his memory from his impassioned broadside. *Meretricious nonsense! Contempt for the great legacy of the medium! Denigration of craft skills!*

He had delivered his harangue to a stunned silence, everyone craning around to look at the back row where he stood. With a magnificent peroration – something to do with the spirit of Michelangelo watching from above – he had turned on his heel and stamped out of the lecture theatre without waiting for any riposte.

He had learned later, from the cherubic Rory Coggs, that the meeting had discussed Sidling's proposal for less than ten minutes before the change of name was approved with a show of hands. The Principal had said that he would ensure the change went through the relevant committees, and the new name would be included in an addendum to the prospectus for the next academic year. Students who had already applied for and been accepted into the Department of Sculpture would be informed that they were now to be ambient interventionists, and given the option to change to another discipline if they didn't like it.

"What about the points I made?" Duncan said.

Rory Coggs shrugged and put on a face of commiseration.

"They weren't discussed. After you left the room, Artjoms made a little speech in praise of the change, and when there was a vote it was no contest.

"Did *you* vote to keep the name Sculpture?"

Rory shrugged again.

"Do turkeys vote for Christmas?"

Late that night in his flat, slumped in a threadbare armchair with a half emptied bottle of whisky on the little table beside him, Duncan ran his eye down the list he had made:

SIDLING
Arsenic
Rat poison
Weedkiller
Radioactive substance
Hit and run with a vehicle
Knife
Sword
Blunt Instrument
Pistol
Rifle
Shotgun
Strangulation
Kidnap and starve to death
Beheading
Axe
Push from high place
Drown in a bath
Smother with a pillow

Garrotte with a washing line
Guillotine
Chainsaw
Chisel
Hammer
Drug and bury alive
Contract killer
Lemmy Stoter?
Cut-throat razor
Boil alive
Dump in septic tank
Acid
Defenestrate
Cook and feed to dogs
Hang, draw and quarter

If only he could subject Steve Sidling to all of these! What a shame that he could only die once! He added some lines to the end of the list:

Must must know who is killing him.
Must know why.
Must be done in a fitting manner.
An AMBIENT INTERVENTION!
Must get away with it.

He put down his pen and stared at the wall. It was the last item that was the stumbling block: getting away with it. Not re-living Lemmy Stoter's twenty years in Shobbs. But for that awful prospect, Duncan felt he could have cheerfully felled Sidling with an axe one morning in the canteen. There would be blood all over the shop – especially all over Arabella, sitting opposite the victim. But it wouldn't do. He might even get more than twenty years. After all, Lemmy's murder was a crime of passion. He would perhaps be judged to be criminally insane, and locked up for good.

He spent an almost sleepless night in a turmoil of incoherent thoughts, laying whatever negative ideas occurred to him at the door of his nemesis. Perhaps Sidling planned to close the stone-carving workshops? Perhaps he was even bending Principal Peabody's ear to get rid of him from the staff? Worst of all, the odious scoundrel had quite likely used his influence with Arabella to encourage her abandonment of himself!

If Sidling could be killed by psychic power alone, then this concentration of hatred that was tormenting him would do it. Perhaps he should create an effigy, voodoo style, and thrust pins into it? He indulged briefly in the fantasy that he would arrive at the art school tomorrow morning to find that Sidling had died suddenly in the night from unknown causes. The whole *ambient* business would disappear like a bad dream. In this rosy future he would even win Arabella back! He revelled in a half-dreaming fantasy in which Arabella came crawling to him – naked, humble – offering to do anything he wished in penance for abandoning him for Hermione Cutter's husband and being the friend of Steve Sidling. He tossed and turned in rumpled sheets until his clock showed four in the morning, when he finally began to feel calmer. An expression had come into his head. *Vengeance is a dish best served cold.* He must bide his time. He must hide his true thoughts. He must even, perhaps, if it were possible, regain the confidence of Steve Sidling. Appear to go along with the changes. Lull the swine into a false sense of security. And then, when it was safe to do so, when it was least expected, when all was prepared, strike without mercy. Comforted by that idea, he fell asleep at last.

CHAPTER 10

Summer 1989

Hermione Cutter knew that what she was doing was harmful to her mental well-being, but it had grown into a pernicious habit that she couldn't kick. At five o'clock every Friday she purchased her coffee in the Star Café in the bohemian Scotsbridge quarter of Forthburgh, and settled herself at a seat with a view out of the window. Occasionally no such seat was available, so she would stand where she could look out, drawing puzzled glances from the serving staff as she loitered on foot in spite of seating being clearly available further back.

Across the street, a tenement door with peeling red paint was the focus of her attention. The door gave access to a red painted hallway and a stone stairway leading to six flats. She knew that fact because she had, in times past, been through the door many times herself. She had ascended, a friend and confidante, to the eyrie at the top that was the apartment of Arabella Wood. An untidy, chaotic apartment with wardrobes not only in the two small bedrooms but even in the living room. In the wardrobes resided Arabella's extensive collection of clothing, much of it made by herself. Outside the living room window was an equally extensive view of Forthburgh, looking north towards the castle perched haughtily on its rock, like an eagle.

She would never again be invited into that flat. It was a torment to her that she could picture its interior so precisely. She could imagine her husband's distaste for the untidiness in there. Their own house in Martinside was appointed with simple, stylish furnishings – Ted never stinted in paying for things – and kept immaculately tidy by herself. However, no doubt Arabella's attentions would make his new bohemian setting more palatable. Perhaps, now that Ted had moved in, some sense of order had been imposed on things? She itched to know everything. Where did he sit when he arrived home from work? Did Arabella make him a gin and tonic or a cup of tea? Did she snuggle next to him on that sofa with its magenta beaded throw? Did they kiss? What did they do – what *exactly* - on that rumpled bed with the gleaming brass frame when darkness fell?

At the art school, Arabella Wood and herself now were as opposing poles of magnets, deviating frostily apart when the geography of the institution threatened to cause a collision. In fact, in the week following Ted's decampment to Arabella's flat, such a collision had occurred in the canteen, witnessed by a sprinkling of horrified and embarrassed staff. Standing up from a table and turning to go back to the Fine Art studios, she had almost walked into Arabella heading from the serving counter with a cup of coffee in hand. For a moment they had stared at each other like two cats suddenly confronting each other in an abandoned garden. Hermione even heard herself making a sort of hissing sound. They were no more than three feet apart. When Arabella averted her gaze and started attempting to sidestep her, she heard herself saying *"You treacherous, conniving bitch!"*

It came out quite loudly. Almost a shout, in fact.

Arabella had flushed with anger or shame or both, turned tail, and left the canteen at speed. Hermione glanced around her. Conversation had stopped, and the dozen or so lecturers in the vicinity had frozen into statues, all looking at their coffee cups or the floor and pretending she wasn't there.

Recently, Hermione had begun entertaining fantasies of killing Arabella, preferably with some torture thrown in beforehand. Since this was impracticable, she had developed this habit of torturing herself instead, every Friday. She watched for the arrival at that red door of, firstly, Arabella herself, in whatever outlandish garb she had chosen for the day, and, secondly, her husband Ted – he was after all, still, her husband – in his sober but stylish grey suit and tie. He always got away from work soon after five on a Friday.

This brief weekly glimpse of him always made her shiver with a passion that she had hardly known she possessed. For all the long years of their married life he had been a steady presence, loved by her in a calm steady way. They had been, looking back, undemonstrative, perhaps. Now that he was gone, she thought obsessively about him, missing everything about him. What a shock it was, that he could stir up such intense feelings in her heart, as strong even as during their courtship all those years ago!

When they had both passed through the door, Hermione would down the bitter dregs of her coffee, jealousy, and resentment, and get the bus back to her empty nest in Martinside, on the other side of town. As she stared, sightless, from the bus windows, she played out imaginary scenes of Arabella and Ted drinking wine, laughing, slipping off their clothes...

She thought also of hit and run accidents, falling masonry, and all the bottles and pills she'd been familiar with in her days as a pharmacist; the ones that could kill.

Hermione had struck up a melancholic sense of mutual understanding with Duncan McBane, expressed in nothing more than exchanged glances as they encountered each other from time to time at the art school. They had an unspoken bond as dumped partners. Before that fateful evening at The Blinking Eye, she and Duncan had barely spoken during their years as staff members at the art school. What an irony that she had been holding her first real conversation with him on the very occasion that his girlfriend – her own closest friend - had been talking to Ted, and beginning to sink her hooks into him! There was a horrible symmetry to it.

Arabella's ditching of Duncan came hard on the heels of that evening, and was soon well known around the art school. Anyone could observe the deepening of Duncan's characteristic hangdog expression into something more like that of a dog that was not only to be hung, but even denied a valedictory bone. The art school's gossip mill soon provided the explanation.

It had been her own fault - that was the most galling thing of all. Blithe, innocent fool that she was, she had actually *introduced* Arabella to Ted. She'd always previously dismissed the idea of bringing them together – say, at a dinner party – because they were so utterly different. But in the heady excitement of the exhibition, she had suddenly been inspired by the idea of putting together this juxtaposition of opposites. Henceforth, when she spoke of her colourful friend in the Fashion Department, he would have a mental image of whom she spoke. Alas, Ted now had a great deal more than mental images on his hands.

As for Duncan, she had enjoyed talking to him at The Blinking Eye. She had been effervescent with the intoxicating combination of prosecco and the attention attendant upon being the artist in the spotlight. Duncan, she remembered, had been highly complimentary about her portraits. Scrutinising his face as he spoke, she had even formed the idea of painting a portrait of him. She had always felt it was important to mix her well-paid commissions with paintings of faces that drew her attention for their own reasons. And Duncan's was a face to marvel at, with its dark lowering eyebrows, small tormented eyes, and deep lines suggestive of mental anguish. In spite of these individually grim features, he was handsome in a rough sort of way, the overall impression somehow surmounting the shortcomings of the individual elements. Also, she had never painted a man with a beard. In fact she had suggested to her son Roland, who was off to start his second year at university in the autumn, that he might grow a beard before he went, in order that she might paint him as a sailorly figure, embarked freshly on his voyage of life. Roland however had declined, pointing out that his facial hair was slow-growing and so fair as to be virtually invisible.

At the end of the summer term, with the students dispatched, there was a drinks party for staff. Since the weather was uncharacteristically mild, a lot of the attendees spilled out of the canteen into the irregular open space of lawn formed by the Old and New buildings of the institution, sometimes referred to as the 'quadrangle'. Hermione observed Duncan standing quietly with a can of beer on the edge of a conversation between some of his Sculpture Department colleagues, and on an impulse she approached him, plastic cup of cheap white wine in hand.

"How are you, Duncan?"

His face lightened a little, as might the face of a man whose family has been slaughtered but who has just discovered that the pet rabbit survived.

"Hello Hermione. Another term over, eh?"

"Yes. Has it been a good one for you?"

The spasm that crossed his face told her that this was not the best topic of small talk to have chosen.

"There's some changes afoot that I need to get used to."

Hermione now recalled the story that had reached her of Duncan's impassioned speech early in the term.

"Oh, yes. Steve Sidling is even changing the name of the department I hear?"

He nodded.

"I've come around to it. But I'll still be glad to get out of here for a couple of months."

"Are you working on anything? Anything of your own?" Hermione said, thinking this might be a tactful diversion from art school woes.

"Aye. A totem pole for the Deil's Glen entrance."

"A totem pole! How interesting! In the Native Indian tradition?"

"Yes and no. I'm just doing sketches now. There'll be carvings of different animals and birds. Things associated with the Glen."

He took a sip of his beer. Low evening sunlight was catching the edge of his profile, throwing that craggy bearded face into high relief. A pity he didn't know how to smile. Her idea of painting him came back into her head. The summer months, free from art school duties, would be an ideal time to do that, if he was amenable. Her interest was not unmixed with the thought that they might converse during the sittings. He might be led to reveal things about Arabella. She knew he was bitter about how she'd dumped him. They could perhaps draw some mutual comfort from assassinating her character together.

"Duncan – you might think this is a little forward of me... but do you think you'd be interested in sitting for a portrait? You have such an interesting face, I'd love to try and paint you."

Duncan looked as if he'd seen a flying saucer land just over her shoulder.

"Just as an exercise for me," she went on hastily. "I mean... of course... not a paid commission. I wouldn't be doing it for money. I just think I'd like to do it. Do you think you'd have a little time over the summer? Just a few hours, maybe on two or three occasions?"

Duncan scratched his ear and took another sip of his beer. Then, wonder of wonders, he smiled!

"Aye, I could do that Hermione. When do you want to start?"

A week later, Duncan sat illuminated by the pure northern light streaming through the high windows of a small painting studio in the art school. Hermione Cutter had been granted the use of this studio for the summer months. He was cradling a skull in his hands, as Hermione had decided that some reference to Hamlet, the Prince of Denmark, was appropriate to his physiognomy.

"It's not that I'm painting you *as* Hamlet," she explained. "It's just that there's a hint of that in the skull – it's such an iconic reference that it doesn't need to be overstated."

Duncan nodded. He seemed indifferent as to whether or not he held a skull. She had given him a comfortable chair to sit in – one she'd borrowed from the boardroom. And from where he was sitting, he would be able to gaze out at the castle looming beyond the studio windows, circled by tattered clouds and squawking seagulls.

Her stretched canvas waited on its easel in front of her, blank and full of potential. She always thought, when about to begin a new work, of the canvas of a sailing ship, rigged and ready to set out on a voyage of discovery. She picked up her 2B pencil.

"I'm going to start sketching in some guidance lines now, Duncan. Are you comfortable in that position?"

"Aye, I'm fine."

"Keep that eye line looking towards the window, if it's okay for you."

"Okay."

She began to put down the marks on the canvas that would serve to shape her composition. They could be laid down freely, rubbed out, re-worked. They would end up underneath many layers of oil paint. She always used paint lavishly, sometimes plastering it on thickly with a palette knife. She would make little ridges and valleys like those that lined the flesh of Duncan's face.

Already she could envisage how the completed portrait would look: almost sculptural, in low relief. She was looking forward to that more intense phase of the work, the only part that would be visible when all was finished.

For now, she was more relaxed, and ready to chat.

"Did you say you lived in Dolry, Duncan?"

"Aye. I've got a flat there."

"What's it like, Dolry? I gather from what I hear and read that it's 'up and coming'. We... Ted and I... we used to eat at a good Thai place there."

Ted and I. How many times did she still use that phrase? It was as if, for as long as it took to say it, it brought him back to her. They'd been married for eighteen years. They were still married. Not divorced. Separated. He was an adulterer. Committing adultery, probably on a daily basis, with the ex-girlfriend of the man in front of her.

These thoughts obliterated Duncan's reply, which was along the lines of he didn't know if Dolry was 'up and coming' and it wasn't an expression he'd have used himself.

"It's still rough around the edges, you know? There's some characters in my local, I can tell you."

"You go to a local do you? Ted and..." she stopped herself this time, "... I've never really got into the habit of going into a particular pub, being a 'regular' as they say."

"When you live on your own it's sometimes good just to go out and talk. Not to anyone in particular. Just other people, you know?"

"Yes, I can understand that."

She thought of her empty house in Martinside. She had anticipated that Roland would be coming back from university for most of the summer, but he'd met a girl and they were going 'travelling' for at least a month. Another month of lonely evenings for her: watching the television, reading historical novels – her favourite genre

– and... grieving. Perhaps she should start going to a pub. But on her own? All her friends in Martinside were married women. One or two of them had made a bit of an effort to keep in touch. But her cosy social life of dinner parties and theatre outings with other couples had vanished along with Ted. She needed to find some other divorcees, perhaps.

She sketched on in silence for a little while. Was she attracted to Duncan, she wondered. The very fact that she had to ask herself that question, in an impassive, analytical kind of way, would suggest that she wasn't. He was about her own age – maybe a tad older. Perhaps fifty. He was nothing like her husband Ted, either to look at or in temperament. But then, equally, Arabella was nothing like *her*. You could find all kinds of different people attractive, in different ways, she supposed. There would be a kind of symmetry in their getting together, given that their previous partners had done so. But he was a gloomy, laconic kind of man, and the last thing she needed in her life right now was more gloom.

That niggling imp of the perverse inside her wanted to get him talking about Arabella; about how they had been together, about how he felt now that she was with Ted. How might she lead up to that in a tactful way? Tact was probably impossible, in such a matter.

Unexpectedly, Duncan started a topic of conversation.

"So... how did you come to be an artist, Hermione? Did you mention that you used to be a pharmacist?"

"Yes, that's right. It seems like a lifetime ago. It was my father's influence, I suppose. He was a doctor - a GP. I did well at science at school but I was squeamish about biology. I didn't like cutting up frogs. The idea of medical training terrified me. So he suggested pharmacy."

"So – you never studied at an art college?"

"No. I started painting in my early thirties. Ted was doing well in his banking career, and baby Roland had come onto the scene. We could afford for me to stop going out to work. I hadn't done any art since leaving school, but I took to painting like a duck to water."

"Did you start with portraits?"

Hermione laughed.

"My first effort was a painting of Roland as a six month old. It looked like a poached egg in a pram!"

"But you stuck at it, obviously."

"I did. It became an obsession, almost. I would paint every day, for hours."

At the end of the session, Hermione felt that good progress had been made, both in laying down the colour foundations of the portrait and in developing a connection with her sitter, even though their conversation had skated along an unruffled surface, leaving the deeper, darker topic that connected them undisturbed. At the end though, as Duncan stood up and stretched his strong-looking limbs, he surprised her.

"I'm sorry, you know, about Arabella and your husband."

She looked up, startled, from the jar of white spirit in which she was dabbling a brush to clean it.

"Oh… thank you, Duncan. You… you must feel upset as well?"

Duncan cleared his throat. His eyes looked into a far distant place. She thought they looked watery. He absent-mindedly picked up one of her paint brushes, one that she hadn't used.

"Yes," he said at last.

"You still feel something for her?"

He swallowed, and dabbed at the palm of his hand with the pointed handle of the paint brush before answering. This revelation of his emotions was clearly a trial to him.

"Aye. Very strongly. But I don't know what it is. It might still be love, but sometimes… it could be hate."

"How long were you going out?"

"It wasn't all that long. Four months or so. Up to last February."

"When she first met Ted at my exhibition at The Blinking Eye."

"Yes. That must have been the start of it. It was soon after that, that things started to go pear-shaped. I didn't know why at first."

"It was because she'd started meeting with Ted in secret. I had no idea."

"Yes. Listen – I'm sorry I brought it up, but it was kind of preying on my mind as I was sitting there and you were working away at your canvas. It was like – I don't know – a stone in a stream that the water was flowing around. Some big thing that needed to be mentioned."

"The elephant in the room, as they say?" Hermione said with a sad smile.

"Aye. A great ugly elephant that I couldn't go without mentioning. Maybe I shouldn't have. I'm sorry."

"I'm not sorry, Duncan. It's a relief to share this with someone... someone so intimately caught up in the same situation. Listen..., the canteen's still open this week before they shut for the summer. Do you want to go and have a coffee? Maybe it will help us both a little if we talk through these things a bit more?"

He looked hesitant, but then nodded.

"Aye. I've got too much bottled up. And we're both in the same boat. It would be good to talk."

That evening, Hermione wrote about their conversation in her diary. She'd started to keep a diary again, after a gap of many years, when Ted deserted her. Not having a living confidant, there was nevertheless some wan comfort in setting down her thoughts and feelings on paper. She intended to destroy this diary one day – she certainly didn't want her son Roland ever to read it when she was dead – and the intention that it should perish in flames liberated her to write freely. Especially she wrote vitriolic passages about Arabella, even once to the point of an elaborate fantasy about luring her to the house and poisoning her.

Had a long chat with Duncan McBane after the sitting. He's really screwed up over Arabella. I think he hates her as much as I do, but it's all mixed up with a longing to have her back. I think he tortures himself the same way as I do: about how she is with Ted, imagining them together. What they do.

He's pretty screwed up in another way too. We didn't just talk about Ted and Arabella. He got onto the subject of his boss, Steve Sidling, and his plans to change things in the Sculpture Department. It's going to be called 'The Department of Ambient Interventions'. He contradicted what he'd said to me before, about going along with it. I think he feels he has to pretend that, to stay safe in his job. But really, I think he hates him, and he trusts me enough to let that show through a bit. I hardly know Steve Sidling, but he and Arabella appear to be great pals, and he's a screeching, camp sort of individual who obviously ruffles Duncan's feathers something awful.

Hermione put the diary back in the bedroom drawer where she kept it underneath a jumble of tights and knickers. As she was doing that, she suddenly had an idea. It would be another outlet for her anger and misery. She went downstairs again and fished out her sketchbook and a pencil. Unusually, it was a set of words that had come into her mind as an inspiration for a visual image. A saying. She took a photo of Ted winning a golf trophy off the wall, and then, after a hunt, dug out an old art school prospectus that contained a photo of Arabella. Her mind a tight, painful, concentrated ball of vicious intent, she started to make some rough preliminary sketches.

CHAPTER 11

Summer 1989

In the quiet vacation-muffled art school, Steve Sidling perused the letter on his desk a second time. It was such an astonishing missive that he couldn't believe he'd read it correctly.

Dear Steve,
If you have read your Bible, I think that what I have to say will call to mind Saint Paul's experience on the road to Damascus, as I have had what is sometimes called a 'Damascene conversion'. In short, I have become the opposite of what I was before!
As you will no doubt recall, I spoke out strongly at the recent meeting, against the proposed change in the name of our department from 'Sculpture' to 'Ambient Interventions'. For some days afterwards, in the knowledge that the change was to go ahead, I must admit that I contemplated resignation from my post. However, I could not see my way to earning a living in any other way, and I love my job. I recognised that I must learn to accept the changed situation, and do my best to quell any doubts about the way forward under your leadership.
This, however, was not the 'Damascene conversion' to which I refer. It merely prepared the ground for it. My attitude at this point was one of grudging acceptance of my lot.
Then, one day in the little library we have in the department, I stumbled across the book dedicated to your own creative practice, 'Steven Sidling, Disruptive Genius". The scales fell from my eyes! What I had previously dismissed as

meretricious nonsense suddenly began to make sense to me! Those gigantic spider sculptures dangling from cranes in Poland! The masterful juxtaposition of your cardboard city of the dispossessed with the frontage of Buckingham Palace! Above all, your awe-inspiring transformation of a town hall in Germany into a vast brooding hedgehog-like creature, looming over the nearby buildings! Although I had seen some of these things before, the combination of the perceptive text and the agglomeration of the beautiful images finally, belatedly, revealed to me the overarching philosophy behind the work.

What was my own artistic achievement compared with these – and many other – wonderful interventions? A few statues scattered about the public places of Scotland: weak, conventional efforts, redeemed only by the craft skills I have learned to employ over the years. How much more ambitious and far-reaching is your vision for your own practice and for the future of our department here at Forthburgh!

I suspect that you will be surprised – even astonished – to read these words. You may even be sceptical about my sincerity, and I must admit that my previous words and actions would invite scepticism. So I am resolved to prove to you, by my words and actions henceforth, that I am now a whole-hearted supporter of the changes you are bringing to our art school.

As a small beginning, I am contemplating something of an ambient intervention of my own, loosely connected with my totem pole commission at Deil's Glen. I will seek your guidance on this and other changes in my creative practice as time goes on.

Sincerely yours,
Duncan McBane, Convert.

Was this fulsome gush of admiration sincere? Sidling was inclined to doubt it. It was an astonishingly crafted missive – he wouldn't have expected the generally monosyllabic McBane to produce such flowing prose. Surely there must be a strong dose of covert cynicism lurking amongst the fine words?

He sat back and mulled it over. Perhaps the sincerity of the letter didn't matter too much? He could live with an *appearance* of acquiescence. The nub of the matter was that Fishface would, on this showing, no longer be a thorn in his side. Time would tell if his protestations of a conversion held water. The main thing was that an enemy had been swept aside – or had, in effect, swept himself aside.

The letter obviously required some follow-up on his own part. During the long summer break, he wouldn't bump into Duncan in the day-to-day business of term time. He was intending to absent himself for the whole of August, and now at the fag end of July he was just in the art school for a few more days, checking details with the Vice-Principal while he tweaked the text for the new course in Ambient Interventions, which would need to be formally approved before the start of the autumn term. Academic Council would meet at the beginning of September, and he wanted all the paperwork to be ready before he went away in August.

He had it in mind to respond to Duncan's declaration with a short letter of his own, but to his surprise he bumped into him the next day in a corridor in the Old Building.

"Ah – hello Duncan," he said. "I didn't expect to see you around now. I thought you'd be busy on your totem pole. You're working on it away from the art school, aren't you?"

"Aye. Forthburgh Parks and Gardens have given me a shed near the Glen. I'm here for Hermione Cutter."

"Hermione Cutter – the painter?"

"Yes. She's doing a portrait of me. This'll be the final sitting, I think."

Steve was doubly surprised – that someone wanted to paint a portrait of Fishface, and that Fishface was diverging so far from his usual taciturn demeanour as to reveal unsolicited information.

"Ah... interesting!" was the only rejoinder he could think of.

Now Duncan appeared to be smiling at him! That could be the only interpretation of the curious twist that his mouth had taken within its bearded den. A couple of jagged teeth were visible.

"I hope you've had my letter, Steve?" he said, widening the smile even further. Sidling had never before seen a display like this. It was unnerving, like a shark masquerading as a dolphin.

"Er... yes, of course Duncan. I was going to write back, but I'm bogged down in paperwork just now."

"No need to write, now we're face to face, eh?"

"No. Well – of course I'm absolutely delighted that you've come around to my way of seeing the future of the department."

"That's great. I was worried, Steve, that after my outburst in the lecture theatre..."

Sidling held up a hand.

"Water under the bridge, Duncan. Water under the bridge!"

"I feel I need to prove myself, after that. I don't expect you just to take my word for it. You'll see a change in what I look for in the students, and I'll be making a change in my own practice. To tell you the truth, I'm excited now that I've seen the light, as it were. I think I was in a rut. All those dull statues and monuments... I was going around in circles, not developing."

"We all need to keep moving onwards, you're right Duncan. Repetition is death for an artist."

Duncan looked at him as if he were the Messiah.

"Repetition is death for an artist!" Duncan repeated, in awe-struck tones. "That's a brilliant piece of advice there, Steve. That's one I'll take to heart!"

This fawning was starting to embarrass Sidling. The proof would be in the pudding. Time to move on.

"Well... good to bump into you and clear this all up, Duncan. When I've finished the documentation for the change of the department's name, we can get together again – in early September – and take all this further."

"Aye! That'll be good."

"I expect Hermione will be er… sharpening her pencils… or brushes?"

Duncan nodded.

"Aye – I'll be getting along. See you later, Steve!"

A week later Sidling had finished his paperwork for the new course, and was as free as a bird. First, he fluttered off to Spain, where he had a commission jointly funded by an animal welfare charity and an eccentrically run arts organisation. There he busied himself in causing the fountain in a large town known for its bullfighting heritage to flow blood red, having planted dozens of black terracotta bulls' heads in the splash pool. It aroused public ire, provoked vandalism, and inspired impassioned debate in the press - just the right recipe to return him to the public eye, which had drifted away to other things during his creatively inactive first year at the art school. He was interviewed on Radio Four, and an article was published in *Sculpture Today*. After that, he went on holiday with Derek to Derek's little Majorcan hideaway for a week, and then spent the last part of the month catching up with old friends in London, where he was careful to avoid any locales where Tiny Prodger might get wind of his presence. He was starting to feel a little more at ease over Prodger. After that threatening phone call last December, he'd scraped together two thousand pounds and sent him a cheque. Prodger wanted five thousand, but Sidling wrote a note with the cheque saying he couldn't afford that, and he hoped Tiny would consider the matter closed. He received no reply, and the cheque was cashed. If Tiny was still going to come after him, he would surely have travelled up to Forthburgh by now? Nevertheless, he thought it would be best not to come to his notice while in London.

At the start of September he returned to Scotland. Following a tip-off from one of his London friends, and taking advantage of the temporary absence of Derek, who was treating his mother to a few days at his Majorcan house, he introduced himself at the door of a hitherto undiscovered venue, *The Devil's Dungeon*. After a short interview with the owner, a leather-clad person by the name of Scragg, he was admitted to membership. It was a club for the gay sado-masochistic community, such as it was, in Forthburgh. He made two visits before Derek returned. He himself was solidly at the masochistic end of the spectrum, but after an enjoyable first experience, he fell in on his second visit with individuals whose complementary tastes were a little beyond his expectations. He was only just starting to be able to sit down again in comfort when Derek returned from Majorca. The wounds on his buttocks were still visible, but he pleaded a mild case of piles and kept that end of himself from view.

In the second week of the month he returned to the art school, and on the Monday of that week the good ship *Ambient Interventions* sailed through an uncritical academic council meeting on the fair wind of the Principal and Vice-Principal's support. So he settled into the start of his second year in the art school with a pleasant sense of achievement. He'd wangled a better office for himself, and spent a pleasant few days arranging its décor to reflect his own decorous credentials as a leading avant-garde artist of the moment. He dipped unstintingly into *Ambient Intervention*s departmental funds to achieve the right look – the zebra-striped wallpaper in particular didn't come cheap. But never mind, the department wouldn't have so much expenditure on traditional sculpting materials now that the students would be out and about devising their own ways to intervene. He intended to encourage low-cost projects, such as fleeting live performances captured on video, or structures that used on-site materials such as litter or twigs. He would draw their attention to the low-budget but impressive work of Andy Goldsworthy. No terracotta bulls' heads for them, unless mummy and daddy were rich.

As September drew on, and the nights drew in, the denizens of the art school began to reassemble, drifting back from their long summer breaks to begin fitful preparations for the coming academic session. There was an atmosphere of more than usual bonhomie in the staff canteen, where morning coffee breaks merged imperceptibly into lunch breaks in the absence of teaching duties. Occasional students started to pop up about the place, like early mushrooms, but there was no obligation to offer them more than a friendly chat and a recommendation that they spend their time elsewhere for another couple of weeks.

In the middle of the month, Arabella Wood reappeared. Sidling spotted her ahead of him in the coffee queue, and when he'd purchased his own coffee and chocolate cookie he swooped down on the small table they habitually shared.

"Arabella! Darling! Where have you been all my life!"

Arabella sprang from her seat and they embraced and air-kissed like a pair of performing seals.

"Oh! It's good to see you, Steve!"

"And you're a sight for sore eyes too! Love the spangly top! Dolce e Zucchini?"

"I made it myself, actually. Or at least, embellished it. Sewing sequins by hand is kind of therapeutic."

"Mmm – worth every stitch!"

They sat down, grinning broadly at each other.

"So tell me, my spangled one, has Derek's friend Ted Cutter been treating you well over the summer?"

"Well, he doesn't have the holidays that we have."

"Ah, no. Same problem for me with Derek. But our other halves do grub up lots of money for us to help them to spend, don't they!"

"We did get away in August for two weeks to Mexico."

"Ahh – *Meheeko* – how divine! Derek told me that you were going there. And was it fun?"

"Fabulous, darling. Absolutely fabulous. I came back with a suitcase of woven blankets and ponchos from Oaxaca."

"So we'll be seeing you dressed as a Mexican peasant lady when the cold weather comes?"

"*Si señor!*"

"That won't be long now, I suppose. I wish they'd move Forthburgh to the south coast of England."

"They have art schools down there too. You could get a job there, I expect."

"Not far enough away from London."

"Are you still worried? About the… what's his name… the bad guy?"

"Just enough to stay clear for another couple of years; although I did spend some time in London in the summer."

"On your own?"

"Yes. Of course."

"I hope you behaved yourself?"

Their eyes met, and they burst out laughing. Over Arabella's shoulder, Sidling caught a glimpse of Duncan McBane settling down with his coffee at a table with the other hairy misanthrope from the fine art department, the one with the John Lennon spectacles. Duncan caught his eye and exhibited that weird shark-like smile of his, and waved a hand. Sidling raised a hand in response.

"Who's that you're waving at?" Arabella asked.

"Your former flame."

"You mean Duncan?" Arabella said with a look of distaste. "Kindly don't refer to him as a flame. More of a wet sponge."

"Or a wet *fish*?"

"Indeed."

They smirked at each other.

After a pause and a sip of coffee, Sidling spoke again.

"You know, I'd never have expected Fishface McBane to come around to *Ambient Interventions* so wholeheartedly!"

"You mean that letter you told me about back in July?"

"Yes, and his new friendly attitude to me."

"Surely he's just protecting his job?" Arabella said. "I mean, now that it's all going ahead, he'd be a fool to keep standing out against it."

"Well, I wouldn't be able to sack him just because we have different views of what sculpture should be all about."

"No, but you could make life pretty difficult for him."

"That's what I thought I'd have to do after that outburst in the lecture theatre that everyone saw. I thought I'd have to try and make his position unbearable. But he genuinely seems to have taken it all on board."

He glanced over Arabella's shoulder again, and found that Fishface was staring at him. When their eyes met, the severe craggy face broke into that strange semblance of a smile that he'd witnessed before. It sent a shudder down his spine.

A few days later, Steve Sidling was walking briskly away from the art school. It was quite late in the day, and he had already switched off the part of his brain that dwelt on art school matters. He was looking forward to a cosy evening in with Derek, who generally got home an hour or two later than him. He intended to cook a Nasi Goreng for them both, while drinking a couple of gin and tonics. He'd put on some nice jazz on the CD player. They'd open a bottle of red. A nice romantic evening in. What ingredients did he need to pick up on the way home for the Nasi Goreng? He had most things... he could pick up chicken at that butcher's on the corner...

"Steve... can I have a word?"

Steve turned around reluctantly. It was Duncan McBane catching him up. What did he want?

He stopped and Duncan came to a halt beside him, slightly out of breath. He was smiling broadly, and Steve coaxed his own features into a pleasant responsiveness. He was beginning to believe that the man was a convert after all. A repentant sinner was, after all, to be valued even more highly than the ready disciples he had found among the students. In less than two weeks time, the first full academic year of the *Department of Ambient Interventions* would get under way, and a compliant, collaborative Duncan was much to be desired.

"I'm sorry to catch you at the end of the day like this, Steve," Duncan said, "but you were busy in meetings I know, and I didn't want to disturb you earlier."

"That's all right, Duncan. Always happy to have a word with you."

He sought for a moment in his heart, and found that he could just bring himself to offer even more.

"Do you want to pop into The Tap of Poverty for a quick one?"

Duncan looked ecstatic.

"That's brilliant, Steve. But... listen, if you've got twenty minutes to spare, could I just run you up to Deil's Glen in my car. I've got a great idea for an ambient intervention up there – kind of complementary to the totem pole thing – and I'd really value your input. It won't take long, and I can run you home afterwards if you like."

Damn! But with his offer of a drink at The Tap he'd already admitted that he had a little time on his hands. Duncan was looking at him expectantly.

"Well... isn't it starting to get a little dark?"

"No, no – plenty of time left before dark. And this won't take long, really. It's only ten minutes to the glen in the car, and then another ten minutes showing you what I've got in mind. I can run you straight home from there if you want."

In Duncan's scruffy little Fiat, Steve was puzzled by the layers of plastic sheeting covering all the seats.

"I'm trying to keep it clean," Duncan explained. "You know, I take different materials about. And sometimes I'm all covered in stone dust or whatever when I've been working. It gets into every crevice, that stone dust."

Steve tried not to imagine that.

They drove past the car park at Deil's Glen, which was empty.

"There's a better place to park just off Cloven Brae," Duncan explained. "Nearer to where I'm planning the art work."

Cloven Brae turned out to be an exceptionally narrow road that climbed up from beside the car park and then ran along parallel with the upper edge of the glen. The deep tree-filled defile could be glimpsed from time to time below them.

"I hope we don't meet anything coming the other way!" Steve said, as they rounded the third in a series of blind corners.

"No worry about that," Duncan reassured him. "There's only an electricity sub-station up at the top. There'll be no one around at this time on a Friday night."

He parked the Fiat at a passing point on the road.

"It'll be fine here – we won't be long."

Steve got out of the car reluctantly. His thoughts were running on the Nasi Goreng again. What time did the butcher's shut? He didn't want to have to trek to the supermarket for the chicken. Couldn't Duncan just have described this project to him verbally? Why did he have to make a site visit, if it was only at an early planning stage? As Duncan shut the driver's door and beckoned to him from the edge of the woods he sighed heavily and followed.

There was a feeling of imminent rain in the air as they made their way down a faint path that plunged into the glen. The trees grew thickly around them, and in the gloaming it was hard to see more than a few yards ahead. What the hell did Duncan have in mind for this secluded place? Deil's Glen was not very far from the heart of Forthburgh, but you could imagine yourself in the depths of the Highlands. There was no sound of traffic and no sign of human life.

Glancing back at him, Duncan said, "Nearly there Steve!" Then he pushed through some thin undergrowth off to the side of the path.

"Follow me! Watch your footing!"

Cursing inwardly, Steve trailed along just behind the broad back of his companion. The ground sloped even more steeply downwards here and was treacherous with tree roots. After a minute or so they emerged into a flat little clearing with a couple of rocks jutting out of the bushes at its edge. Duncan strode towards one of these rocks and picked up a crowbar that had evidently been left leaning against it.

Steve suppressed an irrational shiver of fear. The old Duncan, the Duncan of the vitriolic outburst in the lecture theatre, came back into his mind. There was the same intensity in his gaze now. His eyes seemed unnaturally wide; white, eager eyes staring at him in the gloom. A drop of rain landed on his own head, and he heard the patter of more drops starting to fall on the leaves around them.

"This is the place," Duncan said.

Steve nodded, looking around him for signs of intervention. If the crowbar had been left here, presumably Duncan had been doing some preliminary work. Had he moved those rocks from their original positions?

"What are you planning to do here, then?" he said.

Duncan approached him, swinging the crowbar carelessly.

"If you look down towards that rock there," he said, "You'll see what I have in mind."

Steve turned, following the direction of Duncan's pointing finger. He couldn't see anything but more trees.

"What rock...?"

He heard a sudden, inarticulate grunt behind him, and half swivelled around just in time to see Duncan's face looming at him, contorted like that of a wild animal. Then he felt a blow to the side of his head that was like nothing he'd ever felt in his life. He crumpled to the ground as a wave of excruciating pain welled up to swallow him.

"I'll fucking teach you to call me *Fishface*!" he heard, and then another blow descended on his head and sent him into darkness. Forever.

CHAPTER 12

November 1989

After the three portrait sittings in the art school, Hermione had taken the canvas home late in the summer and worked on it in the room she used as a studio there. Now the portrait was finished, and it was unlike anything else she had ever done. Duncan McBane's face glowered out at the world with an expression of smouldering hatred. The skull that was cradled in his hands was like a threat: this is what will happen to anyone who crosses me! The paint, as she had envisaged from the start, was thick and encrusted, as if the inner spirit of the man was trying to burst forwards and outwards from the canvas. It might be the best portrait she had ever painted, and she felt proud of it.

No-one else had set eyes on it, but now she wanted it to be seen, and it seemed appropriate to her that the first person who should see it was Duncan. They had developed a frank relationship in the course of the sittings and while sharing a coffee afterwards. It was a relationship sustained by mutual sympathy: Duncan, undermined and undervalued at work, and wracked with jealousy and bitterness over Arabella.; herself, equally wracked with jealousy and bitterness over Ted's desertion; both of them still emotionally shackled to their faithless partners. They took some sort of twisted comfort from sharing the same set of circumstances. In their conversations, Arabella's engaging carapace was cracked open to reveal the wicked, manipulative heartbreaker hidden within. Duncan was as damning about her as Hermione, in spite of which she was certain that he'd forgive her in an instant if only she would come back to him.

Hermione decided to have Duncan over for a quiet, informal supper to see his finished portrait. She issued the invitation; it was accepted, and she prepared a boeuf bourguignon and opened a bottle of Merlot. She gave some thought to what she should wear, and opted for jeans and a sweater. The weather was turning a little colder now, but not quite cold enough to put the central heating on. The jeans and sweater would be a clear signal that nothing of a romantic nature was intended by this supper invitation. Not that she thought Duncan would interpret it that way anyway, but it was best to be sure.

The doorbell rang and she went to answer it. Duncan stood on the doorstep, smiling awkwardly. In the night sky behind him, a rocket ascended with a whistling sound and burst into coloured lights. She had only remembered that it was Guy Fawkes night an hour earlier, when fireworks had started to go off and dogs had begun to bark all over the neighbourhood.

Duncan thrust forward a box of chocolates – Cadbury's Roses - probably bought at the corner shop nearby.

"Thank you! Come in, Duncan! Come in!"

Behind him, as she closed the door, she saw Agnes Clore at the window of her house over the road. Now, no doubt, the Martinside rumour mill would start grinding on the subject of this shadowy bearded man entering her home in the darkness.

"I'll get you a drink, Duncan, and then I'll show you the portrait... we'll get that over with!"

She felt a little nervous now. She never let a sitter see the work in progress, so the revelation of the finished painting was always a tricky moment for her. Like any artist, she craved approval.

"I've got whisky, if you'd like that."

Duncan nodded. His jaws must be aching, she thought, with the effort of maintaining that unnatural smile.

"A splash of water in it?" she suggested.

"Aye, that'd be fine."

She dug out the half drunk bottle of Glenfiddich that Ted had left behind him and poured out a shot. She poured a glass of the Merlot for herself.

Drinks in hand, they went along the hallway, with its collection of framed family photographs – her and Ted on honeymoon; her and Ted with the baby Roland; Roland's first day at secondary school – to the back of the house where her studio was located.

"It's a pity you can't see it first by daylight," she said, flicking on the light, "but I've got special bulbs in here that are daylight colour temperature."

Duncan approached the canvas on its easel and contemplated himself, as embodied in swirling paint. The portrait was somewhat more conventional than those he had seen at her exhibition. The story of Dorian Gray came immediately to his mind. The face transfixed him with its fierce gaze, as if upbraiding him for some heinous sin. The skull held in his hands too had a dark blank stare that couldn't be avoided; a stare of accusation. It was the portrait of a murderer, grasping his trophy. For the first time since his slaughter of Sidling, he felt a qualm. Not of guilt, but of fear – an almost supernatural fear. If this portrait could speak, it would denounce him in an instant.

"What do you think?" Hermione asked after the silence had become a little uncomfortable for her.

Duncan shook himself out of his trance.

"It's... well, it's a powerful painting! It's... er, maybe a bit of a shock. A photograph of yourself can give you a bit of a surprise sometimes, but no-one's ever drawn me or painted me before. It's a new thing. Seeing how someone else sees you, I suppose."

He leaned in close to the painting's surface. There was a kind of frenzy in the layered paint, as if a miniature storm had scoured its surface, leaving ridges and little thorn-like spikes.

"It's very intense," he said. "Well done, Hermione! Very well done!"

Now he just wanted to get away from it. He turned towards the door. Hermione flicked off the light and they made their way back along the hallway, leaving the murderous painted Duncan alone in his darkness.

By the time they finished their plates of the boeuf bourguignon, there were two empty bottles of Merlot on the table between them. They seemed possessed by the same urge to drown their sorrows. Their conversation had followed a predictable spiral towards their common preoccupation. Hermione was enjoying discharging more of the poison that had built up in her spleen over the last months.

"She's a piece of work, Arabella Wood," she said, for the third time. She knew that the wine was making her repeat herself, but she didn't care any more. "I thought we were such good friends, you know... confided in each other... had such fun in each other's company... and then... and then she comes sneaking and creeping up like a... like a snake... like a thief in the night. We were happy, Ted and me. Happy! We were! There was nothing wrong... nothing. Maybe some of the fizz had gone out of our... our romance... maybe... who can say... but there really was nothing wrong. Really, there wasn't. If it hadn't been for her, he'd be here now, in the house with me. He'd be here!"

She slapped a hand down on the table between them, making the cutlery rattle on the uncleared crockery.

Duncan nodded. Hermione was going around and around in bitter and somewhat incoherent circles, but he didn't mind. Arabella *was* a treacherous snake! But as Hermione went rambling on, and he nodded occasionally – faked signals of attention - he found his drunken thoughts drifting into a daydream, reliving the memories of those early weeks in his short relationship with Arabella, when he had fallen into that euphoric state of worshipping obsession. He couldn't help picturing her smooth white skin... her smile... hearing the sound of her voice, so much softer than her customary tones, as she lay close in bed beside him... the scent of her... the warmth. None of these fond memories had been entirely obliterated.

To shake them off, now, as at any other time that he fell into these musings, he concentrated on the recollection of Arabella saying the word *Fishface!* The tone of scandalised delight with which she had said it! The collusion with that bastard Sidling! That was the antidote to counteract his infatuation!

It was a thin line between love and hate, and he was teetering constantly on the edge of it. There could be no neutral zone in his feelings for Arabella.

He stood up, and swayed a little on his feet. Hermione was still talking, as if making a case to an invisible judge and jury.

"Is there a bathroom off the hall somewhere?" he said.

She focussed her eyes on him again.

"Turn left and it's on the left."

After he'd pissed and washed his hands, he looked at himself in the bathroom cabinet mirror. Was he really what that portrait made of him? He tried a smile. It didn't look right. On a casual nosy impulse, he opened the bathroom cabinet. Its shelves were jammed with medicine bottles and little packages. One plastic container caught his eye, because there was an image of a rat on the label. He picked it off the shelf and looked more closely. There was a skull and crossbones symbol in a red diamond shape. He put it back in its place thoughtfully.

"What do you think happened to Steve Sidling?" Hermione said suddenly, when he'd sat down again at the kitchen table with her.

It wasn't the first time Duncan had had to discuss this, but he felt fuddled with whisky and wine. He was almost overcome by a terrible temptation to drop a hint. Madness! He thought of Raskolnikov in 'Crime and Punishment'. He mustn't be that sort of fool!

"Who knows?" he said with a shrug. "They say he kept some dubious company."

"I heard that too."

"From Arabella?"

"Yes. She liked to tell me anything a little bit scandalous. She was a bitch about him sometimes. Shows what kind of a friend she was. Two-faced."

"She came across as a big pal of Sidling. They were always having coffee together at the art school."

"So is that how you knew what company Sidling kept?"

"What, from Arabella? No, she liked him and I didn't, so we didn't discuss him. But of course it got all over the art school after the… after the murder. I don't know who started it. Suddenly everyone was talking about his weird sexual practices. It was all a game of Chinese whispers, I suppose."

"My husband Ted was an old friend of Steve's partner, Derek. Did you know that?"

"No. So didn't you socialise with Steve then?"

"Ted met up with Derek once in a while, but I didn't take to Derek. So, no, we didn't socialize with Steven Sidling. Anyway, Derek told Ted, and Ted told me, that Steve had a bit of a wild side."

"Aye. He was the sort of person… you'd expect…"

He tailed off. The booze was getting to him. He couldn't complete the thought.

"There was something else though that struck me," Hermione said. "It was when word got out about how he was found. Stuck all over with paintbrushes. It reminded me of that famous art work of his. The German building, wherever it was. Stuck all over with spikes. I wondered if someone had that in mind. If someone was making a point – if you'll excuse the pun."

She laughed awkwardly and drained the dregs of her wine glass. Duncan couldn't meet her eye. Surely it must only be the whisky and the wine, but he felt she was insinuating… he felt she was on his trail, somehow. He nodded, looking past her at the wall.

"Aye, it's possible I suppose."

Hermione laughed again, drunkenly. She could hear it herself, that she wasn't laughing normally.

"If I could murder Arabella," she said, "I could easily find something to poison her. I can think of lots of things that would work. But I don't know how I'd get her to take it. Maybe I could give her a poisoned apple, like the witch in Snow White."

She laughed again, that laugh that sounded like breaking crockery to her own ears.

"But I'd rather she died in some way that was really *appropriate*," she went on. "I think I'd like to make some sort of portrait of her. Maybe take her head off and put it in a glass case. That would make a lovely portrait!"

She stood up unsteadily.

"Come and look at something I've been drawing, Duncan."

He stood up, and followed her into her studio once more. When the lights came on, his portrait scowled unnervingly at him again, as if it had preferred to be alone in the dark. He tried not to look at it. Hermione went to a plan chest against the wall and slid out a large sheet of paper. She put it on top of the chest and turned on a desk light to illuminate it more brightly.

It was a charcoal drawing, with some coloured highlights. On a bed of vicious thorns two naked distorted bodies writhed together. A man and a woman. Roses, blood red roses, were entwined with the bodies. The faces were turned towards the onlooker, wide-eyed and somehow mocking, as if saying *Look here! Look at us! We don't care!*

Words were scrawled beneath the image; big, bold, looping text adorned with additional little flowers, that proclaimed Love is a Bed of Roses.

The faces of the man and the woman were unmistakeable. He recognized Ted from the family photographs in the hallway and from seeing him at The Blinking Eye. The woman was Arabella.

When Duncan had stumbled off into the night, Hermione set about clearing up in the kitchen. However much she would have preferred just to fall into bed, she had a deeply ingrained habit of wanting to see the kitchen put back in order before she went to sleep.

Scooping up the used cutlery clumsily, she prodded the point of a fork into her thumb. It didn't really hurt, but as she lowered the knives, forks and plates into a sink full of suds, the sensation in her thumb mysteriously brought back a visual memory from the summer; something that she didn't even know she had stored up. It was a recollection of Duncan, standing in the clear north light of the painting studio at the art school after they had finished the third and last of his sittings for his portrait. They were just talking – she couldn't remember about what – and as they talked he picked up one of her paintbrushes. A brush with a point of fine bristles and a long, thin wooden handle. He seemed to have done it absent-mindedly. He ran his fingers along the handle as they talked, and… now she could picture this very clearly… he seemed to be touching the end of the handle repeatedly with his thumb, as if to see how sharp or pointed it was.

She continued to think about this as she finished washing up, and then, on a whim, she went back into her studio and flicked on the light. The portrait of Duncan glared at her. She thought of the newspaper reports of how Steven Sidling had been found, and all the horrified discussions she'd participated in at the art school. *Stuck all over with sharpened paintbrushes – looked like a hedgehog.*

Drunkenly, she spoke aloud to the portrait.

"Are you a murderer?"

It didn't reply. A belated burst of fireworks from somewhere made the windows rattle. Dogs started barking all over again. She turned out the studio light and made her way wearily upstairs. It was high time she was asleep.

CHAPTER 13

November-December 1989

The next Friday, at five o'clock in the afternoon, Hermione was nursing her coffee as usual in the Star Café in Scotsbridge, and waiting for Arabella and Ted to make their appearances across the street. It was like a scab that she couldn't stop picking. She had secured a seat right by the window on this occasion, and a convenient street lamp illuminated the red door on the opposite side of the road like a stage set. She sipped the coffee and tapped her fingers impatiently against the side of the cup. She scanned each figure that approached along the gloomy street. Suddenly her body stiffened and her fingers tightened around the coffee cup. It was her! Strutting, she thought. Strutting like the top ranking hen in the coop, unassailable and smug.

Arabella, clad in a winter coat of some feathery material, paused at the red door and fumbled in her handbag, presumably for the key. Hermione glared through the window as if she could put a hex on her. If a sudden heart attack could be conveyed in a look, then she was sending one across the street with every ounce of will that she possessed.

Arabella looked up, as if startled by something. For just the tiniest fraction of a second Hermione thought that her death-dealing spell had been felt. Then Arabella stared straight at the window of the Star Café. She raised a hand to shade her eyes from the yellow glare of the street lamp. Then, glancing quickly to either side to check for traffic, she strode out into the road and marched directly towards the café.

Hermione had no time to compose herself for whatever was to come. Previously, Arabella had always opened the door and disappeared quickly. She had never before, as far as she could tell, been aware that she was being watched.

The door to the café swung inwards violently as Arabella entered like an exploding feathery pillow. Heads turned at the other tables. The place was quite busy. Hermione had been lucky to secure a seat by the window. Or unlucky, as it was now turning out.

"What the *fuck* are you doing here?" Arabella said in a voice that reached every ear in the café. "Are you spying on me or something?"

She stood over Hermione, hands now on her hips, like an angry schoolmistress.

Hermione had prepared no covering story to explain her presence in this part of town.

"I'm… I'm just having a coffee," Hermione said quietly. This sounded feeble in her own ears. She raised her voice a couple of notches, to show that she wasn't frightened of a scene, if that's what Arabella was here to provoke. "It's a free country."

"Oh yes!" Arabella said sarcastically, in a voice that would carry to the back rows of any theatre, and marched to the counter.

"Has this woman been in here before?" she demanded, pointing an accusing finger towards Hermione.

The plump girl behind the counter was always there on Fridays. She looked over at Hermione and nodded dumbly. She looked terrified.

"I see!" Arabella said, nodding her head vigorously. "A *regular*… well…"

She turned away from the counter and addressed the entire clientele, who were either staring at their table tops in embarrassment or agog for more.

"... this woman here..." She pointed at Hermione. "This woman is what is known as a *stalker*. She's spying on me for reasons best known to herself, and if she doesn't put a stop to it right now, then I'll be getting the police to take an interest."

With a final toss of her head and an imperious scowl at Hermione, she stomped out of the café and across the road outside, causing two cars to screech to a halt. A chorus of hooting horns accompanied her final disappearance into the red door of her tenement.

Hermione felt a prickling in her face – a combination of embarrassment and rage. Tears gathered in her eyes. Leaving her coffee unfinished, she stumbled out of the blurry café into the cold street outside. Only death, she felt, only death could assuage all this pain and humiliation. Hers, or Arabella's.

As the Autumn term wore on and the lonely nights grew longer, Hermione felt as if she were sinking into a pit in the ground. She had nightmares in which she was actually under the earth, and could hear shovels up above, piling soil and stones on her grave. It was Ted and Arabella up there, laughing and kissing as they entombed her. Sometimes her son Roland was with them, and she could hear Arabella explaining to him that she was his real mother, and he must forget all about the imposter down below.

She struggled to find the impetus to go shopping and buy food. Her appetite for eating, her appetite for living, was weak. She started to look thin and wan – she was naturally thin anyway - and occasionally someone asked her if she was ill. Roland spent a week with her in late November – a 'reading week' on his course at Bristol - and she saw the shock on his face when she opened the door to him. Roland went down to Arabella's flat a couple of times while he was in Forthburgh, to see his father, and while he was there Hermione felt so sick in her stomach that she was nauseous and struggled not to throw up the few scraps of food she'd picked at for lunch. She hadn't spoken to Ted herself since August.

"Are you all right?" Duncan McBane said to her one day as they came out of the art school together by chance. She had cut down her teaching there from three days to two days a week this term, and her main preoccupation was avoiding the sight and sound of Arabella. She took a banana or an apple with her for lunch, and didn't go into the canteen any more, for fear of seeing her. She would have quit the art school if she could, but she needed the income. She didn't know what the future held. Ted was still paying the household bills, and putting a little money into her bank account. But it was all up in the air, if he never came back to her. They'd have to have a divorce settlement. But the word *divorce* sounded almost as bad as *death*. She should probably speak to a lawyer, but she preferred to thrust it all aside. She just didn't want to think of it.

"Oh... hello Duncan. Yes, I'm fine. How are you?"

She looked at him, and it occurred to her that he looked thinner and more gaunt than before. Was he suffering as she was?

"Oh, I'm all right."

"I hear you've taken over running the Sculpture Department?"

"Aye – well. They've asked me to be Acting Head. Someone had to take over quickly. Do you... do you want to go for a drink?"

She hesitated a moment, and then thought of the empty house awaiting her return.

"Okay, thank you."

"The Tap? Or somewhere else?"

"It's depressing in there," she suggested. Her real reservation was that it was too near to the art school. There was a faint possibility that Arabella might be in there.

"Okay. Let's go down to the Brassmarket then," Duncan said.

The Brassmarket was a broad trough of a street over which the castle loomed like a vampire from its rocky prominence. From beside the art school they descended without conversation the long flight of stone steps next to the old city wall, and found a corner at one of the dozen or so pubs down there. The pub was almost deserted at this early but dark hour of a November evening.

"So, still no progress on the Sidling investigation I presume? Or have I missed anything?" Hermione commented, when Duncan brought their drinks to the table. It had become a standby topic of conversation amongst the staff and students of the art school, a grim substitute for speculation about the weather.

Duncan mustered an insouciant shrug, but inside he was thrown into consternation. She had raised the topic before, when he had visited her house to see the portrait. Why did she think he would know anything new about the investigation? He tried to meet her gaze, but his eyes slid away to a painting behind her of tartan-clad highlanders wrestling cattle through a burn in spate. He felt, ridiculously, that his face was starting to burn.

Hermione had hit upon the remark without forethought. It was just a conversational gambit. But Duncan's strange reaction piqued her interest.

"Tell me honestly, Duncan... really, truthfully... are you glad he's dead?"

Her eyes caught his own. There was nowhere left to hide.

"Aye. I'm glad."

She nodded.

"From all that you've told me about him, I'm not too surprised."

She took a gulp of the red wine in her glass, and leaned forward a little, lowering her voice. There was no-one within thirty feet of them, but it was something that could only be said quietly.

"I wish Arabella was dead too!"

He said nothing. Was he shocked, she wondered. She'd said it before to him – on that drunken evening when she'd had him to her house. But she'd never said it like this, stone-cold sober, and in earnest.

Duncan wasn't shocked. Sometimes he had entertained the same thought. He mulled over what answer to make while Hermione sipped at her wine. He didn't have to make an answer, of course. He tried to imagine an art school, a Forthburgh… a world… in which there was no Arabella Wood. It would be like cutting out a cancer that had attached itself to his innermost being. The absence of Steve Sidling had made his own life so much better. With Arabella gone, he would also be free of that obsessive longing for her that was mingled so inextricably, so confusingly, with hatred.

"Aye. So do I," he said at last. Then he leaned forward as Hermione had done, and said in a voice that only a rat in the adjacent wall would be able to hear, "and, if you really mean what you say, I think we should think more about it."

The next week, Hermione and Duncan met again at the pub in the Brassmarket, soon after darkness fell. A damp, early December fog had settled over the cobbles and stones of the Old Town, and the floodlit south-facing façade of the castle was almost lost to sight, a mere yellowish blur in the murk, floating over the Brassmarket below.

They sat in a dark corner, well away from the bar, where a handful of early drinkers sat mournfully discussing the weather or the poll tax or the football, intent on depressing themselves as far as was humanly possible. Otherwise, the pub was empty.

They both knew why they had come there. A week had passed in which either of them could have withdrawn. They kept their voices low. They would look like clandestine lovers, at a glance, huddled together over intimacies - unless an observer noticed that neither of them smiled. In fact, observed more closely, they would look like two ghouls, thin and intense, sharing haunted secrets.

"I want it, Duncan, I really do. But it seems more like a fantasy to me. I can't imagine how we could actually make it happen."

Hermione swirled her red wine in the glass and took a swallow.

"You know about how I trained as a pharmacist?" she went on.

Duncan nodded.

"Well… I imagine ways that I could poison Arabella. I've still got my old university text books. I've looked up different poisons and imagined how I could trick her into taking them. But I can't think of a way that I could get away with it."

Duncan nodded again. He had thought of something. Something that might help to move them on from fantasising to planning. Something that would convince Hermione that he was in earnest.

"I've got a story I can tell you," he said. "It's something I've never told anyone before. You'll see why."

Hermione felt a small shudder go through her. Was Duncan going to confess that he had killed Steve Sidling? She had a suspicion – more, an intuition - that he had done that, but she didn't want him to share anything of it.

Duncan noticed her look of alarm, and immediately divined its source. He was sure that Hermione suspected him of killing Sidling, and also sure that it should remain something unsaid between them. He spoke again quickly, before Hermione could have chance to break that silence.

"It's about something that happened when I was a child – or a bit more than a child. When I was twelve."

Hermione looked at him, puzzled.

"Don't worry, you'll see the point soon enough. But you must promise me never to tell anyone about this."

She nodded.

"Of course. I won't say anything. I wouldn't talk about you to anyone else, Duncan. Not ever."

Duncan fiddled with his whisky glass for a moment or two, marshalling his thoughts. Where should he begin?

"When my father died, my father's sister – my Aunt Janet – came to live with us. That was when I was ten."

"I didn't know your father had died when you were young."

"Aye… well… he fell."

"Fell?"

"Fell off of a church spire. He was a stonemason."

"My God! That's awful! How old was he?"

"Fifty. Same as I am now."

"I'm so sorry."

"Aye. Well, at least I didn't have to see him beating my mother any more. Or get skelped myself whenever he was in the mood."

"God!"

"Oh - he loved her. He loved us both. But he drank, and when he drank he got angry. Angry about nothing. Anyway, that's by the by. When he died, my mother was in a state, and her sister-in-law - my Aunt Janet, who was a spinster - she came to help. At first I thought it was just temporary, you know? Just to help out for a while. But she stayed and stayed, and I came to understand that she was there for good. I hated her with a passion."

"Oh… why?"

"Right from day one she was going to be the boss of me. And the boss of my mother, for that matter, because my mum was weak and sad."

"But maybe she needed to... I don't know... create some order in the household?"

Duncan gave a hollow laugh.

"Oh, she did that all right! It was nothing but orders and orders and more orders once she came."

"And you resented that?"

"I wouldn't have, I really think I wouldn't have, if she'd been a normal sort of person. But she wasn't. She was a tyrant, and she enjoyed lording it over us. I got so that going to school was the happiest part of my day, because I'd be away from Aunt Janet for all those hours. Even though I was unhappy at school, it was a better sort of unhappiness."

Hermione looked at him. Those lines of anguish that criss-crossed his otherwise almost handsome face! Had those trenches first been dug in a war so long ago, in his childhood?

"So... what sort of things did she do?"

"I didn't see it straight away, not when I was ten years old, but I think she set out to make Mum consider herself as some kind of relic – or maybe an invalid, almost. Someone who was damaged, and needed to take life very quietly now. For Christ's sake! When I look back... my mum was only in her late thirties! She could have got on with life again, even maybe found a new husband. But Aunt Janet got her bitter, spinster claws into her and turned her into a feeble copy of herself. She turned the house into a prison, and kept the rest of the world away from us. Anyone we'd known before, or knew then – even the few friends I'd made at school – she told us they were all poison. She said everyone was against us, and my mum and me... well, we started to see things that way too."

"You closed in on yourselves?"

"Exactly. The three of us. A little fortified island in a sea of hate. That's how she spun it. Everyone hated us. Maybe she really believed that. And it rubbed off on me all right. I lost the two or three friends I'd had, and I started to get bullied at school. By the time she'd been with us a year or so, I hated everyone except my mother, and the person I hated most of all was Aunt Janet herself."

"It sounds awful."

"It was. But I'm not telling you all this for no reason. It was awful, but I changed it. That's the point. That's why I'm telling you – so you see how we can change things now."

"How?"

Duncan took a sip of his whisky.

"After a couple of years, we moved to Stonehaven, to a rented cottage near the sea. It was Aunt Janet's idea, to move me and my mum away from our home in Forthburgh. To cut us off even more, bring us even more into her power.

"I grew tall and strong early, as a lad. I shot up, and when I was twelve years old I was already nearly six feet tall. They made fun of me for that at the new school. The teachers called me *the lamp post*. So when I tell you this happened when I was twelve, you mustn't picture me as a wee child.

"Anyway, one thing about Aunt Janet was she was a fanatic for fitness. She was a bony, lanky creature. This was in the days before everyone went jogging, but she insisted that I went with her for what she called a 'constitutional' every day after school. That was a brisk walk along the cliffs beside the golf course. My mother had to come too. That winter in Stonehaven we'd all be out there every late afternoon in the nearly dark, with the wind blowing a hooley off the North Sea. It was horrible.

"Well, this one time, my mum had a cold, so she was let off. Aunt Janet and me, we set off as usual, her striding along so fast that, tall as I was, it was hard work to keep up. I was in my school shorts, and the wind was gusting splinters of sea spray up over the top of the cliffs that cut into my bare legs. I could taste salt settling on my chapped lips.

"We were almost at the point where we always turned back, when we heard a sheep bleating. There was nothing unusual in that; there was often a flock of sheep up at that end. But this bleating was loud and went on and on, as if the animal was in distress.

"*That's coming from an odd direction*, my Aunt Janet said. *I wonder if one's gone over the cliff edge?*

"We followed the sound and got as near as we dared to the edge of the cliff. There was a little inlet down there, and on the rocks by the sea we could see this white blob. It was moving a little – only a little - and we could tell that was where the bleating sound was coming from.

"But I wasn't thinking about the sheep. My thoughts were racing. I looked to my right and left. The light was fading fast, and there was no-one else out there. Aunt Janet was standing only three feet from the edge of the cliff, looking down at this sheep. I took a couple of steps back. She started to say something, without turning round.

"*I wonder if we should tell…* she said. I can still hear those exact words that came back to me in the wind, as I ran at her from behind, and gave her a great shove on the shoulder blades with both my hands. She staggered forwards, right to the brink of the cliff edge. She teetered there for a moment, flapping her arms like wings, and then she went over. I heard a long, trailing scream as she plunged down. Like a seagull diving, kind of.

"I got onto my stomach and crawled right to the edge of the cliff to look. In the gloaming I could just make out her shape on the rocks down there. The sheep was still making its noise, but there was no noise from Aunt Janet

– or no noise that reached the top of the cliffs. She'd landed much nearer to the sea's edge than the sheep, and a wave surged in and lifted her body a little and then let it down again. I watched for a while as she rose and fell in the water, until it grew too dark to see. She was either dead already, or she would be very soon.

"I walked slowly back towards town, thinking of my story, and when I came near to the street lights I started running. I ran to our cottage and let myself in. *Mum! Mum!* I shouted as I galloped upstairs. She was in bed because of her cold. Aunt Janet always made her into an invalid. *There was a sheep that went over the cliffs, and Aunt Janet was looking down and then there was a sudden gust of wind and she lost her balance. We need to ring the police, or the coast guard or someone!*

"So, that was how I got rid of Aunt Janet. It had been a favourite fantasy, that she'd get ill and die, or just go away, but in the end it turned into a reality. I turned it into a reality!

"I stuck to my story, and everyone believed me. My mother went to her grave believing me. And, do you know what? I've never had a moment's guilt about what I did."

Duncan went to the bar to get them more drinks. Hermione sat as still as a statue, reflecting on his tale. It had made her go cold all over, as cold as marble. But inside her cold flesh, his words had kindled a little fire. A flickering sense of horror and… excitement. A man like this – a man who had actually killed another human being, who had also perhaps killed Steven Sidling – could he really be the instrument for her revenge on Arabella?

Duncan returned with the drinks and sat down again. He looked searchingly at Hermione. She nodded.

"Go on," was all she said.

"So – I've thought of a plan. I have to say it's a plan that might not work, but if it doesn't then nothing's lost except our time. If it does work, then..."

He let the sentence remain unfinished.

"She... she'd be dead?"

"More than that. We'd make our point."

"What do you mean?"

"You remember you told me you'd like something *appropriate* for her?"

"Yes. When we were drinking so much at my house. So what..."

Duncan's eyes held her in their gaze. She felt almost hypnotized.

"Listen, Hermione. Believe me, this will be exactly what you meant. But it's best you don't know all the details. You'll have a part to play, but you won't know everything. There'll be no risk to you when it happens, and afterwards, when the details come out and the police interview you – and they will interview you as well as me and everyone else at the art school – you won't know much more about it than anyone else. You won't have to act a part, or make up lies... or only small ones anyway. It's safer this way."

Hermione nodded.

"So... when? When will this happen?"

"At the Art School Christmas Revel."

"At the *Revel*? There'll be hundreds of people."

Duncan nodded.

"That's hundreds of suspects. Don't worry. I know where it can be done where no-one will interfere. You'll buy a ticket. You won't drink. Arabella will go. She always does, she told me that once. It's another chance for dressing up, which she can never resist. And she'll definitely drink. She always drinks too much. You'll watch and wait, and look for an opportunity to get her to this place."

"How will I do that? She hates me as much as I hate her. She won't talk to me."

"She will if she thinks you have something to tell her that she really needs to know. Do you think Ted will go to the Revel with her?"

"Definitely not. Not his kind of scene at all. Unless she really twists his arm."

"If he does go, then this plan won't work. But if she goes without him... I'm thinking you could try one of two things. Either you make out that Ted has promised to come back to you. Or you make a big thing of being sorry about everything and wanting to bury the hatchet."

"But even if she talks to me, how will I get her to go with me? Where do you want me to take her?"

"Do you know the corridor that leads to the Sculpture studios?"

"From the Sculpture Court?"

"Not the main corridor. There's a narrow one that goes a back way."

"Oh – I know where you mean. I've never been down there."

"No one much uses it. Only Sculpture staff and the students who have studio spaces at the west corner of the Old Building. There's a toilet and shower room down there, just for staff use."

"I didn't know that."

"Find a moment to wander along there next time you're in the art school. Then you'll know where it is exactly."

"I still don't think she'll talk to me, or follow me."

"Tell her you need to talk to her somewhere quiet. It'll be deafening in the Sculpture Court, where the band will be playing. If you can't get her to come, we'll have a wasted evening, nothing worse. But if she does – if you can find a way to get her down there – then, I promise you - it will be perfect!"

CHAPTER 14

December 1989

The art school's annual Christmas Revel was scheduled for December the fifteenth, a Friday. After that weekend, the students would disperse to the four corners for whatever Christmas festivities – or part-time jobs – were waiting for them. There had been some talk of cancelling it. After all, a prominent member of staff had been murdered and the killer was still at large. But the rumour mill had it that the death was the outcome of aberrant behaviour in the outside world, nothing that touched too closely on the art school itself. Furthermore, with the uneventful passage of three months, the death of Steve Sidling had already started to fade a little in the collective memory. Life must go on, for the young, the talented and the beautiful denizens of the art school.

Arabella had been prominent on the Revel committee in the previous two years, but didn't feel sufficiently committed to revelry this year to devote so much time to it. Ted was away in London – and in any case would not have wished to attend such an event. However, it was out of the question for her not to attend. The chosen theme was *Mythical Creatures*, and her expert advice on costume design was much in demand by her students in the fashion department. Caught up as usual in the excitement, she decided to go herself as a Gorgon, in a greenish floating Greek dress with a headpiece of rubber snakes held in place with threads on an Alice band

In the week preceding the Revel, all other work in the various departments of the art school came to a halt as everyone focussed on their costume or other aspects of the preparations. The Old Building became a buzzing hive of activity, as the Architecture and Interior Design students gradually transformed the interior into a crumbling Cretan temple with the aid of partitions spray-painted as stone, and papier-maché bas-relief sculptures.

Finally the much anticipated night of the Revel arrived, and Arabella in Gorgon mode entered the main central space of the art school, the airy Sculpture Court, which was decorated loosely in the manner of an arena dedicated to Aphrodite, or possibly the Minotaur. There had been two factions at work, but no one cared too much about the anomalies.

A pretty snub-nosed fairy with pointed ears greeted her.

"Hello, Arabella!

It was Sophie, one of her favourite students, presiding with another girl over a table with drinks.

"You look amazing!" Sophie went on.

"Technically you're not supposed to look at me," Arabella replied with a smile. "Or you'll turn to stone."

Sophie looked a little blank. Perhaps she didn't know about Gorgons.

"I love the little snakes. Cute little faces!"

"I didn't want to be too frightening. No one would dance with me."

"Try some of the magic potion we've made! Look, it's blue!"

"What's in it?" Arabella said, taking a glass and sniffing suspiciously.

"Oh, just stuff," Sophie replied vaguely. "Don't worry. They made it with a proper recipe. A fruit punch. With vodka and rum. The first glass is free."

Arabella took a sip. It was surprisingly good, and instilled an immediate inner warm glow. She moved on into the press of people. The band was still setting up on the stage, and only background music was playing, so it was possible to hold conversations. The usual pattern of the evening was that for an hour or so you would mingle and talk and drink. Especially you would drink. After that the live music would begin and the occasion would swiftly evolve, or degenerate, into a delirious bacchanal. If you could remember the evening with any precision the next day, then you had not truly been a reveller. The order of the night was wild abandon. It was like some throwback to pagan times, before Christianity took charge of midwinter festivities. Arabella moved from group to group, exchanging compliments on outfits, engaging in less and less sensible conversations, and replenishing her glass of magic potion from time to time. She felt the tensions of the last few months falling away: the worry over the still-unsolved murder of her good friend Steven Sidling, and the unpleasant antagonism of Hermione Cutter. They somehow mattered less, these things, under the spell of the blue potion. She even saw Hermione at a distance, looking like a ghost in flowing white robes and pale make-up, and felt nothing more upsetting than a sense of slight surprise that she was attending the occasion. Then the band took their places, the drummer and the bass guitarist set up a driving primeval rhythm, the lead guitarist layered in a melody, and the singer began to wail. The crowd stirred and gyrated like some composite many-headed monster of mythology. The Revel had begun in earnest.

Some unknowable amount of time later, she had slumped, exhausted by dancing, onto one of the benches arranged against the walls under the colonnade that formed the Sculpture Court's periphery. Suddenly, arriving from nowhere, Hermione was sitting beside her. Not only sitting beside her, but speaking to her. Arabella shook her head, as if she could clear it from the deafening roar of the revelry around them and the simultaneous sense of being underwater induced by the punch. What was the damned woman saying?

"Come with me, Arabella!"

"What?"

"Come with me."

"Come? Come where?"

"Somewhere quieter."

"Why?"

"I want to talk to you. It's about Ted. Ted has been in touch with me... I wanted to tell you what he says..."

Arabella looked at the ghostly white face of Hermione and shook her head again, feeling the rubber snakes wobbling above her forehead. But shaking her head was a bad idea. The whole of her surroundings set up a wobbling rubbery dance of their own, even the walls and columns. Hermione's voice seemed to come from nowhere specific.

"Are you all right?"

Was that Hermione? Expressing concern? And what did she mean about Ted? Was he here? What was going on?

"I'm... I'm just a little dizzy. And... and I think I need the toilet."

"Come on! I'll help you."

Arabella staggered a little when she stood up. Hermione put a steadying hand on her elbow.

"Are you okay, Arabella?"

"Yes. Yes. Where... the toilets?"

"Come with me. The nearest ones are down here."

Arabella found herself staggering, half supported by Hermione, around some corners and into a corridor that she didn't recognize.

"Is there... are you sure there's a toilet?" she mumbled.

"Yes, just a bit further."

The corridor was deserted, and the sounds of the Revel were muted here; no more than a steady thumping sound as if the whole building had a heart that was pumping blood around its stone arteries.

When they reached the door of the toilet, Arabella put a hand against the wall for support. She stared at

Hermione, as if she had only just appeared at her elbow. Something this damned woman had said came back to her.

"Didn't you say – something – you wanted to say something? About Ted?"

"Yes, but it can wait Arabella. I'll wait out here while you use the toilet."

"Okay. Yes. Okay."

She leaned drunkenly against the door and pushed her way inwards, almost falling over. She steadied herself again with a hand against the wall. Walls were so useful sometimes!

She flicked the light switch on and pulled the bolt on the door shut. Inside the toilet the booming noise of the band was muffled further. It was hardly more than a distant vibration. Her ears were ringing though. The white bowl of the toilet waited invitingly. She noted a mildewed shower curtain off to one side, and now she remembered that she had been in here in the past, when she had a fad for jogging into work. She hoisted her ankle-length robe up around her waist, pulled down her knickers, and subsided heavily onto the toilet seat. With a sigh of relief she let her bladder relax.

There was a bestial grunt from behind the shower curtain and then it was violently swished open. A creature with a great shark's head stepped out and stood towering over her. The trickle of her piss became a sudden torrent, and she flung out a hand to ward off this invader.

"Fishface!" it said in a menacing hiss.

"No!" was the last word she ever heard, and it issued as a shout from her own lips as something metallic came swinging towards her at the end of the monster's bright yellow arm. She felt a massive blow at the side of her neck, and then suddenly the little room spun upside down and then sideways, and she found her eyes at the level of the tiled floor as a cascade of red fell from above her.

"My head's come off!" was her last thought, and then all went dark.

CHAPTER 15

December 1989

The head was not completely severed. Duncan pulled off his rubber shark mask and finished the job with two more blows of the small axe. Spurts of blood pulsed sideways across the tiles from the neck of the trunk, which twitched violently as though it might stand up if it could. The eyes on the head – Arabella's eyes – blinked once and then remained open, staring at him. So, she had come to the Revel as a Gorgon! But she was powerless now to turn him to stone.

He went to the door and drew back the bolt. He was wearing yellow rubber washing up gloves to avoid fingerprints. He opened the door just a crack. He didn't want Hermione to see in there.

"Hermione?" he said quietly.

He caught a glimpse of her face as she leaned towards the crack.

"It's done. Is there anyone out there?"

"No one."

"Good. Put the notice on the door and go home. Leave straight away."

"Did she…"

"No questions. The less you know, the better. I'll deal with everything now. Go home."

He closed the door and bolted it again. He looked at his watch. Half past midnight. The Revel would go on until two. He would have to spend at least the next two hours in here with the door bolted. It was highly unlikely that anyone would try to use this 'staff only' toilet, since there were others much nearer to the revelry. Students and their friends, who formed the bulk of the revellers, would be unlikely to think of it. And Hermione had now taped a note saying 'Out of Order' to the door.

Duncan slumped down onto the floor of the shower cubicle. The blood hadn't got into there. He closed his eyes for a moment. All physical and mental strength had fled from him, as if he were a marathon runner who had just crossed the line, or a puppet whose strings had been cut. He felt a wave of relief. It was done! But when he opened his eyes again and saw Arabella's twisted legs lying on the tiles, an immense sadness hit him, and he found himself sobbing helplessly. Dimly he was aware that he had seen his mother once like that, sprawled on a bathroom floor, either drunk, or beaten by his father. He felt confused and horrified... killing Steven Sidling hadn't felt like this. He cried and cried: for Arabella, for his mother, for himself.

When his tears finally subsided, he marshalled his thoughts. From now on, he must act with military precision. He stood up unsteadily, and with his yellow-gloved finger pushed the light switch off. He didn't want a crack of light to be visible under the door from the corridor. Nor did he want to see what was in there with him. He shuffled blindly back into the shower cubicle and curled up on its floor to wait. His thoughts began to drift, and – the last thing he would have expected to happen - he fell asleep.

When he came to his senses again he checked the illuminated dial of his watch. It was just after one thirty in the morning. The music was still playing faintly in a distant, happier universe. But it would stop shortly, and the art school's janitorial staff, on double wages, would start the job of clearing the building of revellers. There would probably be a few students who had passed out in corners, or who were attempting to bed down together somewhere. It would all take a while. In the meantime, he should start getting organized. He groped his way back to the light switch, turned it on, and out of the capacious black tote bag in the shower cubicle that contained everything he needed he pulled out some big plastic bags..

Paddling unavoidably in the edge of the large pool of blood around Arabella's body, he picked up the severed head with a shudder – how heavy it felt! - and put it into one of the plastic bags. He put that bag into another one, and then that into another one. Then he put the triple-wrapped horror into a zippered red holdall that he pulled out of the tote bag, and stowed it in the corner next to the door.

With the head out of sight, Duncan felt that his previous weakness had passed. It was a time now for action, not for dwelling on emotions that should have died along with his victim! He retreated again to the shower cubicle, where he pulled off his blood-spattered trousers, shirt and trainers, and put them into yet another plastic bag, along with the small axe that had been so useful in the earliest stages of the carving of his totem pole for Deil's Glen. It was a shame that he would have to dispose of it now. The sullied clothes, the axe, the rubber shark mask and the bloodied washing-up gloves all went into another big plastic bag and then into the black tote bag, Without touching any of the shower cubicle's surfaces, he donned a clean pair of trousers, and a fresh shirt and jumper. He didn't put on his spare pair of shoes yet. Finally he put on a clean pair of gloves, thin cotton gloves that were less restrictive than the rubber ones.

It was nearly two o'clock. He should wait another half hour to allow time for the janitors to clear the building. He turned out the light again and settled on the floor of the shower cubicle. He couldn't hear music any more. In spite of his recent sleep, he felt very tired.

Ten minutes later he stiffened in alarm. Voices were approaching along the corridor outside! Of course - the janitors were bound to make a final tour of inspection everywhere... would they try to open the door of the shower room?

He heard a wheezy laugh. It was Miggs, the head janitor. He was presumably talking with one of his underlings. As the footsteps and voices came closer, he held his breath. In these next few moments, all his meticulous plans could unravel! He could even smell their cigarettes. He caught a few clear words as they went by – Miggs's rasping smoker's tones: "... aye, that lassie with her top off wasn't going to..." and then the conversation moved out of earshot again. They had gone past the door without pausing! He exhaled again softly... so softly. At the end of the corridor the two sets of footsteps halted, and there was a click. The thin line of light beneath the shower room door disappeared. They'd turned off the corridor lights. The footsteps receded and silence reigned again.

He thought it prudent to wait another half an hour. The time dragged terribly, and he became more and more aware of a sweetish, metallic smell in the little room. Arabella's blood, presumably. He had never smelled blood before. It was an effort of will to stay in there any longer, but it had to be done.

At last, when his watch said two forty-five, he thought it would be safe to execute the next stages of his plan. He switched on his torch, unbolted and opened the door cautiously, and peered out into the corridor. It was in complete darkness. He picked up the big tote bag and stepped out. There he put on his clean smooth-soled leather shoes, and then removed the Out of Order notice from the door and stuffed that into the bag. He made his way slowly, ears pricked for any sound, through the darkened building to the ground floor window in one of the painting studios that he'd previously identified as his exit route. He left the bag in a corner there behind some easels, and then slipped noiselessly along a series of corridors and up a flight of stairs to the Jewellery

Department. There was a glimmer of emergency lighting here and there, but mostly everything was pitch black. The familiar building was a different, mysterious place by the light of his torch.

The door of the Jewellery Department creaked alarmingly as he pushed it open, and he stood rigid for a few moments and listened. The fact that all the lights were out in the building meant that Miggs must have finished his rounds. He should have gone home by now, but he couldn't afford to take that for granted.

He heard nothing however, so he entered the Jewellery studio and shone the beam of the torch across the shelves along the walls. The glass display cases used for the degree shows were still where he had observed them a week ago on a surreptitious visit late one evening. He selected a case that was the right size, and opened its glass door to remove the internal glass shelf.

Now a problem arose. In spite of his methodical planning, he hadn't thought of this: he needed both hands to pick up the display case and carry it, which meant that he didn't have a hand for the torch. He should have bought one of those torches that attached to a headband! He couldn't carry a fragile – and quite heavy – glass case through the art school to its destination on a route that would mostly be in pitch darkness.

He thought for a few moments, and then wedged the torch between his teeth. Yes, he could manage that. It was fortunate then, as it had turned out, that he had selected the little pocket torch and not the bigger one that he owned. His face fixed in an uncomfortable snarl around the torch's handle, he picked up the glass case and made his way slowly and laboriously to the Sculpture Court. Here, thank God, the torch became redundant, as dim emergency lighting revealed the scene of devastation that it would be someone's job to sort out the next day. He gratefully lowered the heavy case onto a table littered with bottles and plastic cups and wet with spilled alcohol, plucked the torch from between his aching jaws, switched it off, and put it into his pocket.

Now he had to make completely sure that he was alone in the building. If Miggs or the other janitors were still here, they would be in the janitors' office. He crept to the corner of the large double doorway leading from the Sculpture Court to the entrance hall. From this vantage point, he saw a flickering bluish light illuminating the opposite white wall. What the hell was the source of that? He extended his head further, like a tortoise, and brought the glass partition of the janitors' office into his field of view. Fuck! There was a television in there, and silhouetted against its intermittent light was the outline of Miggs, rotund and immobile, staring at the screen. Duncan watched for a few moments. As far as he could make out, the television screen was filled with writhing human flesh. He could hear a faint panting noise emanating from the half-open door of the office. It didn't sound like Miggs. It was too high-pitched. It must be coming from the soundtrack of the television. Suddenly it all became clear to him. Miggs, at three in the morning, was rounding off his night-time duties with a pornographic video.

Withdrawing his head as if returning it to its shell, he stood for a while in his place of concealment and tried to think calmly. It was on a broad shelf behind the temporary stage in the Sculpture Court that he intended to leave the head. The Sculpture Court was an iconic setting, featuring prominently in any prospectus or publicity images that the art school produced. It felt like the right place. He didn't want to leave the head in just any old corner. Was there any risk of Miggs returning to the Sculpture Court? It seemed unlikely, but the very possibility made his heart pound. Should he wait for longer? He felt desperate now to get this thing over with.

He made his way silently to the shower room, this time, thankfully, able to hold the torch in his hand. From there he retrieved the red holdall with Arabella's head in it. As he re-entered the Sculpture Court, he was startled by a loud bang.

He froze like one of the casts of Greek statues – most of them headless like his victim – that had been pushed aside into the corners of the space. As he held his breath, he heard a series of clicking sounds. He exhaled with relief. The sounds were coming from the entrance hall. The bang must have been the closing of the main doors, and the clicking was Miggs turning the keys on the outside.

Just to be sure, he crept very carefully and quietly to his previous vantage point. Yes, the janitors' office was dark and silent. Miggs had finally gone home. Now he could get on with the final stage of his mission without fear of discovery.

He returned to the Sculpture Court and carried the glass case carefully across the rubbish-strewn space to the high display shelf behind the stage and opened its door. Now for the exhibit!

Where had he put down the red holdall? For a moment, his mind was a blank. He retraced his steps, repressing panic, and found it on the floor near where he had been peering into the entrance hall. He must keep his concentration! No mistakes now!

Sitting on the edge of the stage, he unzipped the holdall and took out the heavy, lumpy object inside the plastic bags. Grimacing with disgust, he carefully slid Arabella's head with its headdress of rubber snakes out of the three plastic bags. Half-congealed blood dribbled from the severed neck as he positioned it in its new resting place. Once he had pushed in some stray wobbling snake heads, it fitted perfectly. He closed the glass door of the case and took out of the zipped side pocket of the red holdall the little card he'd prepared. It read *PORTRAIT* in small capital letters. That detail was one he'd thought of for Hermione's sake. She said she wanted something appropriate. He positioned the card at the lower edge of the door, where it met the casing.

He stowed the gore-smeared plastic bags inside the red holdall, and made his way back through the dark corridors to the painting studio where he had left the big black tote bag. He stuffed the red holdall into the bigger bag, and zipped it up. He stood for a few moments by the window through which he would exit the building. Was there anything he had forgotten? He'd removed everything from the shower room – apart, of course, from the headless trunk of Arabella. He had left no clues there or anywhere else. He had worn gloves throughout. He had everything with him now that he had brought into the building.

He fetched a paint-spattered chair from the corner of the studio and placed it next to the window. He undid the window catch, opened the window, stood on the chair and peered outside. It was a dark, moonless night, with a hint of rain in the air. Above and beyond the low windowless building on the other side of the alleyway, a blur of distant yellowish light marked the presence of Forthburgh Castle, looming across the invisible canyon of the Brassmarket. He heard a scuttling noise along the narrow alleyway eight feet or so below him, and thought of rats. Or perhaps it was just a bit of litter, blown on the damp wind.

He glanced at his watch. It was nearly four in the morning. Somewhere far off, a police siren wailed, and then died away.

Stepping down again from the chair, he grasped the tote bag, and re-ascended his perch with it in his hand. It wasn't heavy. He manoeuvred it across the windowsill, lowered it as far down as he could, and then let it fall to the ground. Then, gingerly, he climbed through the window opening, twisted sideways, and lowered himself downwards while holding onto the sill. His feet were not far above the ground when he let go, landing with an involuntary grunt. He shone his torch on the ground. The alleyway was paved, as he'd already ascertained, and he'd made no footprints. Satisfied, he peeled off his gloves and added them to the contents of the tote bag. He carried the bag to the end of the alleyway, and looked out cautiously at the street beyond. It was deserted. Even the Saturday night drunks had gone home long ago. His car was parked directly across the street, in the place he'd bagged yesterday afternoon, outside a defunct shop with a To Let sign.

Now he had to take a risk! There was no alternative. He listened intently. Nothing. Briskly, looking straight ahead, he walked across the street to the car, unlocked it, placed the bag in the boot, which he had lined with a plastic sheet, and climbed inside. So far, so good. He started the engine and pulled away from the kerb.

At the end of the street, he turned right. Left was the way to his flat in Dolry, but he was not going to go home. He could not afford to be seen parking his car and entering his flat at this unusual hour by any insomniac neighbour or early delivery driver. Instead, he drove southwards along deserted roads until he reached Cloven Brae, the little lane beside Deil's Glen. He drove up there until he reached the electricity substation at the top, where there was a turning space. There he parked and settled in for the second tedious wait of the night. At nine in the morning he could drive home amidst the moderate traffic of a Saturday morning. He would approach his flat from a westerly direction, not from the route from the art school, and no-one who happened to see him would think anything of it.

Later, the drive home was as uneventful as he could have wished for. A few cars and lorries were about, as expected, but when he parked and walked back into his flat, the vicinity was deserted. Not even a dog walker. He left the bag in the boot for now. When he'd had a hot shower and some breakfast, and maybe just forty winks, he'd drink strong coffee, put on his rambling clothes and boots, and go on a long drive to the place where all the incriminating items would be disposed of. It was a very clever and unvisited place, chosen after many research trips. Perhaps that black tote bag would somehow turn up in a century or two with its bloodied cargo, and mystify its discoverer. It would be safely and unreachably underground until then, by which time so would he.

CHAPTER 16

December 1989

"Eh, Eleanor, you widnae' believe human beings could leave a place as clarty as this, eh?"

"It's the same every year!"

"Dinnae tell me you do this job every year?"

"Not every year, but I've done it enough times!"

"An' such weird things left lying aboot, eh? What's this?"

"Looks like an ear?"

"Aye, you're right. An ear. Must be made of... what's that stuff?"

"Papier maché?"

"Aye, that'll be it. Papery mashy. Must have come aff one o' they masks they put on. And the number of bottles, eh? They must have drunk a gallon apiece, eh?"

"Woof! Woof!"

"Trudi! Come away from that!"

"What's she found?"

"I don't know. She's always on the scent of something. Trudi!"

"Woof! Woof!"

"Trudi!"

"Woof!"

"It's no good. She won't stop now unless I go and see."

"What kind of dug is she again, Eleanor? Ah cannae mind."

"A Basset Hound... All right, good girl! What have you found?"

"She's excited, eh? Must be a bit of food?"

"Probably."

"Look at her tail going! Looks like she wants whatever's up there above the stage, eh?"

"Yes. I can't make it out from here. Something in a glass case, is it?"

"Woof! Woof!"

"I suppose I'd better go and see... what is it Trudi? What is it, girl?"

"Woof! Woof!"

"Let's have a look then... ohh!"

"Eleanor? Are you all right? What is it, hen? Oh... oh my Lord Jesus!"

"Woof!"

An hour later, Coupar Cruickshank looked at the head, and the head looked at him. *What are you going to do about this?* it seemed to be asking, with its glassy, staring eyes and gaping, terrorized mouth.

The head was in a glass case, with a neatly printed label near the base that simply read 'Portrait'. He had to force himself- really force himself- to look at the head. What made it even harder to contemplate was the fact that he knew this woman, with her long curly hair. Arabella Wood. He'd spoken to her at length, in the course of two interviews, about the previous homicide of her friend, the sculpture lecturer Steve Sidling.

Coupar had the feeling that this sight would lurk in a dark recess of his memory for the rest of his days. But it was his job to look, and to learn what he could from the sight.

Most salient was the nest of green and yellow rubber serpents writhing amongst her hair, attached by threads to a red Alice band. Like Medusa, he reflected. A pool of blood, now congealed, filled the base of the glass case. The skin of the neck, sitting in the blood, had been severed quite cleanly as far as he could make out. That would be one for the forensic pathologists to investigate further. It would be very helpful to know what kind of instrument was used to remove this head from its foundations.

The case and its horrifying contents had come to light this morning following the art school's Christmas Revel – a traditional night of mayhem, he gathered from a white-faced, shaken Principal, who had also been called out to the scene. The building would have been full of people, many in outlandish costumes and most of them drunk. He was going to have to try and track down all of these people and find out if anyone had seen anything useful. Somewhere amidst their number – perhaps – was the murderer.

"You've got a serial nutjob on your hands Coupar!" remarked Detective Superintendent Dennis 'The Menace' Scott , who had just arrived and came to stand at his elbow. He tugged at his bristling moustache. "Odds on that this was the same loony as killed Sidling, wouldn't you say?"

Coupar nodded, but made no reply. It was very likely that Dennis was right, but he had a feeling that the question was a little trap, to see if he retained in his mind the first principles of a criminal investigation, the 'ABC principle' of *Assuming* nothing, *Believing* nobody, and *Checking* everything. The rigorous application of this principle in the case of the murder of Steve Sidling had left him, after almost three months, with a very large list of questions and a very small list of answers.

He didn't like the way that D.S. Scott had emphasized 'your' hands. It looked very like another passing of the buck, such as had already occurred over Sidling. The Menace would no doubt be happy to step into the limelight when the murderer was behind bars, but in the meantime he was going to distance himself from any impatience expressed in the press or elsewhere over the pace of the investigation. No doubt the febrile atmosphere of dread and suspicion that had hung over the art school for three months was about to intensify.

Would the students even return after Christmas, to an institution that was beginning to resemble a charnel house?

D.S. Scott glanced at his watch and left without further comment. Perhaps he had a golf match to get to, Coupar thought. He went outside the entrance doors to Detective Constable Price, who was fiddling with the security tape barrier keeping the curious and the careless at bay.

"Why don't we have a uniformed constable doing that job?"

"They couldn't spare one, sir."

"Where's Waterhouse?"

"Just nipped off to get a coffee, sir."

Without seeking my permission, Coupar thought. He repressed the various comments that came to mind.

"Well, when he gets back, tell him to go up to Principal Peabody's office and inform him that I want the entire art school closed until further notice."

"But…"

"But what?"

Price scratched each ear in turn, a habit that, ever since he had noticed it, drove Coupar into a state of silent seething irritation.

"Well, it's just that there's quite a crowd."

He gestured to the huddle of staff and students beyond the security tape. Only a dozen or so of them. Was that what Price called quite a crowd? It was a cold, frosty morning, and they were all wearing coats and hats and emitting a cloud of steamy breath that drifted away slowly in the still air. They were certainly not attendees at last night's Revel, or they wouldn't have been here this early.

"I thought we were just going to cordon off an area and then send them to some side entrance. That's what I told them all twenty minutes ago," Price went on.

"Did I ask you to tell them that?"

"Well, it seemed obvious."

"When – if - you get a promotion from the rank of constable, Price, you will have some leeway for independent thought. For the time being, just do what I say."

Both Price and Waterhouse needed to be squashed like worms underfoot, whenever possible.

"And once Waterhouse is here, go and fetch that woman, will you… Mrs Brown."

"The one with the dog?"

"Yes, the cleaning woman who found the head. She's in the canteen with her friend. Bring her to me in the office we've got here, please."

"What about the dog, sir?"

Coupar scanned Price's face for signs of insubordination. It was a blank.

"The dog too."

Eleanor Brown sat down opposite Coupar in the little office that he had still got use of as an occasional base in the art school while he tried to make progress on the Sidling case. She was shaking slightly, and the dog was looking unsettled too. It kept looking over its shoulder and sniffing the air, as if still savouring the aroma of decapitated flesh from afar.

"Do you remember me, Mrs Brown?"

"Oh, yes, Officer. I remember you interviewing me after… that poor man in Deil's Glen."

"And now it seems your dog has led you to another murder victim."

"It's unbelievable, isn't it? I was saying to Maggie, it's unbelievable."

"Maggie is the dog?"

"No - the other woman that was on the cleaning job with me. I don't know her well."

"This is a strange coincidence, is it not?" Coupar suggested.

"What?"

"You finding these… these terrible things."

Eleanor Brown nodded.

"Do you have any idea who the person is?" Coupar went on. "The woman whose head...?"

"No, no. That poor thing! What a thing to happen!"

"And you know, now, who it was you found in Deil's Glen?"

"Yes. I can't remember the name now, but it was a lecturer here wasn't it? A lecturer in Sculpture making?"

"Yes. His name was Steven Sidling. Did you ever come across him? When you were cleaning here? You have cleaned here at the art school before, haven't you Mrs Brown?"

"Och, aye. A few times. But I'm not employed here. It's contract work. I go all over."

"And did you ever have any contact with Steven Sidling?"

"Oh, no. Never heard of him until I read the name in the papers."

"Are you still at the same address as when we met in September?"

"Oh yes. I've been there for thirty years or more. I'll leave when I'm carried feet first, no doubt."

"Did you see anything while you were cleaning, before you found the head, that was unusual?"

"No. Just the usual midden."

"Indeed. Well - if you think of anything later, let me know. You and your dog can go home now. You must be quite shaken up."

"I am. It's like the last time all over again. I don't walk Trudi in Deil's Glen any more, you know. We walk along the river path, that goes under the Telford Bridge. It's not as convenient, but... well, I just can't go into the Glen any more. And now I don't know if I could face coming in here to clean any more. That poor woman's eyes! Popping out of her poor wee head!"

"*Another* one Coopsie!"

Lisa's eyes were almost as wide as those of the dead Arabella Wood. Clearly this was exciting news that he'd just imparted.

"Let me get us a bottle of wine, and you can tell me all about it!"

She scurried off into the kitchen, and Coupar was left with his thoughts for a moment. It seemed to him that getting Lisa excited in any way these days was becoming harder and harder. She had grown bored with his fruitless investigation into the 'hedgehog murder' as she called it, taking her cue from the tabloids, who from time to time gave the case a little attention on page four or five under headings such as *Police still clueless in hedgehog homicide hunt!* Their sex life had taken on some indefinable additional impetus in those early days when he started leading the investigation into Sidling's murder. He wondered if the erotic stimulus of a fresh murder might lead to a renewal of those occasions. It made him feel a little queasy, this ghoulish association of ideas. For Lisa, murder was the sanitized version to be seen nightly in television police dramas. She had not seen the sort of thing that he'd been forced to look at today. On the other hand, he wouldn't look a gift horse in the mouth. Would red underwear from *Ann Summers* make a suitable Christmas present, to drive home the advantage? He sighed at the thought of the busy shops on Princess Street. Now he would have to squeeze in his Christmas shopping between the demands of yet another round of interviews.

"So this is actually someone you've met and talked to?" Lisa said, opening the wine and pouring it into two glasses on the coffee table.

"Yes. Arabella Wood. A lecturer in the Fashion Department."

"And where was her body?"

"In two places."

"What do you mean?"

"Well, her head was in one place. We found her body later. Hours later."

Lisa was transfixed.

"She was *beheaded*? Like Marie... Marie..."

"Antoinette. Yes. But probably not with a guillotine. We haven't found a guillotine."

"Jesus!"

She took a gulp of the wine.

"Do you think it might be the same... you know... the same person as the other one, the hedgehog one?"

"It could be. Very possible. But we can't assume that."

"Dan says these things come in threes."

"What?"

"I told you Dan is writing a detective novel, didn't I?"

"Yes."

"Well, he says that psycho killers do it in threes."

"I thought he was a tennis coach?"

"He is. The best one at the centre. I told you to arrange some lessons with him. You need more exercise. You said you used to play quite a bit of tennis."

"I don't have much time now."

"Well, you should always make time for exercise. Healthy body, healthy mind. And Dan says he'd like to meet you."

"You're not going to tell him any details of this are you?"

Lisa snuggled in closer to him on the sofa.

"No, of course not! But tell me more."

CHAPTER 17

December 1989

Coupar started a round of interviews the next morning, in the stuffy office at the art school that had become like a second home during the first month or so of the Sidling investigation. He had spent the day of the head's discovery in the institution, which had been kept closed while the forensics team went over everything. He was at first inclined to think that Arabella's torso must be somewhere else in Forthburgh, but in the end the team tracked it down to an obscure bathroom some distance away from where the head was found. While he paced about impatiently as the forensics people did their work, he thought about the implications of this murder for his ongoing investigation of Sidling's demise. With all due respect to the ABC principle, he thought it very likely that the same killer was involved. The art school connection between the two grotesque killings looked strong. Surely he could discount gay S&M aficionados and Sidling's mysterious 'London enemy' as possible perpetrators of the killing of Arabella Wood? Therefore, by logical extension, they were edged out of prominence in his suspicions over Sidling's death.

Looking over his notes from the last round of interviews he had conducted, Coupar soon found the name of Arabella's boyfriend, or partner, or whatever he was. Ted Cutter, husband of someone else at the art school. This looked like the obvious place to start. After all, ABC or not, most murders of women were committed by husbands, boyfriends, or partners.

It proved impossible to get hold of Ted Cutter all that day. Arabella Wood's address was obtained from the art school's records, and keys were found in a little purse with the torso. Coupar went to the cluttered Scotsbridge flat with the forensics team, but nothing suspicious came to light. There was plenty of evidence of Cutter's co-habitation there but no sign of the man himself. However, documents linking him to his place of work, a bank, enabled Coupar to set Waterhouse the task of trying to track him down through that channel. However, since it was a Saturday, Waterhouse drew a blank, unable to progress by phone beyond pre-recorded messages. Eventually however, late on Saturday night, Cutter picked up the phone at Arabella's flat in response to one of Waterhouse's hourly calls to that number, and agreed to come in the next morning.

It was a pity that Waterhouse told him on the phone that Arabella had been found dead. Coupar should have instructed him not to do that. He would then have been able to observe Cutter's reaction to the information at first hand; cruel, but useful.

Even though it was a Sunday morning, Ted Cutter came into the police station dressed in a suit; a classic, understated but obviously expensive grey suit. His shirt and tie were flawlessly pressed, contrasting with his face, which was crumpled and drawn. He looked as if he hadn't slept. His handshake was firm and business-like, but once he had thrown himself down dejectedly into the plastic bucket chair in the interview room he resembled an overdressed sack of potatoes.

He had carried with him into the little room a scent that Coupar couldn't identify. There was maybe some patchouli in there. Momentarily distracted from his current task, Coupar wondered if Lisa would enjoy him wearing some kind of masculine scent.

He concentrated again, switched on the cassette recorder, and spoke into his microphone.

"Investigation into the death of Arabella Wood. Interview One. Interviewee Ted Cutter. Sunday the seventeenth of December Nineteen Eighty Nine. Interview conducted by Detective Inspector Coupar Cruickshank, in the presence of Detective Constable Neville Waterhouse."

"What happened to Arabella, Inspector?"

Cutter was looking at him with wide, bloodshot eyes.

"She was found dead yesterday morning, Mr Cutter. At the art school."

"And… it wasn't some kind of accident? Or a stroke or something?"

"I'm sorry to tell you it was a murder, Mr Cutter."

"The policeman on the phone said that. I didn't want to believe it."

He ran a hand through his hair and shook his head.

Coupar gave Waterhouse a reproving glance, and then looked down at his notebook with its scrawled list of questions.

"Where were you on the night of the art school Revel, Friday the fifteenth of December – the night before last - Mr Cutter?"

"I was in London. Can't you tell me… tell me more about how Arabella…"

"I need to ask you some questions first, Mr Cutter. Do you have any proof of that?"

"Of what?"

"That you were in London."

"I still have the receipt for my meal in the restaurant of the hotel where I was staying. And my train ticket receipt from Saturday evening, when I travelled back."

"Did you dine alone on the Friday night?"

"No."

"Who was with you?"

"A work colleague."

"Someone who worked at the same bank as you?"

"In the London office, yes."

"What was his name?"

"Why do you need that?

"Corroboration, Mr Cutter. We both want to eliminate you from the enquiry, don't we?"

"The hotel reception staff could vouch for me. They gave me my key in the evening after I returned from the day's meetings, and they checked me out the next afternoon. I got a late check-out."

"Could they vouch for you between early evening and the morning?"

Ted Cutter looked at him with irritation. His prominent Adam's apple took a ride up and down his throat.

"You think I might have travelled to Forthburgh from London in the middle of the night, and then back again? How? How would I do that?"

"No, I'm not saying that's what you did, but in my job Mr Cutter you have to cover every possibility. Your dinner companion... he could vouch for your presence at the hotel until what time?"

"Eleven at night... at least."

"You see, that would put you indisputably in London at the estimated time of the crime."

"I see."

"So... the name of your colleague?"

Ted Cutter hesitated before answering.

"Sylvia Warrender."

"A woman?"

"Do you know any men called Sylvia? I'm sorry... I'm on edge."

"I understand, Mr Cutter. This must all be very upsetting for you. Can you give me contact details for Sylvia Warrender?"

Ted Cutter fished out a slim wallet from his jacket pocket.

"Here... I've got her card. You can copy them off that."

"Thank you."

He leaned back and passed the card to Waterhouse.

"Write down these details will you, and ring Miss Warrender to confirm this."

"Inspector. I can give you the restaurant receipt that shows two meals paid for. I couldn't eat two starters and two mains on my own. You don't have to ring her, surely?"

"Just being thorough, Mr Cutter. Just being thorough."

Coupar was finding that he didn't take to Ted Cutter. He might be upset, and it certainly didn't look as if he was the perpetrator of the crime, but that didn't mean he should have an easy time of it.

"Right, Mr Cutter. Let's go back to the beginning. When did you meet Arabella Wood?"

Ted Cutter looked at him aghast.

"If we've established that I couldn't have killed poor Arabella, then why…"

Coupar cut in.

"The history of your relationship might throw up some clues for us, Mr Cutter. So… please… your first contact with Arabella….?"

It was not a pretty story. It seemed that Ted Cutter had for some time been bored with his marriage. Coupar dragged out of him the admission that he 'played around' whenever an opportunity arose. Arabella Wood had been just such an opportunity at first, but because she was a close friend of his wife it all exploded into the open and he ended up going to live with her in her flat in Scotsbridge. No, he didn't see this as a permanent arrangement. He was looking for a place of his own. But moving out from the family home did have the merit of finally putting into the bin what was, on his side, a marriage that had passed its expiry date. His words.

As the interview progressed, it became clearer and clearer to Coupar that Ted Cutter was a man who was primarily in love with himself. His pale, drawn expression and the bags under his bloodshot eyes spoke clearly enough of his shock and dismay at Arabella's murder. Nonetheless, Coupar was forming the impression that he would not take so very long to put this horrible experience behind him.

What was most important however, was that because of his clear London alibi – once verified - it appeared safe to conclude that Ted Cutter was not the murderer.

The next day, Tuesday the nineteenth of December, the art school was allowed to reopen, although hardly anyone entered the door. Leaving aside the murder, most people's attention had shifted away from art and onto last minute Christmas shopping. As Coupar parked his car in one of the half dozen parking places – all empty - in the central 'quadrangle', he observed that low hanging clouds almost touched the roof of the Old Building, looking like bundles of dirty washing that had been dumped there. Rain dripped half-heartedly out of these clouds and meandered down the walls and windows. An incongruous string of Christmas lights was festooned across the entrance portico, but they were not lit, perhaps in mute acknowledgement that there was nothing to be cheerful about within. Two areas of the school remained cordoned off; the Sculpture Court, and the toilet and shower room at the basement level where the bloody remains of the rest of Arabella Wood had been discovered on the tiled floor. The two parts of the body had been reunited at the police mortuary, but the forensics team were still ferreting around the art school premises in search of evidence. Students had mostly disappeared off home for Christmas, which meant that tracking down the attendees at the Revel would be a slow and tiresome business. The weasel Price had been given this task. In the meantime, Coupar would have to work his way through the academic staff, most of whom were still to be found in Forthburgh, if not in the art school itself. He decided to start with

Hermione Cutter, the jilted wife of Ted Cutter. He must have interviewed her, like all the other art school staff, after the Sidling murder, but he couldn't remember her.

The woman who entered the little office in the art school was tall, very thin, and elegantly dressed in trousers and a beige woollen coat that were lightly covered in water droplets from outside. She had greyish-blond hair, pulled up into a little wooden clasp secured with a miniature knitting needle. He still couldn't remember her. There was something edgy about her eyes. They couldn't seem to rest on anything for more than a few seconds before darting off in search of some new object of interest.

Coupar introduced himself and the walrus Waterhouse, who stuffed a half emptied packet of some unhealthy snack into a pocket. Hermione Cutter took off her coat and sat down, and he started his tape recording.

"Investigation into the death of Arabella Wood. Interview Two. Interviewee Hermione Cutter. Nineteenth of December Nineteen Eighty Nine. Interview conducted by Detective Inspector Coupar Cruickshank, in the presence of Detective Constable Neville Waterhouse."

He leaned back a little and looked at her. Her gaze shot up to the top of his head and then down to his chest.

"Did you attend the Christmas Revel on Saturday night?"

"Yes."

"Did you go alone?"

"Yes".

"Do you usually attend?"

She shrugged. Her regard had settled on the wall behind him. Or perhaps on Waterhouse, who was there somewhere.

"Some years yes, some years no."

"Why did you decide to go on this occasion?"

"My students were excited about it. It sounded like fun. I had an easy idea for an outfit."

"The theme was *mythical creatures* I'm told."

"Yes."

"What did you go as?"

"It was a bit lazy, really. I just put on a white dress with some floaty white netting and made my face white. I was supposed to be a ghost. I probably looked like Miss Havisham."

"Was there a Miss Havisham present?"

Hermione laughed, and for a moment looked straight at him.

"She's a character in a book. *Great Expectations*."

Her eyes went to the surface of the table between them. Coupar, who liked to think that he was good at reading body language, wondered if these wandering eyes were a habitual tic, or indicated extreme nervousness.

"I see. So you went to the Revel. Did you see Arabella Wood there?"

"Yes. I spoke with her."

"You spoke with her? About your husband?"

"No, not about Ted."

"I believe your husband was... with her. Not at the Revel... I mean, he was her partner."

"Yes. He left me to go and live with her."

"Were you on friendly terms with Arabella?

This provoked a violent eye movement.

"No. That was why I took the opportunity to have a word with her. I was tired of the awkwardness – both of us working in the art school – having to avoid each other. It was stressful. I wanted to bury the hatchet."

Coupar leaned forward a little. The press had not mentioned the beheading yet: the first useful contribution from The Menace, who had used his influence with newspaper editors of his acquaintance to get this gruesome detail held back until the next weekend's editions.

"Bury the hatchet?" he said.

Hermione laughed nervously.

"Sorry. That's a horrible expression to use in the circumstances."

"What circumstances?"

Hermione looked puzzled.

"Arabella... being murdered."

"Do you know how she was found?"

"No. I presumed... well, dead somewhere in the art school."

"All right. So, you spoke to her..."

"I wanted to clear the air."

"A crowded hall with a live band blasting out - was that the best place to clear the air?"

"I hadn't thought about it in advance. But I'd had a couple of drinks, and I happened to see her sitting on her own. I went to talk to her on impulse".

"And how did that go?"

"She was drunk. You may know that Arabella had a bit of a drinking problem?"

"Do you mean she was an alcoholic?"

"I don't know if you'd say that. But she often drank too much."

"So was your attempt to bury the hatchet a success?"

"We didn't really have much of a conversation. She needed the loo, and I helped her towards the nearest one. She could barely stand up."

"Was that he staff toilet and shower room near the Sculpture department?"

"Yes."

"Where did you have your conversation?"

"It wasn't really a conversation. Like I say, she was drunk. But we were in the Sculpture Court."

"Then that wasn't the nearest toilet".

"I'd just been in the one that was nearer. It was a mess, and there were queues of girls waiting."

"So you thought the other one would be quieter?"

"Yes. Not many people know it's there."

"Did you go all the way to the toilet and shower room with her?"

"Not quite. I took her to the corridor that led to it. She seemed steadier on her feet by then. I thought she'd be alright."

"Did you see her again after that?"

"No."

"Did you see her go into the shower room?"

"No, I'd turned back towards the Sculpture Court."

"Did you see or hear anything suspicious in that corridor, near the shower room? Was there anyone else around?"

"No."

"Did you wait for Arabella to come out?"

Hermione's eyes fixed on him again, with a look of horror.

"Was that where she was killed?" she said.

"It's best if we keep some information back, for the moment," Coupar replied. "So, what did you do next?"

"I got back to the Sculpture Court. I suddenly felt tired. I decided I'd just go home."

"Without having the chance to *clear the air*?"

"Yes. She was too drunk. It wasn't the right moment. I'd have to try another time."

"And you weren't having fun, anymore, at the Revel?"

"It had been fun, but it was getting late. Everyone seemed more drunk than me."

"How do you feel now, about her death?"

"I don't know. I haven't had time for it to sink in. It makes me feel sick, and sad, and frightened. There's something terrible going on at the art school. Two murders in three months!"

"Did anyone see you leave?"

"Miggs – the janitor - saw me leave. I don't know if he'd remember. He was in the entrance hall. I said goodnight to him on my way out. I didn't say goodbye to anyone else. All my students were flinging themselves about to the music."

"What time was that?"

"It was between midnight and one. I didn't look at my watch when I went out. Probably about half past twelve."

"Have you spoken to your husband – Ted?"

She shook her head. Sadly, he thought. Although he couldn't read this nervy woman's body language at all.

"No."

"So how did you find out what had happened?"

"What? That Arabella…"?

"Yes. That she'd been killed."

"It was the next morning, when I couldn't get into the art school."

"Who told you why the art school was closed?"

"It was a policeman – in plain clothes - outside the entrance."

"Do you know anything else about how Arabella died?"

"No."

"Do you have any idea who might have killed Arabella"?

"No, no idea at all."

"Thank you Mrs Cutter, that will be all for now. Please get in touch straight away if you think of anything that might help us find the killer of this woman."

Hermione Cutter nodded wordlessly, scooped up her coat from the back of a spare chair where she'd draped it, and left.

Late in the afternoon, Coupar glanced at his list. He'd had a parade of staff members through the little office, and also a couple of the fashion students who'd been at the Revel. Price had weaselled well, by his own low standards, in tracking down these two. Price had also established that Arabella had no family connections in Forthburgh. So far then, nothing of much use had turned up.

The last name on the list for today was Duncan McBane. He was that morose-looking sculptor. He remembered his hangdog appearance from the previous round of interviews. He was of particular interest though, because, as Coupar had noted down previously, he had once been in a relationship with this second murder victim.

"Is there anyone sitting on the chairs outside, Waterhouse?"

Detective constable Waterhouse looked through the little wired glass panel in the door.

"Yes. Big guy with a beard."

"Call him in, will you?"

Duncan McBane entered the room. He was nearly as tall as Waterhouse, but a lot leaner. Coupar gestured to him to sit down, started the cassette recorder and made his usual opening statement. McBane watched him impassively.

"So, Mr McBane. I'm very sorry that another of your close colleagues has been murdered."

"Aye. Thank you."

"You must feel very upset."

"Yes."

"When did you hear of the death of Arabella Wood?"

"It was the next day."

"The next day after her death? Saturday the sixteenth of December?

"Aye."

"How did you find out about it?"

"A friend – my colleague – Angus Campbell. He rang me up."

"How did he know?"

"He'd come into the art school around midday and found the place blockaded by the police. He couldn't get into his studio."

"Does he usually come into work on a Saturday?"

"He does his own painting in a studio here, out of term time."

"But how did he know what had happened?"

"He spoke with Miggs, the Head Janitor. He'd seen it. A cleaning woman had nearly had a fit, and Miggs came to see what was the matter. So he saw it."

"Saw what?"

"The head. Severed head."

Damn! Miggs must have blurted this out before he'd been warned not to divulge details. But McBane was the first of his interviewees to reveal any knowledge of it.

"Do you think Miggs or your friend told others about this?"

"What?"

"That it was a… a beheading?"

McBane shrugged.

"And Miggs told your friend it was Arabella Wood?"

"Aye. Miggsy had recognised her straight off."

"How did you feel, hearing that?"

McBane took a deep breath and stared at the desk surface between them, his thick dark eyebrows crouching like beaten dogs.

"I was knocked back. It was a shock."

The large bearded head shook sadly from side to side.

"Were you at the art school Revel on Friday night Mr McBane?"

McBane raised his eyes again from the desk, but they seemed unfocussed.

"No. I haven't been for years. Not my thing."

"Where were you?"

"I was just at home."

"With family?"

"I don't have a family."

"So you were on your own?"

"Aye."

"On a Friday night?"

"When you're fifty, there's nothing so special about a Friday night."

"What were you doing?"

"This and that. Watched some telly."

Coupar remembered Lisa's face that time he had suggested a quiet evening in front of the telly on a Friday night.

"What did you watch?"

"I can't remember now."

"Try to remember."

"Och –I had a few tinnies. I flicked channels".

"So you don't remember any specific programme?"

"I started watching a film on BBC. *Whatever Happened to Aunt Alice* it was called. But I fell asleep. I can't remember much about it now."

"Did you go out to buy the cans of beer?"

"No. I had them in the flat already."

"What about food? Did you cook something, or get a takeaway?"

"I finished off a stew I'd made a couple of days before."

"Did you call anyone on the phone?"

"No."

Coupar glanced at his notes again.

"You and Arabella Wood had a relationship at one time."

One of the beaten dog eyebrows twitched. McBane's hand stroked his beard.

"A short one, aye."

"How long?"

"It wasn't quite four months."

"Who called it off?"

"It was mutual."

"Was there a row?"

"No, no. We just called it a day. It was a long time ago."

"Less than a year, though."

"Aye, it'd be back in March or maybe February or thereabouts."

"You weren't upset?"

"Not especially."

"Or angry?"

"No, not at all."

"Did you try to get back together with her?"

"No."

"Do you feel upset now, finding out that she's been killed?"

Duncan nodded solemnly.

"Of course. Wouldn't you?"

Coupar nodded, and glanced again at his notes.

"Do you know Hermione Cutter?"

More beard tugging.

"Yes. She works at the art school. As you already know, I expect."

"I interviewed her just today. Her husband was living with Arabella Wood. Did you know that?"

"Aye, I did know that."

Coupar glanced at his notes.

"Miggs the Head Janitor said that Hermione Cutter worked on a portrait of you over the summer in one of the studios here at the art school."

"That's right."

"So perhaps it was Hermione herself who mentioned that her husband had gone to live with Arabella?"

"Perhaps it was. I can't remember now."

"But... with your previous attachment to Arabella... Hermione must have known about that, I imagine?"

"I suppose she did."

"Surely, while she was painting your portrait, you must have had conversations?"

"A bit. We chatted a bit."

"So you must know each other quite well? Would you say so?"

"No really. We chatted a bit. I haven't had much to do with her since."

"Was she at the Revel?

"I've no idea."

"She was, in fact."

"Okay."

"So ... did she ever talk to you about Arabella Wood?"

"Not much. Maybe in passing."

Coupar thought he'd fly a little kite.

"Not much? She said you talked about her a lot."

No visible reaction, although he was still playing with his beard.

"Her memory's different to mine then."

"Would you say Hermione Cutter was upset – about her husband going to live with Arabella Wood?"

"I suppose she must have been. Another woman comes along and steals your husband. Bound to be upsetting."

"Did you and Hermione Cutter have a relationship?"

"What sort of 'relationship'? Do you mean were we lovers or something?"

"Yes."

"Not at all. I sat for my portrait. We talked a bit. I'd hardly go as far as 'friends', never mind 'lovers'!"

"Do you think she might have wanted Arabella Wood dead?"

Duncan gave a snort of disbelief.

"I doubt it! A bit extreme, eh?"

"But someone did."

"Maybe. Or else it was a random thing."

"Random? Cutting off someone's head and putting it in a glass case?"

"Must have been a nutcase. Some sort of psycho."

"Do you have any ideas? Of who might have done it?"

"Well… someone who was at the Revel, I suppose."

"There were about three hundred people there apparently. Could you pinpoint a few possibilities?"

"A few? You think it might have been a gang of them?"

"I mean, is there anyone you might think had any kind of reason…"

"It's not just art school people who go, you know. There could have been all sorts of people there."

"But it's mainly art school students, and some staff, I'm told."

"Aye, but back in the day when I used to go there was always friends and hangers-on. Some dodgy characters sometimes. There used to be drugs. Drug dealers would get in.

"Does that still happen?"

"I imagine it does, aye. Maybe some bampot got out of their head on Acid and did it?"

"You think it might have been someone from outside the art school that committed this crime?"

McBane shook his head slowly, expressing mystification.

"I just don't know, Inspector. I just don't know."

"All right Mr McBane. That'll be all for now. Are you staying in Forthburgh over Christmas?"

"Aye."

"Well… Happy Christmas, then."

McBane looked at him as if he'd spat on the Bible.

"Aye, and a Happy Christmas to you, Inspector."

Coupar sat thinking for a while after this interview. Behind him, he could hear Waterhouse accessing a packet of crisps or some such.

Was it at all possible that this McBane was a double murderer? The man had benefited from Sidling's death, to the extent that he was now the head of Sidling's department in the art school. Was that a prize worth murdering for? Then there was the fact of his previous relationship with Arabella Wood. Whether or not it was true that they had parted by mutual agreement, it was quite a while ago, and this killing didn't bear the hallmarks of a crime of passion. Usually a partner, or an ex-partner, was killed in an outburst of rage, responding to some immediate catalyst, such as a revelation of infidelity. Nor, during the interview just conducted, was there anything suspicious in McBane's demeanour. The very casualness of his alibi – that he was on his own watching television on the night of the murder – paradoxically bespoke innocence. Should he ask

McBane for permission to look around his home? But a casual search wouldn't be much use. Full forensics would be needed. McBane could easily refuse such an intrusion. Any innocent person would be likely to resent and refuse such a request, and the refusal would reveal nothing. Nor did he, Coupar, have any argument that he could take to a Sheriff to obtain a search warrant in the event of a refusal.

No, he was clutching at straws. It was time to call it a day.

At the same time as Coupar was thinking about Duncan, the bearded sculptor was engaged in thinking about *him*. How fortunate that Fate had dealt him such a dim-witted adversary! He'd been meticulous in the execution of both murders, but he did have one regret. The little note that read 'ambient intervention' that he'd left in Sidling's nostril had been a bad mistake; an act of hubris that he'd been unable to resist when planning the act. In retrospect, it had been ridiculous to create such a potential signpost pointing in his direction. But clearly this boy-scout of a detective had failed to make anything of it. As for the little card that read 'portrait', he'd done that as much for Hermione as for himself. It was a fitting title for the artwork he'd created, but too generic to be of any danger to him.

He made his way home, complacent and confident, passing unnoticed through the busy Christmas shoppers at the west end of Princess Street like a deadly virus.

CHAPTER 18

December 1989

Coupar got a good look at his reflection as he approached the opaque plate-glass doors of the sports centre. He was wearing a coat, but underneath that he was in his old-fashioned tennis 'whites'. His bare legs projecting downwards from the bottom of his coat looked absurdly schoolboyish. They matched his feeling that he was about to engage in an absurd activity, quite out of keeping with his current preoccupations. On a whim, he stuck out his tongue at the silly schoolboy before he went in.

Today, Wednesday the twentieth of December, was another day that he should have been conducting interviews and gathering information. But the people he most wanted to talk to were proving elusive. Miggs, the janitor, for example, was said to have decamped to Skye. Rumour had it that he spent the Christmas period there with a sister and her family. Waterhouse's informant, one Rory Coggs of the Sculpture Department, had no details of this family's name or address, and added that it might have been Mull, not Skye. The Head of Fashion, Leonora Hunt, was in bed with flu, her husband said on the phone, and Waterhouse, reporting this, pointed out that she would probably infect both Coupar and himself if interviewed now, and that was going to ruin everyone's Christmas. He decided to take the day off, using up the tail end of his annual leave.

Lisa had booked this tennis lesson for him with the much lauded Dan as an early Christmas present. Three more were to follow, at her expense. She'd got a discount, she said, while still managing to imply that it was a generous gift. As for him, he still hadn't made up his mind to go into Ann Summers in search of sexy underwear, and time was running out.

When Lisa had told him about his tennis lesson gift the previous week, a week in which he had only one unsolved murder on his plate, she had pointed out that pairing him and Dan looked to her like a win-win situation.

"Dan's a good coach, so your tennis will improve, and you'll get fitter. And you can give him a few ideas and hints for his novel."

"What kind of ideas and hints? I can't talk about the case I'm working on."

"But you can give him some bits and pieces about things in general, can't you? Police procedures and stuff."

"I'm supposed to be being *taken out of myself* aren't I? That was the phrase you used. That's why you suggested tennis isn't it?"

"Well, you can be taken out of yourself on the tennis court, and then go back into yourself afterwards. Dan would love to have a chat with you over a coffee after the lesson. No pressure though, if you don't want to."

She had looked a little huffy, he thought, as she added the last point.

It was bad enough having the unsolved killing of Steven Sidling still hanging over him, but the grotesque killing of Arabella Wood made tennis lessons and Christmas shopping seem like frivolous activities belonging to a different, more innocent planet. However, there was nothing for it but to get on with it - Lisa would be offended otherwise. Entering the sports centre, he saw her behind the reception desk, already looking his way.

"Why were you sticking your tongue out?" she said.

Before he could reply, her phone went. She picked it up and waved him onwards. He gave her as positive a smile as he could muster and followed the sign towards the indoor tennis courts. It hadn't occurred to him that someone inside the centre would be able to see through those plate glass doors.

Dan was about twenty five years old, Coupar estimated, about the same age as Lisa. He was a handsome, natural athlete who dispatched tennis balls across the net with the same ease as he might stretch or yawn. Easy, gentle shots for Coupar, who was very rusty, although he had been a reasonably competent player a few years ago, when he had more leisure time. At the end of the hour, Dan was as fresh as the proverbial daisy, while Coupar felt as if his lungs had been squeezed through a mangle. He really did need to get fitter.

"I don't have another lesson to give for half an hour, Coopsie," Dan said. He had adopted Lisa's nickname for Coupar without seeking permission. Perhaps he thought it really was his name. "What about a quick coffee in the café?" he went on.

Coupar nodded. At least it was only half an hour, and Lisa would spot him sneaking away if he declined.

In the airy canteen on a mezzanine floor overlooking the tennis courts, Dan was full of enthusiasm for his planned future as a best-selling crime novelist. He seemed to have the same easy confidence about this writing career as he displayed on the tennis court.

"There's so many unsolved crimes everywhere!" he said, as if it was the best news around. "It's like gold dust for a writer. I just need to settle on a crime, change a few names and details, and come up with a solution."

"Where will you get the details of these unsolved crimes?" Coupar enquired, taking a sip of his coffee.

"Oh, there's no shortage of material!" Dan enthused with a grin. He was like a puppy with its first bone. He fished in his tennis holdall and brought out a dog-eared paperback which he passed to Coupar.

Unsolved Crimes America, Volume 28 Coupar read. The cover depicted a figure skulking away along a dark alleyway, silhouetted against the glare of a streetlamp at the end. In the foreground was the prone figure of his victim, a comely young woman of course, splattered with blood.

"These come out every year," Dan said joyfully. "That's the latest – crimes from 1988. They're always a full year behind, obviously. Sometimes the crimes get solved a few months after the book comes out. They have a little section for that in the next year's edition.

Coupar glanced at the chapter headings. There were about twenty crimes listed. *The Body in the Septic Tank. The Missing Twins. The Suicide that Wasn't. The Pine Loop Murders....*

The Pine Loop Murders? Why did that ring a bell in Coupar's ear? He opened the book at the indicated page.

In the woods beside a quiet road on the edge of Portland, Oregon, the bodies of two deer hunters were found, six months apart. The state of their bodies was highly unusual... they were studded with dozens of crossbow arrows, almost like porcupines.

"Can I borrow this book?" Coupar said.

CHAPTER 19

December 1989

Miggs returned from his Christmas break on the day after Boxing Day. Waterhouse, who had been tasked with ringing his home number daily in case Rory Coggs's information was incorrect, set up an interview at the police station for the next morning. Coupar congratulated him on his diligence. Carrot and stick, he thought. Perhaps Waterhouse, a walrus with mulish tendencies, would respond best to carrots?

Lisa had spent Christmas Day and Boxing Day at her parents' house with her brother and sister. The sister's fiancé was one of the party, but Coupar, not having such formal status, was not. Coupar had always spent Christmas in the past with his own parents, but since they had died he had been going to his brother and sister-in-law's place. This year, he seemed to have been appointed chief entertainer of their three year old and their five year old for the duration of the festivities. Coming into the police station felt like a holiday.

Miggs arrived at the agreed time. Waterhouse was on leave now until after New Year, so the weasel Price was stationed in the corner in a freshly pressed striped shirt, tugging on his ears.

Miggs, always a papery white colour, looked a little green around the gills. Coupar, concerned to avoid flu, enquired after his health.

"Och, I'm still getting over the journey back from Shetland on the ferry."

"Shetland?"

"Aye. That's where I spend the Christmas."

"Was it a rough crossing?"

Miggs nodded.

"Thrown out of my bunk three times!"

"I'm sorry to hear that," Coupar said, trying to sound as if he was. "I've never been on a ferry myself. Well, shall we get on with it?"

Miggs nodded again.

Coupar put in a fresh cassette and pressed *record*.

"Investigation into the death of Arabella Wood. Interview Twenty Six. Interviewee Robert Miggs, Head Janitor of Forthburgh School of Art. Twenty eighth of December, Nineteen Eighty Nine. Interview conducted by Detective Inspector Coupar Cruickshank, in the presence of Detective Constable Peter Price."

He turned to Miggs, who was looking glassy-eyed out of the window, where the sky was making its mind up whether rain or sleet would be best.

"Can we just go over the events of the night of the Revel, Mr Miggs?"

"From when?"

"From when you started the evening's work. You were in charge of security, I take it?"

"Aye."

"Go on."

"Well… I had an early tea, and went into the art school. At six o'clock me and the lads went around the buildings to make sure they were empty. There's sometimes students want to get in the Revel without a ticket."

"By *the lads*, you mean… " he glanced at his notes. "… Andy Wallace, George Calder and Charlie Bowman?"

"Yes."

On Christmas Eve, Coupar had interviewed these three blind mice, whose observational powers seemed to have been stunted from birth. He deduced from stray remarks that their consumption of alcohol on the night of the Revel had been only half a step behind that of the revellers. He hoped that Miggs had been more sober and watchful.

"So do you think it's possible someone would have been there that night who didn't come through the main door when the Revel started?"

"No very likely, but no impossible. We cannae open every cupboard, like."

"But you found no-one hiding about the place?"

"No."

"What about the band and the organisers? They must have been in the building before the crowds arrived?"

"Aye, they were all in before the doors opened."

"All in the Sculpture Court?"

"Aye. As far as I ken."

"How many of them?"

"About a half dozen of the students, and mebbe another half dozen to do with the band."

"And the band themselves?"

"They came in for sound checks about half an hour before the doors opened."

Coupar had already got a note of all these people's names from a grubby list that one of the subordinate janitors had produced. Waterhouse – when he was back from his break – would continue trying to track them down.

"Were you in the entrance hall when the doors opened?"

"Aye."

"Did you see anyone coming into the Revel who you didn't recognize?"

"Aye. Dozens."

"Because of the costumes or because they were strangers?"

"Baith. Some were wearing masks."

"And how many attendees would you estimate?"

"There was two hundred and seventy tickets. It always sells oot."

"Did you see anyone come in who… let's say… who you didn't expect?"

"I didnae expect anyone in particular."

"Well, let's put it another way. Was there anyone you particularly noticed, for any reason?"

"Well, there was a lassie wi' her tits oot."

"Your colleagues mentioned her. Did you see Arabella Wood come in?"

"I didnae' notice her come in, no. I saw her later on, dancing."

"Was she dancing *with* anyone?"

"Ach, It wisnae' a Viennese Waltz! It was all a heavin' thrang o' folk."

"Did you notice her for any particular reason?"

"Well… aye, she had this heid of snakes, that was what you might call an eye-catcher. Not as much as the lassie wi' her tits oot though. Big girl."

"Did you see her spending time with anyone in particular?"

"I wisnae following her every move."

"But – try again to remember – did you see her talking with anyone?"

"Well… I did see her one time talking with that weird American feller."

Coupar sat forward a little.

"Do you mean Ricky Love? The exchange lecturer?"

"Aye."

"Why did you particularly notice them talking?"

"There wis nae particular aboot it. I just happened to see them."

"Why do you refer to Ricky Love as *weird*?"

"Have you no talked to him yoursel?"

"I have. I interviewed him briefly about… the other case. Like you."

"And you thought he wis normal?"

"Never mind what I thought. Why do you think him weird?"

"There wis this thing happened when he turned up at the art school before we opened the doors. Two weeks before term."

"Back in September?"

"Aye. He came before the place was open. Must have got his dates mixed up."

"So what happened?

"I'd got the outer door open because I was expecting a delivery. But the inner glass doors were locked. I heard a rattling and went to see. It was this Ricky Love character – of course I didnae know him from Adam then. So I just stonds on the inside of the doors. There was a big notice outside, saying the art school was closed. But he just keeps rattling the doors, y'ken. And then he starts pulling these weird faces."

"Weird faces?"

"Aye. Like a lunatic. Bulging his eyes out. Waggling his tongue at me."

"None of this came up last time I interviewed you."

"No. Well, it had nothing to do with your questions then. Onyways, when he was doing all this gurnin' I just thought he was some nutter that had turned up. When he came again a few days later, after we'd opened up for staff only, I found out he was going to be a lecturer here for a year. So I thought *Och, aye – you'll fit in well with all the other nutters we've got here.*"

Coupar's thoughts went back to his own experience at the tennis centre. Perhaps Ricky Love, like him, had been interacting with his reflection, not realising that someone was on the other side of the glass? Still, it was worth pursuing, this perception of Miggs that Ricky was an oddball.

"Has he acted oddly in any other ways?"

"Och, aye! All the time. Keeps trying to make conversation, y'ken? And all that *have a nice day* crap every time he catches you."

"Isn't that just being American?"

Miggs seemed to reflect on this.

"I don't know. There's just something about him. Smiles too much. Looks like he wants a smile back. Mebbe it's just an American thing. I've never really liked Americans. Come here and talk about how they love being in England. For Christ's sake, you'd think they'd know what country they're in!"

"Do you remember at what point in the evening Ricky Love was talking to Arabella Wood?"

"No. It was after I'd seen him taking photos."

Coupar sat forward again. This could be useful.

"He took photos?"

"Aye. He came in with some fancy looking camera, and he was all over the place taking photos."

He grinned salaciously.

"I saw him getting one of that big girl with her tits oot!"

Coupar nodded. He would make it his business to get copies of these photos. There might be some clues in there.

"By the way, did you see Hermione Cutter leaving?"

Miggs thought for a moment.

"Aye. She was done up like a ghost, I remember. She left earlier than most."

"Thank you Mr Miggs. That'll do for now. I may need to talk to you again though."

"Aye, okay. Best catch this maniac soon eh? Who knows who'll get killed next?"

CHAPTER 20

January 1990

The New Year came in with a bang in Forthburgh. There were the usual fireworks, and a concert in Princess Gardens below the castle. Lisa insisted that Coupar and herself should join the throngs of drunken locals and tourists in the freezing streets. After all, she pointed out, it was not only a new year but even a new decade, and they shouldn't miss being at the heart of it. Lisa, pretty with festive red lipstick and a red bobble hat, was much in demand at 'the bells' for a hug and a kiss. Coupar, jostled and cold, and limping a little with a calf muscle pulled on the tennis court, couldn't wait to get back indoors.

Although he'd managed a few interviews in the gap between the Christmas holidays and the New Year festivities, he was feeling anxious to get on faster with his investigation – or investigations – when the world resumed its routines. He wasn't in the mood for fireworks. At least the red underwear he'd scrambled to buy on Christmas Eve had proved a modest success, so the festive season didn't pass him by entirely.

On the second of January, he was behind his desk again at the police station.

Oregon, on the west coast of the USA, was eight hours behind Scotland, so when Coupar had, with considerable difficulty, tracked down the phone number for the Portland Police Department, he had to wait until early evening to call them. After several rings, a bored, crackling female voice answered

"Portland Police Department. Are you ringing to report a crime?"

"No."

"To whom shall I direct your call, sir?"

"I don't know. I'm Detective Inspector Cruickshank from the Forthburgh Police Department in Scotland. I'd like to speak to one of your investigating officers about a crime that occurred in your city."

There was a long pause. Then the crackling voice came back.

"That doesn't fit with any of my categories, sir."

"What categories?"

"We don't have no-one here who talks with Scotland. Did you say you were a police officer, sir?"

"Yes."

"A police officer from Scotland?"

"Yes."

"Just one moment, sir. I need to put you on hold while I speak with my supervisor."

A noise like a three year-old learning to play a xylophone came onto the line. It was on a loop of twenty seconds or so, and as the third rendition began, Coupar felt that it could send a man insane within five minutes. Then the voice came back.

"Sir?"

"Yes?"

"My supervisor says that you need to put your request in writing. We don't share information on the phone with police forces in Africa."

"Africa? I'm calling from Scotland."

"My supervisor said it was in Africa."

She sounded suspicious.

"No, it's part of the United Kingdom."

"Just a moment, sir."

The xylophone bashing recommenced, and then the voice returned.

"Same thing, sir. United Kingdom or Africa. If you want to talk about a crime that was committed here in

Portland, you need to write. We can't verify who you are on the phone. Have a nice day now!"

And the phone line went dead.

Coupar spent the next hour crafting a carefully worded letter to the Chief of Police in Portland, and got it into priority post the next day. A week later, as he was about to leave the office at six o'clock, his efforts were rewarded.

"A phone call from the States for you Coupar," said Max at the switchboard.

"Oh – good. Put it through please, Max."

A man's voice came on the line. He sounded like an oldish man who'd had a long and passionate relationship with tobacco.

"Am I speaking to Detective Inspector Cruickshank?"

"Yes, hello."

"Hi. I'm Lieutenant Walowski from the Portland Police Department. Your letter came to me."

"Oh. Thank you for calling back Lieutenant."

"No problem. Can we go onto first names Detective Inspector?"

"Yes, of course. I'm Coupar."

"Cooper?"

"Yes."

"Like Gary?"

"Yes, or Henry or Tommy."

"Henry?"

"Henry Cooper. A boxer."

"Or Tommy?"

"A comedian. Dead now. Died live on television with a heart attack."

"My God! Well, okay Cooper. Call me Sam. Now, I see you're interested about this case we've got open here that goes by the name of The Pine Loop Murders?"

"Yes."

"Sure is a strange one. I worked on it myself at the start, but it's not in my hands now. I've got the file in front of me though. What do you want to know?"

"First of all, can you confirm exactly how the bodies were found?"

"You mean, who found them? Or in what condition they were in?"

"In what condition were they, when they were found?"

"Well, both were found in the same condition, which makes us pretty damned sure it was the same person – or persons – who committed both these homicides. They were stuck all over with arrows."

"Arrows? Like bows and arrows?"

"That's right. But the short sort of arrows you use in a crossbow. Bolts, they're called."

"How many?"

"Oh… lemme see now… it says here… ninety four in one body, and eighty in the other."

"That must have narrowed things down a little? I mean, how many people own crossbows? How many places can you buy those things?"

"Oh, you'd be surprised, Gary."

"Coupar."

"Sorry! Of course, *Cooper*! Well - there's a lot of people hunt with those crossbows. These two dead guys who were found, they were deer-hunters that used crossbows."

"So did you think they were killed by other deer-hunters?"

"Hard to say, Cooper. We didn't get nowhere with that line of enquiry. But your letter said you were interested in this guy… lemme see… Ricky Love, right?"

"Yes."

"Nearest property to where the bodies turned up. Ricky Love and wife Boony. Academic. No criminal record. Only thing we got on him was he was one of these anti-gun types. Anti-hunting and anti-gun."

"How did that come out?"

"He belonged to some organisation called *Friends of the Forest Creatures*. Bunch of lefties and tree-huggers. We got a lot of that kind here in Oregon. They used to pull a few stunts. Demonstrations outside gun shops, that kind of thing."

"But Ricky Love?"

"Never got arrested or anything. Just had his name on the list of members. Never bought no crossbow arrows neither. We got nothing on him."

"But the case is still open, right?"

"Sure is. Some crazy is still out there. You know what, Cooper: I seen those bodies, both of them. Made me think of porcupines. You got porcupines there?"

"No. Hedgehogs."

"They like porcupines?"

"A little."

"Why you interested, Cooper? You got a case there?"

"Yes. Kind of similar. A body in woodland, stuck all over with paintbrushes. Like a hedgehog. Or porcupine."

"Jeez. We got more than one of these crazies on this planet, for sure."

"Except that Ricky Love is here in Forthburgh."

"Really? That why you got interested in this Pine Loop case?"

"Yes."

"Well, I wish I could tell you more, Cooper, but he's clean as a whistle over here. You'll let me know if you connect him to your porcupine guy, yeah?"

"Of course."

"Well, good luck, Cooper!"

"Thank you – and please let me know if you get anywhere with your cases too."

"I sure will."

"Goodbye!"

"Goodbye Cooper."

CHAPTER 21

January 1990

"Did you enjoy the book?"

Dan was putting the tennis balls back into a locker by the courts. Coupar, nearby, wiped perspiration from his brow.

"Yes. I'm still reading it, if you don't mind me hanging onto it."

"No problem. Have you got time for a quick coffee? I've got half an hour to kill again before my next customer."

"A quick one, yes."

Coupar felt he owed Dan a little more of his time. After all, he'd put The Pine Loop Murders onto his radar.

Once they were sitting down with their drinks in the cafeteria, Dan pulled a notebook out of his holdall.

"I've written a bit of an opening to my crime novel, Coopsie. Do you want to hear it? It's only short."

This was clearly a rhetorical question. Coupar nodded.

"I'm not a literary expert you know," he cautioned.

"No problem. But you might have some ideas. Here we go then... *The man who walked in the interview room struck Inspector Bowls...* I might change that name, but it sort of came to me.... *struck Inspector Bowls as very ordinary. He was normal height and had normal hair and eyes. But he seemed a bit nervous. Inspector Bowls wasn't to know this, but this normal-looking man was a crazed psychopath, capable of anything. The trail of bloody corpses that had wound about the city led straight to this man, if only Inspector Bowls could follow the clues.*

Dan stopped and looked at Coupar expectantly.

"Is that all?" Coupar enquired.

"So far. What do you think?"

"Well, is it going to be a whodunit?"

"Of course."

"So… aren't you giving the game away straight away?"

"Only for the reader. Inspector Bowls doesn't know this guy is a killer. He's so normal, you see. I read that a lot of psychos seem very normal, so that's my angle."

"Okay…"

Coupar didn't read crime novels very often, but he was pretty sure you didn't generally tell the reader straight away who the killer was. However, he thought it best not to interfere. He didn't want to get drawn into collaborating on Dan's book.

"Sounds good, Dan," he said, as convincingly as he could. "Sounds good."

As he headed back towards his car though, it occurred to him that Dan had unwittingly identified something that might be relevant to these bizarre art school murders. The most innocent and normal-seeming person might turn out to be the killer. Someone like Ricky Love, for instance – although, as it happened, the janitor Miggs didn't see him as normal.

A bout of flu, apparently, was keeping the American at home, but Coupar was itching to interview him as soon as he rose from his sick bed.

The next day, Coupar sat in the 'Art School Murders' incident room at the police station cradling a hot mug of instant coffee in his hands. He had a new pain in his shoulder since yesterday's tennis lesson. Fistfuls of rain struck against the rattling single-glazed windows. An icy, gusting east wind was spitefully dumping dollops of water scooped up from the North Sea all over

Forthburgh's unfortunate citizens. The police station was ill-equipped for such weather, being constructed of the cheapest available materials and with only a parsimonious scattering of undersized radiators in its rooms and corridors.

He had dispatched Price and Waterhouse to conduct outdoor searches for the murder weapon, which had been determined by pathologists to be most probably a small axe or perhaps a meat cleaver. They were still the only assistants allocated to him full time, even though there was now a second investigation. A small rash of domestic murders, always to be expected over Christmas and New Year, was occupying all other available police resources. He didn't have any high hopes of the murder weapon turning up, but Price and Waterhouse were irritants, barely disguising their scepticism about his ability to solve these crimes. There was some satisfaction to be had in sending them off to root about in the city's bins and bushes in this weather, especially Price, who had affected a Burberry trench coat since Christmas – perhaps a present - and could now be identified as a detective from a hundred paces.

One wall of the incident room was dedicated to a pin board with a photograph of Steve Sidling at its centre. Another wall had a similar pin board adorned with Arabella Wood's photograph. Around each portrait were scraps of paper, each containing written details of their closest connections. These were linked to the central photograph by strands of black wool skewered by pushpins, and interlinked in the same way to further connections. The names on many of the scraps of paper were the same on both boards. It looked as if two demented spiders had spun off-kilter webs on the walls. He had been advised to create these visual 'aids' by his superior, Dennis 'The Menace' Scott, who was still nominally the chief investigating officer. The Menace's attention was still almost entirely given to the other case he was in charge of, that of the murdered disc jockey.

He had now ascertained that the chief suspect had taken up residence in a small town in Bulgaria. He contrasted his progress with Coupar's lack of such. Occasionally he would pop into the art school murders incident room and tut-tut over the pin boards.

"Clearly a psychopath, laddie," he remarked to Coupar. "Have you no got someone in your sights yet? And what about this meat cleaver they say? Have you sent the lads around all the butchers to see if one's gone missing?"

"Price and Waterhouse have been to every butchers in Forthburgh, sir."

"And? Any psychos?"

"Most of the butchers seemed to have psychotic characteristics, sir, but we can't yet link any of them to the Arabella Wood murder."

The Menace looked at him with narrowed eyes, suspecting sarcasm, but refrained from comment.

"There's always a motive somewhere to be found, laddie," he went on. "Even psychos have their reasons. Were Sidling or Wood customers of any of these butchers?"

"Sidling seems to have occasionally bought meat from a butcher's in Marchmint. The butcher recalls his unusual appearance."

"Unusual appearance?"

"Peroxide blond hair and so on."

"There we are! Does this butcher have a cleaver?"

"Yes sir, but you'll recall that it was Arabella Wood who was beheaded, possibly with a cleaver. This butcher has no connection with Arabella Wood."

"No connection yet *known*, laddie! Keep an open mind!"

Coupar sighed inwardly. The Menace had caught him out again on his precious 'ABC' principle.

"Yes, sir."

"And what about the laddies in Forensics? Anything there? Fingerprints?"

"None on the glass case or in the shower room. And, as you already know, none at the location of the Sidling murder."

"Hmmph! Do you need more black wool or pins by the way?"

"No, I think I've got enough for now, sir."

"Right. Keep making those connections Coupar. It's time for a bit of progress. We need a breakthrough. The press is impatient for a result. There was another article the other day in *The Daily Record*."

"I saw it. Detective Constable Price was kind enough to bring it to my attention."

"Aye… well, we didn't come out too well. It gave the impression Forthburgh was being stalked by a nutcase with a thing about artists. I had a call from some woman who asked if it was safe for her painting group to meet in their church hall as normal."

"Yes, sir."

"Well… carry on!"

And The Menace moved off, bristling moustache and all, no doubt satisfied that he had instilled new vigour into Coupar's conduct of the investigation. Word in the station was that he was off to Bulgaria quite soon to get his man. Coupar had gained an impression from somewhere that bristling moustaches were thick on the ground in such parts of the world. The Menace would be able to sneak up on his quarry unobserved.

He returned his gaze to the webs of black wool. There were so many connections there! The two victims were close friends, by all accounts, and knew many of the same people. What were the motives though? Who would want both of them dead? Or was this really the work of some psychopath without any of the usual motives? On the other hand, was it possible that the murders were unconnected? Could Arabella Wood's death have been plotted and executed by a person 'inspired' by the killing of Steve Sidling? Someone who knew that the first murder, as yet unsolved, would lead the police on a false trail regarding the second one? It seemed far-fetched. There could not, surely, be two people in Forthburgh capable of plotting and carrying out such bizarre killings.

Then there was the fact that each of the victims was left with a message. In the case of Steven Sidling, the rain had made the message illegible. In Arabella Wood's case, the message was simply *Portrait*. Hermione Cutter, the jilted wife of Ted Cutter, was a portrait painter. In her case, the motivation to murder Arabella might have existed – the old detective's standby of sexual jealousy. But he couldn't persuade himself that the thin, nervy woman he'd interviewed was capable of wielding a meat cleaver – or an axe - with such ferocity. And Miggs had seen her leaving in her ghost costume. That white outfit would have been splattered with blood if she was the killer.

However, 'ABC'... he should keep an open mind.

Coupar's thoughts circled back to Ricky Love. Two unsolved murders in Oregon, bearing a resemblance to the murder of Steve Sidling; Sidling's murder coming shortly after Ricky Love's arrival in Scotland; his apparent cultivation of a friendship with Arabella Wood – the close friend of Sidling - and her subsequent demise...

Were Ricky Love's associations with these four murderous events mere coincidences, just a matter of proximity and bad luck?

CHAPTER 22

February 1990

As grey January blended seamlessly into grey February, Coupar was hounded on further occasions by Chief Investigating Officer Dennis 'The Menace'. He had returned triumphant from Bulgaria, but was immediately preoccupied by two of the additional murder cases that had arisen over the festive season. Coupar was beginning to suspect that The Menace only rolled up his sleeves with crimes he was confident of solving. As far as the art school murders were concerned, he was Chief Investigating Officer in name only, and – perhaps through his golfing cronies in the press – his name had not become associated with the cases, whereas Coupar's had. He felt as if he was going around in unproductive circles. Detective Constables Price and Waterhouse were clearly bored and almost openly mocking. The tabloids revelled in headlines such as *Police Perplexed by Art School Slaughter!* and *Bring in Inspector Clouseau!* Even Lisa, initially thrilled by his involvement in these bizarre and high profile crimes, now had a tendency to tick him off for failing to bring her new developments when they got together. Certainly any aphrodisiac effect had worn off, and the red underwear remained firmly stowed in its drawer.

Dan the tennis coach was a little more encouraging. Coupar still felt that to be taking tennis lessons was an incongruous activity, given his responsibilities. But Dan had been keen to fix up the next session, so he went along with it. In the canteen afterwards, he sat with perspiration still trickling down his brow while Dan treated him to some short passages from his crime-novel-in-progress, which was now tentatively entitled *The Killing Spree*. Dan had been working on 'court coverage' with him today, which meant running him ragged from one corner of the court to another with a languid but merciless series of well-placed shots. It had crossed his mind that his frantic scurrying was a physical re-enactment of his work situation, which never entirely left his thoughts even on the tennis court.

...The police had been set on a false trail by the cunning killer. By leaving the bloody knife at the scene of the crime, he had made sure that suspicion would fall on the chef. After all, the knife had clearly come from the kitchen of the hotel. In addition, the killer had left a small note furled up like a cigarette paper in the victim's nostril. "Haute Cuisine" it said, in capital letters.

Dan finished reading this latest extract and looked at him expectantly.

Coupar was uneasy.

"Where did you get the idea for the note in the nostril?"

Was Dan flushing a little? However, he had an explanation.

"It was in one of those Unsolved Crimes America books. In fact there's a few cases where the killer leaves a note. Anyway, what do you think?"

"Very good, Dan. Very good," Coupar said, dabbing at his forehead with a towel. He had given up offering anything more specific than *very good* in response to Dan's crime novel snippets. He had enough on his plate in the real world without troubling himself with the manifest and multiple improbabilities of Dan's clichéd vision of detective work. He was perturbed by the note in the nostril. He had been indiscreet, he knew, in discussing details of his cases with Lisa on occasion. Had Dan acquired any of this knowledge? If so, what did that suggest about Lisa? Or – and here he experienced a twinge of jealousy – about Lisa and Dan's relationship?

"I've changed the beginning now," Dan was explaining. "You were right about revealing the killer straight off being a mistake. It always turns out that the killer is someone the reader has come across, but has never suspected. There are little clues, when you look back, but nothing that you'd have paid attention to at the time. If there weren't any little clues, then the reader would feel cheated. That's why I put in that the kitchen knife didn't match the other knives in the hotel kitchen, see? Although I'm wondering if it's too big a hint. What do you think?"

Coupar shook his head. "I don't read detective fiction enough to be sure, Dan, as I've said before."

"But you're doing the real thing, Coopsie! Don't you think, sometimes, that the evidence you need is something you've already come across, but you just haven't recognised it?"

These words rang in his ears, in a kind of unpleasant duet with The Menace's admonition *For God's sake get a grip on these cases, Coupar!* And so, almost in desperation, he followed The Menace's recommendation of listening again to the tapes of the dozens of interviews he'd conducted. Maybe some hitherto overlooked clue might come to light, when he played them back?

He started that afternoon, with the tape he'd recorded in early January of Ricky Love, once the American had returned to work after his bout of flu.

"Investigation into the death of Arabella Wood. Interview thirty four. Interviewee Ricky Love. Eleventh of January Nineteen Ninety. Interview conducted by Detective Inspector Coupar Cruickshank, in the presence of Detective Constable Neville Waterhouse…"

"I'm sorry you've been unwell, Mr Love."

"Yeah – worst flu I've ever had. Must be some British strain."

"Anyway, I've been looking forward to asking you some questions, as you can imagine."

"Sure. I understand. I hope the photographs that your constable collected from the house were some use?"

"Yes, thank you."

They hadn't been any use, not so far.

"If I could get the negatives back, that would be great. You see, I mainly went to get some photos for the folks back home. A bit of English… sorry, Scottish… local colour. We don't have revels in Oregon. I don't mind saying I'd never even heard the word before."

"Yes, we'll just keep the prints."

"Thank you."

"Okay. So… can we start with the night of the Art School Revel? I believe you didn't stay for long?"

"No, once I'd taken the photos I went home. I'm not a big drinker. Almost teetotal."

"You went alone to the Revel?"

"My wife Boony had to stay with our little guy, Marcus. So I just came for an hour or so."

"Did you see Arabella Wood there?"

"Yes, she was there. Poor Arabella! God! If only she hadn't been there!"

There was a pause on the tape, and the sound of Ricky blowing his nose. Had he been moved as far as tears at this point? Coupar couldn't remember. His own voice broke the following silence.

"I'm sorry. I'm sure this is upsetting, but we have to find out who did this and bring them to justice."

"Of course… it's fine… just give me a moment… it's just that I haven't lost a friend like this before. It's so shocking."

"Tell me about your friendship."

"We used to talk in the canteen sometimes. I got to know her quite soon after I arrived in September. She'd been a great friend of that poor guy Sidling."

"You stepped in as her new best friend in the art school?"

"I wouldn't go as far as that. But sure, we became friends. She didn't mix a lot with the other staff. She didn't get on with her Head of Department."

"Leonora Hunt?"

"Yes, that was her name… *is* her name, yes."

"Were they enemies, would you say?"

"No, I wouldn't go as far as that. I just think they had professional differences."

"Do you think Arabella had any enemies?"

"What, at the art school?"

"Anywhere."

"Well, if she did, they never cropped up in our conversations."

"So do you have any idea of who might have killed her? Or why she might have been killed?"

"None at all. It's just so bizarre. It must be an insane person, don't you think?"

"It depends on how we define *sane*. What about the night of the Revel – how did she seem?"

"We barely spoke, but she was having a lot of fun, I'd say. Dancing, laughing. Mostly with her students. The Fashion students had great outfits, and hers was one of the wildest! Those Gorgon snakes on her head! You'll see from the photos."

"I've seen for myself."

"Oh… of course. I forgot you'd have seen…"

"Did Arabella ever talk to you about her private life?"

"Well… not a lot. We were friends, but not kind of so close, you know?"

"Did you know that she was going out with the husband of another lecturer at the art school?"

"I did pick that up, yes."

"Did you ever meet that lecturer, the man's wife?"

"I don't know who that was. Arabella never told me a name."

"Okay. Did you also know that she previously had a relationship with a member of the Sculpture staff, Duncan McBane?"

"Yeah, I remember that cropping up some time. But I never knew much about it. She didn't talk about him. I got the feeling she didn't really like him any more."

"Do you know him yourself?"

"I know what he looks like. Big guy with a beard. Usually looks pretty miserable."

"Was Duncan McBane at the Revel?"

"I don't know for sure. I don't remember seeing him – but then, I didn't recognize many people… you know, with the disguises, the masks…"

"Okay Mr Love. Let's move on to something else now. What do you know about The Pine Loop Murders?"

There was a pause of a few seconds. It sounded like Ricky Love was shuffling about in his seat or something. Then he coughed.

"How do you know about those?"

"Just a bit of research. I believe you were interviewed? By the police?"

"Yes… excuse me, I'm a bit taken aback. Why… why do you want to know about those murders?"

"Sometimes we find odd bits of information that fit together. It's like a jigsaw puzzle. So – please, just fill me in a little."

"Well… they happened… they happened in nineteen eighty eight. The police interviewed me – and Boony, my wife – both times. There were two killings, about six months apart. The only reason we were interviewed was that both bodies turned up less than half a mile from our house. That was pretty creepy."

"Did you know either of the victims?"

"No. They both turned out to be hunters. There was a theory that they were killed by anti-hunting folk, but I don't buy that."

"Why not?"

"It was just too bizarre. You know the circumstances? How the bodies were left?"

"Yes."

"Well, to me that looked like something an insane person would do. I think it was just a coincidence they were hunters. I think some crazy guy had a grudge against both these guys who were killed. Who knows why? I once saw a man in Portland shot in the head because he'd pushed in front of a bus queue. You get these crazies with guns in our country."

"Although these murder victims weren't shot with bullets."

"No, crossbow arrows - or bolts, they should be called. But you get my point? People get killed for all kinds of dumb reasons, or no reasons at all."

"The two victims actually hunted with crossbows, I believe."

"Yes. Listen, don't get me wrong: it's a terrible thing, how those guys were murdered. But I can't approve of what they did – shooting at deer in the forest with crossbows. How cruel is that? You think those deer were killed straight out? No way. They'd just be wounded, and they'd limp off in agony with that arrow stuck into them, and the hunters would follow that trail of blood until the deer got too exhausted to go on, and they'd catch up with it where it was hiding in terror, and then they'd kill it with more arrows. A nice easy static target by then!"

Ricky Love sounded more worked up about the fate of the deer than sorry about the dead hunters.

Coupar listened to the rest of the interview, which was inconsequential, and clicked off the cassette recorder. Was Ricky Love a murderous psychopath? Or simply the genial, straightforward family man that he seemed?

CHAPTER 23

January 1990

When the second term of the academic year began in early January, Forthburgh School of Art was awash with rumour and speculation about the second murder of a lecturer. The Christmas and New Year period had dispersed the staff and students to their families all over Britain and the world beyond – but now that they were brought together again, the details of the murder were the only topic of conversation. The beheading of Arabella Wood within the walls of the institution itself was an even more monstrous sensation than the previous fate of Steve Sidling, who had at least been murdered in another place. The obscure location of the blood-splashed shower and toilet cubicle – albeit thoroughly cleaned and re-painted after the forensics team had finished with it – was a place of pilgrimage for the curious, and the hitherto unremarkable shelf in the Sculpture Court had also become an object of morbid fascination. Everyone who passed by glanced up at it, as if picturing a severed head in a glass case still sitting there.

Ricky Love entered the canteen on the first Monday of the new term with some unease. It was a new year – a new decade indeed – but he saw none of the bonhomie and hand-shaking that might normally accompany a first encounter with friends from the old year. He overheard someone saying *half my students haven't turned up yet* and wondered whether or not this was an exaggeration. A couple of Ricky's own students had temporarily withdrawn from the course on medical grounds, and he thought it possible that these were pretexts for avoiding the place in the present circumstances. Apparently several of the Fashion Department students had taken the same course of action. The risks associated with being a student at Forthburgh School of Art had ticked upwards. But perhaps the risks of being a staff member were even higher.

As he waited in line to order his coffee he heard a voice behind him.

"It's Ricky, isn't it?"

He turned. It was a woman with whom he'd had a brief conversation some time last term. A painter, he remembered. What was her name?

"Hi there!" he said, turning. He offered his hand.

"A Happy New Year to you!" he added, although he felt it had a hollow ring in the circumstances.

She shook his offered hand wordlessly. Hers was cold and bony. She looked as if she'd skipped Christmas dinner and most meals since then.

"I'm sorry... your name has escaped me," Ricky admitted.

"Hermione. Hermione Cutter. We chatted briefly at the Principal's sherry party last October. Don't worry, we Brits are generally much worse at remembering names than you are."

"Except in this case!" Ricky said with a smile, a little embarrassed. But then something came back to him.

"I remember now – didn't you say that you trained as a pharmacist, before you became a painter?"

"That's right – my father was a doctor, and I actually worked as a pharmacist for a few years, before my painting started to have some success."

"A sort of false start?"

"Not exactly. I quite enjoyed the work. But... well, the truth is that Ted – my husband – had a very good job, and I could afford to take a chance with my art. Did you go home for Christmas and New Year, Ricky?"

"We didn't. We'd agreed with the Buckleys… do you know the Buckleys…?"

She shook her head.

"Not really. I know who Ernest Buckley is, but I don't know his wife at all."

"Well, we swapped houses for our exchange year. Anyway, we agreed we'd just stay put over the holiday period. Less expense and less disruption."

"Didn't you miss family?"

"Well, sure. But we've got our own little family unit, you know."

"Ah – you have children here?"

"One child, Marcus. He's two years old. Do you have kids?"

"One boy as well. But he's coming up to twenty. He's at university."

They reached the front of the coffee queue. When they'd been served, Ricky hesitated. He'd spotted a table with a few of his colleagues from the Graphic Design and Commercial Art Department sitting there. But Hermione gestured to a small table with only two chairs.

"Do you mind if I join you for coffee?" she said.

"No – of course… Hermione."

They sat down and Hermione took a sip of coffee and said in a low voice.

"I'm sorry I've sort of latched onto you like this, but it's because I don't want to hear any more about this horrible murder. I've only been in the art school for one morning but it's all people seem to be able to talk about. You must think you've come into a strange place."

Ricky experienced a momentary sense of *déjà vu*. In a flash, he understood why. Three months ago he'd sat for the first time with Arabella Wood at this very table, after the murder of the Sidling guy.

"I guess I feel I've come at a strange *time*," he said, after a moment. "Two murders since I arrived. But sure, let's talk about other things. Is your husband an artist too, Hermione?"

She uttered a flimsy laugh.

"No, no. Ted is a banker. And we're separated."

This brought Ricky to a complete halt. But Hermione moved on briskly to another topic.

"What's your wife's name, Ricky?"

"Boony."

"Bunny?"

"No, Boony."

"Oh – I've never heard that name before."

"It's a little unusual. Apparently they called her that as a kind of pet name when she was still in the womb, and then decided to stick with it."

"And is *she* an artist?"

"No. She worked with a TV station in Oregon. She was in their marketing department. That's how we met – I was doing design work at the station. Here…"

Ricky fished out his wallet and extracted a passport sized photo of himself and Boony.

Hermione took it and glanced at it. Then she brought it closer to her eyes and peered more intently. The hair was a little longer in the photo, but there could be no doubt. This was the woman she had seen a few days ago in the company of Duncan McBane.

She handed back the photograph with an attempted smile.

"She's very pretty," she said.

CHAPTER 24

January 1990

A FEW DAYS EARLIER…

Duncan McBane was more at ease with himself than he had been for many months. He felt as if his life could begin anew. The elimination of Steve Sidling and Arabella Wood from the landscape of his world had been liberating, just as the death of his horrible Aunt Janet had cleared the dark clouds that hung over his childhood – or at least some of them. It was remarkable, he reflected smugly, as he put on some of the smart clothes Arabella had once goaded him into acquiring, how little trouble a couple of murders had caused in his conscience. He felt vindicated, not guilty; a bit like Lemmy Stoter.

He appraised his appearance in the soap-speckled mirror in his bathroom. The dogtooth jacket looked good with the open-necked Ralph Lauren Oxford shirt. He snipped a few stray hairs from his beard. He tilted his head to admire the effect of his recent haircut. He winked at himself, and assayed a smile. Who would have thought that was the face of a murderer?

The police certainly didn't see him as a murderer. He'd sailed through his recent interview with that fresh-faced boy-scout of a police detective – Cruickshank. He'd taken an uncomplicated line in response to his questions. There was no point in cooking up anything elaborate. No, he hadn't been in the art school during the Revel. He commented, truthfully, that it was several years since he'd attended one. He'd just been at home, having an early night. He candidly explained that he had been in the art school earlier in the day of the Revel, to deal with some paperwork. He claimed to have gone home at about four o'clock. The janitors in their office in the entrance hall didn't keep any record of who came and went, and were often distracted, or half-asleep, or elsewhere on some task. No one could possibly know that he had been holed up in his office when the art school closed at six, when the final preparations for the Revel took place. He had locked his door, kept quiet inside, and no one had come near. And then, just before the Revel began, he had made his way swiftly and unseen to the obscure staff-only toilet and shower room located quite nearby, where he had lurked for hours with his shark mask to hand, ready to don it and act as a drunken reveller in the highly unlikely event that anyone stumbled across him. In those circumstances he would have aborted the murder mission. Only Hermione knew that he was there.

Cruickshank had made a few notes, asked a few irrelevant questions, and dismissed him. He had dozens of people to interview. Hundreds, potentially. He'd referred to the fact that Duncan and Arabella were once in a relationship, something he'd established during his enquiry into Sidling's murder. But he seemed to accept Duncan's comment that it was water under the bridge long before. Wasn't Duncan upset at the loss of someone who had once been so close to him, Cruickshank had asked. Duncan had nodded solemnly. He was upset. But he had no inkling, no glimmer of an idea, of who might have committed such a hideous crime.

The unveiling of his totem pole for Deil's Glen had originally been intended to take place *in situ*. But the Arts Council, joint commissioners of the work with the Forthburgh Parks Department, had decided that an indoor occasion would be much better attended in the depths of January. Furthermore, it would be the perfect opportunity to showcase their newly refurbished exhibition space in the Georgian Quarter, and a good excuse to start the new year with a few festive drinks. The Arts Council could always find an excuse for a few drinks.

It was for this that Duncan was dressing in his finery; a welcome opportunity to shine a little in public. He was going to give a short talk on the symbolism of the totem, and offer a few remarks about working with natural materials. He wasn't particularly keen on speaking in public, but he was accustomed to addressing groups of students, and it was a chance to assert the values of traditional sculpture, now destined for a resurgence in the art school after the demise of Sidling. Later in the term it would be decided whether his position as Acting Head of Sculpture should be made permanent, and this moment in the spotlight would do him no harm at all. He wondered if Edgar Peabody would attend – he'd certainly received an invitation, along with most of the art school's academic staff.

Boony Love had found the Christmas and New Year period dull and lacklustre. She soon regretted the decision she and Ricky had made, mainly for financial reasons, to remain in Scotland instead of joining their extended families for the festive season in Oregon. Already, since September, she had been feeling that she and Ricky were too much thrown on their own resources, lacking the variety of their Portland life, enlivened as it was by social occasions, friends and other family. The Christmas vacation had only offered more of the same monotony. There was also the unsettling sinister shadow cast over the period by the discovery of another bizarre murder. Was Forthburgh School of Art a safe place of employment for Ricky? Additionally, Marcus had contracted a nasty cold, and was fractious and demanding. Shortly after that, Ricky came down with flu. It was misery every way she looked.

One day early in the new year – a day as dull and featureless as those that had gone before it – she'd gone into Ricky's "office", a shabby back room long dedicated to the accumulation of Buckley junk, in search of some paper and a pen to write a shopping list. Her eye was caught by a printed card with a gilt edging lying abandoned on top of a pile of other stuff on Ricky's desk. It was an invitation to a launch party for a totem pole. A *totem pole*? How weird was that? And it was for the following evening! She read it again, with a small thrill of excitement.

"Were you planning on going to this?" she called out. He was in the living room trying to amuse Marcus.

"What?" he called back.

She carried the card into the living room and handed it to him. Marcus made a grab at it, missed, and started crying.

Ricky read the invitation, which he'd barely glanced at before. It had arrived while he was still down with the flu.

"I hadn't planned to. It's just a drinks party. We won't get a babysitter now anyway."

"Do you mind if I go?"

Ricky looked at her, surprised. Marcus clawed at the air, trying to destroy the invitation.

"No, sure. Go if you like."

Boony felt she had to explain.

"It's just – you know – we've had such a quiet Christmas…"

She raised her voice a little to overcome competition from Marcus.

"… and I sure wouldn't mind a chance to get out of the house and socialize a little."

"Okay, sure. Go for it."

Entering the gallery at six thirty the following evening, Boony felt as if she had just shed a few years. She used to be quite a party-animal before marrying Ricky and having Marcus, and going into a room full of strangers held no terrors for her. She knew she looked good, and was confident of some male attention at least. She was clad in a tight-fitting red dress, just above knee length, and she'd managed to get a last-minute appointment at the hairdresser's that afternoon. In the good old, bad old days she might have expected one or two attempts at a pick-up, to be rejected or accepted according to the quality of the applicant. She'd met most of her pre-Ricky boyfriends at parties.

She was given a glass of fizzy wine at the door, and click-clacked across the wooden floor on her high heels through the gathering – maybe forty or fifty people - towards what she assumed was the principal reason for the event – a broad pole of dark wood, maybe twelve or so feet high, carved and painted. She adopted a thoughtful pose in front of it and soon enough she heard a voice at her side.

"The yellow paint is a bit more garish than I meant. But it'll weather down."

She turned and smiled at the bearded man in the dogtooth jacket.

"Are you the *artist?*"

The bearded man nodded modestly. He was tall and muscular looking, and had an interesting face. Not exactly handsome, but… intense, and *potent* somehow. Boony felt she'd made a good start to the evening.

"I'm Boony," she said, holding out a hand.

"Duncan McBane," he replied, shaking her hand firmly.

"You work at the art school?" she said.

"Aye, for my sins."

This must be some British joke, so she gave him the benefit of her perfect array of dazzling teeth.

"Are you connected with the art school?" he enquired.

"Not directly…"

For the merest moment she thought of leaving Ricky out of the equation, but that was too ridiculous. Besides, she was wearing her wedding and engagement rings.

"… my husband is working there for a year. An exchange with a guy called Buckley, in Graphics."

"Oh, aye. I know Ernest Buckley. And I know your husband – I know who he is, anyway. We haven't talked."

"Are you married?"

Duncan laughed.

"I did try it once. Didn't work out."

Unfortunately, at this point, before they'd properly got going, a third person joined them, someone from the Parks Department, a bald man with a large paunch that suggested he didn't make much use of the open spaces that were his remit. Having introduced himself he began to monopolize Duncan. Boony detached herself after a polite interval and looked around. She observed a woman who was standing on her own a little way off. She looked pale and rather lost, and was very thin. Maybe she had an eating disorder. But she was dressed smartly and met Boony's tentative smile with a smile of her own. Boony was on the point of going over to talk to her when someone else – a short, dark-haired woman in a skirt and jacket redolent of the 1940s - approached the thin woman and began speaking animatedly to her. Boony was momentarily adrift again, but then a pleasant old man in a bow tie addressed her, and soon she was swept up in a group of Arts Council people. A top-up of fizz arrived, and she began to enjoy herself. This was better than sitting at home on that uncomfortable Buckley couch with Ricky, watching the television!

About an hour later, Duncan gave his little speech, and then the crowd began to disperse. It was only eight in the evening, and Boony was reluctant to let go of this lively little occasion. It had been like an oasis in a desert, and only the Buckley couch, a cranky infant, and a lovable but highly predictable husband awaited her at home. Sadly putting down her wine glass on the table by the door, she was about to go out to retrieve her coat from the row of hooks in the entrance lobby when she heard the now familiar tones of Duncan McBane just behind her.

"Bunny!"

She turned. *Bunny* was what most people thought she was called when they'd only heard *Boony* once.

He looked at her, a little sheepishly, she thought.

"We hardly got talking," he said. "I wondered if you'd fancy a drink? There's a nice pub just along the road."

Arriving home by taxi at half past ten, Boony felt a little tipsy. It took her a few attempts to get the key into the lock. The house was quiet. Only the landing light was on. Evidently Marcus had settled, and Ricky had decided to have an early night. Her clothes and hair smelled of smoke from the pub, so she stripped off and took a quick bath. Unbelievable that there was no shower in this house! Just a leaky rubber attachment that didn't fit properly over the weird-shaped taps. Afterwards she slid into bed next to her husband, who stirred a little but didn't wake, and as she waited for sleep to come she reviewed the evening.

Duncan McBane was clearly a complicated person. He was a completely new experience for Boony. She didn't think people quite that complicated even existed in Oregon; or not amongst the people she was used to meeting anyway. He was quite garrulous, but she had the impression that he was not normally so. She guessed that the combination of a lot to drink and the heady experience of being the centre of attention at the gallery had brought him out of whatever shell he usually sheltered in. With a few simple questions and remarks on her side, glimpses of the life of a tormented Scottish artist had come tumbling out: his childhood with a strict disciplinarian father, a Presbyterian stonemason who had died falling off the spire of a Catholic church; a move to somewhere called Stonehaven and the death there – falling off a cliff - of an aunt who had been very dear to him; other women who had failed him – his wife Mary, and the Fashion lecturer Arabella Wood, so recently discovered murdered; his struggles to master the skills required for his creative output; his frustrations at seeing a shift in the fine art world away from traditional media and methods towards conceptual art.

Boony felt she had gained more insight into the Scottish psyche and the world of Scottish art in a couple of hours with Duncan McBane than she had gleaned from all her conversations over the past few months with Ricky about his experiences and discoveries.

The other aspect of the evening – as stimulating as the flow of novel information that was coming her way – was that Duncan was clearly attracted to her. He wasn't exactly flirtatious – she didn't think he would know how to be flirtatious – but as the evening went on, his eye contact grew bolder and his smile appeared more frequently. Of course he was about fifteen years older than she was – at some point he mentioned his recent fiftieth birthday. But, nevertheless, he was a handsome-ish, well-constructed guy who, once upon a time, she might have allowed to make a move on her, had he been bold enough to do so.

Before they left the pub, they exchanged phone numbers. He walked her to a taxi rank, and she was almost a little disappointed when he didn't attempt to kiss her goodnight.

CHAPTER 25

January 1990

Over Christmas and New Year, Hermione had recovered slightly an appetite for food, moderated her alcohol intake, and enjoyed the company of Roland, who, although not a prolific conversationalist, brought the solace of another presence to the too-big house. The girlfriend who had kept him away for much of the last summer break was now off the scene, and he seemed philosophical about that.

But these positive elements were undermined by a kind of sickness always lurking at the back of her mind: the slaughter of Arabella was never very far from her thoughts. Her moments of forgetful happiness were like flowers that bloomed on a dung heap. When she was not engaged in talk or activity, she was plagued by images – actual and imagined – of that night of the Art School Revel; a restless crowd of images, gathered in her subconscious, and constantly knocking for admission at the door of her conscious mind. She couldn't help picturing what must have happened in that shower room while she stood outside. Sometimes it filled her with such a horror that she felt she might vomit. She was once visited by a nightmare in which severed heads were concealed about the house and would come to light at any moment - Roland and Ted were searching for them constantly, and she had to keep moving them to new hiding places.

To combat these black thoughts, the idea that she kept returning to was that with Arabella gone, there was now a prospect of getting her husband back. That, she told herself with wavering conviction, was worth the price that had been paid in blood.

Of course Roland had had to spend time over the festive season with his father too – especially so in the tragic circumstances. Ted was temporarily still in residence at Arabella's flat. At least Roland always returned to spend the night at home with her in Martinside. Also he was around and about during the daytime, as Ted was back at work. Bankers didn't get the same long breaks as university students and art school lecturers, and she imagined he would be glad to distract himself with business anyway after what had happened.

This January morning she felt quite calm. Last night's dream, still faintly lingering on the edge of memory, had been an unusually happy one. She and Ted had been in a boat somewhere, a rowing boat, just bobbing about on a calm, turquoise sea.

Low winter sunlight flooded the kitchen, where she and Roland sat at the long wooden table – long enough to have accommodated the bigger family she would have loved to have had. She regarded her son fondly across the surface of this table. He was wearing a grunge style checked flannel shirt that was too large for him, and his hair flopped off to both sides from a centre parting. She could see both herself and Ted in his features. Later this month he would be twenty. But just now he was dipping thin strips of toast smeared with Marmite into his boiled egg in just the way that he had done as a toddler. Tomorrow he would get the train back to university in Bristol, where he would have to make his own Marmite soldiers.

"So, how did your Dad seem, last night?" she said.
"Fine."
"Quieter than usual?"
"Maybe."

"Did he say anything about whether he's going to stay on in… in her flat in Scotsbridge?"

"He's found somewhere else."

"Oh… where?"

"I'm not sure. He didn't say."

Hermione wasn't sure she believed this. She thought Roland was trying to protect her feelings, not saying too much about his dad. He was growing up: the separation of his parents must have revealed them to him for the first time as completely individual people, with their own foibles, desires and faults. And God knows what turmoil the murder of his father's girlfriend had caused in his young mind. She thought back to that innocent toddler he had been, and wished she could have protected him from all this adult knowledge.

"Do you want more soldiers?"

"No thanks. Is there more tea in the pot?"

"Yes. Pass me your mug."

"Did your father mention me at all?" she prompted, pouring the tea. She just couldn't help herself. She had to dig for information, while an informant was still at hand.

Roland looked out of the window.

"Not really."

Perhaps Ted felt some compunction about discussing her with her son. She had no such scruples. If Ted was to be brought back to Martinside, then she needed any clues that Roland might provide.

"Does he seem very sad?"

Roland shifted in his chair in a way that suggested a strong desire to be elsewhere.

"You don't mind me asking about him, do you darling? I haven't seen him since… since Arabella… you know… died."

Roland gripped his mug, as if it might anchor him to the spot, and stared into it.

"I don't mind, Mum. But I don't know what to say. Dad doesn't open up … he's not himself at the moment.

I'm sure he must be sad – but it's more that he's kind of stunned or bewildered. He has no idea who murdered Arabella, and he says it's lucky – if you can call it that – that he was in London when it happened because otherwise the police seemed to think it might have been him."

"How awful!"

Roland finally brought himself to look at her directly.

"Mum... I know you want Dad to come back to you. I would love that to happen as well. But he's still in shock. I think he was... he must have been... very attached... to Arabella. I'm sorry, but it's true. And for her to be so horribly murdered... it's a shock, like I say. A big shock. So I don't think he's thinking ahead right now, apart from finding somewhere to live for the time being. Obviously he needs to get out of Arabella's flat as quickly as he can. He says she has a sister in Australia who came over for the funeral, and she's going to stay in Scotland and sort everything out. You know... all her stuff and so on. There's millions of clothes in the place."

Hermione nodded. She didn't want to know about Arabella's flat or Arabella's sister. But at least she had got Roland talking, and he had said something for the first time that had been unspoken between them – that he recognised and shared her wish for Ted to return to her.

"We talked about the other murder," Roland went on. "The sculpture guy. Dad can't help wondering if there could have been a connection. Both of them were lecturers at the art school. Both were killed in these weird ways. And of course the sculpture guy was the partner of Dad's big friend Derek. That makes it all even weirder and more upsetting. Dad had to talk a lot with Derek in the autumn, after it happened. And now it's happened to him."

Hermione moved away to the sink, where she ran water to wash the dishes. That sick feeling that frequently afflicted her had come back. After a moment she managed a few words.

"It's possible I suppose. In which case there's a psycho on the loose somewhere."

"You don't have any ideas, do you Mum, about who it might be?"

"No. None at all."

At the railway station the next morning she waved Roland off from the platform in the old-fashioned way, with a fluttering handkerchief. When the train had completely disappeared, she wandered away distractedly through the station concourse. A rack of newspapers caught her eye. *Glasgow off to a flying start as European Capital of Culture!* She thought she would buy a copy. She picked it off the rack, but then she saw a heading lower down the front page; a heading about a beheading. *Police still hunt art school killer!* Arabella's murder could still fill a slack day on the front page more than three weeks after it had been committed. The familiar sick feeling came surging up again, a kind of wave of revulsion that made her feel a little dizzy. She put the paper back and hurried blindly up the steep flight of steps that took her out of the station concourse and into the buffeting cold wind blowing along Princess Street.

A day later, in the evening, she screwed up her courage to ring Ted. Arabella's funeral – which she couldn't bring herself to attend – was over a week ago. Roland was no longer in the house. There was no reason now to delay. She tried the number she still had for Arabella's flat, but it must have been disconnected. So she had to work up her courage all over again to ring him the next day, at work.

"Can I speak with Mr Cutter please?" she said to the receptionist.

"One moment," came the brusque reply. She waited while a message played about the advantages of some new kind of account at the bank until a new voice came on the line.

"Mr Cutter's secretary. Can I help you?"

"Oh, hello. Is that Sharon?"

"Yes."

"It's Mrs Cutter here - Hermione. We've met in the past."

There was a moment's silence. She wondered how much Sharon knew about Ted's private life. She would almost certainly know that they no longer lived together.

"Oh, yes. Hello Mrs Cutter." There was now a note of caution in Sharon's voice.

"I was wondering if Ted was free at the moment to have a quick conversation?"

"Oh, I'm sorry Mrs Cutter. Mr Cutter has just gone out for lunch with a business client. Do you want to leave a message?"

"No, no. I'll try again later. Is he coming back to the office later?"

"As far as I know, yes."

"Okay, I'll try then."

She wondered if he'd instruct Sharon to block her call, but when she rang again late in the afternoon, she was put through.

"Hello Hermione," he said. He sounded weary, and perhaps wary.

"Hello Ted, how are you?"

There was a pause. She'd said the little formula without thinking, but clearly it wasn't an easy question for him to answer.

"Not great," he said at last. "Not great."

"I'm very sorry," she went on, "you know – sorry about Arabella."

As she said these formulaic words it came to her with blinding clarity that she really was sorry. Something that had seemed the most desirable thing in the world now afflicted her with revulsion. But what had she done it for? For this moment! For the chance to bring her husband back to the marital home!

All this, in some fleeting form, passed through her head in the pause before he spoke.

"Thank you," Ted replied.

"Are you... are you still living there... I mean... in her flat?"

"I'm moving out tomorrow."

"Oh... so you've found a place already?"

"Yes."

"Because I was thinking... if you were stuck for somewhere... you could..."

Ted interrupted.

"I've found a place, Hermione."

"Do you want to meet up?" she blurted out, before her courage failed her.

"Meet up? Why?"

The blunt question was as sharp as a sword in her heart.

"I thought... well, perhaps... I thought you might want to talk to someone."

There was a long pause.

"Hermione –that's very thoughtful of you, but at the moment I just need some space and time to myself."

"I see."

There was another pause. Then Ted spoke again.

"I need to get on with things here, Hermione. I appreciate you calling. Goodbye."

"Goodbye..." she said, and then realized that the line had already gone dead. For a moment she fought off the tears welling up in her eyes, and then she capitulated and sobbed helplessly.

She left things as they were for a couple of days, but then she could resist no longer. She *had* to speak at more length with Ted. Her only means of reaching him was still at his work number. She rang three times, and was informed each time by a patient but firm Sharon that he was 'unavailable'. On the fourth occasion the switchboard operator asked for her name when she rang, and then informed her that Sharon's line was busy. The same thing happened two more times. It looked as if Ted had erected a wall around himself, and she wasn't going to get over it. She would have to try another tactic.

She went to the hairdresser's and had her hair done nicely. She had only the vaguest idea of what should be done with it, but leaving everything to the discretion of the hairdresser resulted in a bob – not too short – with blonde highlights. In the mirror at home, she thought it made her look years younger. She had her nails done too, and that afternoon, dressed in a smart dress and jacket combination that had seen service in trips to the theatre or to dinner engagements, and which had been the catalyst for one of Ted's rare compliments, she took up position in the atrium of the swanky building where Ted's bank was located. The atrium was shared by a number of financial businesses that were accessed by lifts. It was a semi-public space with potted plants and a few designer sofas. At five o'clock, she perched on one of these sofas and prepared to wait. As far as she was aware, there was no way of exiting the building without passing through that atrium, unless it was via a fire escape somewhere. She didn't know if Ted was in the building or not, but if he was, he might be expected to emerge from one of the lifts at some point in the next hour or two.

Five thirty came and went, and then six. Hermione was aware that the woman at the concierge's desk had looked at her curiously a few times, but she wasn't about to budge.

The exodus between five thirty and six had slowed to a trickle by six fifteen. Her mind was wandering a little, and she was looking at her shiny fingernails when the faintest waft of a well-known musky scent brought her head up sharply. Ted was half way across the atrium, moving across her line of vision, apparently oblivious to her presence. He was in his business suit, of course, and carrying the black briefcase she had bought him for his birthday many years ago. Her heart lifted a little on seeing it. It was looking a little battered now, but perhaps he had an emotional attachment to it. She hoped so.

He was striding purposefully towards the revolving glass doors that gave onto the street. She jumped up from the sofa and hurried towards him. Just before he reached the doors she called his name.

"Ted! Wait a minute! It's me."

He turned to face her, his eyes wide with surprise.

"Hermione!" he said. "What are you doing here?"

"Trying to see you of course," she replied. "Won't you speak to me?"

He passed his free hand across his brow, and cast a look around the atrium. As if looking for an escape route, Hermione thought.

"Yes, of course," he said. "What is it about?"

"Can we go somewhere nearby?" Hermione said. "There's a nice place just around the corner, that we've been in… in the past."

Ted just nodded, and gestured for her to precede him through the revolving doors. She did so, repressing the thought that he might turn and run back to the lifts and the sanctuary of his office.

They walked in an uneasy silence the hundred yards or so to the bar. A biting wind whistled around Hermione's exposed calves and ankles. It was a relief to get indoors again. The place was quiet, and she led the way to a table away from other customers. She glanced at Ted as he looked around the bar. His hangdog expression made her think of a dog on a leash. She had more or less forced this on him.

"Do you want a drink?" he said, in the tone of an undertaker.

"Yes please, Ted. A vodka and coke."

He went to the bar and returned with their drinks. He sat down, and looked her in the eye for the first time. She couldn't read his expression. It certainly wasn't a happy one.

"So…" he said, and let the word hang there, like a question mark suspended above them by an invisible hand.

She had prepared a few lines of small talk, to lead into the nub of the matter.

"How are you getting on, Ted? Have you moved into a new place now?"

He nodded.

"A temporary place, yes."

"Temporary?"

"Derek's place. He's got a spare room."

"That's kind of him."

"We're in the same boat. Our… partners… murdered. It sort of helps, in a funny way. To have that in common."

She took a long sip of her vodka and coke. He took a gulp of what looked like a whisky, his Adam's apple rising and falling in the way she was so familiar with, and fixed his gaze out of the bar's window. She decided that small talk was pointless. She had to take the bull by the horns.

"Ted… I want you to come back to me. Roland wants it too, of course. I'd love you to come back and live with me in Martinside. I know you're devastated just now. I know you were… that you…. that Arabella was important to you. I don't expect everything to go back to the way it was immediately. You know there's a spare room – three spare rooms. But don't you think… in time…we can put this behind us? There was nothing wrong, was there, before? I never felt there was anything wrong… you know… wrong with *us*."

Ted looked into his tumbler of whisky. He picked it up, swirled the amber liquid gently, and drank it off in a single mouthful.

"Hermione," he said, in a gentler tone than he had used before. "Arabella was a wake-up call for me. Until she came along I hadn't realised how dull my life had become. It was as if I'd been living in a grey world and suddenly a burst of colour came into it. I can't go back now. I hate to say this to you – I'd hoped we'd never need to have this conversation – but to go back to our old life together just isn't an option for me any more."

Hermione felt her eyes stinging. Tears were going to come at any moment. Ted was still talking.

"I've asked the bank to transfer me to the London office, and they've agreed. As it happens, Derek plans to sell up here too and move to London. He feels the same as me. Forthburgh has chewed us up and spat us out. It feels like a cemetery to me now. The whole city feels like death, and I can't wait to get away."

He stood up. Hermione could only see him as a blurry outline now, as the tears started welling up.

"We'll be in touch, Hermione. I won't let you down – financially, I mean. I know your art school work and your painting don't bring in a lot. And of course we've both got Roland close to our hearts. We'll be in contact."

He hesitated. She let out a loud sob. She just couldn't help it. He put an awkward hand on her shoulder, just the briefest of touches, and then he picked up his briefcase and walked out.

The bastard! The bastard! said a little voice in her head. Was *this* all there was? Was it for this that she'd helped to murder another human being? She felt as if she was on the very edge of a dark, bottomless pit of despair, and that shortly she would tumble helplessly into the void.

An hour later, Hermione stood in her bathroom, contemplating the shelves of little brown bottles and packets of pills that she had accumulated, with her pharmacist's knowledge, in the days when she thought vaguely of poisoning Arabella. How different were her feelings now! Used in the right way - in the right quantities or combinations - they offered a range of easy tickets to oblivion. It would just be a matter of falling into a heavy sleep, and never waking up again in this cold, empty house where she had once been happy.

The thing that stopped her now, after going into the bathroom in such a state of desperation – the only thing really – was the thought of her son Roland, now cheerful and busy with his second year at university down in Bristol. There at least there was a certain future – her son. Ted might have removed himself from her life, but Roland would never do that. One day he would marry and have children. She would be a grandmother. She would be connected again to people she loved. It all seemed far-off, a bright island of joy glimpsed from far out in a stormy sea. But it was enough – just enough – to make her close the door of the bathroom cabinet and go to the kitchen.

She opened the fridge, which she had stocked well with fresh food for the potential return of her husband. But what was the point of cooking for one? She dug in the freezer compartment instead, and pulled out a ready meal at random to put in the microwave. She had no interest in food now. But if she had decided to keep herself alive, then it had to be eaten.

CHAPTER 26

May 1990

FOUR MONTHS LATER...

These early mornings along the River Lethe were soothing for the soul. Late May was in full leaf and the birds were singing their hearts out. The dense *haar* that had settled onto the city last night had dissipated in a pleasant morning breeze. Trudi snuffled about, exploring the wooded margins of the path, and Eleanor Brown strolled contentedly, looking at the water bubbling over the stones below. It was a little further to come from her house than her old haunts at Deil's Glen, but that had been spoiled by last year's horrible events. Nor would she ever do a cleaning job at the art school again. But this new dog-walking route was completely free of unpleasant associations, and, at this early hour, as quiet as she could have wished for. So far this morning, she hadn't seen a soul. Up ahead, above the tops of the trees she could see the towering arches of the Telford Bridge. The faintest rumble of traffic reached her ears. Up there, the earliest of the morning's commuters would be driving to work. But down here in the gorge cut by the river, all was peaceful.

Immediately below the bridge there was a bronze sculpture of a figure with a luxuriant beard and a trident. It emerged from the fast-flowing water, and a plaque on the river bank informed the curious that it was Poseidon, otherwise known as Neptune, and that it was the work of one Duncan McBane, commissioned by the city fathers in 1981 to commemorate the hundred and fiftieth anniversary of the opening of the bridge above. Eleanor always looked forward to rounding the corner of the path that revealed the bridge in all its splendour, and to greeting the statue below, which always seemed to be looking at her. Indeed, she had formed the habit – silly, really – of saying quietly *Hello Neptune!* – as she met with it.

Trudi scampered around the bend ahead of her, and then set up a volley of barking. She had probably seen a squirrel.

"Stop fussing, Trudi!" she called out, and followed her around the corner, looking across the water towards her old friend, Neptune. Then she froze into a statue herself. A statue vividly expressive of shock and horror.

Skewered on the upthrust trident of Neptune, like a piece of toast on a toasting fork, was the body of a man. The three prongs of the fork protruded from his back, blackened with dried blood. He must have fallen chest first from the parapet of the bridge a hundred feet above. His face dangled downwards towards the water as if searching for its reflection.

Trudi continued to bark at the ghastly sight in the middle of the river, her paws up on the low stone wall that bordered the edge of the path. Eleanor Brown sat down heavily on an iron bench on the other side of the path, where the wall obscured her view of the river below. The world around her seemed to be spinning violently, the leaves and branches flashing before her eyes like a kaleidoscope. The bird calls had turned into vicious screams. She sat very still, her hands squeezing together as if they could comfort each other, mumbling to herself.

"Not again! Not another one! My God... not another one!"

CHAPTER 27

February 1990

THREE MONTHS EARLIER...

As he walked in the door of the house, Ricky heard Boony's voice. It was coming from upstairs. He paused on the threshold, pulling his key out of the lock, listening, wondering. She sounded unusually animated. She must be up in the bedroom, maybe with the door shut, judging from the slightly muffled quality of the sound. There was a telephone extension up there, and he wondered vaguely why she was using that one instead of the one in the kitchen. Then, as he shut the door, Marcus came down the stairs and along the hall at him like a cannon ball.

He lifted him high in the air and whirled him around.

"Helicopter Marcus to base! Helicopter Marcus to base! Are you reading me?"

Boony's voice ceased speaking upstairs, and she came down. She smiled brightly.

"Hi honey! Have a good day?"

"Sure. You?"

"Yeah, fine."

"I see Marcus is handling the stairs well now on his own!"

He put his son down and leaned in towards Boony. She pecked his cheek, like a bird at a bird feeder, and withdrew.

"What have you guys been doing today?"

"We went swimming, didn't we Marcus? At the big pool with flumes."

"Yeah? Great! Marcus - did you like the swimming pool?"

Marcus shook his head.

"Didn't like man."

"What man?"

"Man with beard."

"There was a man with a beard at the pool," she explained.

"Not at the pool," Marcus said.

"He's getting muddled," Boony said.

"Oh. Well, what about the flume, Marcus? Did Mom take you down the flume?"

"No. Scary."

They went into the kitchen. Marcus retreated under the kitchen table, to resume marshalling his herd of plastic dinosaurs. Boony made them coffee.

Ricky sat at the table, carefully avoiding any intervention with the Jurassic ecosystem surrounding his feet. Boony stayed standing up by the kitchen work top, her hands wrapped around her coffee mug as if for warmth. Her fingernails were freshly painted a delicate shade of pink.

"I've fixed up to go out with one of the other moms from the school tonight, Ricky. I hope you don't mind."

"No. I'm delighted - that you're starting to make friends I mean. Who is it?"

"Someone called Lyndsay. She's got a little boy called Paul who Marcus could play with some time."

"That's great. What are you going to do?"

"Well, we're going to meet for a drink in town, then maybe get some food in a wine bar or something. Lyndsay knows places."

"So, what's Lyndsay like?"

"I don't know her too well yet. She seems really nice, but you haven't got long to break the ice when you're just at the nursery for five minutes dropping off and picking up. Lyndsay and I were talking about maybe setting up something with the other mothers with little ones. Perhaps a swapping system to take it in turns to look after three or four of them a couple of mornings a week."

"Like the arrangement you had with Katy back in Oregon?"

"Yeah - that kind of thing. We also talked about starting a book group."

"This is really great Boony!"

He reached over and took her hand for a moment.

"I know how hard it's been for you, settling in here."

She nodded, detached her hand, and moved towards the door.

"Anyway, I'd like to take a shower… shit, I mean bath! There's some microwave stuff in the ice box for when you get hungry. You just shove it in. Marcus has already had his tea."

"Tea?"

"Gee, I'm getting British already. That's what the other moms call the evening meal. Anyway, see you later!"

Boony headed off to take her bath. Ricky played dinosaurs with Marcus for a while, and when Boony was through in the bathroom he took him up for his bath.

They were busy with a wind-up duck toy when Boony stuck her head around the bathroom door. She looked very pretty. She had on the same shade of lipstick as Ricky had noticed on her fingernails.

"I'll see you later then honey! Goodnight Marcus! I don't want to get all wet kissing you - I'll give you an extra kiss in the morning, okay?"

Marcus was too absorbed in the duck's progress to reply.

"Bye, Boony! Have a good time."

Ricky let Marcus play in the bath a while longer, then got him dried and into bed. He read him a bedtime story and then turned the lights out. Unusually, Marcus fell asleep quickly – maybe the swimming had tired him out. Ricky felt very serene. Things were still a little confusing at work, and of course this latest murder had created a crazy atmosphere there, but at least home life was settling down now. It was good that Boony was getting some social connections. Maybe it would cheer her up.

He'd sat reading the paper for twenty minutes when the phone rang. It was a woman's voice.

"Hello?" said the voice brightly, "you must be Ricky?"

"Yes, that's right."

"Oh lovely! I'm Lyndsay. I have a little boy who goes to nursery with Marcus."

"Oh yes, hello."

"Is Boony there?"

"No - I thought she was meeting you."

"Tonight? No. We talked about getting together next week..... hello? Are you still there?"

"Sorry. I was just wondering how I got it wrong. I must have got mixed up. Is there another Lyndsay?"

"Not as far as I know. Anyway, would you mind telling her I called? It wasn't anything that can't wait until tomorrow. Just tell her I've definitely found another mum who wants to join our swapping group."

"Sure. Okay."

"Bye!"

The phone went dead. Ricky lowered its corpse slowly back onto the hook. The temperature of the room had fallen about fifteen degrees to a tomb-like coldness. His hand had gone numb, and refused to leave the receiver. In contrast to his outward sluggishness, Ricky's brain was racing, looking for calm, rational, sensible explanations for this situation. The coldness reached into the pit of his stomach. Boony had told him a flat-out lie. Where was she tonight if she wasn't with Lyndsay?

First of all, when he'd unwound his nerveless fingers from the phone, he went to look at the new kitchen calendar they'd bought. It hung on the hook in the kitchen, sitting on top of the old Buckley calendar for 1989. There were no entries on it whatsoever for January. He thought he'd go upstairs to the bedroom to see if there were any clues there. What, for example, was Boony wearing? She'd only stuck her head into the bathroom when she was leaving.

He opened the larger of the two wardrobes in the bedroom feeling seedy, like a private investigator on a case. He worked his way one by one along the coathangers, feeling the different textures of her clothes rippling against his fingertips. He wasn't certain he knew everything she had, but he thought it was her favourite 'little black dress' that had gone walkabout. Had she brought that to Scotland? He hadn't seen her wearing it here, but it was unlikely to have been packed away in Oregon. The bedroom had a lingering smell of perfume. She rarely wore perfume these days. He sat on the bed for a few moments, inhaling the simultaneous presence and absence of his wife.

So what was going on? Could Boony possibly be out with another man? Who? What had Marcus said earlier? Something about a man with a beard. Was that it? Was Boony making assignations with bearded men who hung around swimming pools? Boony? An affair?

He looked in at Marcus, sleeping soundly. Then he went back into their bedroom, breathed in the perfume again, and went down to the sitting room. He walked up and down, feeling trapped. He buried his fist in a cushion. He wanted to go out into night-time Forthburgh in search of his errant wife. He would punch the lights out of any man hanging around her and then drag Boony roughly back home- maybe by her hair, like a cartoon Neanderthal. He couldn't though. He didn't have a babysitter.

He made a coffee and slumped on the couch and tried to watch television. But it was some movie with a love scene. He flicked channels, and kept finding the same sort of thing. Couples talking intimately. Kissing. What was the problem with the media? Couldn't they show anything but sex? He switched off the television, and sat thinking about sex.

Boony never seemed very interested nowadays. He'd assumed it was a hormone thing, something to do with being a mother, being fulfilled. But maybe she was as horny as she had been when they were first married? Maybe it was just that she didn't want to do it with *him* any more?

It was time for the late evening news on TV. The Leaning Tower of Pisa had just been closed as unsafe. Another phallus mothballed. In East Berlin, thousands were besieging the Stasi headquarters, wanting to see their secret files. The world was full of secrets. What was Boony's?

At eleven fifteen he went upstairs. In the icy solitude of the bed he lay sleepless on his back, looking at the Arctic wastes of the ceiling and straining his ears for Boony's return. At last, just after midnight, he heard a car draw up outside and then drive off again. The key turned in the lock downstairs. It was a quiet turn, a furtive turn. Then the door opened, creaking, and was shut gently, ever so gently. So she thought he would be asleep did she? His ears followed her to the kitchen. A glass of water. Then footfalls on the stairs. He braced himself for her arrival. But she turned into Marcus's room. A moment there. Then into the bathroom. A long time passed. Much running of water. She was having a bath was she? She'd had a bath before she went out, for Christ's sake! What was she, a fish? Ricky couldn't stand it any longer. He got up, put on a jumper over his pyjamas, and went to confront his wife.

The bathroom door wasn't locked. He walked right in, and she looked up startled from the soapy water.

"What's going on Boony?"
"I'm having a bath, honey."
"Why are you having a bath?"
"What?"

"I don't mean that. I mean, where have you been tonight?"

"I told you before where I was going. Out for a few drinks in town."

"Who with?"

Boony stroked her stomach with the sponge. "There were a few of us.... Annie, Julia, Harriet...all mothers from the nursery, you know."

"What about Lyndsay? Was she there?"

The sponge moved up to her breasts and eased oozily around her nipples.

"Lyndsay? No. Lyndsay couldn't make it after all. Why - did she ring or something?"

A cloud was about to lift. Ricky willed it upwards, driving its shadow away from the calm landscape he knew so well.

"Yes - she rang."

"Did she leave a message?"

"No. She said it could wait until Monday."

"Did you talk to her?"

"Not really. You didn't say there was a whole group of you going out. I was confused when Lyndsay rang."

Boony slid down into the water until it lapped just under her chin. "I'm sorry honey. It was Lyndsay who arranged it all, so I just thought of it as going out to meet Lyndsay. But it was a shame she was the only one who couldn't make it."

Ricky stood like someone who has awakened from a nightmare to find himself safe and unharmed. He shook his head.

"Well... I'll get off to bed again. I was kind of confused, you know, when she rang."

"Sorry Ricky. I should have explained better. You get to sleep now. It must be late."

"Sure. See you in bed."

"Yeah. Go to sleep."

CHAPTER 28

March 1990

"Do you no want the other half of that scone?"

Duncan looked up, startled. He had been lost in a reverie. His friend Angus was pointing at his plate.

"You're in a dwam," Angus said.

"Aye. Sorry, Angus. I kind of drifted away there. Go on- have the rest of the scone, I'm not hungry."

Angus took the half scone, bit off a chunk, and spoke while masticating.

"So – I gather they're going to make your position permanent. Head of Ambient Interventions."

"Who told you?"

"The Vice-Principal."

"He's a leaky bucket. It's not official yet."

Angus fixed an accusatory look on him, through his round spectacle lenses.

"And you never let on, over all our beers at the Tap…"

"I can be discreet."

"Sly and secretive, you mean?"

"Fuck off!"

They laughed.

"So," Angus went on, "how will you be using your new power and influence?"

"I'll be getting rid of the fucking zebra-striped wallpaper in the office. It's doing my head in."

"Is that all? Anything else need changing?"

"Like what?"

Angus winked.

"A change of the department's name for next academic year?"

Duncan grinned.

"Right first time! Back to the 'Department of Sculpture'. I discussed it with the Principal and the Vice-Principal."

"So… are the students on board?"

"They will be. This year's lot are all Sidling disciples. Too late to turn them. Between you and me, there'll be no Firsts in this degree show. But I'm working on the second and third years. I'm softening them up with some illustrated lectures on the greats – Michelangelo, Bernini, Moore, Hepworth – all the big yins."

"I knew you were lying through your teeth when you were all over Sidling last summer."

"Didn't have any choice. I would have been well and truly shafted otherwise. I reckon he'd have found a way to get rid of me if I hadn't come on board."

"Well, I have to say you did it well. I tried a few times to get you to admit it."

"Aye – I was aware of that. I was tempted. I hope you don't mind, Angus. I know we're old pals, but I had to play the part *all* the time. If anyone had got wind of my real opinions…"

"They got that at your famous tirade in the lecture theatre did they no?"

"Aye, but that was before I saw which side my bread was buttered."

Angus stuffed the final piece of scone into his mouth and wiped the crumbs from his ginger beard with a napkin.

"Well," he said, "you're in clear water now laddie. Captain of the ship. Lucky you!"

Lucky? Duncan thought to himself later, as he made his way down the steep steps beside the old city wall towards the Brassmarket and The Bull's Tail. No, it wasn't luck that had brought him to where he was today. It was the vigour and determination of his own actions. He felt like a man who had grasped his opportunities, a man who had controlled his own destiny.

In the Brassmarket, he glanced behind him. He sometimes had a feeling that he was being watched, or followed. This was new. It had started in January and now it had become a frequent fancy, causing him to turn his head without any good reason, and to use shop windows as mirrors to check if anyone was on the other side of the street observing him.

Once, he had thought he saw Arabella. That was illogical. Stupid. It was just a woman with a passing resemblance to her, with her long, rather unruly hair. Nonetheless, it had sent a horrible shiver down his spine.

There was no-one of any concern behind him now. A couple of young women hurrying through the rain together, huddled under the shelter of a single umbrella held over their heads. Further off, anonymous people walking head down with hunched shoulders and upturned collars. Across the road, someone was loitering under the entrance to a shop, their face invisible under the canopy of an umbrella. He pushed open the door of The Bull's Tail.

In the shop doorway across the rain-splattered street, Ricky Love shivered a little with the cold, and watched him disappear into the pub.

It was through the merest chance that Ricky had been put on the trail of something odd going on this evening. A couple of days ago he'd thrown a magazine in the bin in the kitchen, and then remembered that there was an article in it that he'd intended to read. Fishing it out of the trash, a scrap of paper had got stuck to it. Half of a torn envelope. The adhesive was formed by some remnant of Marcus's food. Peeling it off the magazine cover he observed that there was a little bit of Boony's handwriting on the scrap of paper. It read *Bull's Tail. 5 pm Thursday 15th*. That was all.

This caused him a definite twinge of unease. He didn't want to ask about it, because it would look strange – as if he were rooting about suspiciously in trash cans, checking up on her. No doubt by Thursday the 15th she would have told him anyway what was happening at the *Bull's Tail*, which sounded like a pub.

It stuck in his mind, reviving unpleasant memories of that night when she was out so late. Finally, on the 14th, Boony broached the topic he had been waiting for.

"Oh, Ricky... could you pick up Marcus tomorrow after work?"

"Sure, I think so. What time?"

"At five – or five thirty at the latest. I'm meeting up with one of the other moms for a drink and a chat again."

"That's good. Lyndsay?"

"No. Harriet."

"You're getting a bit of a social life going!"

"Yes."

"Where are you meeting?"

"Just at a pub. Her little girl's gonna be at her grandmom's with her dad, so it'll give us a chance to chat without having to deal with the kids all the time."

"Great."

It preyed on his mind all that day at work. At lunchtime he took a walk down into the Brassmarket, only five minutes away. There were about a dozen pubs down there, and as he had already vaguely recollected, The Bull's Tail was one of them. At four fifty, feeling sleazy and furtive, he took up position in the doorway of a closed shop on the other side of the road. Rain was falling steadily. He was under cover in the doorway, but he put up his umbrella anyway. An anonymous black umbrella. He kept it low over his shoulders and peered out from under its cover, like a spy.

At five o'clock on the dot, a tall man walked quickly along the street and entered the pub. It was that moody guy from the Sculpture Department, Duncan McBane. Marcus's words came into his head. Was McBane the man with the beard?

At ten past five, just when he felt he had to leave in order to go and collect Marcus, he caught sight of Boony's red umbrella approaching the pub. She was moving fast in the rain, in spite of the high heels she had chosen to wear. He hunkered down even further under his own umbrella, but she didn't glance about her. She dived into the pub like a rabbit going down a rabbit hole.

He made his way out into the cold and wet, feeling as if the usually even keel of his ship was now pitching in a storm. Was Boony meeting in secret with this Duncan McBane guy? Or was it coincidence that had taken them both into the same pub at this early hour for drinking? Was the woman Harriet, the nursery gate acquaintance, already in there? No one else had entered while he was watching. He was burning to just walk into that pub and see if Boony was with McBane. But something was preventing him – and it wasn't just fear of being late to pick up Marcus. It was fear of provoking some dreadful rupture in his marriage, some confrontation from which neither he nor Boony would be able to draw back. He walked away quickly.

He said nothing to Boony about his suspicions in the following days, but he found it hard to maintain an air of normality. When Marcus was awake, they didn't have opportunities to talk much, and after he'd gone to bed they slumped in front of the television and watched strange British programmes: *Coronation Street; Last of the Summer Wine; 'Allo 'Allo*. The accents were almost impenetrable.

Boony didn't seem to notice that he was less communicative than usual. Only a week later, she announced another get-together with Harriet, the mum from the nursery gates. Once again the time was to be five o'clock - an early evening drink at Harriet's house, and once again Ricky was contracted to collect Marcus at five thirty after work – usually Boony got him late afternoon. Ricky didn't know this time where Boony was really going, so rather than stake out The Bull's Tail on the off chance, he thought he'd try to check his hunch about McBane's involvement. Maybe it was a long-shot, but at around four forty-five he positioned himself as unobtrusively as he could behind one of the broad pillars in the entrance hall of the art school. He pretended to be looking at some papers. It might look a little odd, but he didn't care what anyone happened to think about that. It was of no concern compared with the importance of his objective.

Five minutes later, Duncan McBane walked briskly through the entrance hall. He didn't see Ricky, but acknowledged Miggs with a nod. Miggs was standing behind the counter outside the janitors' office, and, as usual, offered no visible response. As McBane disappeared through the front doors, Ricky came out of hiding, stuffed his papers into his backpack, and headed for the doors himself, not too quickly – he didn't want to catch up with McBane. A faint woody aroma hung in the air near the exit – an aftershave? McBane's beard had looked freshly trimmed and he was wearing a smart dogtooth jacket. He looked very much to Ricky's tormented eyes like a man heading for a romantic assignation.

Chapter 29

March 1990

A little earlier that afternoon, Duncan McBane was in his office trying to work out how much limestone and marble he could afford to order for the stone-carving workshops he planned for the next term. It was high time that traditional skills regained their place in the curriculum. Not that the art school was a great follower of curricula – students were generally left to sink or swim by their own devices. However, in the Sculpture Department at least, he was going to introduce a bit more structure now that he was in charge. He prided himself on being a good planner. After all, he'd carried out two outrageous murders undetected, thanks to meticulous planning.

"May I have a word, Duncan?"

Duncan looked up from his desk. It was Artjoms – not Duncan's favourite student. He nodded non-commitally, and the black-clad figure insinuated itself further into the room. Duncan did not invite him to sit.

"I was wonder if you could give me some guidances about my final year project."

"What sort of guidance?"

"You know I am hoping to get good degree. Good high level degree. First, I hope."

"Everyone hopes for that, I dare say," Duncan said with a shrug.

"But I am confusing now, Duncan, a little. Because I send my work in a direction, you know. The direction that Steve tells me, when he is here. The ambient interventions. But now I don't know the direction any more. I don't know if my make the kratts at the different crossroads in Forthburgh is going to get for me the First class degree."

"Oh yes. The *kratts*. All to do with selling the soul to the Devil, aren't they?"

"Yes."

"Have you sold your soul to the Devil, Artjoms?"

"Me? I don't really believe. The only devils are people. Like the devil that kill poor Steven. And this new lady, with her head taken off. That is real devil at work. But I think idea of the *kratts* is very interesting."

Duncan nodded.

"Listen, Artjoms. This is my advice. You still have three months or so. Forget about *ambient interventions*. When you came here in the first year of the course, you did well in the carving and casting workshops. You produced some good work. You've gone off more recently in the wrong direction, but you can still find your way back, if you start on something now, drawing on those traditional sculpting skills. I'd recommend doing something with wood. It's quicker for you to work with. Make some small pieces in wood. Nothing too ambitious."

"But if I'm not ambitious, how do I get the First? You see, I need the First because I want to go on in this field. I want to be like you or Steve, one day, lecturer in sculpture somewhere. In my native country perhaps."

"Well, I'd suggest you think differently now, Artjoms. To be honest, with the time you have left and the time you've wasted messing about with ambient this and that, you'll do well to get a decent degree at all. As for a First, your hopes are dead in the water as far as I'm concerned."

Artjoms stood as though stunned. Duncan looked down at his calculations again.

"You are telling me now, Duncan? You are telling me now my degree result, before the work is even submit?"

Duncan raised his head again, and made a face, raising his eyebrows and turning down the corners of his mouth. It was an admission, only not in words.

"But it is a committee, no? The examiners. It's not just you?"

Artjoms sounded desperate, pleading. Duncan nodded.

"It's a committee, as you say Artjoms. A committee chaired by the Head of Sculpture. That's me now."

He left it at that, and looked down once more at his papers. He heard Artjoms moving, and only looked up again when he was sure that he'd gone. He'd teach that insolent Estonian to call him *Fishface*!

An hour later he glanced at his watch – nearly a quarter to five. He had another date with Boony at five, at a wine bar at the west end of Princess Street. It was slow going, wooing this American woman. This would be their third encounter after their initial meeting, and he hadn't got so far as kissing her on the lips yet. But he felt a growing confidence that her scruples would be overcome. She wouldn't be meeting him like this at all if it was going nowhere. Sure, he lent a sympathetic ear to her complaints of boredom here in Forthburgh: how she wished Ricky wasn't so completely taken up with his work at the art school; how she wished they could do more cinema going, theatre going, eating out; how having little Marcus was lovely but she missed her independence. He could put up with all of that. Their meetings weren't entirely taken up with humdrum chatter on her side - she also exhibited a charming fascination with his own discourses on art and life. Her eyes stayed fixed on him as he talked, as if he were dropping pearls of wisdom. It was a sure sign, that eye contact. A sure sign that he was onto a good thing, if he was patient. He hadn't had sex with anyone since Arabella. It was 'a consummation devoutly to be wished' as Hamlet put it – but Duncan didn't mean death, on this occasion.

It was drizzling a little outside, and the late March light was almost gone from the sky. He turned up his coat collar and set off. His route took him along a path that skirted the Castle Rock, as it was called. High above him, the castle itself seemed to be exuding moisture like a squeezed sponge, causing thin streams of water to dribble down the granite cliffs below.

Yet again he had that unsettling feeling that someone was behind him. He stopped for a moment and looked back the way he had come. It was murky – even a hint of fog was forming among the trees beside the path. He could see someone - a man - moving towards him. It looked a bit like that annoying Artjoms, although he couldn't be sure. He was a long way back, and someone else was coming along behind that figure too, with an umbrella. Well, there were always people coming and going along this path, which was a short cut to the West End. Up ahead he heard a train tooting as it pulled out of Walter Scott Station. He shrugged off his sense of unease and moved onwards, turning his thoughts to the lovely pink lips, as yet unkissed, of Boony Love, and the delightful tête-à-tête that was awaiting him.

Ricky had Duncan McBane well in his sights, and felt safe from observation. Not only was he under his umbrella, and a long way back, but there was also an intervening pedestrian, a young man with long dark hair who seemed oblivious to the rain.

As McBane crossed the footbridge spanning the railway line that took the trains westward out of Forthburgh, he made a sudden, strange, sideways lunge. Ricky was too far away to make out why he did that, and the young man about twenty yards in front of him partially blocked his view. Above the sound of an approaching train, there was a piercing squeal, as of an animal in distress. Ricky felt a cold shiver at that sound.

McBane however seemed to be proceeding just as before after this odd movement, walking on at a steady pace towards… Ricky's wife?

Now the young man with dark hair was on the footbridge. He paused, at about the same place as Duncan's sideways lunge, and peered over the parapet. There was something down there that held his attention for a few seconds. Ricky held back. He wanted to look too. Then the young man walked onwards, and Ricky stepped onto the bridge and went to the parapet. The sound of the train on the tracks diminished westwards, and in the silence left in its wake Ricky looked down at the bloodied furry corpse of a cat on the edge of the tracks. A cold fury rose in him, as it always did when he saw animal suffering. Had the bastard pushed this innocent animal to its death? It very much looked like it.

He withdrew his gaze, trembling with anger. McBane belonged to the same bloody fraternity as those deer hunters with crossbows! Looking ahead again, he saw that the killer was getting too far away. Soon he would ascend the steps out of Princess Gardens and merge with the bustle of Princess Street. The young man with the dark hair had diverged onto another path. Ricky quickened his pace so as not to lose sight of his quarry.

CHAPTER 30

March 1990

Coupar was getting ready to call it a day when his phone rang.

"Inspector Coupar Cruickshank speaking."

"It's Miggs here. From the art school."

"Oh yes. Hello, Mr Miggs."

"I've got something for you."

"Oh?"

"Aye. It might be nothing, but I thought I'd pass it on."

"Go on, Mr Miggs."

"You might remember I was saying about that American fella? Ricky Love he calls himself."

"Yes?"

"You remember I was saying he acted strange?"

"Yes, I remember."

"Right. You know our Head of Sculpture? Or whatever they call it the noo."

"Duncan McBane? Is he made head of that department now?"

"Aye. Anyway, this evening, Duncan McBane was coming out of the art school. He was coming through the entrance hall here. Well, this Ricky Love guy, he was kinda hangin' aboot – I'd wondered why – and when McBane came through, this American dodges behind one o' they pillars, y'ken."

"As if he was hiding?"

"Aye. He was hidin' all right. And when McBane goes oot through the main door, this Ricky Love comes oot of his hidiehole an' goes oot on his tail, like he's following him."

"Do they know each other?"

"I dinnae ken. They might do. They both work here."

"But you've never seen them talking?"

"No, no that I can mind."

"So you have no idea why Ricky Love would surreptitiously follow Duncan McBane?"

"That's it in a nutshell. Genius."

Coupar bridled. He'd had enough sarcasm, open or covert, over these murder investigations.

"Do you have anything useful to add?"

"No."

"Thank you, Mr Miggs. Please let me know if you see anything else odd."

"Aye."

The phone went dead before Coupar could hang up himself. Well, he supposed he should be grateful that Miggs was passing on information. Although he had a feeling that Miggs simply had some grudge or dislike for the American – he hadn't passed on any unsolicited information about anyone else. He called over to Price, who was poring over some paperwork and scratching his ears alternately in a corner of the incident room.

"Price. Get photocopies done of the photos of Duncan McBane and Ricky Love. They're for you. I want you to hang out near the door of the art school for a day or two, discreetly, from around four in the afternoon onwards and watch for either of them coming out. I've had a report that Ricky Love is following Duncan McBane in secret."

"How do you know they'll come out at that time of day?"

"Well – they've got homes to go to I suppose."

"It's bloody freezing, just standing about."

"Are you questioning my instructions, Price?"

"No… just saying…"

"Wear warm clothes. Take a thermos flask if you want. Find a good vantage point where you won't be seen from the door of the art school."

"If I can see the door, then I can be seen."

"Not if you're careful. No one will be looking out for you."

"People will think I'm a pervert or something. Those pretty art school lassies…"

"Well, that's just part and parcel of being a detective, Price. One is often misunderstood by the general public."

Driving home from work, Coupar got stuck in traffic. As he sat in the stationary car, or edged forwards a few tantalizing yards, he mulled over the new information that had come to light: Ricky Love surreptitiously following Duncan McBane out of the art school. Did this have anything at all to do with the crimes he was trying to solve? He had already discounted certain other strands that had preoccupied him before this second crime – the thwarted investigation of the members of the Devil's Dungeon, and trying to identify the mysterious 'London enemy' of Sidling. He was completely concentrated now upon the denizens of the art school itself. Around two hundred academic and non-academic staff, including part-timers, and about a thousand students. Somewhere in this collection of people lurked the killer, like a cancer cell in an otherwise healthy body. Whoever had killed Arabella Wood, at least, was someone who had an intimate knowledge of the art school - a familiarity with its details. They had chosen an obscure and out of the way place to commit the crime. They had known about the glass display cases in the Jewellery department. They had left the head in the prominent location of the Sculpture Court. They had made their exit through a ground floor window in a painting studio. This was almost certainly the work of a student or a member of the staff. If the previous murder of Steven Sidling out in the woods of Deil's Glen were not an outrageous coincidence, then surely the same maniac was at work. Also, in both cases, a kind of message had been left – the illegible rain-soaked note and the little card that read *Portrait*. These details also argued for the same perpetrator.

His thoughts circled back to Hermione Cutter. It was she who had led Arabella to her place of slaughter, like a lamb. Was the killer already in that shower room? Or did he enter afterwards? Could it possibly have been Ricky Love? Why would he have done it? And he'd barely arrived in Forthburgh when Sidling was murdered...

A car honked behind him, making him jump. A thirty yard gap had opened up in front of him. He edged forward to close it.

Finally he reached the roundabout that was causing the hold-up. Cars were edging slowly around it, blocking the entrances and exits. It was a shambles. At first he couldn't see why this problem had arisen, and then he observed that in the centre of the roundabout – usually just a grassy space – a large and strange object had appeared. It looked as if it were constructed from old bicycles and scraps of corrugated iron. It was imposing – over ten feet high – and it seemed to be a gigantic figure, a kind of giant in fact. What was most arresting about it was the sense of menace it gave off. Its metallic arms were both raised. One claw, made from barbed wire as far as he could make out, wielded a kind of scimitar, and the other clasped a doll-like figurine. The head was huge, out of proportion with the body, with dustbin lids for eyes and a jagged tin nose projecting downwards almost like an elephant's trunk over a shaggy tangle of beard made from multi-coloured strands of electrical wire.

It was drivers rubbernecking this inexplicable apparition that was causing the hold up, and Coupar was aware that he was as guilty as the rest of them, edging around the roundabout slowly and cautiously so that he could get a good look at it. Had the city council erected this monstrosity? Or sanctioned its erection? It was hideous! It exuded an aura of threat and chaos, of evil he might almost say. What was strangest of all, to his eyes, was that in spite of its peculiar constituent parts, it bore some uncanny resemblance to that bearded sculpture lecturer at the art school, Duncan McBane.

CHAPTER 31

March 1990

Sometimes Hermione could barely rouse the necessary volition to get out of bed and fulfil her duties at the art school. But she forced herself to do it because walking around the studios to talk to the students about their work, conducting life drawing classes, and interacting, however superficially, with other human beings were the only palliatives she knew for her wretchedness. She came out of her dejection on these working days, only to relapse quickly in the aching silence of her house in Martinside. It was not only the dashing of her hopes of getting Ted back that was putting her on the rack – it was also guilt and regret. Never a person with many close friends, she looked back now with a painfully ironic fondness to those wine-fuelled evenings with Arabella in the years before she introduced her to Ted. If only she had a friend like that now!

She fell in with Ricky Love sometimes in the art school canteen. Talking with him was another easement for her suffering. His quiet, straightforward manner and his sympathetic readiness to take the reins of the conversation when he could see that she was in the doldrums, and tell her things about life in Oregon and about America in general were a little ray of light in her gloom. He seemed to exist in a better, simpler world, and his family life at home shone in her mind's eye as a radiant little vignette of happiness. That was how she remembered the early years of her marriage with Ted, when little Roland came along and life was full of joy. If this was a sentimental weakness – even, perhaps, a fantasy - she didn't care. She needed a little comfort in these dark days.

She and Duncan didn't speak to each other now, at the art school or anywhere else. Their partnership, such as it was, had existed for a single murderous purpose. She still had the sinister, powerful portrait of him in her home studio, and that was as much of him as she wanted in her life now. But she observed him surreptitiously, when she happened to see him at the art school because he now held a horrid fascination for her. It was like being trapped in a room with a poisonous snake, never knowing when it might emerge from a hiding place. He seemed, to her, to slither about with a new energy and confidence. He had been appointed head of his department now, and she noticed that everyone had reverted to calling it the Department of Sculpture. No doubt he'd get the name changed back again officially, as soon as he could do that through Academic Council.

His appearance had smartened up as well, she observed. He seemed to have dug out once more the clothes that first appeared when he was in a relationship with Arabella. She remembered Arabella telling her about their shopping trips together – how she had to force open Duncan's wallet with a crowbar in the attempt to make him presentable. How they had laughed together over those stories, she and Arabella! It was a distant, innocent, world away now.

It happened, one evening, that she was passing through the entrance hall of the art school when she saw Ricky Love detach himself from behind one of its classical pillars and hurry out of the doors. The janitor, Miggs, was staring after him. She passed Miggs herself, saying "Goodnight!", and paused in the portico to put up her umbrella, as it was raining lightly. She saw Ricky Love a few yards ahead of her, out in the rain, putting up his own umbrella belatedly, getting wet. His attention was obviously focussed on something else. He was watching a tall figure receding in the evening gloom, coat collar turned up and shoulders hunched. That figure was unmistakeably Duncan McBane. As it turned a corner out of sight, Ricky hurried off in the same direction.

Hermione brooded over this for much of the next day. It looked very much as if Ricky was following Duncan. What could that mean? Could it be that Duncan had continued his connection with Ricky's wife – the connection she had observed at what was probably its inception, at the private view of the totem pole? Had Ricky somehow got wind of that? Try as she might, she couldn't think of any other explanation. Was she mistaken about Ricky following Duncan? She pictured his anxious movements again, the way he'd put up his umbrella with his eyes fixed on the other man. No, she was not mistaken.

This incident poured fuel on the fire of a sense of anger and outrage that was already building up slowly within her towards Duncan. Knowing what she did, she could only wonder in disgust at the way he seemed to be flourishing, like a poisonous toadstool on decomposing remains. But – worse - if he had now embarked on a secret affair with another man's wife, the wife of lovely, harmless Ricky Love… well, that really did twist a bitter knife in her guts. That made him exactly the same sort of marriage-wrecker as Arabella had turned out to be. Weren't there enough unattached women in the world for him to turn his attention to? She began to see a hitherto unperceived connection between Duncan and Arabella. Ruthless egotists - narcissists even- the both of them, who would trample each other, and the rest of the world, if it was necessary to attain their own satisfactions. Yes, perhaps that was the connection that had drawn them together into that short-lived relationship of theirs - and perhaps why the relationship contained the seeds of its own destruction.

The next day, at the art school, she saw Ricky ahead of her in the coffee queue. Should she speak with him about his wife? What could she say? What if she was wrong? And if she was right, what did he know already?

He certainly didn't know how dangerous a man Duncan McBane was. But she couldn't tell him much about that.

Ricky came past her with his coffee. Still undecided, she didn't avert her eyes from him and he looked at her in a slightly startled way, she thought.

"Are you okay, Hermione?"

"Hi Ricky. Yes, just a bit tired that's all. I'm not sleeping well. Do I look so bad?"

He probably thought she did, but he smiled.

"No, no. *Tired* covers it. You just look rather tired. Do you want to sit together? Over there?"

He indicated one of the small tables with only two seats.

"Yes, of course. Good idea."

When she sat down with him, she said, feeling her way, "you have a worried look."

Ricky thought to himself that if anyone had a worried look, it was Hermione. Perhaps not so much worried as *depressed*. She'd raised a smile when he first spoke to her, but it was like a winter sun just barely penetrating the mists over a frosty field.

However, he nodded, unable to deny her observation. He *was* worried.

"I don't want to pry," she went on, "but is there anything I can help with? I mean… is it anything here at the art school?"

"Yes and no," Ricky said slowly. "Its not a work-related thing. More personal."

He hesitated. He wasn't given to sharing confidences, and he didn't know Hermione very well. On the other hand, he was burning to share his problem. Maybe another person's perspective would help. He cleared his throat.

"It's... well... I can tell you something in confidence can't I, Hermione?"

"Of course."

He took the plunge.

"It's to do with my wife, Boony. I think she may be having an affair... or, at least, she's meeting someone without telling me."

"Duncan McBane," Hermione said.

Ricky looked stunned. He even moved back a little on his chair, as if she had pushed him in the chest.

"God! Does everyone know?"

Hermione made a wry twist of her lips and shook her head.

"No. I don't' think anyone else has noticed anything. But I was at the unveiling of his totem pole sculpture for Deil's Glen. That's when I think he first met your wife. I saw them going off together afterwards."

"So that's when it happened! Back in early January."

He looked so crestfallen! She felt a sudden flare up of that anger she had stored up like tinder inside her.

"It's so awful! Breaking into a perfectly good marriage like a... like a thief! Not giving a fuck if they destroy it.! It's unbearably selfish!"

Ricky was surprised by the depth of feeling in her voice, and he had never heard her swear before. This had obviously struck a chord with her. He knew she wasn't with her husband any more, but he didn't know why.

"Did you... is that what happened to you?" he said hesitantly.

"Yes. A predatory, selfish... someone who I thought was a friend..."

She choked on her anger. Ricky was struck by a thought.

"What... what was your husband's name again?"

"Ted."

Ted. That name had cropped up from time to time in the weeks last autumn when he and Arabella had become friendly. Belatedly, he put two and two together. How had he been so slow to see this connection? Arabella – poor, murdered Arabella – was the woman who had stolen Hermione's husband!

Hermione was pulling herself together. She wiped a corner of her eye with a paper tissue.

"I'm sorry," she said. "It's all a bit raw."

"I'm sorry I've brought it up. I can see it's touched a nerve with you."

"No. No – it was me who brought it up. I'd noticed you looked sad."

She put the tissue away and leaned forward.

"Listen, Ricky. You have to confront this before it goes any further. Speak to your wife. Tell her you know what's going on. And..."

She hesitated for a long moment, and then leaned even closer. Her voice was hardly more than a whisper.

"... and tell her... tell her Duncan McBane is a dangerous man to get mixed up with."

Ricky went home that evening with his stomach churning. He had to tackle Boony about what was going on, and he had no idea how she would react. Would she try to deny it? Brazen it out? Would she reveal some yawning chasm in the surface of their marriage that he had been unaware of? Had she stopped loving him? Would she take herself – and Marcus - back to Oregon? Or away to live with Duncan McBane! How could she associate with such a man? The bloodied corpse of that dead cat came into his memory. A man who could do that to an innocent animal! And – according to Hermione – a *dangerous* man! He felt as if his whole world was on a shaky footing, and might fall about his ears.

At home – or the Buckley house that they called such - he had to act normally for around three hours until Marcus was finally settled. He tried to respond to Boony's account of the day, delivered in her usual tone of putting a brave face on a round of tedium. They ate a Spaghetti Bolognese, which he forced down as if he were chewing on socks and string. Boony drank three glasses of red wine. He just had one. He needed his wits about him. He read Marcus's bedtime story and waited until his eyes closed and his breathing slowed. He lingered a moment longer, treasuring this precious moment of time with the little guy, and worrying about how assured he could be of such moments in the future. Then he descended the creaky staircase slowly as if labouring in the opposite direction, upwards to a gibbet.

Boony was in the living room watching television. She didn't look up as he entered the room. It was a soap opera which she'd taken to viewing, set in some part of London where everyone was nasty to each other. An irate man was confronting a woman in a kitchen. *You're lying to me!* he said, face torn between thespian versions of anger and incredulity. One hand clutched at his hair, as if in response to a hand signal from the director. The woman carried on slicing tomatoes at the kitchen work surface. *Calm down*! she said. *You're making a mountain out of a molehill!* She faced the camera, talking with her back to the man, who moved up closer behind her until his agitated face looked as if it were perched on her shoulder, like a piqued parrot. This was how people frequently talked in soap operas, both facing the camera for maximum facial display.

"Mind if I turn this off?" Ricky said, pointing to the television.

"I thought I'd watch it." Boony said, not taking her eyes off the screen.

"I'd rather talk, Boony. I think we should talk."

Anyway! said the woman, turning and pointing the tomato knife uncomfortably close to the man's throat. *You're no goddam angel! You.....*

Ricky pressed the off switch on the television's remote control, which was held together with sellotape. He sat down in the easy chair. Boony was on the couch. Once, not so very long ago, they had sat on couches together. Boony would put her legs up on his legs, and he'd maybe massage the soles of her feet. She loved that. She said her feet were her second most erogenous zone. But she'd never had her feet up on his legs on this Buckley couch, and maybe never would. He glanced towards her feet now, tucked defensively underneath her, impregnable.

"What's going on, Boony?" he said.

She continued to look at the television, as if the soap opera were still dimly visible on the darkened screen. She wasn't making this easy.

"What do you mean, *going on*?" she said eventually, still not looking at him. Her face was hard; the colour of her flesh was all wrong. His wife had been replaced by an unfriendly wax effigy.

He tried to find words that were not clichés, tried to ignore the sensation that they were actors in another soap opera.

"I mean.... Boony...I mean, well, in a nutshell...you don't seem to be very loving towards me any more. And now you've started going out and lying to me. What's the story?"

Boony looked at him now. Her eyes were wider than normal. She spoke aggressively.

"What do you mean, *lying* to you?"

"Boony, I know about this. You're meeting up with a guy who lectures at the art school. Duncan McBane."

Aggression was replaced with doubt in Boony's face. It looked as if she was uncertain whether or not to continue with outright denial.

"How do you know?" she said, still with a note of challenge in her tone.

"There's someone I have coffee with there occasionally, a lecturer in Fine Art. She was at the private view of the McBane guy's totem pole thing. She saw you going off together."

"That was nothing. He just invited me for a drink."

"And then there was that time you were meeting up with Lyndsay and she rang?"

Boony's eyes flickered away upwards. She was still going for denial.

"I explained all that."

"And I saw you and McBane going into a pub in the Brassmarket – The Bull's Tail. And another time I saw you meeting him in a wine bar in the West End."

"You *saw*?"

"One time I found a note you'd written, the other time I followed him from the art school and then saw you too."

"You were *spying* on me!"

It looked to Ricky like Boony had now decided that attack was the best form of defence. He was right. She launched an offensive.

"What do you expect, Ricky? You drag me away from my home to this God-forsaken place and just leave me to get on with it as best I can! You've got your work, your Forthburgh Art School. What have I got? You knew I didn't want to come here!"

Ricky felt caught out in an unexpected downpour without an umbrella. He knew she'd needed talking around, but this negativity now was a shock.

"Well....I knew you were reluctant at first. But I thought you came to see it like me in the end…" he pictured briefly the conversations they'd had last spring, sitting on their deck under cherry blossom, sunlight and shadows dancing across Boony's face, "… a chance to live in a different culture. See a different way of life. It's only for a year."

"Only! God! Every week lasts more than a year for me! Stuck in this cramped little hutch looking out at the rain! Trying to keep Marcus amused with the crap these Buckleys left behind them. God! It's been desperate Ricky! Desperate!"

She glared at him accusingly, the author of her misfortunes. Her wax face had become suffused with angry red.

"It would be raining more in Oregon right now than it does here, Boony. You can't blame rain."

She dismissed this pathetic point with a gesture.

"You're so bound up in your work Ricky. What do you know about the weather? Or anything else? You haven't wanted to know about *me* since we got here, about how *I* might be feeling!"

He felt thoroughly wrong-footed. He had to get this conversation back on the right track.

"Listen, Boony, we go home in three months. It's not so long. But what's more important, what you have to tell me… are you in love with this guy?"

She stared at him as if he'd turned into an extra-terrestrial.

"*In love*? For God's sake, Ricky! I've met the guy a few times in a pub. Sure, he's attractive. Sure I get a kick out of it. It's a bit of excitement in this desert of boredom. But *in love!* Not in a million years."

"Have you… I have to know this…"

Boony interrupted him.

"Ricky, I haven't even kissed him goodbye. We just talk, that's all, we just talk."

"Why have you had to lie to me then?"

"Oh, come on! Use your head. Would you have liked it? Me meeting up one-to-one with another man? Look at how you're reacting!"

"That's because of the lying, Boony. It's not because of what you've done – or haven't done. It's the lying that hurts."

Then, quite suddenly, the hard, defiant face crumpled. Sobbing, Boony scrambled to her feet, ran out of the room, and up the stairs. He heard the bedroom door shutting up there. So – now what did he do?

He moved to the vacated couch and after a while he saw it was time for the evening news programme. He turned it on. Anything was better than just sitting there. Down in England it appeared that everyone was running riot over the Poll Tax again. He watched images of burning barricades and police baton charges. Soon he and Boony and Marcus would be back in their quiet backwater Oregon once more – wouldn't they?

Upstairs, he heard Boony running a bath. He thought maybe she'd just go to bed early. But twenty minutes later she surprised him. She came into the living room in her white fluffy bathrobe, sat down next to him on the couch, and snuggled into his side. She got hold of the remote control and banished the noise and fury of the rioters to a blank screen.

"I'm sorry, Ricky!" she said softly. "I've been thinking it all over. I shouldn't have done what I did. And you're right, it's only three more months here. And now maybe you know better how I feel... maybe you can pay me more attention?"

He turned towards her. Her lips were slightly parted. She gave him a long look, and then leaned in and kissed him. He moved his hand to the shoulder of the bathrobe and slid it downwards. She was wearing nothing underneath. Her kiss grew more passionate, and then she pulled away a little and shrugged the bathrobe down further, revealing her breasts.

"Let's have sex, Ricky. Right here! It's been too long."

A few days later, Duncan was drinking his fourth whisky in The Bull's Tail. The scent of Boony's perfume still lingered faintly in the air about him. She'd been in there sitting opposite him for about three minutes.

"I can't keep seeing you, Duncan. I wanted to tell you in person, not with a phone call. I owe you that much. I'm sorry. Ricky's found out, and I've promised to stop this. I've told him nothing's happened between us, that we've just been talking. Of course... you know... it might have gone further. But... it didn't. I've got to be sensible now. I'm very fond of you, Duncan. And there *is* something between us – I *am* attracted to you. But it's got to stop now."

Duncan shook his head regretfully, like a lion that has just seen a gazelle twisting nimbly out of his reach and running off into the long grass.

"We've been so careful," he said. "How did he find out?"

"Someone said something to him at the art school. Some woman had seen us, and told him."

"A woman?"

"Yes. One of the lecturers. She was at the unveiling of your totem pole apparently, and saw us leaving together. And then later he found a note with the name of this pub on it in the trash. Duncan - it doesn't matter how he found out. The lies I was making up about meeting other mothers... sooner or later I'd have slipped up. We shouldn't have let it get as far as this. I'm so sorry."

Then she'd stood up, leaned in quickly to peck his cheek, and walked quickly out of the pub. Like a vanishing dream, leaving a half- finished glass of white wine and a zephyr of perfume.

The feeling that suddenly overwhelmed him then took him by surprise. He felt a stinging sensation in his eyes. This was the same place where Arabella had ended their relationship. His feelings for Boony didn't remotely match that intense feeling that Arabella had inspired in him. But this sudden withdrawal brought all that old misery and anger bubbling to the surface once more. As he drank steadily, it was the anger that began to predominate. The ultimate bedding of this attractive

American woman had become a sanguine expectation: no more than what was due to the new triumphant Duncan McBane, Head of Sculpture and lord of all he surveyed. A man with power over life and death, like a tyrant. When he'd read about Nero and Caligula at school, he'd imagined himself in their shoes – or sandals – and how he would deal with anyone who crossed him. In his imaginings, he tore the wings off the tormenting gadflies who called him Fishface!

Well... he'd been too complacent in his pomp, and now he'd been thwarted! He had little doubt about who had betrayed him. It must have been Hermione Cutter. He'd observed her and Ricky cosying up at coffee breaks in the art school. Seeing her talking to anyone, anyone at all, always made him feel anxious. Her agonized appearance gave him the feeling that she might not be relied upon with the heavy secret that she carried. He knew that her husband had not come back to her – she'd told him that in a brief exchange of words one day. The look that she gave him then seemed to convey that it was his fault: that the elaborate and extreme act of removing Arabella had been a failure. She – who should have been grateful! She was an accomplice to the crime, but would that stop her blurting something out, deliberately or by accident, in the depths of her despair? She was a liability, a weakness, and now she had meddled in this other matter deliberately to undermine him!

With three successful murders under his belt, why not a fourth? A Nero or a Caligula would not hesitate.

CHAPTER 32

April 1990

It was the end of term at Bristol University, and Hermione was looking forward to having Roland with her again over the Easter break. She thought he would perhaps have preferred to stay down south – apparently he had started seeing a new girl – but he had been definite about coming up to see her. She felt a glow of maternal love and pride. He was an affectionate boy, and she could tell that he was worried about her.

When the doorbell rang at around eight in the evening she was surprised. His train wasn't due in for another fifteen minutes, and then it would take him at least that long to get a bus up to Martinside. Perhaps the train had arrived early? Or maybe he'd splashed out on a taxi because of his baggage? She went to the door in a state of happy anticipation. She was determined to be as positive and cheerful for Roland as she possibly could.

When she opened the door and found Duncan McBane there, it was a big surprise, and certainly not a pleasant one. The only time they'd exchanged any words since the murder of Arabella was in one very short conversation: he'd asked her if she'd got back with Ted, as their paths crossed outside the main door.

So, as he stood before her in the early evening gloaming, she took an involuntary step backwards. He smiled a ghastly smile and she summoned all her strength to return it, as if they were normal people and the world was a normal place.

"I thought we should have a chat, Hermione," he said. "Can I come in?"

How she longed to shut the door on him! It would be better if he didn't even exist! But she stood aside and he entered, wiping his feet carefully on the mat.

Duncan had planned this evening's visit much less meticulously than his elimination of Sidling and Arabella. But, after all, he had killed Aunt Janet in a very ad hoc fashion, and got away with it. Hermione's death was going to look like a suicide. She'd been going around looking like a corpse since January. He presumed that her errant husband Ted hadn't come back to her since he'd enquired. It certainly didn't look like it. No one would be too surprised if she took her own life. She'd amassed all those pills in her bathroom cabinet. Her pharmacist's collection. Who would be surprised if she was found dead somewhere in her house, with an empty bottle of pills and an empty bottle of spirits nearby?

They went into the living room. The curtains were drawn. That was good.

"Can I offer you a drink then, Duncan?" Hermione said. She sounded as if she would rather offer him poison.

"Have you a whisky in the house?"

"Of course. Macallan?"

"Fine."

He'd have to remember everything he touched. He had a clean handkerchief to wipe things down. Not that it was essential. He'd been in the house before, after all. He wouldn't deny that. The portrait painting was the reason. This would look so very much like suicide. An open and shut case.

Hermione went into the kitchen and got the whisky bottle out of the cupboard. She poured one for herself too and returned reluctantly to the sitting room. She gave him his glass and sat down opposite him.

"Cheers!" Duncan said.

She raised her own glass, mechanically, and they both took a sip of whisky.

"So... how have you been, Hermione? We haven't spoken for a while."

"I'm all right, Duncan."

She put her glass down on the little table at her elbow.

"Why have you come?" she said.

Duncan smiled that shark-like smile of his. It made her go cold all over.

"I was concerned about you, Hermione. I've seen you about the art school, and I've thought to myself, *poor Hermione doesn't look well.* In fact, I've thought you look depressed. Can I ask you something?"

She looked blankly at him.

"What?"

"You told me that you and Ted... that you hadn't got back together. I wondered if that had changed. Have you been in contact with him again?"

She looked at him. The hypocrite! That voice of fake concern! What did he care about marriages surviving? She gestured to the empty house around them.

"He doesn't seem to be here, does he?"

Duncan nodded, as if sadly.

"Well, nothing's changed since we spoke before," she went on. "In fact, he's going off to London shortly. He's sick of Forthburgh. And me, apparently."

"That's a shame, Hermione. That's such a shame."

Again that tone of sympathy that made her sick! She wanted to show her anger. She wanted to tell him to leave Ricky Love's wife alone. But she didn't dare. Alone with this man, she didn't dare show her anger.

"I've started seeing a therapist," she said.

It wasn't true, but she was thinking about it. She thought it would put Duncan on his guard. The question kept coming back to her: why had he come?

"A therapist?"

"A psychotherapist. Someone to talk to."

"Isn't that a bit risky, Hermione? Knowing what you do. Having done what you did?"

"You're worried I might blurt something out?"

"Well... you need to be careful."

"Not as careful as you need to be, Duncan."

"What?"

She couldn't hold it in any more.

"You should lay off Ricky Love's wife."

Duncan took a big gulp of his whisky before replying. His eyes were wandering oddly about the room.

"It's too late," he said.

"What?"

"She's broken off with me. Someone told her husband, and so she broke off. That was you, wasn't it Hermione? You told him, didn't you?"

Now his cold eyes settled on her, and she felt a wave of fear. Had he come here to kill her? She knew he was capable of it. How long would it be until Roland arrived? What should she do? Her mind raced.

Duncan's mind was also busy with calculations. Hermione was thin and most likely weak. She wouldn't be able to put up much of a fight. He didn't want any signs of a struggle. He thought he would get her onto the floor, and then get one of these plump cushions over her face, and push it down hard onto her nose and mouth until she stopped breathing. Then he'd get some suitable pills from the bathroom cabinet and pour whisky and pills into her mouth. He'd prop up her head so that gravity would take the mixture down her throat.

He downed the rest of his glass of whisky and stood up decisively. It would be best to act swiftly, without giving her time to be on her guard. Hermione shrank back in her chair.

The doorbell rang.

"Who's that?" Duncan said, startled.

"My son, Roland," Hermione replied.

Duncan stood for a moment, perplexed. Hermione stood up herself. She was trembling all over.

"I'll go and let him in. He's come back for Easter."

Duncan nodded. He felt like a punctured balloon; all the adrenaline that had coursed through him a moment ago had dissipated.

"I'll go then. But, Hermione, listen to me. Don't mess with me, all right? I don't need you poking your nose into my affairs."

"Or else what?" Hermione said.

Duncan shook his head. The doorbell rang again, a long ring.

"I'm the one with the power here, Duncan," Hermione said. Now that she was safe, she felt angry and emboldened. "So don't threaten me."

"Who was that Duncan guy?" Roland said. Hermione had introduced him as 'a friend from the art school' as they crossed each other's paths at the front door. They had shaken hands, and then Duncan walked off quickly without any conversation taking place.

"Don't you recognize him?"

"Wait a minute… is he the guy in the portrait?"

"Well done!"

"I didn't know you still kept up with him."

"I don't. He was just passing, and wanted another look at the painting."

"Is he going to buy it?"

"It's not for sale."

Roland gave her a penetrating look.

"He's not a new *boyfriend* is he?"

Hermione laughed. A genuine laugh, but with a slight edge of hysteria in its notes.

"No. Definitely not a boyfriend!"

With the help of a few drinks – several drinks - and a more than usually communicative and voluble Roland, Hermione gradually relaxed and enjoyed the evening.

But when she was in bed, sleep evaded her. She kept replaying Duncan's unexpected visit in her head. She was frightened that he might come back to the house when she was alone. She would never open the door to him again, but he might find a way in, or catch her in some deserted place. Did he want her dead? What could she do? Could she denounce him to the police without revealing her own hand in Arabella's death? And what evidence did she have? None. The problem went around and around in her head, without a solution. There was really only one good solution. The best thing that could happen in her world would be that Duncan would die.

CHAPTER 33

May 1990

JUST OVER A MONTH LATER...

"*Another one!* For Christ's sake, Coupar, get a grip. At this rate there'll be no fucking lecturers left at the art school!"

"Yes, sir."

"Yes, sir, no sir, three bags full sir! And that's *body* bags, Coupar. Who the hell is doing this?"

"That remains to be discovered, sir.

"Oh, that's very helpful, Coupar. *Remains to be discovered*. Remains *are* being discovered at an alarming rate. Spiked full of paintbrushes, beheaded, and now skewered on a trident for Christ's sake! You must have *some* inkling as to what's going on? You've been poking around the art school for the last... what... eight months. There's a raving psycho on the loose there, and you still haven't got a clue who it is? The press are going to murder us over this one!"

"Yes sir."

The Menace looked wistfully out of the window of his office. His moustache appeared to twitch a little, as if keen to make a run for it. A perfect June day out there. Ideal for a few holes of golf. The killing of the disc jockey, the case that had preoccupied him for the duration of these art school murders, was in sight of a satisfactory conclusion. The presumptive murderer had been dragged back to Scotland from his bolthole in Bulgaria and was safely locked up in Shobbs prison on remand. That was all well and good, but The Menace was now belatedly realising that he should have been a lot more proactive in these events nearer to home. There was a limit as to how much shit he could shovel over Coupar Cruickshank. The press were sure to turn their attentions on him sooner or later, as notional chief investigating officer. So far his cordial relations with local newspaper editors – two of them regular members of his golfing four – had kept the focus elsewhere. There had also been generous coverage of his triumph in the disc jockey investigation. But now the chickens would come home to roost. Three bizarre and interconnected murders in eight months right on his doorstep! If he didn't get to the bottom of this quickly, he'd find himself banished to some ghastly windswept outpost of the police service. Shetland perhaps.

Coupar also looked forlornly out of the window. There was a sunny world of happiness out there. Young people were stretching out on the grass of the city's parks, aware that such a day had to be grabbed and milked to the full before the stern rigours of normal Scottish summertime set in once more. Why had he chosen this career? Grubbing about in an underworld of sinister murders, trying to understand…

"Well?"

It was The Menace again. Apparently he was waiting for something from himself. Coupar sought for some positive spin that he could put on things.

"This one might be a suicide, sir. The Telford Bridge. It's a popular place for it."

"Does that really help us, Coupar? Are we to suppose that Arabella Wood cut off her own head and put it in a glass case? Or that Steven Sidling stove in his own head in Deil's Glen, after adorning himself with sharpened paintbrushes?"

He paused, and assembled his features into a display of exaggerated delight.

"*I* know…."

Here The Menace leaned forward with simulated enthusiasm.

"*I* know... *I'll* tell you what, Coupar! Why don't we just say that this Duncan McBane topped the other two and then threw himself off the bridge in remorse, happening to land right on top of his own bronze sculpture? That would tie it all up neatly, wouldn't it laddie?"

Coupar was no stranger to irony. Lisa employed it frequently in their conversations. He shrugged his shoulders in a defeated manner.

"It might be the case, for all that. It might be that that's what happened."

"Do we have a shred of evidence to support this story?"

"Not as yet, sir."

"Well, go and get some. Have you been to McBane's flat yet?"

"It's the next thing I'm doing sir. If you remember, you told me to come straight to see you this morning."

"Yes. Well, off you go now then. And take some forensics people with you. Look for paintbrush handle shavings on the carpet and a DIY book on beheadings. For Christ's sake, we need to turn up something soon!"

Later on, Coupar waited in a little café on Dolry Road while the forensics team finished their work. Eventually his impatience got the better of him, and he paid for his coffee and made his way towards McBane's flat. He headed up the dismal stone staircase and went inside. The three forensics guys were just packing up in the hallway.

"Anything promising?" he said, hopefully.

"Fingerprints, hairs. Wood shavings. A weird rubber mask. We've taken a few things for further examination. You'll get the list."

"Okay. So it's clear now for me to go in and root around?"

"All yours."

The forensics guys clattered down the stairs and Coupar shut the door behind them. He turned into the living room and ran his eye around it. It exuded the melancholy of a place belonging to someone who had just died. It was as if the very furnishings lamented their abandonment. Duncan McBane had walked out of this room for the last time only two nights ago. Had he expected to return? Or was he, as Coupar fervently hoped, suicidal? If the latter, then would he have been in a frame of mind to think beyond his death, leaving his home and belongings for the last time in some sort of order? Or would the depth of his despair make him careless of such considerations? Never having felt suicidal himself, Coupar couldn't make up his mind on this matter.

The room was certainly untidy and uncared for. There was a thin layer of dust on the mantelpiece and the television stand. There were two plants dying for lack of water. There was a scattering of crumbs on the worn-looking sofa. On the coffee table, unwashed mugs and a disordered newspaper jostled for space. There were no pictures on the walls. For a man whose occupation was artistic, it seemed to Coupar that there was a strange lack of anything of aesthetic value in the room. It could have been the room of any depressed middle-aged male living alone. A room, then, that although not promoting the idea of suicide, certainly proposed no argument against it.

Moving to the bedroom, he found a little more evidence of personality. The room was the same size as the living room, and set up in a corner was an old-fashioned bureau with a litter of books and papers on it. On the wall above this was a set of shelves, jammed with books. Coupar ran an eye over the titles. Books on art, mostly, but also books on cinema, and a few novels.

He opened the drawers of the bureau. They were stuffed with folders, sketch books, notebooks and miscellaneous odds and ends. He sighed. This would all have to be gone through. He'd send Waterhouse back here later in the day with some bags. He could cart it all down the stairs and bring it to the incident room at the police station.

On the way back to the station, Coupar was held up for a while at a busy junction with traffic lights. His eye wandered to the side of the road, where an arresting figure stood half-concealed in bushes. It was human in form, but taller – perhaps eight feet high. It seemed to be constructed, as far as he could make out, with twigs and branches. He might almost have thought it was a Guy for Bonfire Night, except that the fifth of November was a long way off. Where the face should have been, a black cowl obscured the head. One of its arms pointed towards Coupar, and the other pointed downwards to the ground. It was sinister, and coming just after his visit to a dead man's home, it struck him as a kind of reminder of the Grim Reaper, pointing out that he too, Coupar Cruickshank, would one day be in the ground. Or, perhaps, below it, in Hell.

A horn sounding just behind him alerted him to the fact that the lights had turned to green. He was in an unmarked car – you didn't get tooted at in a squad car. Engaging first gear, he moved on.

It was one of his twice-weekly 'nights in' with Lisa. After checking in at the station, where Waterhouse informed him there was no news, he drove home to shower and change, and then headed for her flat. On impulse, he bought a bunch of red roses on the way from a garage shop.

The flowers made a good impression. Lisa gave him a kiss on the lips and went to fetch a vase. There was a nice aroma coming from the kitchen and the flat was tidy. He went to stand at the kitchen door.

"I see there's been another art school lecturer found dead," Lisa said, pouring water into the vase.

"I know," Coupar replied glumly.

"It's all over the evening paper!" Lisa remarked. "Dan showed me a copy when we left work."

Coupar felt that now familiar twinge of jealous suspicion.

"You leave work together, do you?"

"Sometimes. It depends on what classes he's got. So are you in charge again?"

"In practice, yes. The Menace is still keeping his hands clean. Lisa, do you mind me asking something?"

"What?"

He took a gulp of air. It had to be faced.

"Do you and Dan… do you fancy each other?"

Lisa turned around with a laugh.

"Dan fancies me like mad, I think."

"So…?"

She put down the vase of roses and came to him. She wrapped her arms around his torso and squeezed him hard.

"Silly Coopsie! Are you jealous? I'm not interested in Dan. Not a bit! He's just a big kid. Why would I want him when I've got a *real* man?"

She gave him another squeeze, and then stepped away.

"Now – let's have a drink and you can tell me about this latest case!"

CHAPTER 34

May 1990

The natural starting point for a murder investigation was the victim's partner. They were frequently the culprit, especially if the victim was a woman. However, Duncan McBane wasn't a woman, and he didn't have a partner, so Coupar drew up his list of initial interviewees with an eye to the previous cases. Surely there had to be some link between this death and those of the other two art school lecturers?

He thought he would start with the two individuals who had clear connections to McBane. Ricky Love, who, according to the janitor Miggs, had been mysteriously following him; and Hermione Cutter, who had painted his portrait. He couldn't see what bearing these connections had on the cases, but the connections were there, and were all he had to work with for now. After them, he would have to trawl through the Sculpture staff and students once more, as he had done with the Sidling case, and then spread his net wider and wider through the art school. He felt discouraged before he had even started. Maybe he just wasn't very good at this job?

However, before he had embarked on these first interviews, a phone call came through to him from one Angus Campbell, who identified himself as Duncan's best friend at the art school. He offered to come in and tell them anything that he knew. Coupar allowed himself a glimmer of hope. Could this unexpected offer provide the key piece of information that would unlock this baffling and bloody puzzle?

Angus Campbell duly appeared at the police station where he was shown into the interview room. Coupar vaguely remembered him from one of the dozens of fruitless interviews concerning the previous cases, and started the cassette recording. As he pressed the 'record' button he tried to supress his recollection of how many times he had done this over recent months, and how so far it had led him nowhere.

"Investigation into the death of Duncan McBane. Interview One. Interviewee Angus Campbell. 27th of June Nineteen Ninety. Interview conducted by Detective Inspector Coupar Cruickshank, in the presence of Detective Constable Peter Price."

Angus Campbell was looking intently at Price through his round spectacles.

"Haven't I seen you hanging about outside the art school sometimes?"

Price nodded, and scratched both ears.

"You were wearing one of those detective type raincoats. I thought you were a pervert or a flasher or something."

Peter Price gave Coupar a look that said *I told you so!*

"Detective Constable Price was conducting some discreet surveillance on my instructions. Anyway, I'm very sorry, Mr Campbell, that your good friend has been found dead."

"Aye. It was a shock."

"Do you have any information that might help us establish the cause of his death?"

Angus looked surprised.

"Plummeting off the Telford Bridge onto a metal trident would kill most people."

"I mean, do you know anything about how this would have come about?"

Angus ran a hand through his beard.

"I've nothing definite, no. But I've been thinking about things since I read about him in the paper yesterday morning. I've been thinking if it could have been suicide."

"That's our first line of enquiry, Mr Campbell, although we have to keep open minds. Did he seem depressed? You said on the phone that you spoke with him often at the art school."

"Aye, we had coffee together most days, and the odd bevvy after work. I've known Duncan for years."

"So, what was his mood in recent days?"

"Hard to say for sure. I knew him well, like I say, but he was the kind of guy who didn't let on too much, even to me. But I would say that he had something on his mind, definitely."

"Something on his mind? What kind of thing?"

"Well, his mood had turned a bit sour, I'd say. Right through the Spring term and up to now he'd seemed… I don't know… in his element. He was made Head of Sculpture – well, it's still called Ambient Interventions for now, but I never heard him call it that after Sidling was killed. So he was happier in his work than I'd seen him for a long time. I think he was enjoying having a bit of power. And then – I don't know any details – but he let on that he'd got some lassie on the go."

"On the go?"

"Aye. Since about January or February time it was. He never said much about it, but he did let on that he was seeing someone."

"Never a name?"

"No – I got the impression – and I'm guessing here, Inspector – that it might have been a married woman, and it was taking a long time to get going, if you know what I mean."

Coupar nodded.

"Go on, Mr Campbell."

"So... I'd say Duncan was pretty chuffed with himself up until a week or two ago, and then he came in one day with a face like someone had just trodden on it."

"What, he'd been in a fight or something?"

"No, no. I was just meaning he looked kind of flattened. I asked him if anything was wrong, and he just said that this lassie had dumped him. It wasn't like him to come out with even that much plain information. We had more of a jokey kind of relationship, you know? Skated over the surface of things."

"I see. And from that time up until... until he was found, would you say he was depressed?"

Angus took off his glasses and give them a polish with a dirty handkerchief while he gave this a long moment's thought. Coupar was beginning to wonder if he had forgotten the question when he spoke again.

"Well, maybe depressed, aye. He wasn't too sunny at the best of times. But I'd say it was something else as well. I got the feeling that he was very angry about something."

"Why did you think that?"

"It was just... well, whatever subject came up – say the Poll Tax for instance, or Margaret Thatcher – he seemed to be more stirred up about it than was normal. He said he'd hang Margaret Thatcher publicly in the Brassmarket, for instance, if he had the power. Or behead her, even better."

Coupar leaned forward slightly.

"Behead her?"

"Aye."

Coupar leaned back again. It was an interesting comment to come from Duncan McBane, but on the other hand there were probably a few thousand would-be executioners for the Prime Minister these days.

"Do you think he was angry about the woman who'd dumped him?"

"I never got him onto that subject. Once he'd told me it had happened, he just wanted to drop it. But very possibly, aye."

"Was that woman someone who worked at the art school, do you think?"

"I don't think so. I think I'd have worked out who it was if it had been."

Coupar decided to play his ace.

"Mr Campbell, do you think it's possible that Duncan McBane killed Steven Sidling, or Arabella Wood, or both of them?"

Angus took a deep breath, and then leaned forward.

"You know, Inspector, it's a relief to hear someone say that aloud. It's crossed my mind many a time, but I've never had the tiniest bit of proof that he did those things. Like I say, he was a man who always held his cards close to his chest, and he's been a good friend over the years. We see... we saw... eye to eye on so many things. I'm going to miss him like hell. We're... we were... what you might call on the traditional end of the art school spectrum – we shared a respect for tradition, and craft skills, and aesthetics. And we were on the same wavelength about politics; the people we liked and didn't like; TV programmes and films... anything, really. You know how it is? When you've got a friend who you just know what they're going to think about anything? So, when it crossed my mind that he might be a murderer, which it did both times – with Sidling and with Arabella Wood – I was what you might call *hyper-alert* for a while, wondering if there'd be anything that would come up to make me think that he... you know. And there was never anything, never the smallest thing, in all the... I don't know... hundreds of hours we spent drinking coffee or beer together. And of course, like everyone else in the art school, we discussed the murders and who might have done them. So, no, I don't think he was a murderer. Or if he was, he was the most devious bloody actor the world's ever seen."

CHAPTER 35

May 1990

Later the same day, Ricky Love was seated opposite Coupar in the interview room, and the cassette recorder was making its gentle whirring sound between them.

"So, Mr Love, you fly back to Oregon next week?"

"That's right."

"Glad to be going back?"

"Yes. And my wife too, she's especially looking forward to being back with the family and the folks we know."

"It's been a strange year for you."

"Extraordinary."

"Three murders."

"Yes. But... this latest one... Duncan McBane..."

"Yes?"

"*Is* it a murder?"

"We don't know yet."

"But... you think...?"

"We could say the circumstances are suspicious."

"I see."

"Three violent deaths of art school lecturers in nine months. And two of the victims being persons closely associated with yourself."

"Closely associated? I knew Arabella Wood a little, yes. What a horrible shock that was!"

"What?"

"That... what happened to her. Something like that happening to someone you've known and talked to."

"Terrible, yes."

"But... I never had a connection with the others. You said closely associated with two of them? The Sidling guy I only set eyes on once or twice, when I'd just arrived."

"We know that's the case."

"So... you mean Duncan McBane? Who's just died?"

"Yes."

"I don't think I've ever had a conversation with him. So – what do you mean by *closely associated*?"

"Can you not think of any connection?"

"Only that we work... worked... in the same art school."

"Mr Love, you've been observed following Duncan McBane."

"What? Who says I was doing that?"

"Miggs, the head janitor."

"That guy! He's a real screwball! And he doesn't like me."

"Do you deny you were following McBane?"

"God! Why would I? Maybe he happened to be going in the same direction as me. Maybe that's what happened."

Coupar was suddenly struck by an idea. Something that Angus Campbell had come up with – that maybe McBane had been seeing a married woman. He decided to fly a kite.

"Was he on his way to meet with your wife?"

Ricky looked stunned. He slumped back in his chair.

"Oh. I see. You know about that, do you?"

Coupar could have rubbed his hands with glee. Mentally he did so. Such a simple trap and this naive American had walked straight into it.

"Yes, I do. It would appear that your wife was having an affair with Duncan McBane."

"It never came to that. It was nipped in the bud."

"Nipped in the bud? How did that come about?"

"She stopped seeing him."

"When was this?"

"A couple of weeks ago. We had it out."

"You and McBane?"

"No. I told you, I've never spoken to the man. Me and Boony. We had it out."

"You confronted her?"

"I guess you'd call it that."

"You had a row?"

"It wasn't a row. It was a conversation."

"And she told you... what?"

"She told me... she admitted she'd been meeting him. Maybe four times they'd met. I think four or maybe five times."

"Where was that? Did you follow McBane there?"

"Yes. I followed him one time. They met that time in a wine bar in the West End. But it wasn't an affair. It might have been headed that way. She found him attractive, she told me that."

"Do you think she told you the truth? That they'd only met up and talked?"

"I think so. Why? Do you know any different?"

"No. But we'll be interviewing your wife today as soon as we can get hold of her."

"She's at home with Marcus."

"Marcus?"

"Our little boy. He's not at nursery today."

"We'll pick her up. Did you come in a car here?"

"No, I got the bus."

"I'll get an officer to run you home, and you can look after your little boy while your wife comes here for her interview. And I'll ask the officer to ensure that you don't speak to each other. He'll explain what's happening to your wife."

"Why? Why can't I speak with my wife?"

"Do you know what collusion is?"

"Of course I do. Are you suggesting Boony and me would cook something up?"

"Not at all. But it's best to get independent accounts of things."

Ricky looked discontented.

"Are we done here, then Inspector?"

"Not quite, Mr Love. How did you feel about Duncan McBane, when you found out he was seeing your wife?"

"I didn't feel anything. He was a stranger to me. My feelings were all about Boony."

"Anger?"

"More sadness. And regret. Guilt, even."

"Guilt? Why should you feel guilty?"

"Oh... this whole coming to Scotland thing. It was all for me. She tagged along because of me, but she felt... I don't know... not great about it. I was busy here – crazy busy sometimes – but she didn't have a life here. She was bored and neglected. That's the only reason that... that something might eventually have happened with the McBane guy."

"So you *nipped it in the bud.*"

"Yes."

"So you didn't feel angry towards McBane?"

"I didn't feel anything towards him. I just wanted him out of my wife's life."

"Okay. Let's move on. Can you tell me where you were and what you were doing the night before last? The night of Tuesday the 31st of May?"

"This is crazy! Are you trying to pin a murder on me?"

"Not at all, Mr Love. I want to eliminate you from the enquiry if I can."

"Two nights ago. I don't specifically remember, but we're at home every night. So, I was at home. Like normal."

"With your wife and child."

"Yes. Now I remember – we ate a takeaway Indian meal. We've got a taste for that stuff now."

"So you went out?"

"It was delivered."

"So your wife... did you say her name was *Boony*?"

Ricky nodded.

"So Boony can back you up?"

"Of course she will. Listen, Inspector... I know you've got a job to do, but I'd be grateful if you could *eliminate* us, as you put it, as soon as you can. We're really busy getting ready to fly home, and I've still got a lot of loose ends to tie up at the art school."

Coupar thought he'd fly another kite. His first one had been such a great success.

"Just one more thing..."

"Yes?"

"The Pine Loop Murders."

Ricky looked as if he might explode. His eyes widened and he ran a hand wildly through his hair.

"Not that again! God! I had enough of that with the police back home! Just because they happened near my house!"

"And you knew the victims."

"What? Didn't I tell you before? I have no idea who they were!"

"Hunters, weren't they"?

"Yeah, they were hunters. But I don't hunt."

"Crossbow hunters".

"That's what the papers said."

"So you didn't know them?"

"No. Definitely not."

"You're quite anti-hunting, aren't you?"

"I don't like it. Crossbows... guns... I don't like anything to do with that stuff. The US is crazy over guns."

"Did it strike you that there was a similarity between the way they were found and what happened to Steven Sidling?"

"No. I never thought of that."

"Both stuck all over, like hedgehogs. Or porcupines."

"Horrible."

"It seems that you're a bit of a magnet for murders. Unsolved murders."

Ricky Love looked even more agitated. His face was flushed.

"Where the fuck are you going with this?"

"Nowhere, Mr Love. Nowhere at all. I just wondered if you had any observation on the matter."

Ricky suddenly half-rose in his chair, thrusting his chin forward, his voice rising to a shout.

"Fuck! Yes I do! It's very shitty, Inspector, to be an innocent person and to have the police in two countries treating you like you're a suspect, just because you happen to have been in the wrong place, or you know the wrong people. It's extremely shitty!"

Coupar observed this transformation with interest. Ricky's calm family-guy persona was suddenly like a cracked egg shell in fragments on the floor around him. Now he resembled a newly hatched pterodactyl: beaky, bug-eyed and belligerent.

Another kite usefully flown, Coupar congratulated himself.

"Okay. Thank you, Mr Love."

He clicked off the cassette recorder, and turned to the weasel Price sitting by the door.

"Please run Mr Love home and pick up his wife as you heard us discuss, Price. And please ensure they aren't left alone together out of earshot."

CHAPTER 36

May 1990

An hour later, Ricky Love's wife was seated in the chair recently occupied by her husband. She was an attractive woman with high cheekbones and a well-groomed appearance. Coupar thought she must have spent a few minutes changing her clothes and putting on make-up. She didn't look like a woman who'd just come as she was from an afternoon at home with a two year old.

She looked edgy, and fidgeted purposelessly with her handbag, which she eventually put down on the floor beside her.

Coupar nodded at Price as the detective constable sidled sinuously into the chair by the door.

"No communication?" he enquired.

Price shook his head.

Coupar introduced himself, and then pressed the record button on the cassette player.

"Investigation into the death of Duncan McBane. Interview Three. Interviewee Mrs Boony Love. 31st of May, Nineteen Ninety. Interview conducted by Detective Inspector Coupar Cruickshank, in the presence of Detective Constable Peter Price."

He looked at Boony Love again. She bore a passing resemblance to his girlfriend Lisa; Lisa as she might be in ten years time, perhaps.

"So, Mrs Love, you'll understand why we want to talk to you?"

"Not really."

"In connection with the death of Duncan McBane."

"Oh. Yeah. I heard about that. It's really upsetting."

"Because you knew him a little, didn't you?"

She hesitated.

"A little, yes."

"When did you last speak with him?"

"That would be around a couple of weeks ago maybe."

"Were you alone together? Was it a conversation just between the two of you?"

"I… yes… it was."

"Where did this take place?"

"In The Bull's Tail, in the Brassmarket."

"And was there any particular reason why you were meeting him there?"

"You've interviewed Ricky, my husband already, haven't you?"

"Yes."

"What did he tell you?"

"Just answer my questions for yourself please Mrs Love, if you wouldn't mind. Was it just the two of you there?"

"Yeah, it was."

"How did you come to know Duncan McBane?"

"I got friendly with Duncan a while ago. We first met at the private view of his totem pole. At the Arts Council place."

"And you met frequently after that?"

"Not frequently, no. Just a few times."

Time to fly another kite. Coupar spoke neutrally, as if it were a statement of fact.

"You had an affair with him."

"No! Is that what Ricky said?"

"I'm asking you."

"No. No way. We were just friends."

"Friends who met in secret?"

"It was innocent."

"An innocent secret?"

She looked flustered. She smoothed a loose lock of her blond hair away from her forehead.

"Yes. It was just that. We just met and talked sometimes over a few drinks. God! We never even kissed each other!"

"But you might have done that. If Ricky hadn't found out? You might have become lovers?"

Now she flushed a little, either from embarrassment or anger.

"I'm not saying that. That's you saying that."

"So when you met Duncan for the last time, quite recently, how were matters left? Why didn't you see him again?"

"Ricky had found out about us, and it was sensible to stop."

"While it was still innocent?"

'If you like to put it like that."

"Did Duncan agree it was sensible?"

"He didn't need to agree. I was just telling him the way it was."

"So was he angry? Upset?"

"I didn't hang around after I told him we weren't meeting up any more."

"You just got up and left?"

"Yes. It was a little brutal maybe. But at least I'd come and told him in person, and said I was sorry."

"How did he look when you told him?"

"He didn't look very happy."

"Would you say Duncan was generally a happy person?"

"No, that's not the first word you'd use about him. He was pretty serious."

"But not depressed?"

"Not while I knew him. Serious, yes, but an interesting person, to me at least. And definitely he didn't come over as depressed. Actually, things were going well for him. He'd just been made Head of Sculpture."

"Steven Sidling's job."

"The guy that was killed?"

"Yes. Didn't Duncan ever mention him?"

"Maybe he did some time... yeah, he mentioned him. He told me it was time to change the way things were done in the department; do things more traditionally."

"Because he didn't like the way Sidling had run things?"

"I guess so. We didn't touch on it much. He didn't talk art school politics with me."

"Did you ever think he might have killed Sidling? Or the other art school lecturer, Arabella Wood?"

Her eyes widened in horror.

"God no! Is that what you think he did?"

"We don't know. We're looking into all possibilities But you're quite sure he didn't ever say anything about those deaths that you can remember now?"

"No. Like I say, he mentioned Sidling at some point. I don't remember him ever saying anything about that poor woman, except he said he'd once gone out with her. That was when we first met."

"So he *did* talk about her?"

"No, it was only that one time. He said he was sorry she'd died. But he didn't say any more than that, and he never mentioned her again, and I sure wasn't going to bring her up."

"Okay. Did he ever say anything to you that would suggest he might be suicidal?"

"No, never. Like I say, it seemed like things were going well for him. But I haven't seen him recently of course."

"Could you breaking up with him have made him depressed?"

"Maybe. I don't know. I didn't get the feeling…"

She hesitated.

"Go on…

She fiddled with her hair some more.

"I don't know… I think he liked me… liked me a lot, but… no, there's no way he'd have killed himself over me. No way."

"Is there nothing at all that he ever said, or any other impression you ever formed, that would make you think he killed himself?"

"He sometimes had a kind of… I don't know… a kind of anguished look when his face was at rest. But that was just part of him, I guess. Once he told me he'd been bullied at school. But hey, that happens to lots of kids. It happened to me one time."

"Okay. Just one final quick question, Mrs Love. Where were you and your husband two nights ago?"

"Two nights ago? Tuesday?"

"Tuesday the 29th of May, yes."

"We were at home. We're at home every night."

"Do you remember what you had for supper?"

"The night before last – sure, we had an Indian takeaway delivered."

"Thank you."

Coupar clicked off the cassette recorder.

"Okay, thank you Mrs Love. I'm sorry we've had to drag you and your husband in here at such short notice. But I believe you're leaving soon to go back home?"

"Yes, in a couple of weeks."

"Okay. I may have to get back to you. If I don't, have a good trip back to the US."

"Thank you Inspector."

"Price – will you please take Mrs Love home now."

CHAPTER 37

June 1990

The next morning, the first day of June, Hermione Cutter took her place opposite Coupar. He put the cassette player into operation and recorded the usual details of date and interviewee. The cassette tapes were building into quite a collection. Hours and hours of material, stacked in two boxes labelled 'Steven Sidling' and 'Arabella Wood'. Now there was an equally capacious box labelled 'Duncan McBane' just waiting to be filled up.

Hermione Cutter's demeanour struck him as more relaxed than he remembered from their previous interview. She was still thin and haunted-looking, but there was a new air of... something. Positivity? Her eyes still darted about, but much less frantically.

"I don't know why you think I can help you, Inspector," she said.

"I'm interviewing everyone who was connected with Duncan McBane, however slightly. Obviously that includes everyone who works at the art school."

"Like you did with the previous two murders?"

"Do you think this is a murder?"

"I've no idea. It looks more like he jumped off the bridge, doesn't it? The Telford Bridge is Forthburgh's Beachy Head, after all."

"I'm sorry?"

"Beachy Head... in Sussex."

"I don't understand."

"It's a cliff by the sea. Famous for suicides."

"Ah... I see. So you think Duncan McBane killed himself?"

"I don't know. I'm only saying people go to the Telford Bridge to do that."

"When did you last speak with Duncan McBane?"

"It must have been quite a while ago. I can't remember exactly."

"Try to remember."

"I don't know. Maybe a few words in passing at the art school some time. I really can't remember."

"You painted his portrait last year, didn't you?"

"How did you know that I did that?"

"It cropped up when I interviewed you about the death of Arabella Wood."

"Of course. I'd forgotten."

"You specialise in portraits, I believe?"

"Yes, that's mostly what I paint."

"Did I show you this before? When I interviewed you about Arabella Wood?"

He slid a little clear plastic envelope that contained a card with the printed word *Portrait* across the table towards her. The card that had been found with Arabella's head. Hermione looked at it blankly. It didn't appear to him that she was in any way disturbed by it.

"No. Why? What is it?"

"It was found with the head of Arabella Wood."

"My God!"

She regarded it now with a wide-eyed look of horror.

"Shocking, isn't it," he said, sliding it back to his side of the table.

"Yes. It's so... I don't know. So horrible! So... warped... to leave a kind of label!"

"And we still don't know who committed that crime - or who killed Steven Sidling. But this little card, Mrs Cutter... this little card, and an illegible note we found at the scene of Sidling's murder, they point towards someone trying to make a point, if you understand me.

Someone who not only wanted to kill, but wanted some kind of significance to be seen in the killings."

Hermione nodded, but she appeared to be lost in thought.

"Mrs Cutter?"

"I'm... I'm thinking, Inspector."

"About what?"

"About whether it could have been Duncan."

"Has that occurred to you before?"

"No, of course not. He... well, we never became what you would call friends... but... you know.. to think that someone you've actually talked with... that they could be a murderer... it just seems too fantastical."

"How do you feel now, thinking of that?"

"It's frightening. Last summer I was in a studio alone with that man. For hours. He came to my house too, to see the painting. That was last October. If he'd killed Sidling, he was already a murderer by then. In my own house!"

She gave herself a shake, as if the thought had made her go cold all over.

"Is there anything definite you can remember, Mrs Cutter? Anything at all that he said or did that was suspicious, now that you look back?"

She sat silently for a few seconds, and then shook her head.

"No, nothing that I can think of."

"Can I ask you please, Mrs Cutter, to come back to me with anything that occurs to you, looking back on things in the light of the idea that Duncan McBane may have been a killer?"

She shook herself again, as if trying to shrug off a ghoul clinging about her neck.

"Of course, Inspector. Of course I will."

Coupar clicked off the cassette player, and Hermione Cutter took her leave. As she stood up and left the interview room, again he had that fleeting, intangible impression of positivity in her manner. Perhaps she was just glad to leave the subject behind her.

When the last of the long day's interviews were over, Coupar returned to his office, where the contents of Duncan McBane's writing bureau had been dumped on his desk in two black plastic bin bags. A typically shoddy effort by Waterhouse, whom he had dispatched earlier to gather the material. What if a cleaner had come in and assumed they were actually rubbish? Why hadn't Waterhouse taken out the contents and placed them neatly on one of the tables where the sparse bits and pieces relating to the murders – those that were not under lock and key in the forensics store – were assembled? He couldn't help wondering if, instead of Price and Waterhouse, he'd had a couple of eager, intelligent and efficient deputies, he might not have got to the bottom of this affair by now. Was it entirely his fault that he was going around in circles? And what about The Menace? Why wasn't *he* doing his job properly?

He felt tired and frustrated. He'd interviewed a dozen people today, and there were a dozen more to speak to tomorrow. But his head was so full of theories about Duncan McBane that he couldn't resist starting to look at the contents of the bin bags. He fetched himself a coffee out of the machine in the station canteen and got to work.

As he got everything out, he arranged the materials into three piles. On one pile he put printed items like bank statements and bills. Then there were a lot of pencil sketches and technical notes presumably related to his sculpture work, which he put into another pile. And then there were folders containing handwritten material – possibly they were diaries or some such? Once everything was in order, he turned first to the folders. Perhaps they would offer some glimpse into the mental workings of that taciturn and unhelpful individual who had ended up skewered on a trident of his own design. Two crucial questions had somehow to be answered. Had McBane killed himself? And had he killed anyone else?

Two hours later, Coupar was still reading. He had learned a great deal about the dead man. It seemed that McBane, in a tortured instrospective fashion, had needed at some time in the past to set down in writing a detailed catalogue of the various trials and traumas of his childhood and early years. There were long descriptions of his early memories of growing up in a household prone to sudden outbursts of violent behaviour from his father, who was a stonemason. There was an account of how he discovered, at about the age of eight, that the bottles of gin that his mother referred to as her 'medicine' were in fact not medicine at all. It was a certain Aunt Janet who had made it very clear to him at that time that his mother was a weak and useless person, and only such people needed recourse to gin. When his father died – of injuries sustained after falling off a church spire while doing restoration work – Duncan was ten years old. The previously mentioned Aunt Janet – who seemed to be a spinster - had then taken over the little household of Duncan and his mother and moved them all to Stonehaven. There, life appeared to have become even more unbearable. Salient memories from Duncan's Stonehaven days were being 'interfered with' by a man who lived next door, and being taunted and abused by schoolmates who christened him 'Fishface'. The worst of these incidents – which he described in great detail – was when some older boys waylaid him on his way home from school and thrust handfuls of rotting mackerel down his shirt and trousers. They were severely punished by the headmaster after his Aunt Janet had marched to the school and denounced them, but not severely enough in Duncan's view.

This Aunt Janet featured in the most harrowing part of Duncan's narrative. Like Duncan's father, she had perished by plummeting from a height – in her case from the sea cliffs near their home while out on a walk. A page had been torn out of the diary at this point, so it was unclear how or why she had fallen. It struck him that Duncan's own death made a trio of such falls. Did that argue for suicide? Did jumping off a high place present itself to Duncan as the obvious and natural way to end it all?

The writing was intensely, almost obsessively detailed, as if McBane had wanted to re-live every fleeting impression of those sad days. There must have been over a hundred pages of closely written text, contained in half a dozen folders. As he read, Coupar felt a cloud of gloom gathering over his own head. It was as if the man was explaining himself to himself, perhaps setting out for his own satisfaction why he had become the morose adult individual that Coupar had briefly encountered in his interviews: a man with a vast range of chips on his shoulder.

Eight o'clock. There were only two more folders, and they contained only a few pages each. He might as well finish the job.

The next folder contained two brief factual accounts – although again full of detail – of events that must have occurred when Duncan was a young man in his early twenties. They were dated 1962 and 1963. Coupar checked his own notes. McBane was born in 1940.

In the 1962 account, Duncan had returned to Stonehaven and paid a visit to the man who had 'interfered' with him as a boy. He still lived in the cottage next door, alone as before. Duncan had confronted him with what he had done in the past, and offered him a choice. Duncan would now denounce him to the police as a paedophile, or the perpetrator would submit to a small revenge to be exacted there and then by Duncan himself. Coupar felt a cold dread mounting as he read. The man – Archie, he was called – reluctantly agreed that a swift and summary justice was preferable to being dragged into public notice. Duncan had then strapped the man's arm to the kitchen table with a length of washing line he had brought with him, boiled up a kettle, and slowly poured boiling water over 'the hand that did the dirty deed', as he put it. He had taken the precaution of stuffing a dishcloth into Archie's mouth to stifle his screams.

Coupar felt as if he might be sick. There was a pitiless, stony precision both in the act and in the description of it. There was no crowing or exultation in the revenge, but equally there was no sense of doing anything wrong. The Duncan McBane who had carried out this torture, and the Duncan McBane who had written about it later, were apparently devoid of any compunction about inflicting pain on another human being.

The second event, which had occurred in 1963, was of a similar vengeful nature but more spontaneous. Duncan had by chance seen in Forthburgh, in a pub, the schoolmate who as a boy had come up with the hated nickname of 'Fishface'. He had been in no doubt that it was the same person. His voice, overheard, was deeper but familiar. He had stayed out of the man's sight, and then followed him as he left the pub. On a street corner, the man - whose surname was Ransom - had said goodbye to his two drinking companions and struck off on his own. Duncan had followed at a little distance, without any definite plan of action. However, when Ransom turned into a steep, narrow close leading down from the Regal Mile towards the railway station, Duncan quickened his pace to catch up with him. There was no-one else around. "Ransom!" he said, just behind him. As the man turned to see who it was, Duncan swung his fist hard into his face and he fell to the ground. Duncan then administered a series of hard kicks into the ribs, as hard as he could muster, and finished off with one to the head. Then he ran away as quickly as he could. He didn't think that Ransom had recognised him, and he never heard of the man again. Perhaps he'd killed him, he wrote.

Coupar paused when he finished reading this, and looked out of the window. It being high summer, it was still light out there, and the sky was an innocent blue. These self-confessions of McBane argued for a man capable of murder, did they not? Capable of murder and with enough anguish and desolation in his past to provoke suicide.

He opened the last folder. It contained several sheets of paper, but only one had writing on it. At a first glance, he thought it was a shopping list, and might have put it aside if the first word in the list hadn't caught his eye.

SIDLING
Arsenic
Rat poison
Weedkiller
Radioactive substance
Hit and run with a vehicle
Knife
Sword
Blunt Instrument
Pistol
Rifle
Shotgun
Strangulation
Kidnap and starve to death
Beheading
Axe
Push from high place
Drown in a bath
Smother with a pillow
Garrotte with a washing line
Guillotine
Chainsaw

Chisel
Hammer
Drug and bury alive
Contract killer
Lemmy Stoter?
Cut-throat razor
Boil alive
Dump in septic tank
Acid
Defenestrate
Cook and feed to dogs
Hang, draw and quarter

Must know who is killing him.
Must know why.
Must be done in a fitting manner.
An AMBIENT INTERVENTION!
Must get away with it.

Two emotions swept through Coupar in quick succession. The first was a cold sense of horror and regret that he had failed to identify Duncan McBane as the probable killer of Steven Sidling. That mysterious piece of paper with the mostly illegible letters found in the dead man's nostril came before his mind's eye. How many times had he puzzled over it without seeing that it might have read a*mbient intervention*? He felt irredeemably stupid. That was a piece of evidence that could have led him to pay much more attention to McBane. He might then have prevented the murder of Arabella Wood. It seemed crystal-clear to him now that McBane must have perpetrated that crime too. He was exactly the kind of man who would kill a woman who had spurned him.

The second, more self-interested emotion was a wave of relief that all the jigsaw pieces were finally fitting into place: McBane was a double murderer, who had then killed himself in a fit of remorse or despair in the way that seemed most appropriate, even perhaps calculating his place of death with such grim precision that he could fall on his own sword, as it were.

The piece of paper he now held in his hands did not constitute proof, by itself. There was more work to be done, especially to establish the link with Arabella's killing. But he had no doubts now in his own mind. He had his man, albeit that man was beyond the reach of earthly justice in the police mortuary.

CHAPTER 38

September 1989

EIGHT MONTHS EARLIER...
No visitor from the art school or anywhere else in the known universe had ever penetrated Artjoms's rented flat, except for his hero, the Head of Ambient Interventions, the divine Steven Sidling, who had additionally penetrated his body and his heart. A photograph of Sidling, carefully cut from the art school prospectus, was lovingly displayed in a small silver frame beside his bed.

He was only the second man with whom Artjoms had experienced a sexual encounter. The first was long ago, in the enshrouding forests of his native Estonia, in the days after school when he had worked for a year as a logger to save money for his education. That fumbling madness in a summer bed of moss had been a recognition, but Sidling had been a revelation.

On this late September morning, Artjoms was sitting on the edge of his bed, staring at the photograph. The dried tracks of his tears pulled at the skin of his face. He had just returned, blindly blundering, from the art school, where he had learned the reason for Steven Sidling's unaccountable absence over the last two days.

Murdered!

It was Fishface who had given out the news. McBane had toured the studios, informing students of the tragic event. He had also put up a notice on the Ambient Interventions Department notice board – which was still labelled 'Sculpture Department'. It read *We regret to inform you of the untimely death of Steven Sidling, Head of Department. Please continue with your work as normal. Duncan McBane.*

'As normal'! For Artjoms there would be no more *normal*. He was bereft of normality. His mentor, his guiding light, his lover, had been struck out of his life! He barely left his room for days. He brooded obsessively. Murdered! *Noslepkavots!* Who could have wanted his darling Steve to be dead? And in such a manner!

He knew so little of Steve's life outside the art school. The long, intimate conversations of that wonderful night together had given him a glimpse of a world he longed to be part of, but since then Steve had gently kept him at arm's length. He could easily perceive that it was with reluctance. He still had a place in Steve's heart; he was sure of it.

With a little discreet surveillance, he had discovered where Steve lived, and that he had a partner. That started a little fire of jealousy in his heart. Nevertheless, their relations at the art school remained cordial – more than cordial. He felt like the 'chosen one' amongst the students, and Steve was wont to tell him that he was his right-hand man, his most important disciple in the cultural shift of the department from 'Sculpture' to 'Ambient Interventions'. There had even been, in private places, hints of the physical desire that Steve must be holding in check – a hand on a knee, a stroke of the arm… once, a quick peck on the cheek. He treasured these moments; they were signs that gave him hope that Steve would come back to him one day – perhaps when he had completed his degree in the summer of 1990. After that, they would no longer be divided by that invisible barrier between staff and student. Steve would be able to declare his love for him, Artjoms, and break free from the shackles of what must only be a temporary and unsatisfactory relationship with the other man. He allowed his thoughts to take wing further into the future. Together, Steven Sidling and Artjoms Ubags would be a force to be reckoned with in the art world! Two creators with hearts beating as one, collaborating on their ground-breaking, convention-defying projects.

Now this dream was over, a glorious Grecian urn shattered into fragments; a coat of many colours ripped and shredded.

The destroyer of his future must be found! Henceforward he would dedicate himself to this task. It would be the bitter replacement for the sweetness of his trampled dream. He hoped – oh, how strongly he hoped – that he would unearth the murderer before the police did. The police would take away the perpetrator's freedom, but how much worse that killer deserved! An eye for an eye, and a tooth for a tooth: no less was required, and he burned to be the avenging angel who would deliver that justice.

Artjoms's suspicions ranged far and wide. His first thoughts were of the man Steve had lived with. He had never discovered his name, but he knew what he looked like. Older than Steve, with the beginnings of a middle-aged belly. Dressed to look younger. Dyed hair. Less flamboyantly gay than Steve, but with that slightly mincing walk that some gay men affected. Artjoms had hated him on sight.

He started to hang about near the man's flat, lying low, driven by a compulsion to find out more about him. No doubt the police would have made him an early focus of their enquiries. But here he was, walking about town a free man, weeks after the murder. They couldn't have found out anything incriminating about him, or at least not yet. Artjoms racked his brains for a way to scrape acquaintance with him. The man might put him on the track of something, either deliberately or accidentally.

One Saturday morning, the man emerged from his door while Artjoms was hanging about nearby, and set off walking somewhere. Artjoms tailed him at a distance with a vague hope of something turning up. After a while it became clear that the man was wandering without purpose. It was an unusually warm and pleasant day for late October in Scotland. Artjoms glided almost invisibly behind his quarry through the dappled shadows of the trees that lined the streets. The sunlight made a golden roof of rustling, dying leaves above him. It was a day that might have gladdened the hearts of others, but Artjoms's heart was as impervious as a stone.

The man turned into a small park and sat down on a bench, where he commenced staring at the duck pond in front of him. He appeared lost in his own thoughts. Artjoms felt there could be no better opportunity than this to make an approach. He must seize the moment without any hindrance of shyness or embarrassment. Pushing closed the creaking metal gate of the park behind him, he made his way straight to the bench and sat down at the other end of it.

Since there were other benches nearby without occupants, Artjoms could feel the surprise that radiated from the man. There was a slight stiffening of the body, and just the suggestion of an intake of breath. The awkwardness of the moment was palpable, and Artjoms spoke quickly to break the silence.

"I think you're Steven Sidling's partner, aren't you?"

Now the man stared at him as if he'd fallen from the sky and landed there like a meteorite. He didn't reply. Artjoms pressed on as quickly as he could get the words out.

"I was one of his students – at the art school. A student of Ambient Interventions. And I think I see you with Steven once there… at the art school… I… I just see you here by chance, and I… I want to say that I like Steven very much, and I'm so sorry, you know…"

The man nodded at last, and heaved a long sigh.

"Thank you," he managed to get out.

"My name is Artjoms. Artjoms Ubags. It is an Estonian name."

"Ah…"

The man nodded again. Artjoms waited, but there was no sign that he wanted this conversation to continue. He didn't offer his own name.

"I wonder…" Artjoms blurted out, "if you have any idea who might have done it… kill Steven, I mean."

In spite of his embarrassment, Artjoms watched the man's face keenly for his reaction. Could you read guilt in a man's face? But the man's face registered only surprise; surprise and then anger. He frowned at Artjoms and made a gesture with one hand, as if to sweep this intruder off the bench and into the pond.

"I'm sorry, but this isn't something I want to discuss. The police have it all in hand. I await the result of their enquiries."

"But… you were the closest person…"

"Mr Bags… was it Bags? I don't know what the customs of your country permit, but here in Britain we don't approach perfect strangers with intimate questions. Now, either you will leave this bench, or I will, and there's an end to the matter."

Reluctantly – what a wasted effort this had been – Artjoms stood up, made a slightly formal and foolish-looking bow, and made his way out of the park and back into his world of tormented suspicions, none the wiser.

Artjoms's preoccupation with Steven Sidling's murder had pushed his creative efforts into temporary abeyance. He began, little by little, to feel that he should channel his anger and frustration into his work somehow. He still planned to pursue the *kratts* concept he had discussed at length with Steven, but he felt he was now on uncertain and shifting ground. Duncan McBane had taken over leadership of the Sculpture Department. It was supposed to be The Department of Ambient Interventions, but he had never heard Duncan use that phrase since Sidling's death. He remembered the fierce denunciation of *ambient interventions* that Duncan had delivered at the big meeting when the change was approved. His subsequent conversion to the cause had always seemed odd to Artjoms – and to others – and now the word 'sculpture' was freely bandied about once more, as if the change had never taken place. In this uncertain…ambience… what was the surest way of achieving the first class degree so necessary to his ambitions? The dream of a future of collaborative work with Steven had been shattered, but he still longed to make his mark in the art world. In a way, he owed that to the dead man as much as to himself, as a tribute to Steven Sidling and his ideas. He needed a first class degree as a launching pad into an academic career. That would give him a secure financial base from which to practise his art. He didn't want to starve in a garret.

He decided that he must tackle Duncan about his prospects of that good degree, but for the moment he couldn't trust himself to speak calmly. Duncan McBane's blithe reversion to 'sculpture' enraged him. It was an insult to Steven's legacy.

One day, chance threw him in the way of Arabella Wood, lecturer in Fashion. She was struggling to lift an awkwardly large, and apparently heavy, box onto a trolley in the entrance hall. Artjoms glanced at the janitors' office. There was no-one visible in there. There was no-one else in the entrance hall either.

He had observed Steven and Arabella talking and laughing intimately on two or three occasions over the few months before the murder, and he wondered if he might glean any insights from her. He feared another abortive conversation such as that with Steven's partner, but he would have to try.

"Can I help you?" he offered, approaching.

Arabella looked up at him from the awkward stooping stance in which she was wrestling with the burden. She was slightly flushed from her efforts.

"Thank you! I just can't get a grip on it properly. Where are the janitors when you need them?"

Artjoms nodded. The box was wide, but he managed to get his long arms around it and lift it. It was heavy, but nothing like the logs he had learned to shift around with chains in Estonia. He lowered it gently onto the trolley, in case it was fragile.

"Thank you! You're a lot stronger than you look!"

It was true, he had a slender build, but he had become strong during his year as a lumberjack, as well as adept at moving heavy objects.

"You take this to the Fashion Department?" he said.

"Yes."

"I can wheel it there for you, if you like, and help you to unload it again."

She smiled.

"That's very kind of you. The janitors seem to have been abducted by aliens today."

This was a joke, and he turned up the corners of his mouth accordingly. The British loved their jokes.

"How did you know I was going to the Fashion Department?" she said, as they set off.

"I know you are Arabella Wood, lecturer in Fashion. I see... I have seen... your picture in the prospectus."

"Oh... how nice that someone reads that thing! Actually, I know who you are as well. You're the Latvian student in Sculpture. Artjoms? Is that your name?"

"Yes, Artjoms. I'm Estonian. Also it's *Ambient Interventions*."

She glanced sideways at him.

"Oh yes. That. We'll have to see if that name sticks, now poor Steven's gone."

This was the perfect opening, and Artjoms grabbed it.

"I think you were good friend of Steven Sidling, Arabella? I just want to say that I admire him greatly. You must feeling very sad."

She looked surprised, but she didn't close down the subject as Steven's partner had done on the park bench.

"Yes, it did make me very sad. I'm still very sad."

They arrived at the lift that would take them to the floor where Fashion was located.

"It's frustrating, no? How the police not find out who did it," he said.

"Whoever it was, they were very careful to leave no clues."

"Do you have any ideas?"

The lift arrived and they went in. Arabella was looking at him doubtfully now and he wondered if she was going to pull back from this topic.

"I do have ideas, but it would be wrong to speculate without any proof."

The lift doors closed, and made a strange intimacy in the little space. It was like a confessional box in the church, and Artjoms instinctively lowered his voice. He chose his words carefully. He wanted to test one of his theories.

"There is someone who I think hate Steve, although he pretend not to."

Arabella nodded, but didn't comment.

"Like you, I feel very sad about what happened," he went on. "Also I feel angry. I don't like it that whoever kill Steven is still free."

She nodded again. Her gaze wandered around the lift a little, and then she looked him in the face.

"I'm angry, but I'm also frightened."

"Frightened?"

"Yes. Because a person who could do a thing like that… well…"

"Do you think it's someone in the art school?"

"I don't want to say."

"Because you're frightened of… him."

"Perhaps."

The lift had arrived at the upper floor. Artjoms decided it was time to lay his cards on the table and see what happened. He put his hand on the button to keep the doors closed.

"Do you think it might have been Duncan McBane?" he said, almost in a whisper.

He could read the answer in her face, although she shook her head a little.

"We can't say that. We don't know that. It would be wrong."

Artjoms sensed that she wanted to say something more.

"*But?* Is there something else?"

"Only that he's a... someone with strong passions. A forceful man. But that doesn't mean..."

"No, of course not. It's not meaning he's a murderer."

Arabella looked at her watch.

"I've got a meeting starting soon. Do you mind...?"

"Of course. I'm sorry to take away your time."

"No, it's okay – I'm grateful for your help with this box."

He let the lift doors open, and wheeled the trolley into the Fashion Department with her, and unloaded it where she directed him. In the long bright studio there were only two students working. They were at the far end, well out of earshot.

"I'm sorry again, to bring up..." Artjoms said quietly. Arabella made a gesture of acceptance.

"It's okay. We've all stopped talking about Steven's death, and it's only six weeks ago. It's normal to want to discuss it. I don't mind, Artjoms. I'm glad to hear his name again."

Her eyes were a little watery now. He felt a sudden wave of emotion himself, so he made his quick formal little bow and retreated. As he walked back to the entrance hall and left the building, he felt he had made some progress. Like him, Arabella had some suspicions of Duncan McBane.

That night, he had an inspiration for a new *kratt*. It would be a kind of bearded face, something like the face of Duncan McBane, and it would be looking out from behind a screen of thorns. It would have marbles for eyes, and hazel twigs for its beard and hair. Its nose would be made of jagged tin, and its mouth would be crimson. It would be larger than a real head, set on the ground, as if it had no body, or had a body that was buried in the earth beneath it. He would make it look somehow threatening. He would find a crossroads somewhere in Forthburgh and it would be half-concealed behind its screen. When drivers or other passers-by glimpsed it, they would be a little frightened.

Perhaps he might make a series of kratts in the image of the sinister Duncan McBane?

Christmas approached, and Artjoms went home early to spend three weeks with his family. When he came back, he found out that Arabella Wood had been murdered. Beheaded.

He felt stunned, and spent many bleak hours considering this new atrocity. Like everyone else in the art school, where the killings were avidly discussed in a prevailing atmosphere of dread, he felt sure there was a connection between this event and the previous murder. He watched Duncan McBane carefully, wondering if he was capable of such acts. The man seemed the same as ever – taciturn and undemonstrative. He certainly didn't appear anxious or display any behaviour that might argue guilty feelings. Time passed, the police came and went, and the new unsolved murder sank slowly into the fabric of the life of the institution, like a bloodstain that everyone could see but mentioned less and less.

As the Spring term progressed, Artjoms began more and more clearly to understand that Duncan McBane had set himself firmly against him and his work. At first only stray remarks suggested this, but finally, in March, he brought himself to go into his office and tackle him about it squarely. He was shocked when Duncan gave him to understand, without saying it explicitly, that he would not get a good degree mark.

Artjoms was thrown into a panic. This was a threat to his whole future! The first class degree was the vital key that would open the door to postgraduate study and his subsequent hoped-for career as a teacher and artist.

Burning resentment made him determined to redouble his efforts to find a connection between the man and the murders. Brooding constantly over the injustice of a pre-determined low degree mark, and the unjust slaughter of his hero Steven, he took to tailing Duncan McBane whenever he could. He didn't expect it to lead to anything definite, but he was starting to become obsessive about him. In fact, he now hated Fishface with a passionate hatred, the dark mirror image of his passion for Steven Sidling.

One rainy afternoon he had observed his bearded nemesis leaving the art school as he himself was approaching its doors. On an impulse he decided to follow him again. It was a kind of self-torture even to look at him, but he couldn't help himself.

Trailing well behind, he came into Princess Gardens just as McBane, ahead of him, was crossing the railway bridge spanning the deep cutting that smuggled the trains invisibly out of the city towards the west. There was nobody else on the bridge, but a cat was sitting miserably on the parapet, most probably a stray. He could hear it set up a mewling whine as McBane came near. Maybe it had some hopes of food.

With a sudden thrust of his arm, too rapid for even a cat to evade, McBane swept the animal off the parapet onto the tracks below. A train was passing down there. McBane walked on without a second glance, as if nothing at all had happened.

When Artjoms got to the bridge, he stood on tiptoe to look over the parapet, which was chest high. Down below on the tracks was a black bundle of fur and blood.

He felt suddenly sick – as if he might actually vomit. He stood for a few moments, abandoning the idea of following Fishface any further. His thoughts were in as much turmoil as his guts. This random act of cruel violence proved nothing at all, but a man who would do a thing like that... of what else might he be capable?

From this moment on, in Artjoms's own mind, Fishface was a double murderer. It was just that he had no proof. But then, he wasn't constrained like the police: he didn't need definite proof in order to act.

Artjoms had never murdered anyone. But then, he had never hated anyone as he hated McBane. He started to think of the matter in judicial terms: it was a sentence of execution, and he was both judge and executioner. He felt sure he was capable of doing it, and bent his thoughts to the practicalities. He was naturally methodical, and approached the matter as if it were a logistical task – like designing and installing one of his *kratts*.

The first consideration was timing. It was essential that when the degree work in Ambient Interventions was assessed, Duncan McBane should no longer be on the scene. There was no cast-iron guarantee of a high mark for his own work from other assessors, but there was a guarantee of a low mark from Fishface, if he was still alive. It was now early April. The assessments would take place in June. So Fishface must be dead in two months' time.

The next consideration was that he must carry out the execution without arousing any suspicion. If a poor degree mark would jeopardise his future career, a long prison sentence would sink it beyond all hope, along with the rest of his life. How might he kill Fishface without anyone finding out?

One element in his favour, ironically, was that two previous murders had been committed with which he was utterly unconnected. The untimely death of another art school lecturer would almost certainly be taken as the third in a series. On the night of Sidling's murder, he had been at a classical concert in Glasgow with a cousin who had married a Scot, and had stayed with them overnight. At the time of the murder of Arabella Wood he had just arrived in Estonia to be with his parents for the Christmas season. No one could think of linking him with the other murders therefore.

Even better, although obviously they had not uncovered any proof, surely the police must have Fishface high on their list of suspects? He had no way of knowing that for sure, but logic suggested that if he had his suspicions, so must they. That being the case, how perfect it would be if only Duncan's death could look like suicide! Stricken with remorse for his hideous crimes, Fishface had decided to end it all. How could this come to pass?

Most people committed suicide by taking an overdose of pills – sleeping tablets or some such. They would almost invariably do this in the privacy of their own home. Artjoms could conceive of no way to inveigle himself into Duncan's home and administer an overdose of sleeping tablets.

Slitting of the wrists – sometimes in a warm bath – also had many devotees, but presented even more formidable obstacles to Artjoms in terms of its accomplishment.

Jumping off a high place was the simplest means of achieving the objective of self-immolation, and could be done in an instant. But how on earth would Artjoms lure Fishface to a high place in order to push him off? At first sight, it seemed as wildly unattainable as the other methods.

Every day on his way to and fro between his flat and the art school, Artjoms crossed the Telford Bridge, a highly suitable location. He stopped occasionally and craned over the high stone parapet. It would certainly kill you, a drop from this place into the river below. There seemed to be some kind of figure down there, on a rock or little island, with the fast-flowing water breaking into flecks of white foam as it struck the obstacle and parted to either side. What was that? One day, he made his way down there to find out.

The next morning, Artjoms awoke with a plan half-formed in his drowsy mind. He got up, made himself a coffee, and focussed all his powers of concentration on bringing this vague formulation to light. At last the vague notions coalesced in his mind: a step-by-step scenario for the execution of Duncan McBane.

Artjoms had only visited his doctor once before during his three years in Forthburgh. On that occasion, he had been suffering from a boil on his back. Now he sat nervously in the busy waiting room, wedged between two overweight people, a man and a woman. He might have thought they were a couple, they were so well matched. But they weren't communicating and they had left a regular person-sized gap between them, the only seat available.

Artjoms had kept himself awake with strong coffee and videotapes of films throughout the previous two nights, and he felt dizzy and disorientated. He had dark rims around his eyes, and they were suitably bloodshot. It had perhaps been unnecessary, but thoroughness and fortitude were both parts of his character. He would need to call on these qualities again in the near future.

Eventually his name was announced.

"Artjoms Ubags!"

He stood up. The doctor at the door to the waiting room looked at him without much enthusiasm. In fact, she looked almost as tired as he was. He followed her into her consulting room.

"Please take a seat, Artjoms. Am I pronouncing your name correctly?"

"Yes. Artjoms."

"Good. Now, what can I help you with?"

"I can't sleep, doctor."

"I see. How long have you had problems sleeping?"

"For over a week. I not going to sleep at all."

"Are you anxious about anything?"

"I'm a little anxious of my future, but nothing in particular. I'm mostly anxious about the no sleep."

"Do you drink tea or coffee, or alcohol in the evenings?"

"No, never after about six o'clock."

"No wine or beer?"

"Almost never. Not during last week at all."

"Is this a new problem?"

"Yes. I normal sleep like the log."

"Have you tried having a warm bath before bedtime, or other ways of relaxing?"

"I've try everything, doctor. I feel desperate."

He had kept his eyes from blinking since he had entered the consulting room, and now he managed to squeeze out a tear.

The doctor tapped her pen a few times on her notepad and her eyes flickered towards the door. Perhaps she was thinking of the crowded waiting room out there.

"Well... I could give you something to help you sleep. But it's only for short term use. Dependency on sleeping pills is not a solution for the longer term. Are you taking any prescription medicines now?"

"No."

"And what about other drugs? Have you taken any recreational drugs – amphetamine for example?"

"No. I don't have nothing to do with those things."

"All right."

She scribbled on her pad and handed him a prescription.

"Here. This is only to sort out your immediate problem. It's a sleeping pill called Ambien. Take one just before bedtime – it should make you sleepy very quickly. Don't take more than one at a time, even if it doesn't make you sleepy – which is unlikely, actually. Taking two or more at a time can be dangerous. Don't use them in the daytime, and don't drink alcohol with them. I'm giving you a prescription for ten tablets, which should give you some good nights' sleep. If the problem comes back after that, we may need to refer you to a sleep therapist."

"Thank you doctor. Where do I get the tablets?"

"From a chemist's. There's one just down the road if you turn left out of the surgery. Give them the prescription. They'll have it in stock."

"Thank you."

That night, ignoring the tablets, Artjoms enjoyed a glorious ten hour sleep. The next night, feeling refreshed and back to normal, he decided to try the effect of one tablet dissolved in whisky. There was no strange taste, as far as he could tell, or perhaps just a hint of something unusual that might be due to his *knowing* what was in the whisky. He noted the time: eight o'clock.

After the drink, he sat reading for a while. After only ten minutes he realised that he was re-reading the same page. He made an effort to concentrate. At some point the book dropped from his hands. When he looked at his watch again it was nearly midnight. He felt groggy and disoriented, and groped his way to the bathroom, had a piss, and stumbled into the bedroom where he fell asleep again in his clothes with the light on.

So, he reflected ruefully the next morning, one tablet in alcohol would do the trick.

In spite of these successful preparations, he still dithered for some weeks. It was a formidable, daunting undertaking. But his hatred of Duncan McBane burned as fiercely as ever, and the dates for the degree assessments grew closer and closer.

At last, he screwed up his courage and put his plan into action.

It was the merry month of May. Scotland sat on the edge of a spell of hot settled weather on the continent. The easterly breezes brought the warm air across the cold North Sea and caused thick sea fog to roll into the city of Forthburgh, poking its damp fingers into every nook and cranny, and denying the inhabitants the sunshine they felt entitled to. On some days the heat of the sun would disperse it a little during the afternoon, but as night fell it would gather again like a smothering blanket.

This weather pattern suited Artjoms's plan perfectly. At the crucial moment, in the early hours of a weekday morning, a dense fog would be a welcome accomplice to his actions. He did not need to rely on it, however. If ever he was interviewed by the police, he would not deny that Duncan had visited his flat. He might even offer the information that he had helped him out to the street. He had his story well prepared. With a slightly shaky hand, he wrote the note that would set the wheels in motion, and pushed it one morning under the door of Duncan's office.

CHAPTER 39

May 1990

I know things that the police would like to know about you. You must talk to me about this. Come to my flat at midnight this Tuesday. The address is Top Flat, 80, Belgrove Crescent, near to the Telford Bridge. There is buzzer at the street door. Artjoms Ubags.

Fuck! What did that toe-rag Estonian know?

Duncan stared at the note as if he might will it out of existence. If he could will Artjoms Ubags out of existence, that would be even better. Could this just be a bluff? He had been so careful! Artjoms couldn't have got hold of any definite evidence of either of his crimes. There wasn't any. The only mistake he'd made in the two murders was something that, as it happened, had turned up just a few days ago, scrunched up in the corner of his car boot. The rubber shark mask. How it had slipped out of the tote bag when he disposed of everything else he had no idea, but he brought it back into his flat and shoved it away in a drawer. He thought vaguely that he might be invited to a fancy dress party one day, although in his fifty years on the planet no such invitation had yet arisen.

Anyway, that was irrelevant. Artjoms couldn't possibly have come across that.

He thought over what he knew about Artjoms. It was clear enough that he had idolised the upstart Sidling from the moment he arrived at the art school as the new head of sculpture. Furthermore, it was possible that the Estonian hadn't been taken in by Duncan's toadying to

Sidling in the months before he killed him. He had most probably cottoned on to the fact that in fact he hated Sidling.

Perhaps he'd been wrong to let the arrogant Artjoms know that his first class degree was doomed from the outset? Maybe this note indicated no more than a desperate attempt at leverage to obtain the good degree for which he was so desperate? And why this ridiculous meeting time? Tomorrow night at midnight! Midnight? Artjoms was a weird one. Perhaps midnight had some significance in Estonian folklore. Well, if Artjoms had any peculiar, sinister intentions, he would find he'd met his match in Duncan!

He spent much time during the rest of that day pondering what he should do. In the end he decided that he *had* to go to this meeting with Artjoms, if for no other reason than to find out if he really did know anything incriminating. He racked his brains to think of what that could be. If he was bluffing, then it was crucial that he himself should say nothing that was an admission of guilt. Was turning up at Artjoms's flat in itself an admission? Should he perhaps adopt an air of benevolent concern, an anxiety to clear up what was obviously a delusion or mistake on the part of this exasperating student?

The next day, the day appointed for his midnight meeting with Artjoms, dragged horribly. He looked for Artjoms in the studios and the canteen, in case he could forestall the meeting or somehow steal a march on him, but he wasn't to be found. He looked in his file for a telephone number, to propose a more sensible appointment, but the only number was in Estonia.

At home after work, he watched two films on videotape, eating his supper in the interval. But he couldn't keep his attention fixed on the screen. His thoughts kept wandering to the meeting ahead of him, and what he should say and do. Might it be necessary even to kill Artjoms at some point in the future?

Artjoms and Hermione. Two more murders, to cover up the first two? How many murders might it be possible to get away with? He thought of Macbeth. How did those lines go? He looked them up in the dog-eared copy of the play that he should have returned to the school stockroom at the end of his school days:

I am in blood
Stepp'd in so far that, should I wade no more,
Returning were as tedious as go o'er

Emerging from his flat about twenty minutes before midnight, he found that a *haar* had descended on the city, a dense, damp fog that rolled in from the river estuary and sometimes robbed the unhappy citizens of sunlight for whole days during summertime. An eerie silence pervaded the street outside. As he walked to where his car was parked, the sound of his footsteps was stifled by the heavy air. Everything was swaddled in murk. A Tuesday night at midnight, and the city was blind and deaf.

He drove through the centre of town with hardly a glimpse of human life. Only an occasional ghostly taxi glided by, and – once - a night bus, its illuminated interior looming up and then swimming past him in the mist like some huge phosphorescent creature of the deep.

He knew the street where Artjoms lived: Belgrove Crescent. It was quite an upmarket address for a student, a graceful curve of Georgian terraced houses facing south over the deep ravine through which the River Lethe made its way to the sea. Sometimes though, these splendid facades concealed an interior partitioned and diminished in ways the original architects could not have imagined. Artjoms's top floor flat might well be as squalid as his own dwelling place in downmarket Dolry.

He drove over the Telford Bridge, and turned into Belgrove Crescent. There were no parking spaces, so he had to drive back across the bridge and find a space on

Balls Brae. There was a rubbish bin there, and after checking the number of Artjoms's flat, he paused for a moment to rip up Artjoms's message into tiny fragments and deposit it in the bin. It was best that such a document, bearing its veiled accusation of murder, should not exist at all.

At number Eighty, Belgrove Crescent, an illuminated panel revealed that six flats existed within. He pressed the buzzer for *Ubags*, and a couple of seconds later heard the disembodied 'click' that told him the street door had been unlocked. He pushed it inwards and entered the narrow stone-flagged passage that led to the foot of the stairs. A single fluorescent light spread an unwelcoming sheen on the dark green walls. It was more deathly cold in here than it was in the fog outside.

He climbed the long curving stone stairway that brought him finally to Artjoms's abode. A door with peeling paint – the same dark green as below - faced him, the only door on this upper landing. It opened as he raised his hand to knock, and he found his raised fist hovering in front of the pale face of Artjoms, as if he would knock there if he could. He lowered it with a grimace.

"Come in, Duncan."

Somewhere a church clock started to strike the hour. Midnight. A suitable time for a dark purpose, Duncan thought, passing Artjoms as he held the door open.

"Turn left at the end of the hallway, that's the living room."

The room was quite large. The windows were closed with the traditional wooden shutters still often found in this part of town, a better protection from the hostile elements than single glazed windows and a fluttering curtain. Not that there was any wind tonight.

At least this room was warm. A double-barred electric fire stood in the chimney place. A threadbare sofa and two armchairs were arranged conspiratorially around it. There were some posters on the walls – odd looking figures and faces by some artist that Duncan didn't recognize, probably some outlier of the Surrealist movement. They made a kind of waiting audience for whatever act was to transpire. There was a higgledy-piggledy bookcase half filled with books and dotted with maquettes. Duncan recognized them as tiny prototypes of Artjoms's kratts.

"Have a seat, Duncan. Wherever you like."

He chose the armchair nearest to the electric fire, which made a steady, low buzzing noise, like a metallic bee.

"Would you like a drink?"

Duncan felt that he would very much like a drink. He'd had two small whiskies earlier on in the evening, but their effect had worn off completely. He could keep a clear head now if he went easy.

"Aye, I'll take something."

"Beer or whisky?"

"Whisky."

"It's only a cheap blended one, is that all right?"

"Aye, anything. Just with a drop of water in it."

Artjoms went out, and Duncan could hear him getting out glasses and pouring liquids in what was presumably the kitchen. Also he heard a teaspoon stirring in a glass. Stupid Estonian! You could mix whisky and water without a teaspoon!

Artjoms returned with two whisky tumblers and handed one to Duncan. Neither of them offered to clink glasses and say 'cheers!' It wasn't that kind of occasion. Artjoms sat down on the sofa, and Duncan took a large sip of his whisky. Christ! This must be the worst blended Scotch on the planet! But at least it warmed his insides, and gave him a feeling of being, in some obscure way, more in control of the situation.

For a few moments they sat in silence. Duncan wasn't going to break it. This meeting was at Artjoms's behest, and it was for Artjoms to lay out his position. Then he would know how best to respond. He sipped some more of his whisky. The second sip tasted marginally less bad than the first.

"So, you've read my note, Duncan," Artjoms said at last.

"I wouldn't be here otherwise, would I?" Duncan replied. "Obviously," he added, to make sure Artjoms realised what a stupid opening remark it was.

"What have you done with the note?" Artjoms said.

This was an unexpected query. Why would Artjoms care what he'd done with the note? But there was no harm in telling him.

"I've destroyed it of course. I don't want a piece of paper with a lying accusation lying about the place."

"I thought you would do that. You see it as an accusation?"

"What would you call it?"

"It was meant in a friendly way, Duncan. If I want to accuse you of something, I would go straight to the police, no?"

"*Friendly!* I took you to be saying I had something to hide."

"You do. Something to do with Steven's death."

"You suspect that, do you?"

"I *know* you did have something to do with it."

"Well, you can't, because I didn't."

This sounded feeble even to his own ears, like a child denying stealing sweets. But he let it stand, and waited for more from Artjoms.

"Why did you come tonight then? You could have shown the note to police. Blackmail is a crime itself, I believe."

"Exactly. It's you who's the criminal here, Artjoms. I came because I wanted to help you. To put you straight."

"How can you help me?"

"I can persuade you that you're wrong about Sidling. Put your mind at rest on that score. I know you were very fond of him. A disciple, one might even say. Would you agree? A disciple?"

"He was inspiration, yes. I wanted to follow his way of doing things."

"And that's where you went wrong, Artjoms. Sculpture is much more than what Sidling brought to it. No Steven Sidling could have created Michelangelo's David, not a hundred Sidlings working for a hundred years could produce something sublime like that."

He downed the rest of the whisky. He had reconciled himself to the taste, and the fire in his belly gave him courage. He would outface this icy Laplander.... Estonian... whatever he was...

Artjoms didn't say anything. He knocked back the rest of his own whisky, stood and took up Duncan's empty glass and returned to the kitchen. A few moments later he returned bearing replenishments and sat down again.

"I want to tell you some things about myself, Duncan, before I say why I believe you killed Steven Sidling. Is that all right?"

"Fire away! I've come out on a wild goose chase and you're the goose."

This didn't particularly make sense even to himself.

Artjoms looked at him with a disconcerting stare, and then eased himself back on the sofa with a sigh.

"I'll begin with my mother and father..."

Duncan put up a hand, as if stopping traffic. As he did so, he had a strange sensation that the whole room had been moving towards him until he had brought it to a halt.

"Is this going to be your whole fucking life story, Artjoms? Because I don't want to be here all night."

"You'll see that I get to the point quite quick, Duncan."

"I hope so. This isn't my idea of fun, you know."

"Relax, Duncan. We can help each other."

Duncan took a deep breath. As he exhaled, his sense of impatience and anxiety seemed to flow out of him. What the hell did it matter if Artjoms wanted to talk about himself? It would allow him to assess the situation while he listened, give him some hints as to whether the Latvian... Estonian... really knew anything about Sidling's death. He took a gulp of the fresh whisky. It didn't seem to taste so awful now, somehow.

"So... my mother was quite old when I was born, thirty eight, and my father was a younger man..."

"... so that was when I decided to come to study in Forthburgh."

Duncan jerked convulsively. He must have fallen asleep. He'd been aware of Artjoms's voice droning on, but somewhere along the line he'd lost track of the words. The warmth of the electric bar fire beside him, the whisky, and the monotonous monologue had all conspired to make him drowsy.

"You were saying..." he heard himself say, but couldn't finish the thought. He tried to pick up his whisky glass to take another sip, but found it was already empty. Artjoms was looking at him oddly. He had begun to look like one of the disquieting posters that adorned the walls. His hair seemed to have a life of its own, writhing about slightly on his head, as if composed of worms. Duncan blinked the unsettling image away. Artjoms resumed his story.

"So, when I arrive in Forthburgh..."

"... Duncan! Duncan!"

"What? What's the matter?"

Someone was shaking him. Was it his father? A sudden terror made him open his eyes. Someone behind him was shaking his shoulders.

"No! Don't hit me!"

"Duncan!"

It wasn't his father's voice. Who was it?

"Duncan, wake up! It's time to go."

"Time? Time?"

"Yes. Come on, I'll help you up."

Now the stranger's hands came up under his armpits.

"Stand up!"

He put some weight on his feet and felt the floor pushing up against them, as if he was being lifted by some force coming up through the building below. He was quite certain that he was in a high building, and a force, some supernatural force, was surging upwards from the ground through all the intervening rooms, through the carpet, flowing into him...

"Good. Stay on your feet. I'm getting your coat."

He stood swaying until the stranger came back and put him into his coat. He didn't remember taking it off. How did he get into this place?

"All right? Ready to go?"

"Thank you!" he mumbled. This man was helping him, somehow. He was looking after him. He needed to be looked after. He had a strong feeling that he *did* know the man. A young man. Was he dreaming this?

"Come on, we've got to go down the stairs now, Duncan. Lots of stairs, and we've got to go quietly."

Suddenly they were outside. It was all grey and swirling. He had a memory – it seemed like long ago – of walking down, down, down an endless staircase. He'd thought they'd never reach the bottom of it.

"Where..." he heard himself say, and then he lost the thought.

They were walking through grey nothingness. There was no sound. The stranger was guiding him, half-supporting him, with an arm linked with his own. Sometimes he wanted to stop and lie down, but the man would then put his other arm under his armpit and guide him forwards. Where were they going?

They had stopped. He wanted so desperately to sleep. He could sleep right here, in this grey nothingness, standing up. He felt himself being lifted. He was all floppy. He was a dead weight, in his father's arms.

"Don't hurt me Dad. Don't drop me."

His bed was narrow and stony. But still he could sleep on it. He could sleep anywhere, he was so tired. His father pushed him towards the edge of the bed. He teetered there, rolled, and slid off. He waited for the floor to come up and meet him. Cold air rushed at his face. For a second he thought he had learned to fly.

As Artjoms had hoped, there was no traffic at this dead hour of the night. No vehicle had appeared out of the fog during their short progress from his flat to the bridge. He rubbed away the almost invisible little chalk mark he'd made on the parapet earlier in the day. He'd brought a damp cloth in his pocket to do that. He'd been meticulous about everything, and it had all gone perfectly. Duncan McBane had committed suicide.

CHAPTER 40

May 1990

**Editorial in the Forthburgh Evening News:
SCOTT GETS HIS MAN!**

At last the mystery of the bizarre and gruesome murders of two lecturers at Forthburgh Art School is solved! Detective Superintendent Dennis Scott (affectionately known as 'Dennis The Menace' to his colleagues) told this paper how the dramatic suicide of Duncan McBane, another lecturer at the art school, revealed the identity of the perpetrator. The killer was none other than McBane himself.

McBane's first victim, as readers of this paper will remember, was Steven Sidling, Head of Sculpture at the art school. His body was found last September in the woods at Deil's Glen, grotesquely pierced with the sharpened handles of hundreds of artists' paintbrushes.

Before any progress had been made in discovering the author of this outrage, another killing occurred in December of last year on the premises of the art school itself, when Fashion lecturer Arabella Wood was decapitated and her head left in a glass case.

"It was a case of two kinds of jealousy," Detective Superintendent Scott informed us. "In the first instance, it was professional. Steven Sidling was an outsider who had been appointed as Head of Sculpture when McBane himself was a candidate for the post. In the second case it was sexual jealousy: Arabella Wood had been romantically involved with McBane, but had left him for another man."

Scott told us that it was the discovery of written materials in McBane's flat, following his death, that had provided the answers. Not only did these include accounts of violent retributions undertaken in the past, but also a list of possible methods by which the recent killings might be carried out.

"Everything added up," Scott said. "And to cap it all, our forensics team found tiny slivers of paintbrush handles in the cracks between the floorboards of the living room, and minute traces of Arabella Wood's blood on a rubber shark mask among McBane's possessions."

The irony that McBane, a double murderer, should have ended up impaled on one of his own artistic creations has not escaped notice. It seems likely, indeed, that it was his intention to throw himself off the Telford Bridge at that precise point, presumably motivated by an overwhelming sense of guilt and remorse. There will be few who mourn the passing of a monster, who plotted his murders in cold blood, and apparently donned a shark's mask to perpetrate them. McBane was indeed a vicious predator of the deep, merciless and calculating. Forthburgh and its citizens are much the safer for his demise.

See our main article for more details of the gruesome events and Detective Inspector Scott's brilliant investigation.

Coupar put the paper down with an exasperated sigh. As he had anticipated, The Menace had stolen all his thunder, no doubt by bending the ears of his journalist golfing cronies. But at least the case was wrapped up at last, and the torturing uncertainties of the last few months were put to bed.

Lisa looked at him with concern.

"Well, *I* know it was all *your* hard work that solved these cases, Coopsie!"

He nodded.

"A lot of people are unsung heroes," she went on. "Dan... don't get jealous now... Dan was telling me that a lot of famous writers died unrecognised and penniless in garrets... what *is* a garret by the way?"

Coupar shrugged.

"Well, never mind. But anyway, as I say, you've got the satisfaction of knowing it was down to you. And The Menace and your colleagues will all know that too, whatever the papers say."

That, at least, was true. The Menace himself had been generous in his praise; Price and Waterhouse had given him a box of chocolates with no detectable undertone of irony, and positive remarks from the other detectives at the police station gave him a gratifying sense of having at last made his mark here in Forthburgh.

Lisa put her hand on his and gave it a squeeze. He gave it a squeeze back. This stressful period in his professional life - after some rocky moments - seemed to have finally brought them closer together. He was beginning to think... think seriously... of asking her to put a ring on one of her lovely slim fingers.

Hermione had put the house in Martinside on the market. The summer was a slow time for house sales in Forthburgh, but she was impatient and didn't want to wait for the autumn. With Ted in London, she had finally given him up for lost. The ghastly murder of Arabella had not brought him back to her, and every time she set foot in the art school now, she had to fight down a wave of revulsion that was almost a physical feeling of sickness. Roland would be at university in Bristol for another two years, and here in Scotland she felt stranded and left behind, like some unfortunate fish washed up onto a beach by a storm. Through an old friend, a painter like herself, she had secured a prospect of two days a week of teaching at the Bristol School of Art - the equivalent of what she was doing at Forthburgh. With the house in Martinside either disposed of, or left in the hands of an agency, she could rent a modest place down in Bristol and have a fresh start, with the added bonus of more contact with Roland.

She had started the task of clearing some of her possessions from the house. In her studio, she contemplated the charcoal drawing of Ted and Arabella with its inscription *Love is a bed of roses*. She weighed the heavy paper in her hands and then slowly, deliberately ripped it in two. She then gradually reduced the two halves to smaller fragments and put them into a black bin liner.

Now she turned her attention to the portrait of Duncan McBane. He glowered malevolently at her from the canvas. It was without doubt the most powerful portrait she had ever painted. The eyes seemed to hold her own in a hypnotic gaze, while the mouth, half-hidden in the dark tangled beard, twisted in an animalistic snarl. It made her feel the same sickness as she experienced entering the art school nowadays, and she couldn't imagine anyone else ever wanting to own it. She took a pair of scissors from a drawer and slashed repeatedly at the image, until the canvas was just a mess of holes and tatters. Then she stamped on the wooden stretchers until they broke, and dropped the whole ruin into the plastic bin liner.

In the busy departures zone of Forthburgh Airport, Ricky Love put down the newspaper he was reading to assist Boony in retrieving Marcus from under a row of seats that he had decided to explore. They were awaiting the departure of their plane to Heathrow, the first leg of a wearisome journey back to Portland in Oregon. Ernest Buckley and his wife would be commencing the reverse journey at about the same time. Ricky had reflected on the fact that his exchange partner had missed the most eventful few months in the history of Forthburgh Art School. In contrast, he and Boony had been embroiled in the extraordinary situation and closely connected with two of the three individuals now pushing up daisies. It was not a year that they would ever forget.

Boony enticed Marcus from under the legs of a bemused Asian gentleman by brandishing a lollipop. Ricky was returning to his seat when he caught a glimpse of a young man sitting a couple of places away. At the same time, the young man, an intense looking dark-haired guy, looked at him. There was a confusing moment of mutual recognition without certainty. The look was too prolonged to be ignored.

"Aren't you…?" Ricky said.

The young man nodded.

"I've seen you at the art school," he said. "I'm Artjoms. I've just finished my degree."

"Ah. Yes. You were… I know… you're the Sculpture student who made all the strange things at crossroads, aren't you?"

"That's right. You saw them?"

"I only saw one of them *in situ*. But I remember the maquettes and the photos in your degree show space. And you were there weren't you, at the degree show private view. Didn't we speak?"

"You congratulate me on my first class degree."

"That's right. I did. So where are you off to today?"

"I go home to Estonia for a while, to see my family. And also to have some time of peace. Already I imagine myself walking alone in the endless woods there."

Ricky nodded, and thought of the endless woods that also surrounded his home in Oregon. There was certainly peace to be found in such places… although the unsolved Pine Loop Murders cast a dark shadow amongst the whispering pines.

"Well, congratulations again, Artjoms. I hope you find the peace and calm you're hoping for."

"Thank you. I'm sure I will."

THE END

Printed in Great Britain
by Amazon